THE LAST V

THE
LAST
VICEREINE

A NOVEL

Rhiannon
Jenkins Tsang

PENGUIN BOOKS

An imprint of Penguin Random House

PENGUIN BOOKS

USA | Canada | UK | Ireland | Australia
New Zealand | India | South Africa | China

Penguin Books is part of the Penguin Random House group of companies
whose addresses can be found at global.penguinrandomhouse.com

Published by Penguin Random House India Pvt. Ltd
7th Floor, Infinity Tower C, DLF Cyber City,
Gurgaon 122 002, Haryana, India

Penguin
Random House
India

First published in Penguin Books by Penguin Random House India 2017

10 9 8 7 6 5 4 3 2 1

This is a work of fiction. All situations, incidents, dialogue and characters,
with the exception of some well-known historical and public figures mentioned
in this novel, are products of the author's imagination and are not to be construed
as real. They are not intended to depict actual events or people or to change the
entirely fictional nature of the work. In all other respects, any resemblance to
persons living or dead is entirely coincidental.

ISBN 9780143441106

Typeset in RequiemText by Manipal Digital Systems, Manipal
Printed at Manipal Technologies Ltd, Manipal

www.penguin.co.in

For Mum and Dad

TIMELINE OF KEY EVENTS

8th May 1944	War in Europe ends
5th July 1945	UK General Election; wartime leader Winston Churchill defeated; Clement Attlee becomes Prime Minister of a Labour government after a landslide victory
15th August 1945	War in the Far East ends
February 1947	Lord Louis Mountbatten appointed Viceroy of India by the King; his wife, Edwina, becomes Vicereine; UK Parliament debates India Independence Bill
24th March 1947	Lord Mountbatten sworn in as the Viceroy at Viceroy's House in New Delhi; negotiations with Indian leaders on a deal for transfer of power begin
March–April 1947	Nehru hosts Asian Relations Conference in Delhi in his capacity as head of the Provisional Government

15th April 1947   The Viceroy hosts Governors' Conference at Viceroy's House

28th April–1st May   The Viceroy and Vicereine visit the North West Frontier Province and the Punjab; they inspect riot-torn areas and refugee camps, including the village of Kahuta

3rd May–14th May 1947   The Viceroy and Vicereine go to Simla for rest; informal negotiations take place; Pandit Nehru and the Chinese Ambassador, Chia-Yuen Lo, among the guests; draft plan on transfer of power rejected by Nehru

3rd June 1947   Announcement made of agreement on a new plan for the transfer of power

14th August 1947   Pakistan created as a new independent country with Dominion status; Jinnah sworn in as Governor General

15th August 1947   India created as a new independent country with Dominion status; Mountbatten, now Earl Mountbatten of Burma, is sworn is as Governor General; Nehru sworn in as Prime Minister of India with his cabinet; mass exodus of refugees in the Punjab and Bengal

December 1947   The Mountbattens attend the Silver Jubilee Celebrations of the Maharaja of Jaipur

1948	Edwina Mountbatten, now Countess Mountbatten of Burma, continues her relief work in her capacity as wife of the Governor General of India
30th January 1948	Assassination of Mahatma Gandhi
21st June 1948	The Mountbattens leave India; C. Rajagopalachari sworn in as Governor General
26th January 1950	India becomes a republic; post of Governor General abolished
23rd March 1956	Pakistan becomes a republic; post of Governor General abolished
21st February 1960	Edwina Mountbatten dies in her sleep in British Borneo; she is buried at sea off the coast of Portsmouth; Nehru sends the Indian frigate *Trishul* to accompany her and to cast marigolds on the sea in her honour
27th May 1964	Death of Pandit Nehru

THE LAST VICEREINE

PART I

India, Full Speed Ahead
Early February 1947 to late May 1947

I was hiding and I was freezing.

I was in an office above the main post office in Oxford. It was ridiculously early. There was no need for me to be at my desk at such an unholy hour. I wasn't even sure why I was there.

No, that isn't true.

I won't lie to you. The truth is, I had run away. I blocked my ears and pretended I didn't know what people were saying about me.

'Did you hear about Letty? Poor dear! Such a shame!' But work was all I had left. It was my bulwark against the nightmares. That is why I was hiding.

The morning hours dragged past and my black pen scratched carefully on the ledger, my figures neat and precise despite my fingerless gloves and the biting cold. I had to keep things organized, everything in its place. Miss Meticulous, the postmaster often called me. It was meant as a compliment, then why did I take it as an insult?

I removed my reading glasses, rubbed my eyes and rose to blow warm air from my mouth on to the window panes that bore flowers of frost on the rippling old glass. With the back of my glove, I cleared a spyhole. The sky was a flat sheet of pewter. Opposite me the glorious towers of Christ Church Cathedral and College were thick with snow, while the cars ground up and down the icy hill of St Aldate's in asthmatic bursts. How I hated that winter. I hated what the cold was doing to people, what it did to me. I craved warmth. I craved sleep, real deep sleep, and peace in my heart.

The snow was piled up seven feet high on the sides of the road, so that the pavements looked like trenches with doors cut in them for entering the shops. The war had been over for more than a year, yet the country was still battling unending months of ice and snow. Suddenly, directly below me, I spotted a purple feather emerging from a taxi. I stared transfixed. The owner of the feather straightened up and surveyed the street as if she owned it. No one had a look quite like hers. It was unmistakable. She glanced up as if she could actually see me at the window, although I knew she couldn't. She was short-sighted. Ashamed of myself and my situation, I stepped back. Yet I smiled at the way the feather on her hat bobbed jauntily along the ridge of the ice trenches and into the post office.

Oh Edwina!

It was that moment before a fall from a horse, that stab of panic as you struggled to regain your balance but realized you could not stop it from happening. I knew there was nothing I could do. Whatever it was that had brought her here, I could not fight it. I was forced to reveal myself. With a pounding heart, I hurried downstairs.

She was standing in the queue. In her purple tweed coat with her fox fur elegantly draped over her shoulder, she was like a lone crocus in the middle of the winter. Wherever she went she brightened everyone's day.

'It isn't—it can't be?' I heard two old ladies in black whisper behind their gloved hands.

'It is, I tell you. It's Lady Mountbatten!'

An old gentleman turned around at the sound of her name, shuffled forward, removed his hat and offered her his place in the queue.

'No, thank you.' She rewarded him with her most charming smile. 'I'll wait my turn.' But the old man did not go away. It was always like that. There was a magic about her. She drew people to her, held them in her orbit the way the sun holds the planets. No one could ever escape. The man leant heavily on his stick.

'My son, Arthur, was a Jap POW in Burma,' he said simply. 'I want to thank you.'

She smiled again and offered him her hand, but there was more to it than that. It was as if a light had come on behind her violet-blue eyes. She knew better than to ask and waited for the old man to continue.

'Arthur says the day Lady Mountbatten came to the camp was the day he knew he was going to survive.'

'And how is your son now?' Her forehead wrinkled with genuine concern.

'Aw, he's just fine. Married his gal, Peggy, last month.' He tapped the side of his nose. 'Here's hoping I might become a grandad before too long.'

'That's wonderful! His Peggy waited for him, all that time?'

'She did.' The old gentleman seemed to think there was nothing remarkable about a girl waiting for years for a soldier who might have been given up for dead in the Burmese jungle, but Edwina thought differently. Leaning forward, quick as a flash, she dropped a kiss on the old man's cheek.

'Give him that from me!'

I had seen Edwina working her charm, night after night, when I laboured with her at the St John's Ambulance during the London Blitz. I would squeeze into the front seat of her car and we would drive through the blackout to inspect air raid shelters in the East End, with me calling out the hazards that loomed along the way. As always in life it is the poorest people who get the worst of things and those living near the docks in dense housing had suffered the most during the bombing. I was never sure which was worse—being up top to face the bombs, fire and smoke, or being buried deep underground in the airless shelters with thousands of others, where the floor was wet with urine and the buckets, which served as latrines, overflowed with faeces.

'Hello. What's your name? What do you need?' Edwina Mountbatten would smile and ask of the toothless old dockers and exhausted young women who looked twice their age and were shivering with babies at their breasts. Cowering in dingy smoke-filled chambers, they would stare up into the torchlight, bewitched by her, and when they talked she would listen. Unlike me, who always wrote things down in a notepad as best I could during each visit, Edwina seemed to be able to hold it all in her head. Of course, she always wore an expertly tailored uniform and bright red lipstick, and kept perfect nails, but the thing about her was that it was not all just show. She cared about those people and knew how to get things done to help them.

'Letty, get this request to the Secretary of State first thing in the morning and if he's bolshie, you jolly well tell him it's coming from me!'

And before long I, Brigadier Letticia Wallace of the St John's Ambulance Brigade, had learnt to emulate Edwina's ways. If I could not be a barrister in the man's world of the Inns of Court, then I would be a woman, but by God, I would be one who got things done! I pulled rank. I wore lipstick and Joy perfume. I tightened my belt to show off my not insignificant curves and donned the highest of heels for meetings in Whitehall. I accepted smokes, flirted outrageously, stomped my feet, bossed, shouted, wheedled and cajoled; all of this to get things done, to make things better for people.

I could be ruthless too. Like Edwina I did not tolerate fools gladly and could not stand pompous incompetence, laziness or complacency. Edwina taught me that rank brings responsibility and if things were not right, heads would roll. In time, I came to see what Edwina had understood from the first day, that when we delivered light bulbs, bandages, blankets and eventually latrines, we also brought humanity and hope.

Edwina placed a small crocodile-skin handbag on the counter and removed her left glove to pay for some stamps with a shilling. While her change was being counted, I put on my shabby pre-war black hat and coat and waited for her by the door. I didn't know why she had come. But I knew she had come for me.

We walked the short distance to the little house I was renting in Holywell Street. I had wanted to take her to lunch at the Randolph Hotel but she had taken one look at me, known at once that something was not right and was determined to get to the bottom of it. So, my house it was.

The curtains in the front parlour were drawn and the ashes in the grate unraked. She headed straight to the kitchen in the back, the scent of powder, soap and perfume wafting in her wake. She stood in the middle of the room, staring at the unwashed dishes in the sink, smelling the rancid odour of the bacon I had fried for breakfast and the dank laundry left to dry higgledy-piggledy on the rack in front of the range. Pursing her lips, she pulled out her hatpin and removed her hat.

'Letty,' she said, 'Why on earth didn't you come to us, to Dickie and me? We are just so sorry. We'd no idea that Charles had died.' She looked at the photographs of my boys lined up on the mantelpiece and at the formal portrait of my husband, Charles, in his wig and gown, taken when he had become King's Counsel. He was smiling slightly and resting his chin in his hand. Beside this portrait was George, tall and looking squarely into the camera, dressed in the uniform of a midshipman; and Robert in his flying kit, standing with his friends in front of his Spitfire; and all three of them in cricket whites, father and sons, red-headed and freckled in the summer sun, arms around each other, grinning at the end of a veterans versus first eleven game at Charterhouse in 1937. I tried not to look at them but failed.

On 7th September 1940 my elder son Robert's Spitfire had been shot down over East Anglia. He was killed. On the

5th of August 1944 my second son George's ship had been sunk
by a German U-boat; all hands were lost. It had destroyed
Charles. He had clung to life for no more than a few months
after their deaths. So there I was. Alone in my untidy rented
house, hiding away in Oxford. Letticia Lady Wallace was my
title, but it lay like lead on my heart.

'Don't worry, Edwina,' I said, 'I'm all right. I'm well-provided
for financially. Charles left money and there is my family trust.'

'That's not what I mean and you know it,' she snapped.

Taking a poker, she began to stoke up a fire on the range,
adding coals and blowing gently to coax it to life. Embarrassed,
I knelt at her side with the bellows.

'You came all the way from London to Oxford on the train
in this weather to see me?'

'Of course! I needed to see you.' She hesitated and I knew
she was deferring to my grief, holding back her own agenda. 'I
went round to your place in Argyll Street in London yesterday
and your housekeeper told me what had happened.'

I got up, my knees cracking, and went over to the sink to fill
the kettle. Bringing it back, I hung it on its hook over the fire.

'That's better,' Edwina said. 'Have you got anything to eat?
I'm famished.' Her face was pinched from the cold and for the
first time I realized that she too might not be in the best of
health.

'Eggs,' I said, 'and some bread and milk. The bread might
be a bit mouldy though.'

'Don't worry, we'll cut it off. Scrambled eggs would be
good. I don't suppose you've got any Worcester sauce?'

I shook my head, salivating at the thought of it.

'Nice try!' I said, managing half a smile. Both of us knew it
was a long shot. We had not had little luxuries like that since
before the war.

But finding it suddenly easier to motivate myself in her company, I set about getting the utensils together to make the simple meal.

'Your housekeeper said that you nursed Charles at home yourself until the end?'

'Yes.'

I was sitting by the fire with pieces of bread on the end of the toasting fork and Edwina, with her sleeves rolled up, was vigorously beating the eggs in a bowl.

'It was awful,' I said, remembering against my will. 'But at least it was quick. Less than three months. The cancer was too advanced for anyone to do much about it.'

She dished up the eggs and I buttered the toast. Removing our coats at last, we sat at the tiny table near the fire. She ate quickly yet daintily, like a little bird, pecking at her food. But I knew the inquisition was coming.

'I manage well enough when I'm at work, really, I do. It's just at home, especially these last few months, the cold and the dark, I can't seem to get myself organized,' I said.

'What on earth possessed you to leave London and move out here all alone?'

'It seemed like a good idea at the time, letting Argyll Street and starting a new life here in Oxford where, a long time ago, I was once a student. I thought I might use the Bodleian to brush up on my criminal case law and eventually get a teaching post at the Society of Oxford Home Students. You know me, always keeping busy.'

I wanted to say that I had planned to go riding eventually. That I had hoped in time I would feel able to take Communion again. But neither of these things had happened. I had visited Pusey House for High Mass once. They were singing Byrd and I had calculated that the simplicity and beauty of the Latin mass might open the door to prayer for me once more. But the sight of the priests in white and gold serving the pretender they called God filled me with such rage that I almost threw my hymn book at the stained glass window. I walked out before the end of the Credo.

Edwina picked up a piece of toast, bit it and looked at me with her piercing violet eyes.

'Well, it clearly isn't working, is it?

'No.'

The kettle whistled and I got up to pour the tea. Mine was black; hers white, with one sugar. Cradling the cups in our cold hands, we sat in silence in front of the range. The fire roared angrily at me as if admonishing me for my neglect.

'Look at us!' she said. 'Like two old harpies.'

'Double, double, toil and trouble,' I joked, and was surprised to feel the muscles of my face stretch into something forgotten, something I had once known as a smile.

'I had a partial hysterectomy just before Christmas, you know,' she announced briskly. 'God I hate getting old.' She clenched her teeth. 'And I tell you now, Edwina Mountbatten is not going to accept her fate and degenerate into some fat, wrinkly old matriarch. I'd rather die on parade than trussed up in a wheelchair in a draughty old stately home.' And this time it was my turn to say sorry. She nodded and sipped her tea. And then she got to it. The reason she had come to Oxford in her fur and feather. I knew too well that quick intake of breath and haughty lift of an eyebrow.

'Something has come up, Letty.' She paused.

I waited in silence for more. She placed a despairing hand on her forehead. Overly dramatic, the pose might have been funny if she had not been so upset.

'A horror job. Dickie says he absolutely doesn't want it, but I think it's a front. I suspect he's been angling for it ever since he left South East Asian Command. He's doing it to spite me, damn him!'

I tilted my head to one side by way of a question.

'The PM called him into Downing Street just before Christmas and then he went to see the King. He says he tried to wriggle out of it.' She gave a harsh bark of laughter. 'The thing is, and I've told him so, I really don't want to go. I've got my relief work here in Europe. But even the King was all for it and I can't say I blame him. Dickie has been hassling the poor chap for months about Princess Elizabeth marrying Philip. He probably thinks good riddance. With Dickie dispatched, he will finally get some peace and quiet! But Noel Coward is saying it's a scandal and that Attlee and the Labour Party are lining Dickie up as the fall guy.' She pulled at her hair with her fingers—so unlike her—and took several shallow breaths. 'Letty, it's awful! We will probably come back with bullets in our backs.' She spoke quickly, and I was mesmerized by the bright red of her lipstick and the urgent lilt of her voice.

But I still could not understand what the devil she was talking about.

'What is it, Edwina?' I said.

'India! India, of course!'

Edwina then explained it all to me in detail. It seemed that Lord Wavell was a lame-duck Viceroy of India and the Indians didn't like him. The discussions were deadlocked with the Indian National Congress and the Muslim League. So they, Prime Minister Attlee and King George VI, wanted Dickie to be the next Viceroy of India.

I stared at her open-mouthed. Edwina in India? It would be like throwing a firecracker into a petrol tank.

'Don't look so shocked, Letty. Dickie is to replace Lord Wavell, and take India through to independence, which, unless we get divorced in the next few months, will make me the Vicereine!' She laughed long and hard, almost hysterically. For a second I was alarmed. 'What a turn up for the books! Me of all people! The pariah of the British establishment, Queen of India in her Majesty's place!'

'Has Dickie said yes?'

She said that he had and that things in India were an appalling mess with the potential for civil war between the Muslims, Sikhs and Hindus. Indian army and navy units had mutinied and the country was in general chaos. Edwina assured me that Dickie had laid down all sorts of conditions before accepting the position: a deadline of June 1948 for Britain's withdrawal from India, a mandate to negotiate with the Indians on independence without reference to London and the right to pick his own staff. 'Of course, he wants us all to fly out in his stupid toy airplane. Typical!' She talked faster and faster, gesticulating wildly, throwing up her arms and for a moment I thought she would fly up off the chair in agitation.

'The thing is, it's not just Dickie who can choose his own staff. I can too. Letty, I trust your judgement. You're steady, whereas me . . . Well, we've been friends a long time!' She gave me her biggest, most enchanting, most seductive smile. 'That's why I want you to come with me as Special Adviser to the Vicereine.'

Then I really did laugh, giddy with the occasion, the hot food and the conversation.

'Me? Look at me!' I held up my chapped hands and unfiled nails and then pointed at my reflection in the mirror on the wall surrounded by the neglected domestic debris of the kitchen. My thick black hair had not been cut in months and was gathered in an untidy bun at the nape of my neck, revealing to their best advantage the long streaks of grey. I was unmade up and my woollen cardigan bagged unflatteringly over my old dress. 'Anyway, I don't know much about India. I'm not qualified.'

'You're more qualified than you realize. You've always supported the India League and you know Krishna Menon.'

I sucked the air between my teeth at the thought of the tricky man who had co-founded Penguin Books and the India League to campaign and lobby for Indian independence in London.

'I've met him several times at meetings, but I don't like him. Mephistopheles in a Saville Row suit, they call him!'

She half laughed.

'The point is, there is no going back to the way things were before the war. Winston Churchill and the old India hands still don't understand that the British Raj is finished. We'll never get an agreement with the Congress and the Muslim League if we rely on them. If we are to succeed, Dickie and I will need to be a new kind of Viceroy and Vicereine, reaching out to the Indians and building bridges. To put it bluntly, I need people on my staff who are not afraid to shake hands with an Indian.'

Slowly, she finished her tea, eyeing me as if assessing a new recruit. 'Look here, Letty, I'm going to be cruel to be kind. It's not that I don't understand. I do, more than you realize. After Bunny got married I could barely tie my own shoelaces. I used to wander along the riverbank at Broadlands and think about throwing myself in and being found dead in the reeds like Ophelia.'

I knew that she was talking about her long-time lover from before the war, Bunny Phillips.

'Well, and then the war and St John's and the Red Cross came along and the flighty playgirl grew up at last. I found a new purpose to my life, one might say.' Looking again at the pictures of my boys gazing down at us like saints from an altar, she went on, 'And I must add that I'm probably the worst mother the world has ever known, but I cannot imagine how utterly devastated I would be if anything ever happened to my Patricia or Pammy.' She shook her head as if with surprise at all the confidences she was suddenly, uncharacteristically, sharing with me. 'Do you remember when we were at school and the other girls were so abominably cruel? And how, sometimes, I used to come home with you for exeat weekends?'

'Cabbage and Patch,' I replied, referring to our childhood nicknames for each other.

My reply prompted a young girl's open smile, not her forced one for the press, modelled on American film stars. 'Yes. Once, your father took us collecting conkers and climbing trees. And one rainy Saturday afternoon your mother threw the cook out of the kitchen and made apple crumble with us—just you and me—and in the evening we ate it, like we are doing now, from big bowls in front of the fire. The truth is, I think that if I'd been loved like that by my own parents as a child I might have been a better person. I've always cherished the memory of those happy days with your family.'

'I had no idea,' I said. 'But I'm glad.'

Already she had opened up enough and the mask of rank and class slipped firmly back into place. Standing up, she picked up her hat and coat, and then faced me squarely.

'So, Brigadier Wallace, what are you going to do? Stay here torturing yourself with the memory of your boys and weep yourself into an early grave? You were the best I ever worked with at St John's. You think on your feet, won't take no for an answer and unlike my usual female secretaries, you have rank and get on with senior people on equal terms.' Plonking her hat back on her head, she stabbed it with the pin.

'The Vicereine needs you in India.' Edwina Mountbatten turned to leave but looked back over one slim coquettish shoulder. 'In fact, I think I shall tell my husband, the PM and the King that I will not go to India unless you, Lady Wallace, agree to come too!'

he engines of the converted Lancaster bomber droned through the blackness, over the endless deserts of Iran. I had left Northholt airbase yesterday morning with the Mountbattens, their seventeen-year-old daughter Pamela, and some of their staff. With extra fuel tanks and a replacement crew, we were aiming to make the 6500 mile journey to New Delhi in less than twenty-four hours. I lay with my feet carefully tucked up, so they didn't kick the head of the Viceroy Designate, Lord Louis Mountbatten, known to his friends and family as Dickie, who was snoring in the next bunk. But I could not sleep.

The noise rattled and grated and the cold tightened my muscles so that my skull felt as if it had been forged from metal plates. I pulled the green army blanket around me and imagined myself dozing against a warm rock on the beach in Malta, where we had stopped to refuel the day before. But was it just yesterday? I did not know many hours ago, I, this Englishwoman who had flown only once before to Austria for a holiday in 1935, and who had never been outside Europe, had stood at the tiny airplane window, watching the vast tracts of moon-like landscape far below, and wondered if I would ever see green again. I was losing all sense of time, scale and place, my Englishness already diminishing with the flight into something bigger, greater than I had ever known.

Suddenly the plane began to shake. Just a little at first. Enough to rattle the teacups on the shelf in the galley and stir a few of the

sleepy heads in their bunks. Then with a bang and a violent judder
the plane began to fall. I was thrown upwards. Gasping with
shock, I grabbed the side of my bunk and clung on desperately.
The women were screaming; the men shouting commands.

'Turbulence. Buckle up! Hold on!'

A box fell from an overhead locker, hitting me sharply on
the head, and I raised one arm to protect myself as more boxes
tumbled and avalanched like rocks down a hill. And then, as
suddenly as it had started, it stopped. Cautious smiles broke
out around the cabin. People picked themselves up, cleared
away the debris, strapped themselves down again and wearily
settled to try to sleep again.

I thought that I ought to have been more afraid and
wondered why I had not been. Perhaps because I felt I had
nothing left to live for. Pulling the blanket over my head, I
cradled a tatty old shoebox that had fallen out of the locker. It
comforted me, although I didn't know why.

What was in that box? I had a suspicion. If I was right, our
departure from Northolt had nearly been delayed because of it.

I could see them now in my mind's eye, the two men standing
in the spring sunshine on the tarmac prior to take-off. One was
Lord Louis Mountbatten, son of Prince Louis of Battenberg and
Princess Victoria of Hesse, and grandson of Queen Victoria.
The other was his nephew, the young Greek Prince Philip. Tall,
athletic and blond, Philip was a lieutenant in the Royal Navy. He
was handsome and self-assured. It was easy to see how he had
turned the head of the young Princess Elizabeth, or so they said.
The manners of the two men were virtually identical. Relaxed,
confident, polished. To the manner born.

They had mingled with the assembled company, posing for
photographs, exchanging a word here, a word there, shaking
a hand, Dickie patting the occasional shoulder. He had not
looked like a man who expected to get a bullet in his back. At
last the final boxes had been stowed, over sixty in all, and it was

time for us to leave. The older man had patted the younger one on the shoulder one last time and turned towards the stairs leading to the aircraft when he caught sight of me.

'Good morning, Pippi!' he said. 'So pleased you've agreed to come along!'

He had offered me his hand. For reasons best known to him 'Pippi' had always been Dickie's nickname for me. How I hated it! Yet at the same time, I was drawn in by him. Damn him! He could charm the hind legs off a donkey. It was Dickie Mountbatten's way of dealing with people. He might only speak to you for a few seconds about a matter of no interest to him at all, but during that time he would look at you with his beautiful blue eyes, his head cocked to one side, focusing his full attention on you. He would give the impression that you, and you alone, were the most important thing in the world. It was always like this with Dickie Mountbatten. He was a gentleman and a diplomat. A showman and a charmer.

'Good morning, Lord Louis!' I had smiled despite myself. 'I'm honoured to be invited. I hope I won't let you down!'

'Can't do without you, Pippi!' he said with a grin. 'Been damned difficult to persuade Edwina to come at all. Weight off my mind with Pippi at her side!' Leaning forward he had carefully straightened the collar of my coat and whispered in my ear. 'I'm counting on you to keep Edwina on an even keel.' And in that second my time was up, my moment in the sun was over. He had gestured with his chin to indicate that I should board before him, waved to Prince Philip, to the Secretary of State for India and Burma, to the press, and then bounded up the steps behind me.

But no sooner had we got on the plane than we nearly all had to get off again.

'Where is it?' Dickie Mountbatten had taken off his trilby hat and demanded of the valet, the maid, of Elizabeth Ward, Edwina's permanent private secretary, and lastly, somewhat desperately, of me. 'Well, someone must have packed it? We can't leave without it.' One after the other we had all shaken our heads and a search had begun.

Now, in the cold and dark of the night, high over the Himalayas, the temptation was too much. Carefully, I slipped off the large red elastic band keeping the lid in place. In the gloom, the diamonds of Edwina's tiara glistened like a miniature silver Christmas tree decorated with crystal snowflakes. My eyes feasted on the shimmering vision of beauty and perfection. It reminded me of an old life from a long time ago, imagined round, full and complete. The window displays in Fortum and Mason's, the smell of mulled wine, ham and Christmas pudding, and my little boys in their dressing gowns, whispering as they tiptoed downstairs on Christmas morning.

But my mind would not be still. It wandered back to Northolt again.

'Here it is! Damn stupid thing! I don't know why you brought it in the first place!' Edwina in her brown Prince of Wales check suit had finished her round of formal farewells on the tarmac, climbed the steps to the plane and casually slung the shoebox with the tiara into the locker.

Dickie had grimaced at the slight and the two of them had squared up to each other like boxers before a fight. Dickie balled his fists, his eyes darkening with anger; Edwina tensed her shoulders and gritted her teeth to the point you could see her receding gums. But conscious of the presence of the rest of us they had pulled back, Dickie turning on his heel and quipping to his ADC Ronnie Brockman, 'Hey ho! Ready for the off! They don't want me out there, and I certainly don't want to go.'

Lying there in the darkness I wondered how it was that they were still together. Edwina had told me that the sex had stopped years ago. Dickie was loyal to his French mistress, Yola Letellier, and Edwina had never made a secret of her lovers.

But now, after nearly twenty-five years, they were imprisoned by each other: Edwina by Dickie's royal ambitions and fixations with service, honour and glory, and he by her, a once beautiful woman he had loved and tried to please but never understood or been able to satisfy or control.

My narrow bunk creaked as I tried to ease myself quietly to the floor. Around me in the cabin people still slept or snoozed in various postures. Dickie Mountbatten's feet in grey socks stuck out of the blanket. Elizabeth Ward was on her stomach, her face squashed to the left. Pamela with one leg hanging off her bunk, was puffing gently as if blowing bubbles.

At the front of the cabin, in the seating area, Edwina's old maid was knitting, her matronly form expanded over nearly two seats. I took out my notebook from my bag and with a nod and a smile moved to sit opposite her. There was no response. They didn't like newcomers, the other women on Edwina's staff. They knew I had gone to school with Edwina, so by that token I counted as one of her friends. They knew also that I was Letticia, Lady Wallace, on account of my husband who had received his knighthood after becoming a King's Counsel. But I was now a widow being paid for my work in India, which reduced me somewhat to the rank of a servant. All in all, very confusing for them. They were struggling to place me for I was neither fish nor fowl. I would have to tread carefully. Putting on the reading light, I looked over my shorthand notes, taken during meetings and briefings over the last weeks.

It was my brother-in-law, Victor, who had first suggested the meeting. I had been staying with him and his wife Margaret in London while preparing to leave for India.

'You want to know about Indian politics?' Victor had said to me over breakfast. 'Sir William Staffs is your man. Spent most of his career in the Indian Civil Service, stationed in the

Punjab. He worked with Lord Willingdon and Lord Linlithgow when they were Viceroys. A good dinner and a couple of bottles of wine will oil his tongue. In fact, you won't be able to shut the old devil up!'

Now, in my mind, I was back in the Savoy Grill that night, trying to make sense of it all. The letter. The message. The old man's breath hot on my face as he whispered in my ear. Surely matters couldn't be that bad in India? But what if it were true? Then we were doomed to fail. And what were our chances of returning to England alive?

'The irony is that the Sikhs, Hindus and Muslims can live in relative peace under the British Raj, but not if left to rule themselves. The only reason they don't eat each other is because Hindus are vegetarian!' Sir William Staffs roared at his crude joke, before tipping back his head, slurping an oyster and chasing it down with a gulp of Muscadet. 'And we, the British, are damned by our fidelity to the notion of democracy and our perverse sense of duty and doing the right thing. Not at all sure that democracy is the right thing for India, mind you, but one isn't allowed to say that.' Another oyster disappeared. 'And out of the quagmire, hey presto! comes the ridiculous idea of Pakistan, a new state for Muslims where they can have a voice and govern their own affairs, free from the tyranny of the Hindu majority.' Yet another oyster and Sir William's Adam's apple wobbled up and down excitedly. He ate with such gusto that I found myself wondering if he didn't actually swallow his food at all but stored it in the great folds of his neck like a pelican. Eyebrow raised at me, Victor eventually poured the last of the Muscadet into Sir William's glass.

'But why, if Muslims cannot live under Hindu majority rule, is Pakistan such a bad thing?' I knew I was playing devil's advocate.

When Sir William smiled, his reply took me by surprise. 'My dear lady, that was just what I said when I first heard about the idea in Simla in the 1930s. Perhaps it might solve all the problems; two Muslim states, one in the west, one in the east, not ideal, but nevertheless.' When all the oysters were gone, the waiter began to clear the table in preparation for the main course, brushing the crumbs away and catching them in a little silver tray. 'But you see, it is all far more complicated than that. The populations are mixed, and the creation of a Muslim state would be an invitation to the Muslims in those areas to slit the throats of any old Hindu.'

The waiter poured the wine carefully from the claret jug. It flowed rich and red into the glass. The main course arrived— beef Wellington for the three of us. I salivated at the sight and smell of it. I had not eaten like that since before the war.

'But surely, the hostage theory will apply?' The meat was tender and the juices oozed into my mouth. 'There will be Muslims living in other parts of India and vice versa, so neither community will want to risk the lives of their brothers and sisters.'

The old man looked at me, his red face distended, pudgy eyes suddenly sad. This time he sipped his wine, speaking slowly now with an effort that reflected pain.

'No. You see, my dear, India is like a long ball of string. It has been unravelling for decades already. Perhaps we should not have given the Muslims electoral reservations in 1909.' He sighed and wiped his chin with his napkin. 'If it comes to pass, Pakistan that is, and I very much fear it is too late to stop it, there will be a rush for land and power. In fact it has already begun. To all intents and purposes it's a war of succession. I predict a bloodbath, a slaughter of catastrophic proportions and there will be nothing anyone, Indian or British, can do about it.'

It was time for dessert, and Victor casually cracked the top of his crème brûlée with a spoon. Sir William had gone uncharacteristically quiet and Victor filled in the gap in conversation.

'Seems to me that Mountbatten has been handed a poisoned chalice. We might have won the war, but the coffers are bare. We all know that there is neither the money nor the political will to hang on in India. Who is going to pay for us to garrison India with reliable forces while the Hindus, Sikhs and Muslims argue it out? The Americans certainly aren't. Churchill is right: Mountbatten's mission is Operation Scuttle.'

Sir William Staffs played with his apple crumble, describing yellow rings of custard with his silver spoon. Then he looked me straight in the eye.

'Trouble is, Mountbatten is already a lame duck and he doesn't even know it.'

'How so?' I asked, sensing I was on to something.

Veins pulsing in his neck and face, Sir William Staffs leant forward and whispered across the table. 'He's Krishna Menon's man. Don't tell anyone I told you, but the Indian National Congress has been secretly lobbying for Mountbatten to be appointed Viceroy for some time.' He slumped back into his chair, his great belly threatening to pop the buttons on his blue shirt. Eyes narrowed, he watched me to see if I could join the dots. I realized that if Jinnah, leader of the Muslim League, knew this, it would make Mountbatten's task of producing an agreement between the Hindus and Muslims that preserved a united India and effected a smooth transfer of power virtually impossible.

Slowly, Sir William Staffs reached inside the jacket of his pinstriped suit and pulled out a brown envelope. He placed it on the table and smoothed it tenderly with the flat of his hand.

'Lady Wallace, I wonder if you might do me a favour?' He handed me the envelope. It was slightly bulky in one corner. 'I have a friend in Simla, Mrs Jane Ovington. I could post it, of course. Silly, really! But if it wouldn't be too much trouble?'

I took the envelope, protesting that of course I would be delighted. He went on, 'And when you bump into Field Marshal Auchinleck, tell him from me, *Non illegitimi carborundum!*'

When dinner was over Sir William helped me with my coat and wished me God speed. At the last moment, he forcefully grabbed my arm and pushed his face right up against mine. I was revolted. I could smell the wine, garlic and tobacco on his breath. Urgently, he whispered in my ear.

'Final word of advice, my dear. Never ever be tempted to carry a side arm in India. Despite what people say, believe me, you'll be safer without one.'

My God, India was hot! Standing on the tarmac at Palam airport, the heat took my breath away. Everything was white. My eyes ached from the brightness. Had I been living so long in the darkness that I had forgotten the light?

Where I sweated and wilted, Edwina was as cool as a cucumber. We had landed ages ago and the boxes were mostly unloaded. The Viceroy and Vicereine Designates had been received by the waiting dignitaries and Dickie had long since finished inspecting the guard of honour. Yet she tarried.

She stood about ten feet away from the foot of the steps to the aircraft. All fizz and sparkle, her weight resting seductively on to one hip, she was deep in conversation with two Indian men. Already, they were under her spell. They were Liaquat Ali Khan, General Secretary of the Muslim League, and Jawaharlal Nehru, Vice President of the interim government. Both of them were famous and I recognized them immediately from newsreels, papers and books. The handsome, charismatic Nehru was the man most likely to be the Prime Minister of the new independent India after we left. But it looked like Edwina knew them personally. She had greeted them like they were long-lost friends. Now she was chatting animatedly, talking French style, with her hands and shoulders, as was her way.

The rest of us were gathered by the cars, waiting to leave the airport. Dickie's face was inscrutable. But he pulled awkwardly at the hem of his jacket as if trying to straighten it when it was not creased. It was getting embarrassing. She was almost flirting. Did she know she was keeping everyone waiting? If she did, she didn't seem to care.

Squinting and shading my eyes against the sun, I saw that now Nehru was doing the talking. He must have said something very funny for Khan rolled his eyes to the sky and all three of them burst out laughing.

It was a relief when at last we got in the cars.

'Best keep the windows up as much as you can once you enter Delhi,' the young British officer from the 14th Punjabi Regiment warned. He closed our car door gently, almost as if he were tucking children up in bed.

I was squashed between the side of the car and Ronnie Brockman who seemed owl-like in his spectacles. He, in turn, was wedged against a bulging padlocked briefcase and Elizabeth Ward. Just after we landed Edwina had thrust the shoebox containing the tiara into my hands for safe keeping. Tenderly, I cradled it in my lap as the cars sped towards New Delhi.

On the outskirts of the city we stopped so that Edwina and Dickie could transfer into the horse-drawn landau for the final leg of the journey to Viceroy's House. I could not see the point of such a show for there was a marked lack of crowds to welcome the new Viceroy and Vicereine. Out of nowhere, I remembered that in 1912 someone had thrown a bomb at the elephant carrying the then Viceroy, Lord Hardinge, and his wife when they were passing through Chandni Chowk in Old Delhi. The Viceroy had sustained serious injuries, and the mahout had been killed. And now Dickie and Edwina were out in front in the open-topped carriage. They smiled through clenched teeth at the non-existent crowds, and hated one another. They had not exchanged more than a few words during the whole flight.

Through the windscreen of the car I watched the landau with its mounted escort of the Viceroy's bodyguard, wheel past

India Gate. Facing the Gate was a high stone canopy underneath which stood a monumentally square, almost Soviet-style statue of King George V.

'Look!' Ronnie Brockman pointed to the great cupola dome of Viceroy's House. In the distance, it seemed to float on a cushion of the palest blue. 'Designed by Sir Edwin Lutyens. Isn't it magnificent?' Ronnie had been in New Delhi during the war when he was Secretary to Lord Louis in his capacity as Supreme Allied Commander South East Asia. He was gearing up for the role of tour guide. 'The city of New Delhi was commissioned in 1911, and designed by Lutyens and his colleague Herbert Baker. It is in a unique style, as you will see, combining Western classicism with Indian decorative motifs.' Elizabeth and I nodded dutifully. Judging the danger of bombs, stones and Molotov cocktails to be minimal by this point, I rolled the window down.

There was no wind, not even the promise of a breeze. The pennants on the lances of the Viceroy's bodyguard barely moved. The men were tall in their turbans, splendid in white breeches, black jackboots and red jackets. The hooves of their horses clattered as they rode a neat collected trot.

'North Block, South Block.' Ronnie Brockman was feeling at home, proudly indicating the two great administrative blocks of red sandstone, one on either side of the road, each topped with its own miniature dome. Here was the heart of the British Raj that ruled over four hundred million people. I wondered who might be looking down at us from behind the black unblinking windows. The size and the scale of the buildings made Whitehall look like a toy town. Surely it was Britain that was ruled by India, not the other way round?

The great gilded wrought iron gates to Viceroy's House had been thrown open. The cavalcade of horses and cars, including ours, followed the landau up the long drive until it stopped in front of the great house.

Another honour guard, this time made up of Royal Scots Fusiliers, stood to attention. Even as we lesser folk got out of the car, photographers pressed in, keen for pictures of us all.

'You'll be in the papers tomorrow,' Ronnie Brockman quipped. 'Mark my words!'

Shading my eyes against the sun, I looked up at the house. Judging by scale, it was incorrect to call it that. It had to be a palace. But for a palace it was not delicate, subtle or ornate; there was no stucco or gold leaf. There were no visible windows on the front and this left a faceless, blind construction relying on ranks of Greco-Roman columns which seemed to bite down on the earth like a lion's teeth.

Edwina and Dickie descended from the landau. Regally, they climbed the red-carpeted stairs to the entrance of the house. At the top, waiting to greet them were the tiny matchbox figures of the outgoing Viceroy and Vicereine, Lord and Lady Wavell.

'Witness the moment!' Brockman said. 'Never happened before; a meeting of an incoming and an outgoing Viceroy on Indian soil. Usually the one sails in as the other sails out, two ships passing.' He drew the palms of his hands silently at a distance past each other.

For one cannot have two incarnations of the great King Emperor in the same place at the same time, lest one eclipses the other, I reflected, but kept my thoughts to myself.

Edwina curtsied to the Viceroy and Vicereine. It was a neat, practised little bob. Patting a curl with her right hand, she smiled and chatted as photographers clicked and clucked about like hens.

We had time for a quick tidy and were back on parade. Dickie, in full dress naval whites, descended with Lord Wavell to inspect the guard and the band struck up. No one had thought of providing a chair for Edwina, and she was left to perch like a heron on the edge of the fountain for the duration of the inspection.

Everything was familiar and yet, at the same time, so unfamiliar. I let myself be guided by the momentum of the occasion, Ronnie Brockman, the ADCs and viceregal servants. We were taken to tea in a grand teak-panelled yellow drawing room. You could cut the atmosphere with a knife. Lord Wavell's staff were lined up stiffly on one side of the room. They did not smile. They were minimally polite. It was clear we, the newcomers, were not welcome. It fell to a couple of elderly khidmutgars to break the ice. Smartly dressed in white uniforms with red bibs and turbans, they served the tea and cake. At the sight of Ronnie Brockman their faces broke into big grins. It seemed they remembered him from his previous visit with Lord Louis.

I stared at the array of neat sandwiches, sponge cakes, scones and caramel custards. Unable to help myself, I sub-consciously calculated the sugar rations required for such a spread.

'Well, go on! Dig in!' Ronnie said. I took a small caramel custard. Struggling to balance the teacup on its saucer, the plate and the box with the tiara, I hurried to sit down at the side of the room. I found myself next to a morose-looking Field Marshal. The fact that he had company forced him to look up from his Victoria sandwich cake which he was demolishing in big chunks with the aid of a fork.

'Auchinleck'—he, at least, gave me a friendly smile— 'Claude.' And I recognized him immediately from the newsreels. He was The Commander-in-Chief India and I had a message for him.

'Letticia Wallace,' I put my teacup and saucer on a side table and offered him my hand, adding as an afterthought, 'Special Assistant to the Vicereine.'

'Welcome.' He nodded, and took a mouthful of cake. His hand was big, with prominent hairs on the back. He gripped the cake fork with a thick fist, like a child.

'I had dinner with Sir William Staffs in London just before I left. If I might be so bold, he asked me to pass on a message.' I leant forward and whispered.

A spark of something flickered behind his ice blue eyes and he managed a small laugh.

I judged him to be in his late fifties or early sixties. He had a chiselled face and a neatly clipped grey moustache. But something was not right. It was as if he were hollow within and the uniform, with all its pips and medal ribbons tight across his chest, was the only thing that was holding him together. I expected him to ask me about myself, to enquire about my credentials for the job. He would have perhaps expected me to say then that I had been born in Calcutta or Lahore and that my father had been in this or that regiment and that I spoke Bengali or Punjabi. But he did not ask, and that was the point: What on earth was I doing here?

I got up and made to leave the room. But just at that moment I was saved. A thin gentleman with his hair neatly slicked back bounded up to me as if I were a long-lost friend.

'Hello! You must be Pippi, SA to Her Ex?' He was about ten years younger than me, and was all grins and enthusiasm. Relieved by his offer of friendship, I held out my hand. But I still had no idea what 'SA to Her Ex' might have to do with me.

'Alan Campbell-Johnson, Press Attaché to His Ex.' He must have seen the confusion in my face for he helped me out. 'The Viceroy told me you were on the team. Special Assistant to Her Excellency the Vicereine. Welcome!'

'Oh yes, that's me!' I laughed, getting up to speed with the jargon.

'Looks like you survived the flight?'

'Just about!' I smiled.

Two York aircraft had left London carrying the new Viceroy's staff. The earlier, which Campbell-Johnson must have been on, had made more stops than Mountbatten's plane.

Even so our plane with its extra fuel tanks arrived in Delhi only a few hours later.

'I rather fear you might have been bumped off our leisurely flight in favour of Lord Ismay. He flatly refused to fly with Mountbatten, you know.' He cupped his hand to his mouth giving a muted impression of the new Chief of the incoming Viceroy's staff. 'I want to eat at civilized hours and sleep in a bed. Damned if I will fly hell for leather over "The Hump" with Mountbatten. That man knows nothing but speed!'

My low-heeled court shoes click-clacked through the labyrinth of rooms and corridors of Viceroy's House. I was lost. I still had the tiara in its shoebox and I was looking for Edwina's suite. After the formal welcome, Lord Louis had gone straight into the study with Lord Wavell and the heavy teak doors had been firmly closed. Edwina too had disappeared with the maternal figure of Lady Wavell and not been seen since.

I wandered through the vast ceremonial rooms of Viceroy's House, with their chandeliers, oil paintings, archways and mirrors. But there was no one there. It was as if a magician were playing a great trick. He had waved his wand and made all the people, guards and servants disappear. All was still, fixed by his spell. Even though the open windows begged for it, there was no breeze in the mushroom-shaped trees in the Mughal gardens; the birds too were mute. Only in the Durbar Hall underneath the huge dome, did I find another living soul. A mangy monkey that must have sneaked past the guards into the house. He sat on the top of the steps in front of the viceregal thrones. I was about to shoo him away but in that moment he looked at me with large wise eyes. A few seconds passed. He blinked, then turning his full pink bottom to me, scampered up a column and out of an invisible opening high in the dome. I heard him chattering briefly with his friends before silence fell.

A distant tinkling of water drew me outside, where I came across a fountain with eight sprinkling marble lions. A servant in white with a turban, balancing a tray on his shoulder, cycled past. He seemed to be dragging with him a trail of cornflower blue. It moved between one arch and another and I recognized it as the cotton dress of Edwina's maid. Quickening my pace, I called out to her, but she did not stop.

I was now inside the Viceroy's private quarters, climbing stairs, round and round, like Alice chasing the White Rabbit. The air was musty and already paint was starting to peel from the walls of this great British palace that had been finally completed barely sixteen years ago. It hung in great curls or had flaked on to the floor and the window sills, where it lay like bits of Parmesan. I stopped at the top of the stairs to catch my breath. The maid had disappeared, but Edwina's dog, Mizzen was there, whimpering at my feet.

'Where is she then? Show me!' I bent down and patted him. The dog cocked his head to one side as if in answer to my question then trotted obediently down the corridor and through a door that had been left ajar.

I found myself in a bedroom. The fan whirred nonchalantly over the bed on which were laid out several of Edwina's dresses and gowns. Clearly her maid had already prepared the outfits to be worn for Wavell's early departure tomorrow morning and the swearing-in ceremony on Monday.

Mizzen padded over to a closed door in the corner of the room, whining and scratching at it. It was too quiet. Something was wrong. I forgot protocol.

'Edwina? It's Letty. Are you all right?' I asked as loudly as I dared.

There was a metallic clatter as if a tray had been dropped.

'Cabbage?' Edwina's voice came from near the floor behind the door. She was calling me by my schoolgirl nickname. 'Is it just you? No one else with you?'

'Yes, Patch!' I answered. Now I was worried. We had not used these silly nicknames for each other in years. There was a moment's hesitation and then the heavy teak door creaked open. Mizzen shot through it, like a rabbit returning to its burrow.

Edwina was slumped on the marble floor of the bathroom like a rag doll. Her long thin legs were splayed out in front of her, her stockings and shoes had been discarded at her side and her dress was hitched up above her knees. My first thought was that she must have slipped but then I saw that she was picking up pieces of roast chicken which had fallen from the silver platter resting on her knee. What was going on? Surely she had not been hiding in the bathroom, gorging on chicken? But her eyes were red and her face was stained where her makeup had run. She had been crying.

'I've brought the tiara,' I said, holding out the cardboard box to her.

She wiped her eyes and her greasy mouth with the back of her hand and forced a smile. 'Come in, Cabbage, and lock the door!'

Suddenly exhausted, I sat next to her on the floor of the bathroom, both of us leaning against the cupboard.

'Want some chicken?' She proffered a chicken drumstick in my direction. I shook my head. 'I asked for something to feed Mizzen and they brought this.' Guiltily, she looked down at the half-eaten roast chicken on its silver platter. 'Far too good to give to the dog. Don't you think?'

I nodded. I could not remember the last time I had seen a whole roast chicken.

'Are you sure you don't want any?' she asked again, her eyes narrowed.

'I've just had tea.' The truth was I was revolted by the sight of the chicken torn apart on the plate and the thought of Edwina devouring it in secret. And yet with this revulsion came a greater realization of the true extent of Edwina's unhappiness. She must have finished her meeting with Lady Wavell, run up to her suite and locked herself away. She shrugged as if to say have it your own way, then carefully started to pick bits of meat off the bone and feed them to Mizzen. He snuffled with delight but was soon sated.

'I've brought the tiara,' I repeated, somewhat at a loss. Leaning forward, she put the chicken platter on a rattan chair by the bath. Then she took the shoebox with the tiara, but made no attempt to open it.

For a long time the two of us sat in silence, looking at the large bath with its little golden feet, each in the shape of a viceregal lion couchant. There was mould around some of the grouting and a patch of green in the corner next to the fly window. Out of the corner of my eye I saw the two of us reflected in a long mirror. Edwina looked shrunken and emaciated in the glass. It was difficult to believe that she had once been considered a great beauty and that she, like me, was only forty-five.

We had always been an odd pair, even as schoolgirls. She had been terribly bullied as a girl because her grandfather, Ernest Cassel, was Jewish. I too had always taken flak, in my case because I had been a tad porky. And so it was that our 'Cabbage and Patch alliance' had come about, as a mutual self-preservation pact. But now Edwina's face was gaunt and pale, her skin wrinkled and lined by too much sun and self-neglect, while my cheeks with their two dimples had filled out, minimizing the ageing, although I had too much darkening and sag under my eyes. She sat hunched, her upper spine slightly curved, while I was taller and straighter. Yet it was the confused, beseeching face of Edwina the child I saw in the mirror. She looked at me with unfocused watery blue eyes. And suddenly it was as if all the girls from our boarding school dorm were here to torment her. Nails scratching at her face, pulling her hair, they screeched, 'Jewish witch! What a bitch!'

Distractedly, Edwina pinged the elastic band round the shoebox a couple of times, then removed it and opened the box. She blinked critically at the tiara, took it out and, grabbing Mizzen by the collar, balanced it behind the dog's ears. He looked so ridiculous that both of us laughed. Sensing approval, Mizzen gave one woof, wagged his tail and sat back on his haunches to show off.

'Do you think all Queens and Vicereines feel like this in the days before?' Edwina asked. She was thinking of the swearing-in ceremony which in some ways would amount to a proxy coronation of Dickie and Edwina as Viceroy and Vicereine, representing the King Emperor and the Queen Empress.

'Like what?' I said, knowing her tendency to bottle herself up.

'Like this,' she said, gesturing towards her half-eaten chicken and her dishevelled ragdoll self in the mirror.

'The good ones, the ones worth their salt, almost certainly do.'

'Thing is, Cabbage. I don't believe in it, any of it. But Dickie loves it, the dressing up, the pomp and ceremony, the glorious final days of the great British Raj. What tosh!' Briefly she puffed herself up and pretended to be trotting on a horse in the manner of a great general. 'And on Monday I have to put on my finery, get out there before all those people, sit on the throne and represent all that I despise.'

People had always ridiculed Edwina Mountbatten, one of the richest women in the world, for calling herself a socialist and championing the cause of Asian nationalists. But then my own socialist inclinations might also have been considered a bit odd given my background. Although I had never lived the high life like Edwina and shuddered at the thought, perhaps there were parts of both of us that refused to be restricted and defined. Maybe this was why, even in her wildest years, I had always found it in my heart to make excuses for her.

'I can't do it!' Her eyes darted anxiously from side to side.

Now it was my turn to be cruel to be kind.

'Yes, you can. You can because you have to, because Dickie is counting on you, because you have no choice.' And in that moment I understood the weight of responsibility on this woman and I was clear what my role had to be. It was to support her. And yet, I thought, she was not afraid for herself, or of the bullet or the bomb. She was afraid that she might not match up to what she expected of herself, what the world expected of her—afraid of failing as Vicereine. And if we did fail . . . well, it is always the decadent temptress empress who is blamed for the rot and final toppling of an empire.

'Want a cigarette?' she asked, taking a packet of Pall Mall and a lighter from the floor beside her. I nodded. Neither of us was really a smoker, but had sometimes lit up, particularly in times of stress during the Blitz. I got up and opened the little fly window in the bathroom to let the smoke out. It was the exchange, the touch of hands, the flicker of flame, the ritual that counted.

'It's not good, you know, the situation.' She waved her hand in front of her as if a map of India were laid out on the floor before us. 'They're all terrified: Lord Wavell, the generals and governors. They're expecting full-on civil war and have battened down the hatches in the government houses and cantonments. They're preparing for the worst. All Lord Wavell has got to offer Dickie is Operation Madhouse, a province by province evacuation plan for British citizens. And dear old Eugenie Wavell is well-meaning with her Bengal famine relief, but really, she is like Marie Antoinette sitting in Versailles and eating cake.' She drew on the cigarette, not really inhaling, and puffed it out quickly through her mouth.

Abruptly she sat up straight, rolling her shoulders, calling herself to attention. 'Cabbage, we've got to get out of Viceroy's House, and on to the streets. We must reach out to the Congress and Muslim League ladies, throw open the gates, invite the Indians to dinner, supper, garden parties, tea. Otherwise the day will come when they will storm the ramparts with pitchforks. At best they will stick our heads up on spikes, at worst . . .' Wincing slightly and holding her side, she stood up and smoothed down her badly wrinkled dress. She went over to the sink, took a tablet from a pillbox and, pursing her lips in the mirror, swallowed it without water.

'God, I look awful!' She tipped out a bar of soap from the soap dish and used the empty dish to stub out her cigarette. Perhaps it was the unaccustomed effect of the nicotine on me, but a storm of ill-formed images rushed through my head: The French painter Delacroix's bare-breasted Liberty—red, white and blue tricolour in one hand, musket with fixed bayonet in the other—leading the revolutionaries through the fire and smoke, over the bodies of the fallen. Hundreds of tiny bloodstained handprints and footprints on stone walls like bizarre cave paintings. But looking around all I could see instead were the white hands and feet of the English children who had made them and been hacked from their bodies. I was thinking of the 1857 Indian mutiny when Englishwomen and children were massacred at the Bibighar and their bodies thrown down a well. In retaliation, Indian villages had been burnt and the citizens of Delhi pulled out of their houses and butchered. I remembered a photograph of three brown bodies with drooping black heads hanging from a tree, people standing about in the manner of a painting of the crucifixion. Edwina handed me the soap dish and I stubbed out my cigarette next to hers. I imagined a finely drawn black-and-white lithograph of sepoys strapped to the mouths of cannons set out in orderly lines, that strangely, I had no recollection of ever having seen before.

'Take a look at this!' Alan Campbell-Johnson dropped a copy of *Dawn* newspaper in front of me at breakfast. 'Yesterday's clanger!'

Putting down my toast, I looked at the picture of Ronnie Brockman and Elizabeth Ward taken the day before yesterday as we were getting out of the cars in front of Viceroy's House.

'Lord and Lady Mountbatten arriving,' I read out the caption.

'What did I tell you!' Ronnie Brockman quipped from the far side of the table. 'I said you'd be in the papers!'

'But they cut me out!' I protested lamely although I was not surprised to have been removed from the frame. I always looked out of place in photographs because I was usually taller than the men. But it was good at least to laugh at something. We had been in India just over twenty-four hours and it was already clear that the British Raj was on its knees. Yesterday there had been riots in New Delhi between Muslims and Sikhs. Whatever the truth, the papers reported that the whole situation had been ignited by the recklessly provocative behaviour of the Sikhs who, as the Muslims were holding a meeting in a mosque in favour of Pakistan, had arrived in the marketplace in lorries and jeeps and careered about, brandishing swords. The upshot was that the District Magistrate had imposed a curfew from 6 p.m. until 7 a.m. Furthermore, for a fortnight no group of more than five individuals would be permitted to assemble for any purpose, and for a week all newspapers, commentary, photographs and cartoons would be subject to official censorship.

Against this backdrop we were up bright and early, dressed in our best bibs and tuckers. Apparent high spirits masked the frenetic preparations and anxiety about the Viceroy's swearing-in ceremony set for 10 a.m. that morning. It was a formal occasion and most of the preparations had already been done prior to our arrival under the supervision of George Abell who had been Private Secretary to Lord Wavell and was carrying on in the job for Lord Mountbatten. Yesterday Edwina had sent me down to see him with some enquiries about the guest list and there had been much last-minute tinkering of seating plans.

'Viceroy's House, lesson one: Live or die by protocol,' Abell had said to me as we went through the list together and rearranged chairs in the Durbar Hall. 'And if we sit Patiala next to Bhopal'—he was referring to the Maharaja and the Nawab of these princely states—'I guarantee it'll be pistols at dawn!' He was carrying a stopwatch and had made me walk at a stately pace into the hall and up the carpeted steps to the thrones in the manner of the Viceroy. From there I read the oath of office while he timed it with the watch that he polished on his trousers in between times as if it were a cricket ball. The whole ceremony had to run to fifteen minutes precisely, otherwise, he said with a nonchalant shrug, 'I'll be for the chop.'

After all this preparation, I found myself standing in the shadow of a column in the Durbar Hall, counting in the guests for the swearing-in ceremony as they arrived. The Indian princes, some in spurs and jewelled turbans, others in Western-style suits, clattered down the staircase into the hall. There were British generals proud in polished leather gun belts and well-hung medal bars and British judges in wigs and gowns. They all towed white-gloved wives with shiny handbags in the crooks of their elbows. There were a couple of maharanis in brightly coloured saris, members of the Muslim League in black astrakhan hats, and members of the Indian National Congress, both men and women, in homespun white khadi cotton. The atmosphere was quietly subdued as if in anticipation of a solemn church service. Nevertheless, the men were alert for any opportunity offered by the occasion, their eyes bright, glinting in the tumbling shafts of sunshine like dagger tips. They milled about, shaking hands, having a quiet word in someone's ear, someone here, turning and side-stepping, neatly avoiding all eye contact with someone else nearby. All the main players in the drama were there, except perhaps the most famous one. The man Winston Churchill had once called a seditious, half-naked fakir was missing. The 'Great Soul', Mahatma Gandhi, had been invited but was not able to come because he was among the peasants in the countryside, trying to calm communal strife. I surveyed the diverse bunch before me, representing the Muslim League, the Indian National Congress and the princely states, and realized why it had been impossible to get any agreement on a plan for a transfer of power to India to date. Surely there were as many different visions of what India was and should be as there were conversations in this room. The Muslims were agitating for Pakistan, many of the Princes wanted to be independent states when the British left and Nehru, leading the Congress, favoured a united India under strong central control. How incredible it was that they were all here beneath one roof, especially considering that many of the Congress members had spent years in British jails as a result of their campaigns for Indian independence. Yet, despite the obvious differences of class, religion, politics and background, as I watched them mingle, it seemed to me that everyone there appeared to share an absolute conviction in themselves, their rank and position, their right to lead. Gradually people began to settle down. They took their seats in front of the empty red and gold thrones under their great scarlet canopy which was illuminated from above by arc lights. For a moment I imagined the scrawny monkey sitting before the thrones. High in the gallery, one of the trumpeters puffed out his cheeks and polished the bell of his instrument on his sleeve.

I looked at my watch: 9.45 a.m. Alan Campbell-Johnson herded the press pack like a sheepdog with a flock. I calculated that nearly everyone was present but noted that there were still two empty chairs in the front row of the Princes' ranks.

'Pippi!' George Abell tapped me on the shoulder. His brow was furrowed and he was sweating. How quickly he had adopted Lord Louis's nickname for me! But for the first time in my life I took it as a compliment, not a put-down.

'Bikaner and Bhopal.' He jutted his chin towards the two ominously empty seats. 'Could you look around, see if you can find them? The Princes are two of Lord Louis's closest friends. He played polo with them when he was here with the Prince of Wales. If they don't show it won't look good.'

I nodded. 'But how will I recognize them?'

He wiped his brow and managed a laconic half grin, twiddling an imaginary moustache and making a gesture over his head which I interpreted to be a feather stuck in a turban. 'You'll know them when you see them. I'm going back to the library. If you could check the staterooms . . .'

I went first to the front of the house and, shading my eyes, stared down towards the Jaipur Column and King's Way. Already the chauffeurs were lining up the cars to pick up the dignitaries after the ceremony. Of the missing Princes, there was no sign.

I hurried down the stairs into the Durbar Hall and through to the state dining room: 9.52 a.m. The doors had been left open to allow the air to circulate. The floor-to-ceiling windows let in slabs of sunlight so that the room was chequered with light and dark. I began to walk the length of the long dining table, touching chair after chair, as if I were a child running my hands along a set of railings.

He strode through the open doors next to the huge Union Jack which hung from the wall at the far end of the hall. He was in a shaft of light. Eyes wide with surprise, he slowed ever so slightly to look at me then looked again. He smiled softly, almost as if he recognized me from somewhere long ago and was pleased to have found me once more. He hurried towards me now, crossing into a square of shade.

He walked stiffly at the knees, leading slightly with the right leg. He was a big man, well over six feet tall. An Indian, he wore a well-cut Western suit with a double-breasted jacket and tie which made him look even broader across the shoulders than he actually was. There was no one else in the hall and he did not take his eyes off me. Now he was in a square of light. He brought with him a gentle breeze, which tugged at the hem of my new cotton summer dress and ruffled the little decorative frill at my neckline and arms. After months in heavy woollen skirts, jumpers and coats, bundled up against the bitter English winter, now in a summer dress I was suddenly conscious of myself, the tiny beads of sweat between my breasts, the air around the tops of my silk stockings and thighs. He came on, in the shade, in the light. I shivered. Every hair on my body stood up on end, yet I was not cold. I wished I had brought a handbag with me. It would have been something to hold on to.

And now we were going to meet. Perhaps in the shade, perhaps in the light. But there was no avoiding it. It would happen halfway down the dining table, perhaps a little less than halfway from my end, I calculated. His stride was longer and quicker than mine. Was he the Nawab or the Maharaja? How was I to tell? The Maharaja perhaps, without jewels and feather? He was nearly upon me and I stopped first. A little short of him, I made my stand. For an instant I thought that he was not going to stop, that the momentum of his walk would carry him past me and all would be lost. I was holding my breath. Still he came on, in the shade, in the light. I rolled back ever so slightly on my heels. We were in the light.

'Excuse me!' I managed to steady my voice and it came out stronger and more assertive than I felt. 'Your Royal Highness?' That should cover it—both a Maharaja and a Nawab. The skin under his large eyes was folded and creased and had just begun to darken with age. His hair would have been black, perhaps curly, but it had been cropped short to hide the grey. Such a huge man. Perhaps he had been an athlete. And yet he had the heart-shaped face of a beautiful woman with high cheekbones and a tiny mouth. He was in his late fifties or very early sixties but there was still youth and vitality in his brown eyes. I ought to have looked away, but he held me in his gaze. My breath was hot on my top lip. I noticed that he had cut himself shaving, probably that very morning. A small nick on the left cheek. He stood right in front of me, near enough for me to reach out and place the palm of my hand on his cheek. I felt ridiculously English, gawky and, strangely for me, small. My hand fluttered to my breast where, in honour of the occasion, I had pinned my Order of St John medal. The pin through my dress felt cold on my chest.

'Who is asking?' His voice was deep, the vowels vibrating long in the empty room.

'Pippi Wallace,' I said, 'Special Assistant to the Vicereine.' I don't know why I called myself Pippi. Perhaps because it was catching on among the Viceroy's staff. Perhaps because it gave me a chance to leave grief behind. Either way, this was the first time I had ever called myself by my own nickname. I offered my white-gloved hand and almost curtsied but he withheld his hand, just for a few seconds, long enough to speak, long enough to save me.

'Well, I am sorry to disappoint you, Mrs Wallace.' He grinned. Then slowly, deliberately, he put his tongue into his cheek, and pushed it out as if he had just popped a grape in his mouth.

'I'm merely Hari Rathore.' He extended his hand. I shook it, feeling it cool and firm through my glove, flushing until the tips of my ears burned.

'I'm the doctor in the house,' he said, and I remembered his name in bold black letters typed at the bottom of George Abell's guest list.

Emergency: Dr Hari S. Rathore

'Ever since the 1911 Durbar, they always make sure to have a doctor on call,' he explained. 'Someone always keels over on these occasions. There were three at Lord Wavell's swearing-in.'

I tried to smile but thought of George Abell with his stopwatch waiting back in the Durbar Hall. It was 9.56 a.m. Dr Rathore saw me looking at my watch.

'You're seeking Bikaner and Bhopal?'

I nodded and wondered how he knew and, briefly, why he had taken so long to tell me. But time was running out and I had to get back to the Durbar Hall.

'Well, it looks like they're not coming. Too busy fighting amongst themselves.' His brow furrowed, highlighting the deep creases between his eyes. 'Damn Princes, like spoilt children! High time they grew up! Before it is too late—for themselves and for India.'

George Abell saw me return to the Durbar Hall unaccompanied except for Dr Rathore. He nodded slightly as I shook my head. It occurred to me that he must know Dr Rathore, and might even have dispatched him to look for the Princes too, for he did not seem in the least surprised to see us together. Dr Rathore hurried to help George Abell remove the two empty chairs. Pandit Nehru, sitting on the front row in a black sherwani and white khadi cap, raised a quizzical eyebrow. Abell handed Dr Rathore his black doctor's bag. He must have been keeping it for him. Then the three of us took our rather cramped seats at

the back of the hall. But almost immediately the trumpet fanfare
began in the gallery above and we scrambled to our feet again.

Edwina, elegant and slim in a long gown of ivory brocade,
stood with Dickie on the threshold of the hall. She was pale.
Her shoulders hunched and tense, she held on to a ridiculous
ostrich feather fan as if her life depended on it. I had seen this
before. She always shook uncontrollably in the minutes before
climbing the rostrum to make a public speech. Despite this, I
had never known her to give in to her nerves or shirk her duty,
and in the end she always had the audience eating out of the
palm of her hand. Dickie, on the other hand, had no self-doubt.
He was splendid in full naval dress whites, sword at his side.
His chest was decorated with the Order of the Garter, the Star
of India, the Star of the Indian Empire and the Royal Victoria
Order. I knew this because his valet had reeled off all Dickie
Mountbatten's honours to me at breakfast this morning with
the utmost pride.

'There are more, you know. But that is all he is allowed to
wear at once.'

When Edwina hesitated at the sound of the trumpets,
Dickie took her right hand without looking at her, patted
it and put it on his arm. Slowly, regally, the Mountbattens
walked down the aisle towards the thrones. Next to me,
George Abell stared at his stopwatch which he held in the
palm of his hand. All eyes were now on Edwina and the
glittering tiara that she had so carelessly allowed her dog to
wear. And as she walked, with every step she seemed to grow
taller, to swell within herself until it was her presence, and not
Dickie's, that dominated the room.

The Mountbattens stood in front of the thrones. Dickie
raised his right hand and the Chief Justice, in long wig and
gown, administered the oath of office.

'I, Louis Francis Albert Victor Nicholas Mountbatten . . .'
To the right of the Mountbattens stood Nehru and Vallabhbhai

Patel for the Congress, on their left, Liaquat Ali Khan and
others for the Muslim League. Edwina looked at her husband,
her chin jutting out slightly. She was the picture of the perfect
Queen, dignified, intelligent and a little aloof. I knew she
could not see me at the back of the hall. She had once told me
that being short-sighted helped during public occasions, for
without her glasses she could not see the faces of the people
in the audience. As Dickie repeated the oath of office, which
I myself had stumbled over the previous evening, I watched
the countless particles of dust in the wide shafts of light that
tumbled into the hall from the top of the dome. They moved
at random, without ever seeming to fall. I wondered if he were
sitting up there on the top of Viceroy's House, that monkey,
with his crowd of friends, watching us all.

The oath was faultlessly completed, and Dickie turned
with Edwina to face the hall. Suddenly there was loud bang. I
gasped and half jumped up. A tremor of fear rippled through
the audience as people tensed and turned, preparing to run. A
bomb?

'It's all right.' Dr Rathore put his hand on my bare
forearm. His touch was courteous, brief, feather light. 'Just
a photographer's bulb bursting.' The rest of the bulbs went
off in salvos, recording for posterity the last Viceroy and last
Vicereine of India in the Durbar Hall, and the audience heaved
a collective sigh of relief. The only ones who appeared unruffled
were the Mountbattens; they hadn't even flinched.

'Now for the speech,' George Abell mopped his brow with
his handkerchief and we all sat down. The three of us settled
ourselves as best we could. It was a dramatic break with tradition
for a Viceroy to give a speech at the swearing-in ceremony and
there had been rumblings in the ADC's mess last night. Clearly
the speech took the majority of the audience by surprise. They
sat up alert in their seats to listen.

'This is no normal Viceroyalty on which I am embarking.'

The Durbar Hall was built for King Emperors and Queen Empresses, not democracy and speeches. The Viceroy's words bounced off the marble walls and those that were not mixed up and distorted in the process, were half gobbled up by the great expanse of dome.

'Everyone of us must do what . . . can to avoid . . . word or action . . . might lead to further bitterness or add to the toll of innocent victims . . .'

Next to me, Dr Rathore twisted in his seat, leaning forward slightly with his head to one side. He was squashed between Abell and me and there was not enough legroom for us between the chairs in front and his doctor's bag. Abell, who had the aisle seat had done his best for us by putting his legs out to the side to create some space. But even with my legs held to the right, there was no way Dr Rathore could stop his knee skimming my left thigh. Both of us were doing our best for propriety, holding our muscles tense to keep the distance. A fly buzzed around our heads, the strange acoustics amplifying the sound so that it drowned out the Viceroy's words. In my mind it droned ominously and low like a bomber. The fly flitted from the back of the chair in front, to a stripe on my dress over my right knee, then on to Dr Rathore's left thigh. I was filled with a sudden rage towards the poor creature and wanted to swat it right there and then. But really, it was Dr Rathore I was cross with, not the fly. It had settled peacefully next to his folded hands. With long delicate fingers, they were incongruous in proportion to the bulk of the rest of his body. Dr Rathore made no attempt to shoo the fly away. It hopped to the point where the muscles of his leg could be seen tight under his trousers, knotting together just above his knee.

'I am under no illusion about the difficulty of my task . . .'

At the front of the hall, Pandit Nehru also had his head cocked to one side. He was listening intently to the Viceroy, but looking at Edwina. Her eyes were fixed on her husband. As

I watched these three great players in the drama, I realized with a shiver that Dr Rathore was looking at me. His right eyelid drooped slightly lower than his left, giving the impression of sleepiness. Suddenly I wanted him to put his arm around me. I wanted, just for a few seconds, to rest my head on his shoulder. Damn the fly!

'I shall need the greatest goodwill of the greatest possible number and I am asking India today for that goodwill.'

The rest of the Viceroy's words were lost in the goldfish bowl of acoustics. But I had heard enough to anticipate the horror with which the speech would be received in London. I could see them in their clubs and Inns of Court! They would be tut-tutting over tomorrow's *London Times*. For here was the great British Raj admitting its vulnerability and weakness. The old guard would not like that one little bit. The second hand on George Abell's stopwatch concluded its final round. Pursing his lips with satisfaction at a job well done, he pressed the stop button. At that precise moment the canons of the Royal Horse Artillery rumbled into action, booming outside in the grounds, the first shots of a ponderous thirty-one gun salute. I imagined the troops in all the regiments in all the military garrisons all over India. Like us in Viceroy's House, they too must have risen at dawn and were now on parade, ready to present arms. The moment the first gun exploded in New Delhi, the salute would be picked up by their own cannons, sounding the last thundering roar of the Imperial British lion.

I was sitting at my desk by the window of my room. It was pleasantly cool; with a partial view of the Mughal Gardens. Soon it would be dusk, the gardeners ambled about turning off the fountains in anticipation. The shimmering plumes spluttered and died quickly, to order, in lines. Somewhere in the distance the guard was changing. The soft clip-clop of horses' hooves and the tired murmur of men's voices as they went off duty, and then it was quiet—too quiet and still.

Picking up my fountain pen, I hurried to be busy, to fill the space and time. It was a habit born of fear. If I did not keep occupied, exhaustion born of despair would rush to fill the vacuum. Clumsily, I unscrewed the cap of my pen. It had been a present from my father and was engraved with my maiden name: Letticia Thomas. Holding it now, smooth and cool in my hand, it occurred to me that the young woman I had once been had died the day her first son was killed. Unhooking a frayed elastic tie, I opened my leather notebook. Inside were the 'letters' I had written to my husband, Charles.

Writing to him was my way of coping after his death. Back in London, every evening after supper, I had picked up my pen. I was like a mediaeval priest shut away in a stone chapel, writing letters as prayers. I had imagined my words fluttering up to heaven, binding Charles and me together. I would see him sitting right there at the head of our big dining table in Argyll Street, with his mop of curly red hair and freckled faced, grinning like a pirate at our boys.

That was the man he had been, and I had chosen to fix him in my memory in this way; a hard working criminal barrister who would take on the most challenging and controversial cases without a second thought.

Here now in Viceroy's House, I flicked through the pages and began to read. All my letters began the same way. *My dearest darling*. Page after page. I had told him about the general election at the end of the war. It had been a Labour landslide and Clement Attlee had replaced Winston Churchill in Number 10. How pleased I had been! *But let's not quarrel about it,* I had written, for things really could not go on as they had before. I told him about my visits to the East End with the St John's Ambulance and the woman with three thin, dirty children and a newborn, who did not have enough coal to boil water to make a cup of tea. I hoped that the nationalization of the coal mines would help. *Really, we have to offer people something better or all our sacrifices will be in vain.* I turned another page. *The doctor has given me some pills to help me sleep. Damn it! I'm not going to take the bloody things!* Another page, another letter. I sighed, for it was the summer of 1946 that prompted my move. Alone in the house in Argyll Street, memories jumped out at me from every corner. I hoped that he would forgive me, for I had decided to let the house and leave London.

By this point my handwriting had deteriorated to border on the illegible. The ink and the words had run into senseless black tides with my tears. I swallowed hard to control the sense of panic at the memories of 1940 and 1945. They choked me with the heavy scent of summer flowers. The long summer nights when the sun had hardly set and there was only worry and nowhere to rest. The sweet peas at the side of the house commiserating uselessly in the breeze. The first raspberries from the canes which were bittersweet and tasted of blood. The bees buzzing on the lavender. Didn't they know I had lost two sons in the space of four years? Oughtn't they to stop?

I looked at the picture of Charles on my desk that I had brought with me from Oxford. I looked and yet it was not the handsome young QC I saw, but a gaunt old man wasted suddenly, cruelly, by disease. In his last weeks the housekeeper and I had brought our big double bed into the drawing room. Many times at night I had climbed in beside him and held his bony body in my arms. The physical contact, he had said, eased the pain far better than any morphine. That night, the last one, he had reached out and stroked my hair away from my forehead in the way he knew I liked, just once, for he did not have the energy for more.

'Take me with you,' I had whispered. 'To be with you all. I can't go on alone.'

'Yes, you can. You must. For me, for George, for Robert. You must live on. Find a purpose, find a way.' Exhausted, he had rested a while before struggling on. 'Say it now. The Lord's prayer. Like you used to for the boys when they were little.'

And I had.

'Our Father, who art in heaven, hallowed be thy name. Thy kingdom come, thy will be done on earth as it is in heaven. Give us this day our daily bread and forgive us our trespasses and we forgive those him trespass against us. Lead us not into temptation, but deliver us from evil. For thine is the kingdom, the power and the glory, for ever and ever. Amen.'

A few hours later when I had awoken, my husband was cold in my arms.

There was a knock at the door.

'Come in!'

It was my bearer, Zamurad Khan, with the tea I had requested. I had written to Charles about him the day after our arrival in India.

My dearest darling,
It's a strange thing, but all the staff in Viceroy's House are men. There is not one single woman in service. All of them wear white uniforms with the initials of the Viceroy sewn on to their chests, just like the Yeoman Warders at the Tower of London. Imagine them the night before the swearing-in ceremony, feverishly sewing on their new badges! Rather ridiculous, don't you think?

It will take some getting used to, having a man for a personal servant. He is a Muslim, of course; seems very diligent and has an honest demeanour. You will certainly want to ask me how old he is and although he is certainly a lot older than we are, I cannot begin to guess his exact age. He is a small, energetic, wiry man who gives the impression that his joints are made of springs. There is something about the shape of his face, his narrow eyes and the way his skin is tight over his face with not one wrinkle, that reminds me of a Chinaman. So far so good and we get along with a certain caution between us, rather like a cat and a dog who have been thrown together. Although, I confess, at the moment Zamurad Khan is probably the dominant partner. He has a definite air of authority about him in the way of a man whose family might once have been something and had fallen on hard times. The younger men certainly jump to it when he gives orders and he knows all the ropes here in Viceroy's House.

'Shall I pour, Memsahib?' Zamurad Khan stood in front of the tea tray. I nodded and sat back in my chair, letting him do his job. I had seen immediately in our first meeting that he took great pride in it and realized that any socialist pretensions I had would undermine his profession and status and be a great affront.

The crockery clinked as he took the tea strainer. Sitting it on top of the cup, he poured the tea. He added water, making it just the way I liked it, not too strong. Out of the corner of his eye I saw him looking at the photographs of my husband and boys on my desk. He had been eyeing them for days and I knew it wouldn't be long before he asked me about them. I felt a wave of dizziness coming. It was always like this when I anticipated the inevitable questions.

This time I decided to take the initiative, hoping that by doing so it would be less painful for me. I pointed to the picture of Charles and me taken after our engagement at my parents' house. It was late spring. We had been riding and were just entering the yard. Reins loose, our shirts open at the neck, we were looking at each other and laughing.

'That's me with my husband, Charles. Sadly, he died of cancer.' I talked quickly, wanting to get it over with. 'And these are my two sons Robert and George. They were both killed during the war.' There, it was done.

But Zamurad Khan looked as if I had taken out a pistol and shot him in the stomach. Such was the mixture of horror and confusion on his face. And I regretted that in my rush to protect my own feelings I had not gone about it in a better way. His hand flew up to touch his turban and he stared wide-eyed, struggling to believe. Somewhere deep inside, I screamed. For, some days, even I could still not fully comprehend that my beloved family was gone, just like that.

'I am sorry, Zamurad Khan . . . It's just that . . .'

'So they are all dead, and Memsahib is alone in the world?' He was still not sure if he had heard me correctly but followed my cue for bluntness.

'Yes, Zamurad Khan.' I picked up the teacup, willing my hands not to shake.

'*Inna Lillahi wa inna ilayhi raji'un.*' He paused and although I did not understand his words I realized that this man whose race and background were so different from mine, was feeling my pain as if it were his own.

'It is from our holy Koran and is meaning, we all belong to Allah and to him are going back.'

Ashes to ashes, dust to dust.

'Thank you, Zamurad Khan.' I nodded at him and stared into my teacup, steadying myself. After a few moments I looked up.

'Have you worked a long time at Viceroy's House, Zamurad Khan?' I asked brightly. His face lit up with relief and enthusiasm. This was clearly a comforting question.

'Ah! Memsahib, I am happily knowing no other life. I have served six Viceroys of India and before me my father's grandfather and his grandfather and his grandfather before him and so on. All served at the court of the great Mughal emperors. My great great greatest grandfather was a mighty general in the court of Shah Jahan. And today my sons . . . .' He stuttered to a stop and looked at his feet.

'It's all right, Zamurad Khan,' I said. 'Please tell me about your sons, I would like to know.'

He smiled shyly and continued.

'My eldest, Iqbal, is the chief mechanic here on the estate and my younger son, Musa, is risaldar in the Viceroy's bodyguard.' He shrugged as if his son's senior rank as a viceroy commissioned officer was a small matter. 'Iqbal, we are putting him once on a horse when he was three years old, and he is never wanting to go back on again. Musa, he has been riding here on the estate all his life. He lives for horses and the army—we are so proud of him.' He hesitated, his eyes searching my face, wondering perhaps if I would understand. 'He is restoring our family honour.' He played his ace.

I smiled, wondering in my turn whether I might risk broaching a subject.

'Zamurad Khan, I too very much enjoy riding. Yesterday, I rode out with His Excellency on The Ridge. But it was a circus. Far too many people in the escort, police, bodyguards and so on. I know what His Excellency really wants is to be able to ride out privately in the early morning with his daughter and his wife. I was wondering if you might be able to ask your son. Does he know anyone in the stables who might be able to find me a steady horse and accompany me on occasional rides? Of course, there would be an arrangement.'

His brow furrowed. Like the men in the Viceroy's equestrian entourage, he was thinking of all sorts of reasons why we, and specifically I, a woman, should not ride out on The Ridge that ran behind Viceroy's House. He looked again at the picture of me. The young woman that once I had been, laughing with her handsome fiancé, feet hanging out of her stirrups, hair dishevelled by the wind. Smiling, he tapped the side of his nose to indicate secrecy.

'Not to worry. Memsahib, I am asking. See what old Zamurad can do!'

*P*eople often underestimated Edwina Mountbatten. The chicken incident apparently behind her, she had pulled herself together and stepped up to the role of Vicereine with elan. Deliberately smashing rules and conventions from day one, she began as she meant to go on. In this she was aided and abetted by me. We attacked the Court Circular first, redrafting it to make it less condescending, more inclusive. After that we changed the dinner menu in Viceroy's House to offer Indian and vegetarian food. Small steps perhaps, and they may have been considered ridiculous, but our little revolution met with quite some resistance.

'But Her Excellency doesn't understand the way things are done out here!' they complained, threatening appeals to higher authorities.

'She understands all too well,' I responded curtly. 'This is how it will be done from now on.' And it's about bloody time, I thought. Heaven knows, our departure from India was long overdue!

But if only all change were that simple. The political situation was critical. It was clear that if a deal with Indian leaders on the transfer of power was not made soon, India risked falling apart. Every day that leaders postured, procrastinated and stalled, the death toll rose.

We, the staff, found ourselves back in our old war-time routines. Starting with breakfast briefings, we worked twelve- to sixteen-hour days. There was so much to do and time was running out. The violence in the Punjab escalated daily and the Governor was tearing his hair out. A tour of the trouble spots in the province had been scheduled, as had an urgent All India Governors' Conference. I was busy organizing the parallel conference for the Governors' wives, to be hosted by Edwina. It would focus on welfare and nursing. Added to this was the reception for the delegates of the Asian Relations Conference, hosted by Nehru in a week's time. A garden party had been planned on the same day for the members of the Legislative Assembly and senior officials in Delhi. I was astonished to learn that the guest list for this ran to a mere seven hundred! I had been working on it with a rather stressed George Abell. It was fair to say my feet had not touched the ground.

Operation Seduction, the beleaguered Viceroy optimistically called his offensive aimed at producing an agreement on the future of India. He was meeting with senior Indian leaders, Nehru, Jinnah and others daily. His aim was to build a personal rapport with each man and thus break the deadlock. Edwina was certainly his secret weapon in this. And she, in turn, was unforgiving of herself and her staff. For every meeting her husband had, it seemed to me she had to have at least two more with prominent Indian ladies, wives and daughters of senior leaders, members of charities and nursing organizations. But, by Jove, she was good at it! Once, she sailed, smiling, into a meeting with Nan Pandit, Nehru's sister.

'You know, we think that Gandhiji is quite right, and we are going to do our best to make it happen.'

Nan Pandit looked as if she had been knocked over with a feather. Who would ever have thought to hear such words from the lips of a British Vicereine?

But Edwina did not fool me. Since our conversation in the bathroom, she had let her mask slip just once. But it was enough.

It was during a hospital visit. All the doctors and nurses had stood on the steps, waving as she departed. Graciously, she smiled and waved back. But as soon as the viceregal car rounded the bend, she slumped into the back seat and heaved a sigh of relief.

'Letty, don't you miss England? A cosy fire, the sound of church bells ringing?'

I had nodded in response, but said nothing for I was not missing England at all. In India, with so much to do, I was thinking less and less about my husband and my boys. This meant I was mostly sleeping better than I had in years, but at the same time it troubled me. One night I had dreamt I was alone in a lifeboat on a wide sea. In panic, I was rowing away from a shipwreck, abandoning the three of them to their fates. I turned round just once to see the stern tip up and disappear. For a few seconds their hands reached out of the foaming, churning waves and then they were gone. Once, it would have been all too easy to give up and let myself die with them, weighting myself down with bricks and jumping into the Thames one dark night. I had often thought of doing such a thing. Why was it that I had survived when they had not?

However, here in India, I began to feel a cautious sense of relief. But that brought with it guilt. The beginning of release meant a betrayal of the memory of my husband and my boys and the happy little family we were once. Deep inside, somewhere under my ribcage, a giant iron claw still tore and tormented. Try as I might, I could never pray. It was better not to think of England. I was afraid of home. Afraid I would get drawn back in, drawn back down and lose myself in the pit of blackness again.

A thin trail of smoke escaped from the incinerator at the back of Viceroy's House. They had started burning files as dusk fell so that the smoke would be smothered by the night. But even if we could not see it, we could smell it, and taste it, acrid in our throats and nostrils.

It was after dinner and I was in the office drafting a speech for Edwina. She was to give it on a visit to Lady Irwin College which taught home economics to young Indian women. 'No point pulling punches.' Edwina had sat at the head of the table by the swimming pool at that morning's staff meeting. 'I'm determined to say what I think.' Even after all these years I was not always sure what she thought. But I knew how passionate she and I were about nursing and education for women. I wrote accordingly. One thing was for sure—if she did not approve, she would have no hesitation in amending the draft speech. Her schoolgirl handwriting was not too different from mine and she would scrawl all along the margins in vehement red pencil.

'It is clear that India's problems are largely economic and social, not religious or political, and that urgent improvements are needed in the standard of living, standards of education, employment and health.' Ping, thump, carriage return. I imagined the ranks of fresh-faced young women. Their hair neatly tied back, they looked up earnestly at Edwina as she stood on the platform, her left hand grasping her right so it did not shake.

'Ninety two per cent of the population is illiterate, twenty women in a thousand die in childbirth, a hundred and sixty-two babies die in the first weeks of life, four hundred and thirty children in a thousand die before they reach the age of five. In India, for a population of four hundred million there are fewer nurses than in London. So here is the task that lies before you ladies . . .'

When I was done, I rolled out the draft from the top of the typewriter and peeled the copy away from the carbon paper. The carbon copy I filed, but the top copy? I thought about going up to Edwina's suite to give it to her along with some other letters that I had typed earlier in the day. Through the window I saw that her lights were still burning. Brow furrowed underneath her heavy spectacles, she would still be working through briefs and speeches, signing piles of official letters. But after last night's experience I was having second thoughts. Unwittingly, I had walked into the middle of a blazing row. Rather, I had heard it, the mercifully muffled voices coming from behind the heavy teak door.

'Do you deliberately set out to make my position untenable?' Dickie was trying to sound calm.

'Don't you ever think of anyone other than yourself?' Edwina screeched. 'Everything is for the great glorification of Dickie Mountbatten. What about me?'

'Hell's teeth, woman! No one has a better husband than you. No one else would put up with you. You're a disgrace to me, to the family and most of all yourself.'

A pounding of feet. A thump as if a chair were being overturned. Heavy breathing. Both sides waiting.

'I bid you good night!' Dickie was curt and crisp.

A door slammed, then silence and sobbing in the darkness.

Here in the office, I took the top copy of the draft speech and placed it in a folder to give to Edwina in the morning. Work done for now, I picked up my pen, opened my diary and began to write.

Dearest darling,

Everything here in Viceroy's House is being recorded at least in triplicate. So you see that with my taste for administrative order, there really is a use for me and it is all far from a jolly holiday! We are kept busy all day and into the night and there is always a mad rush just before the London airmail bag closes at 9.30 a.m. The office chaprasis hold on to their turbans and skid helter-skelter down the corridors in their soft shoes. Quite a sight!

Right now half the house is probably busy scribbling late into the night. Everyone is keeping diaries. There is no doubt we are on the cusp of a great historical event, the independence of India. I wonder if by recording our work we feel that somehow we might influence the outcome and keep the record straight? I doubt it, for already it is clear to me that even the big players in this game are at the mercy of forces far greater than they care to admit. I admire Dickie, ever the optimist, fully of energy and drive. He is doing his best to create a fresh start and the Indians have certainly warmed to him which is progress on Lord Wavell. The problem from our point of view, and darling, your legal mind would be sure to appreciate this, is to whom exactly are we to transfer power and under what legal structure? The Indians won't have dominion status like the other white colonies because they think it will not mean full independence. But if we transfer power to a united India under the interim government, this means essentially the Congress, which will exclude the Muslim League and almost certainly lead to civil war. And that is not to mention the Sikhs. I know you have always had a poor opinion of Dickie, 'the nincompoop'. But this time he really has been dropped in the proverbial. Even you might have some sympathy for his dilemma! It is all one grand pôt de chambre!

The positions of the Muslim League and Congress are completely entrenched and no one trusts anything anyone says. Liaquat Ali Khan for the Muslim League thought that the Congress had put Dickie up to his speech at the swearing-in. He was very surprised when the Viceroy said it was completely his own idea. Lord Ismay, Chief of the Viceroy's Staff, says that Nehru sees the black hand of Churchill in everything.

And yesterday, when I came back to the office, I found Alan and
Krishna Menon whispering together in a corner. Menon is Nehru's
man, you know. Anyway, the two of them blushed as purple as beetroots
when they saw me, like naughty schoolboys caught doing something
illicit. I have not got to the bottom of it yet. In sum, it is all rather like
living in a mediaeval court. Dickie and Edwina row almost daily, and
there is constant whisper, rumour and counter rumour.

Even tonight, as I write, there is smoke coming from the
incinerators. Deals are being made and top-secret documents are being
burnt in batches. They relate to some aspects of Gandhi's life and,
shall we say, the more salacious and sadistic activities of some of the
Indian Princes. Last night I dined at Lord Ismay's. He told me that
the intelligence services knew Gandhi was in the habit of sharing his bed
with his eighteen-year-old niece. Discretion and the loss of a few files
was quite in the best interests of India, or so he said. 'Best not to attract
the attention of the Congress or the Muslim League, who would dearly
love to get their hands on all these aspects of British intelligence and use
them for their own purposes!'

I looked up from my writing. The thin trail of smoke, almost
invisible now, slightly blacker than black, was disappearing into
the night. I picked up a cigarette and lit it. Relaxing, I imagined
Charles dressed in the white panama hat that he used to wear
when he went down to Lord's to watch cricket. He would kiss
me on the cheek and pat me on the bottom by way of goodbye.
'Toodle-oo! Are you sure you don't want to come too?'
Normally I told him everything, unshakeable in my belief
that in his cricket stand in heaven, he could read my diary, but
not tonight. I had omitted any reference to Dr Rathore in my
account of the swearing-in. It was late. I snapped the diary shut
as if swatting a fly.

*I*t was early and the dawn air still smelt peppery. But already I had felt the first nip of the morning sun on the pink flesh of my forearms. I had just returned from a ride on The Ridge with Lord Ismay and Risaldar Musa Khan. It was time to shower and change before breakfast, and the first staff meeting. It was going to be a long day. But when I saw Zamurad Khan and one of the office chaprasis waiting for me on the top of the steps to Viceroy's House, I knew something was wrong.

Untying my scarf from under my chin and using it to wipe my face and neck, I went straight to the Vicereine's office. I stopped only to wash my hands. Still in my jodhpurs and riding shirt, I smelt of horse, leather and hay.

They were waiting there, the two of them—she with her white khadi sari drawn modestly over her head and he, Dr Rathore, dwarfing her, reading the newspaper. They stood up when I came in. Rajkumari Amrit Kaur, Personal Secretary to Gandhi, offered me her hand in the English way.

'I am sorry,' I said, embarrassed. 'Pippi Wallace, Special Assistant to the Vicereine. I'm afraid I have come straight from the stables.'

She was small and slight, about fifty years old, although she looked younger. I saw that she had been crying.

'It's we who are sorry, Lady Wallace, turning up so early and unannounced. It's just that my driver was indisposed and Dr Rathore kindly offered to drive me over. I wanted to speak to Her Excellency before she gets caught up in the day. It really is a matter of the utmost importance. I must see her.'

My mind ran on. I knew that Edwina would not want to turn Amrit Kaur away. She was a significant person. Indeed a meeting between the two of them was coming up soon. My mind trawled through the secret briefs on prominent Indian ladies we had received before leaving for India. From these I knew that Amrit Kaur had been born a princess and educated at Sherborne School in Dorset and Oxford University, and then had given it all up to follow Gandhi and fight for Indian independence. At the same time I knew that even with the strongest will in the world there was no way Edwina would manage to squeeze in another meeting this morning.

'Rajkumari, I am so sorry. It's just that with the Asian Relations Conference and the garden party later, Her Excellency really is completely booked up today. I really don't want to ask you to hang about here on the off chance. You will certainly have better things to do.'

She wrung her hands in agitation. All the while Dr Rathore's gaze never wavered from me despite my sweaty shirt and jodhpurs. It was as if he had never imagined meeting me again, least of all with me looking so dishevelled and gamine.

'Have you had breakfast?' I fastened the collar button of my shirt, feeling a tad self-conscious. 'What is it? Perhaps you could tell me, and I could tell Her Excellency. Then she could get back to you?'

Amrit Kaur pushed her sari back from her face revealing her curly hair that had been cut into a neat bob. She raised her eyes to Dr Rathore who gave a curt nod.

'I'll leave you ladies to it and pop down to the dispensary and the stables. I want to check on a young syce whose appendix I removed some months ago. Poor boy had smallpox as a child and his face is much blighted. Shame I couldn't fix that too.'

'Ravi?'

'Yes. You know him, Lady Wallace?'

I thought of the smiling but greatly disfigured groom who had tacked up and delivered our horses this morning. Eyes downcast, holding the bridle as I mounted, he had mumbled something to me in Hindustani that I had not understood.

'He is telling you to be careful.' Risaldar Khan had translated. 'This mare is a good girl. Lady Wavell liked to her ride her, but she is very quick from trot to canter.'

But already this morning's ride seemed like weeks ago. I wondered what Amrit Kaur's matter might be that it could not be discussed in the presence of a man.

Dr Rathore started to leave. 'Amrit, send someone to fetch me when you are finished. I'll drive you to the Secretariat for your next appointment. Your cover driver can fetch you from there.' At the door he turned, his face grave. 'If I might be so bold, Lady Wallace. There should be proper minutes and records of this. History needs to know.' He closed the door behind him softly and suddenly I felt drained, as if my day had gone with him.

We sat, two women together, in the large teak chairs on either side of the coffee table. I took up my notebook and pencil. Amrit Kaur folded and unfolded the hem of her sari.

'Such terrible things,' she said, 'I hardly know where to begin ... Yesterday a delegation of Sikh and Hindu women came to see me. They are refugees from Kahuta in the Rawalpindi division.' She looked me firmly in the eyes to check that I was following while my pencil worked to transcribe her words to shorthand. 'Really, it is the most harrowing of tales; I barely slept a wink last night.' A khidmutgar knocked at the door and brought us a tray with tea and toast. He waited to serve but I asked him to leave.

'The worst thing is that it is all organized; part of a deliberate military campaign to wipe out the Hindu and Sikh minorities in the region and pave the way for Pakistan.' She stopped and took a deep breath. I poured the tea which she took with milk and sugar.

'No one can ever lose more than these women have. They simply have nowhere else to turn. It's the Muslims, you see. They're calling for jihad in the mosques, jihad against the minorities in their areas. The ladies say the men came to raid Kahuta in organized brigades with tommy guns, Brens, hand grenades and field glasses.' She was thinking hard, making sure to give an accurate account and not leave anything out. 'The mujahidin brought petrol. Even locksmiths to break locks and barbers to shave beards and forcibly circumcise the men. And last of all gangs came with camels for the loot.'

I looked at her not quite comprehending and she paused to give me time to write it down. I stopped to pour more tea which she gulped in distress.

'The women were raped, and then forced to watch their eleven-and twelve-year-old daughters being raped in front of crowds. Young children were burnt alive. When they tried to escape the mujahidin picked them up and threw them back into the flames or strangled them and hung their bodies from trees.'

Her words fell disjointedly, out of time with the movement of her lips. My pencil stalled and I looked at her in disbelief. Her hands wrapped around the teacup, she sat watching the steam rising to the ceiling.

'Yes.' She said in answer to the question I could not put into words.

She was speaking quickly now with a more marked Indian intonation, rushing, wanting to get it over with. 'And if the girls were not carried off they were murdered. One girl by having her legs pulled apart, another by being stuck inside with a pole.'

I wrote: 'Looting, arson, abductions, forced conversions, rape (awful details).' At last she had said her piece and I put down my pencil, staring at the swirl of my shorthand and at the toast on the tray between us that neither of us had touched. Bile rose in my mouth. We sat for a while nursing our teacups, listening to the cheeping of the birds. Then gently, very gently,

I asked in the way my husband would have asked of a vulnerable witness in court.

'Do you know these women, Rajkumari? Do you have any way of verifying their stories?'

'Amrit. Please call me Amrit,' she whispered.

'Pippi. Everyone just calls me Pippi.'

She folded, unfolded and refolded her hands in her lap and smiled. Suddenly calm and serene—it was as if, paradoxically, nothing mattered and there was something bigger and more beautiful beyond us that could make all things right. 'Pippi, if you had seen their wounds and their faces you would not have doubted them.' And looking at her face and thinking of how Dr Rathore had put himself out to drive her here, I realized I did not doubt her either. To my mind, it had to be true.

$\mathcal{V}$iceroy's House was built for nights like these. Out front the cars dropping off guests circled back to the Jaipur Column, their headlights flickering like stars orbiting a great sun. Inside, light danced off the chandeliers and silver platters and fractured into rainbow shards. Tides of people flooded the staterooms and out on to the terraces which were strung with fairy lights. So much light! It made me uneasy. My instinct was still to run and hide from the bombs which would surely fall on such an obvious target.

For most of the evening I had been acting as a guide, taking small parties of Indian ladies on tours of the staterooms. Shy, curious, they told me that they had never been in Viceroy's House before. Nor had most of their husbands, although many of them were senior men who had been in public life for years. Indeed quite a few of them had also spent time in British jails. My mouth dry with talking, I took a drink of lemonade from one of the khidmutgars. Following the music, I went out on to the terrace. It was then that I saw them—Edwina and Jawahar. Caught in a halo of light from the stage, they sat in the centre. In that moment everything that was happening seemed to spinning off them, happening because of them, and in some way connected to them. Edwina was sitting on a sofa, watching a performance of Indian dance. He was cross-legged at her feet. It was written on their faces, in the turn of her head and the angle of his back against the sofa, pressing too close to the hems of her skirt. Whether they knew it or not, it was unveiled for all the hundreds to see. Shocked, I realized that this was what those red-faced schoolboys, Alan Campbell-Johnson and Krishna Menon, had been gossiping about the other day.

'Hush hush! Just between ourselves, Edwina and Jawahar.'
Surely not?

Embarrassed, I looked away and then back again. The
Vicereine and the future Prime Minister of India; he responding
to a remark, lifted his face earnestly up to hers, and she, smiling
a little, lowered her eyes.

Yet how could it be? They had barely known each other
a week. Was that enough time for two people to develop an
attachment? Now I was cross. Certainly Edwina had been lonely
and unhappy, and Jawaharlal Nehru was a handsome widower,
his wife having died some years ago. Surely they would have more
sense? But it was the political implications of their potential
liaison that really troubled me. The Viceroy was already being
seen as favouring the Congress to the detriment of the Muslim
League. If it came out that his wife was close to their leader,
Dickie's position would become untenable. He would have to
resign and there would be more delay in arriving at a settlement
for India and more bloodshed. Turning away, I walked back up
to the house, passing a group of middle-aged Englishwomen.

'It's disgusting!' one of them brayed like a donkey.

'Disgraceful,' snorted another, 'that the Viceroy should let
all these filthy Indians in.'

I had had enough. I stopped right in front of them.

'I think you ought to leave.'

To my satisfaction, their saggy jaws dropped. I wanted to
slap them on their fat powdered faces, to stun them out of their
narrow little worlds. They ought to shut up or one day it would
be their own good Christian bodies hanging from trees. But
anger drained my will to fight. It was late. I had done my duty.
I turned my back on them and walked away.

As I headed to my room, I came across Alan in a quiet lobby by
the library. He was with a pink-faced Chinese gentleman in a long
black gown, and Krishna Menon, Iago-like, loitered at their side.

'Pippi!' He called out to me with a big smile. The men had
all undone the top buttons of their jackets. They looked as

if they had come from a modestly successful day at the races. Even Krishna Menon might have been said to appear pleased underneath his sullen black eyebrows. I forced a smile.

'You must meet the Chinese Ambassador, His Excellency Mr Lo. Your Excellency, may I present Lady Pippi Wallace, Special Assistant to the Vicereine.'

Letticia was increasingly going by the board in India. It appeared just on seating plans and arrangements. But I didn't mourn her passing. Pippi gave me a new identity, a fresh start, a chance to make my life anew.

'Enchanté.' Mr Lo kissed my hand. 'Such a splendid event at the end of what has been a momentous day at the Asian Relations Conference. Please be sure to give my compliments to the Vicereine, although of course I will write to her myself.'

'And now you too must come!' Krishna Menon grinned like a tiger and spread his arms in an uncharacteristic gesture of munificence which was actually an order, not a request. 'Jawahar is having a small at-home at York Road. We're all going.'

Spirits danced in the shadows at 17, York Road. A tall, elegant heron stretched its neck amongst the gliding, fluttering swans. A fisherman stalked through the water to throw his net. Mesmerized by the dancers, we were drawn into the wordless narrative of the shehnai and walked across the lawn in time to the beat of the dhol.

There was no reception line. Dickie had not come to the party. Together, Jawahar and Edwina mingled amongst the guests. She was the steadying influence while he appeared to leap about like a leprechaun, embracing and shaking hands.

'Welcome!' Jawahar greeted our little party made up of the Chinese Ambassador, his wife, Alan and me, with his hands pressed together in namaste. 'Traditional masked dance from the state of Seraikella for your enjoyment here tonight. Please make yourself at home.'

Krishna Menon called the men away. This left me in the
company of the diminutive Mrs Lo in her seductive green
and gold cheongsam. The two of us made our way through
the milling guests. Many of them were Asian delegates in the
bright silks and satins of their respective national dress. We
were offered drinks. Giggling, Mrs Lo took a small beer in a
glass tumbler. Why not? Infected with the spirit of the evening,
I took one too. We found a space on a rug under a tree. Mrs Lo
sat elegantly with her legs to one side, revealing a slim thigh. For
my part, I was conscious of my chunky knees under my skirt.

'Gan bei!' She raised her glass and took a startlingly large swig
for such a delicate-looking lady. The dhol beat faster, the shehnai
reaching its climax. The swans, herons and other quasi-mystical
creatures jumped, twirled, swooped and disappeared into the
night, leaving only the moon hanging in the sky over the house.

In the interlude I noticed a plump Indian girl sitting alone
a little further along the rug. She wore an expensive pink sari
which unfortunately made her look like a strawberry sweet.

'Hello,' I said, 'we haven't been introduced. I'm Pippi Wallace.
I work with the Vicereine.'

Shyly, she reached out her hand and smiled. 'I'm Tania. I go
to Lady Irwin College.' She looked at me, at Mrs Lo, hesitated,
then took a deep breath as if plucking up all her courage, and
announced, 'I'm going to be a nurse,'

'That's super! ' My words were half drowned by the beat of
the dhol as it started up again. But Tania's face seemed to fold
around what I had said, as if netting a trophy fish and pulling
it in. At the same time she stared defiantly at the far side of
the garden at a woman looking splendid in a green and red silk
sari who was resting her hand softly on Hari Rathore's arm.
My heart skipped a beat. Was she his wife? The woman was
stunning, the sort of lady who would draw men's eyes wherever
she went. She was not petite and her sari was tied in a way that

expertly highlighted and flattered the curves of her body. She had pale skin, large dark eyes ringed with kohl and generously made up lips in a luscious rosebud red. Hari was frowning as she talked, but she had his complete attention. I could not help myself. I too stared. Genetically speaking, it was obvious that his lady was Tania's mother. But it seemed that all of nature's blessings had been bestowed on the mother to the detriment of the daughter. It was as if some cruel god had deliberately chosen to distort the best features of the mother and pushed them to the extreme in the daughter.

Thankfully for me, at this point, two masked dancers pitter-pattered, barefoot on to the stage; a blue painted faced man and a white faced woman in a red wedding sari. They were greeted by the mournful notes of the shehnai, leading them into a breathless weaving dance; every movement of head or finger or foot of one, however tiny, mirrored perfectly by the other, together and apart, together and apart.

'The story of Radha and Krishna,' Tania sighed, 'the greatest of all Indian love stories.' The dhol rumbled and Radha, hands cupping her face, prostrated herself at Krishna's feet.

Making a clumsy excuse, I escaped into the house to find a bathroom. On my way I caught sight of Edwina and Jawahar though the glass doors to the drawing room. Beer and fatigue had gone to my head. Conversations were muffled and I had the queasy impression we were all swimming in a goldfish bowl. Jawahar had taken off his jacket. He sat in his shirt with its buttons open; I could see the hairs on his chest. Edwina had removed her sandals and folded up her legs under her skirt on the couch next to him. But they were not alone. They were listening to an oval-faced Chinese man. He was talking animatedly to them and the others sitting around in easy chairs. Malays and Indonesians, I thought. One of the men offered cigarettes from a packet. Edwina and Jawahar each took one, she lighting hers from the tip of his, the tops of their heads touching, but for just a moment.

I wondered what on earth Westminster and Fleet Street would make of this: a barefoot Vicereine smoking with a gang of Asian nationalists and anti-imperialist revolutionaries. Just then Nan Pandit appeared at my side with a tray of sweets. Her jaw dropped at the sight of her brother with Edwina.

With pursed lips, Nan Pandit pushed the tray towards me in a manner which expected me to take one. I scrambled for small talk.

'I was talking to such a nice girl just now—Tania. She's at Lady Irwin College and told me with great pride that she wants to be a nurse.'

Nan Pandit wrinkled her nose. 'Well, I'll believe that when I see it, Lady Wallace. Not with a family like hers!'

'Oh?'

'She comes from a very well-born family. Her mother is considered a beauty. Such dirty menial work would be considered beneath her.'

High above Viceroy's House, the Indian man in the moon lay cheekily on his side. Or did he? For as our jeep sped round to a side entrance of the sprawling estate, I didn't think I was entirely sure. Everything jiggled in my mind. The moon bouncing like a ball around the dome of Viceroy's House. The Indian navy ADC sitting in the front seat by the driver, singing at the top of his voice in Hindi, 'Jana Gana Mana'. Alan in the back seat next to me, gently crooned, 'Swing low sweet chariot, coming for to carry me home.' There was no animosity in the duet, and the strange counterpoint between the two of them seemed to sum up the spirit of the day. Here in India, there was something which we had lost during the long years of war in Europe. For a moment I had to think what it was. It was hope.

Suddenly, I was looking at the moon again, holding it in my hands, drawing it close, trying to work out whether the Indian man in the moon really does lie to one side. But now the moon was the face of my alarm clock, the hands telling me it was way past midnight. I had probably been asleep about an hour. Someone was tapping lightly, but urgently, at my bedroom door.

'Letty! Letty! Are you there? It's me. Let me in.'

Edwina stood in the shadows of the corridor, holding her high-heeled sandals in her hand. She must have taken them off so as not to disturb people.

'Sorry, Cabbage. Did I wake you?' she whispered like a conspiratorial schoolgirl, finger on her lips. The leftover heat of the day was stifling in the corridor. Quickly, I ushered her into the cool of my room and closed the door.

'What is it?'

'Stupid, stupid, stupid!' Her face was flushed, glistening with sweat. Her curls which had been carefully set in the morning, now drooped at the back of her neck.

'I left something at Jawahar's, on the sofa in the drawing room.'

'What?' We knew each other too well to pussyfoot around.

'My evening bag. There are things in it that, well . . . you know.'

I didn't but I could hazard a guess.

'Cabbage, could you be a darling?' Cabbage was all I got; she didn't even bother to try to charm me with a sparkling smile. 'Are you riding in the morning? Could you pop round to York Road first thing and pick it up for me instead? Take the duty ADC with you. Here!' She thrust an envelope into my hand. 'You could say that you're just passing and delivering a thank-you note. It would be such a weight off my mind.'

I decided not to trouble the duty ADC and took a jeep myself from outside the white post office with its little clock tower at the back of the estate. The dozy guards at the gate nursed rifles between their knees. They protested not about the jeep, but the earliness of the hour and the fact that the curfew had not been lifted yet. But I was desperate for the luxury of twenty minutes alone. Between the office, the army of staff and the mess, there was no privacy at Viceroy's House. Waving aside their offers of an escort, I indicated my St John's Ambulance khakis which I always wore like a suit of armour, floored the accelerator and shot out of the back gate. This rear section of road was not yet laid. I bumped along a dirt track, the frayed remnants of the pink dawn fading in the east, birds flying up, monkeys chattering in the trees. Holding the steering wheel with one hand, I took off my cap, letting the softest of early morning breezes play with my hair.

At 17, York Road the gates had been left wide open. I drove in. No one came out to either challenge or greet me. Apart from the rattan chairs stacked up in the corner of the porch, there was no sign of last night's gathering. Ghosts and shadows, all had vanished, and the right-angled corners of the two-storey bungalow, with its isosceles triangle portico, were clear-cut against the blue of the day. Leaving the jeep at the bottom of the drive, I made my way to the back of the house.

The sun was in my eyes as I turned a corner and I didn't see him. He must have been bending down, working in the flower

bed and when he stood up and took a step back, I bumped right
into him. The momentum on impact was such that we grabbed
each other to stop ourselves falling over. He was wearing a
long white khadi shirt and white trousers, and holding a pair of
secateurs and a freshly cut red rose. These were now pressed up
against my chest and my battered old leather briefcase which
had come between us in the crush. I moved to pull back but he
held on to my arm and roared with laughter.

'Panditji! I am so sorry. I didn't see you!' I stuttered.

'And I didn't see you either, Lady Wallace. Have you had
breakfast?'

I was surprised that he remembered or indeed knew who I
was. Caught off-guard by his informality, I answered truthfully.

'No.'

'Nor I, then you must stay and have some with me.'

'I couldn't . . . Her Excellency sent me,' I said limply.

'Did she?' He raised an eyebrow and turned back to the rose
bushes, gently parting the leaves and branches with the back of
his hand, letting them rustle against him, playing at avoiding
the thorns. Carefully he examined first one flower and then
another. There were only about half a dozen shrunken blooms
left. After some deliberation he snipped one with his secateurs
and gave it to me.

'Alas, the season is over, Lady Wallace, and my offering is
poor. Come!' Hooking my arm through his, he led me on to the
veranda and in through the French windows at the back of the
house.

Not for the first time in twenty-four hours I was cross.
Cross at being disarmed with a rose. Cross at this man for a
friendship with Edwina that risked so much. Cross at being in
this embarrassing situation at 7.20 a.m.

We were alone in the sparsely furnished dining room.
There were no pictures on the walls, no clocks or collections
of fine China in glass cases, just stark white-washed walls. And

I remembered that many years ago Panditji and his father, Motilal Nehru, had given all their wealth away for the cause of Indian independence and Gandhi.

'Tea and toast, eggs and tomatoes; we live a simple life here,' he said quietly.

Breakfast had been laid out on the sideboard at the end of the room. Panditji dropped his chin and I heard his breath as he threaded his own red rose through the top buttonhole of his shirt. There, it drooped more than a little. Somewhat at a loss as to what to do with my own rose, I opened the top pocket of my St John's uniform and popped it in so that it peeped out of the right side under my medal bar. I hesitated over food, but already he had taken a plate from the pile.

'Tuck in! Won't be long before the hordes arrive!'

Without his jacket, in just his shirtsleeves, he was a private man, a different person from the evening before. Gone was the exuberance, effort and show. His movements were now slow and calm, and he exuded a sense of peace which reminded me of Amrit Kaur. Despite myself, I was drawn in. And yet there was something of the boy in him too, bashful in expression and a little shy. In his late fifties, he was still undeniably handsome and young-looking, with a very fair complexion, aquiline nose and large sad eyes. His wife had died tragically some years ago. He was probably one of the most eligible men in India.

He sat at the head of the table and motioned me to his side. A boy appeared with tea. Panditji waved him away and took charge of the pot himself.

'How do you like your tea, Lady Wallace?'

'Black please, Panditji.'

'No milk? No sugar?'

I shook my head.

He smiled softly. 'Then perhaps you were an Indian in your past life?'

Carefully, he poured the tea; the gurgle of water and clink of porcelain the only conversation between us. I was deeply embarrassed that this man, second only to Gandhi, who had been one of the most famous political prisoners in the world and spent years in British jails, was serving me. But he was hungry, focusing on his food, buttering his toast and taking big careful bites.

'It was a most lovely party last night; a pleasure to meet so many Asian delegates.'

I was making small talk.

He nodded, eating more quickly now, talking between mouthfuls.

'And how do you find India, Lady Wallace?'

'I can hardly say, Panditji. I've been here such a short time, under such extraordinary circumstances. I've not seen much more than Old Delhi, the office, a few schools and hospitals, and your back garden full of mango trees!'

He laughed. 'Believe me, that's already more than many. Indeed some of our very own high-society ladies with their fine clothes and shiny handbags would never think to roll up their sleeves as you and Edwina do.' I was taken aback. 'Don't think I don't know that you and the Vicereine have been out and about,' he said mischievously, with a twinkle in his eye.

'I am afraid neither of us is a woman who can sit on her hands.' I hesitated. 'I promise you, Panditji, whatever happens we will work hard and do our best for India. Edwina wants to be a different kind of Vicereine.'

Oh heavens! Formality was falling away. Loyalties were getting confused and I couldn't stop. I had to be careful. It would be all too easy to be charmed by this man.

He nodded, popping a piece of egg into his mouth. Then waved his right hand as he talked, giving the illusion of picking words most precisely out of the air.

'Well, you must visit the Qutb Minar when you have time and, of course, see the Taj Mahal before you leave. Did you know that Delhi is, as a matter of fact, made up of seven cities? Layer upon layer of history, ruins all over the plain, if you have eyes to see.'

'I fear work leaves little time for sightseeing.' I sipped my tea, waiting for the right moment. 'Yesterday Amrit Kaur came to see Her Excellency. Unfortunately she was indisposed so the poor lady had to make do with me.' I was wearing my lawyer's face, looking him in the eye. 'She told me the most horrendous tales of Muslim violence against Sikhs and Hindus in the Punjab.'

He raised his hand like a traffic policeman to stop me.

'Such violence is temporary. I assure you, Lady Wallace, it'll stop as soon as the British leave.' He mopped up the remains of his egg with his toast. We were silent again and he stared back at me intently, this time with a glint of barrister's steel in his eye. He was also a barrister; in fact most of the Indian politicians I had met in recent weeks were lawyers. Knowing lawyers as I did, it did occur to me that perhaps this was part of the problem facing the Viceroy. Nevertheless, as we sat there alone over the teapot, I thought it rather unfair that I knew so much about him when he knew so little about me. A breeze rattled the window blinds. Suddenly, I was afraid of the silence between us, afraid of where it was leading.

'If I might take the opportunity of this quiet moment, Lady Wallace'—he hesitated; I braced myself—'I had the honour of knowing your husband personally when I was a pupil at Chambers in London. I saw him in court on several occasions. He was a superb advocate—one of the best. I was so sorry to hear . . .'

My teacup shook in my hand and I bit my lip to pre-empt any tears. People should not be so kind. From his face it was clear he also knew about my boys. He reached towards me and, stopping short of my hand, patted the tablecloth instead.

'And, please, do call me Jawahar, as Edwina does.'

But how did he know about my family? Perhaps Edwina had told him, although I thought that unlikely. Or maybe the Indian National Congress Party had its own secret briefs about the new Viceroy and Vicereine and their incoming staff, just as we did about them? Perhaps Krishna Menon had prepared them? I shuddered to think what he might have put in mine.

Upstairs, footsteps and voices echoed along a corridor. After their late night, the household was finally on the move. Jawahar took a deep breath.

'We've met before, you know, Edwina and I.' He spoke uncharacteristically quickly, as if wanting to get if off his chest. 'In Government House in Singapore last year, as a matter of fact. She and Dickie received me most kindly, giving me tea. Later she was nearly crushed by the crowd in a St John's Ambulance canteen she had set up. Dickie and I had to link arms and barge our way through to drag her out. Did she tell you?'

'No, she didn't.'

'All quite hilarious, really! Poor Edwina was quite literally flat on her back in the mêlée! She might have been crushed to death if we hadn't come to her aid!'

Suddenly, the French windows were thrown open from the outside.

'Where is he then? The Bharat Bhushan!' Dr Rathore's voice boomed throughout the room. He kicked off his sandals before entering but stopped short on seeing me. He was wearing a long, creased cotton shirt over a pair of blue swimming trunks, and carrying a bath towel over his arm. His wet hair dripped on to his collar.

'Jewel of India, you fraudulent quack! I'll give you Bharat Bhushan.' Quick as a flash, Jawahar was out of his chair and the two men were laughing, sparring, wrestling affectionately with each other like puppies.

'I waited for you at the pool, but you didn't come . . . again!'
Dr Rathore struggled out from under Jawahar's grasp but let
him get him into an armlock.

'Meet Dr Hari Rathore.' Jawahar announced with Hari's
red face peeping out from under his arm pit. 'Letticia, Lady
Wallace, Special Assistant to the Vicereine.'

'Pippi. Just Pippi, please.'

'Hello again!' Hari grinned. 'We've met before. A couple of
times actually, at Viceroy's House'.

Jawahar raised his eyebrow, just a fraction. I flushed and
was cross with myself for it. Then Hari was released and the
two men embraced, slapping each other on the back.

'My apologies. I'm afraid Hari and I were at Cambridge
together, a long time ago. As you can see we picked up some
rather bad manners. Although, I must say Hari was always
a much better student than I was. At least he came out as
something useful. He is the best surgeon in Delhi.'

Hari stared at the rose peeping out of the top pocket of my
uniform.

'Lady Wallace kindly delivered some urgent papers this
morning from Viceroy's House.' Jawahar lied, swiftly gesturing
to my briefcase which sat prominently on the empty chair next
to me.

Smoothing down his hair, Dr Rathore picked up the towel
that had fallen to the floor. He used it to wipe his face before
throwing it to his friend who urged him to eat.

The main door to the house banged open and the dining room
filled with people; Nan Pandit, Jawahar's grown-up daughter,
Indira, a rotund businessman from Bombay, servants, children,
others. The house boy brought me Edwina's little evening bag.
With it was a letter addressed in tiny black handwriting to
Her Excellency, The Vicereine. Rising to leave, I looked around for
Jawahar. But already he had been dragged into a conversation
with the businessman who was urgently pressing his suit.

'Leave him! He's lost to us now.' Dr Rathore was at my side, clutching an egg sandwich that he must have hastily knocked together for himself. In the main hall, a crowd of people had gathered. Fat men with briefcases in well-ironed white shirts, three scrawny men in dhotis yellowed with age and red turbans tied in peaks at the front, their faces tanned almost black by the sun—all had been let into the house to be heard. As Jawahar came out of the dining room, there was a clamour and a rush. A peasant woman in a filthy sunset orange sari threw herself at his feet, wailing. In the end he and the men in the red turbans had to pull her up.

'Come,' said Dr Rathore. 'It's all in a day's work for the Jewel of India.' Munching on his sandwich, he walked me down to the jeep, all the time eyeing Edwina's little gold clutch. Stupidly, I had not slipped it into my briefcase. 'My house is a few doors down. I have a pool and swim or ride every morning before going to the hospital. It keeps me sane. Jawahar loves to swim too. As a matter of fact he's quite the water baby.' His smile met mine as he found himself using Jawahar's habitual phrase: As a matter of fact. 'I do encourage him to join me as often as he can. To get him away from all this, even for half an hour.' He gestured back to the front door, where, already, a queue of petitioners had lined up with more coming up the driveway. With narrowed eyes he looked again at Edwina's evening bag. 'You must not misunderstand my friend, Lady Wallace. Power, glory and the weight of expectation, it makes for a very lonely man.'

*I*t was the in-between time at the end of the formal working day and before dinner; the hour between 6 p.m. and 7 p.m. The Viceroy's senior staff would leave their ties on the backs of chairs, undo their top buttons and roll up their sleeves. Sighing with exhaustion and relief, they would go into the gardens, or descend to the tennis courts and swimming pool. Work was never-ending. It was an opportunity to unwind a little, a time for informal soundings, for a pat on the arm and a word in an ear, a time for gossip, intrigue and scandal.

Eyes half-closed to filter the heat and the light, I sat in the shade by the pool. Taking advantage of one of the walls around the pool, some garden trellis and old parachute silk, someone had set up a cricket net. Every now and then, amid the chatter of monkeys and parakeets, there would be the sharp whack of bat on ball. Stretching and wiggling my bare feet, I opened my eyes, shading them against the sun. George Abell was bowling to the Maharaja of Patiala, his shadow swinging larger than life through the parachute silk at the ball. From where I sat, it seemed to fly like a meteor through the Milky Way. The cricketers were supervised by two little boys dressed in white, with old men's faces, whose normal job was as ball boys on the tennis courts. There was rhythm in the men's game, a measure in the pauses, the whole thing running like a very slow and peculiar clock. Abell walked in and out, the soft thump of his plimsolls on the grass as he ran up, the pause as the ball spun through the air and the final whack. There was tension too. Both men had serious faces. Before they had begun the Maharaja had carefully unwound yards of turban. Round and round as if he were a spinning top, until he was left with a black cloth tied around his head. No word passed between them. They concentrated on the ball, working with the myriad possibilities for pace, bounce, trajectory and spin. And it seemed to me that they were not just marking time, but slowing it, holding back the day. I was grateful for it, even if for a few minutes. Ever since our arrival in India it was as if life had been running at super speed. Each day, so full and busy, was a life within itself. Already, the change within me was so great, I was beginning to wonder how, when all this was over, I would ever go home. This had particularly been the case during the past week when the Viceroy's official stenographer fell ill with Delhi belly. I had had to step in. It meant that I had been spending long days in the Viceroy's office. After every private meeting Dickie would open the door to his study and call, 'Where's PWP?' He had given me a new nickname: Pippi Without Portfolio. And I would go, notepad and pen in hand, to take dictation of his record of what had been said between him and whichever Indian leader had been to visit.

Sitting on my sun lounger, I picked up the letter I had been writing to my brother-in-law's wife, Margaret, in London. She and I had always been good friends but I was careful what I wrote, not wanting to reveal too much of the conversations I had been recording. It was Dickie's quick clipped dictation voice that sounded in my head as I read

Things are looking up! At last Mr Gandhi has come to tea with the Viceroy. He actually came twice in two days and threatened poor Dickie with a daily visit until power is transferred. The first time he arrived leaning on the shoulder of Maniben Patel who is the only daughter of the senior Congress Leader, Sardar Patel. The poor woman looked terrified. She is the main confidant of her father and keeps house for him. She puts me in mind of a Catholic nun I once knew, for as she walks, large iron keys clink on a string at her waist! Mr Gandhi is quite a tall man, although painfully thin with his shoulder and collar bones sticking out. Despite his age and apparent infirmity, it has to be said he walks with quite a bounce. The first time he came around 5 p.m. He talked for over two hours in the study with Dickie about his early life in South Africa. It was all rather hilarious as the air conditioner was on and Mr G, bare-chested in just his dhoti, sat there shivering. In the end Edwina went in and turned the machine off, chiding Dickie for letting the poor old chap get cold. The second time the two men sat on the terrace and Dickie offered Mr G tea and scones. They were declined in favour of a meal of goat curd that Mr G had brought with him. Later, when Dickie was dictating a record of the meeting to me, which actually was quite insignificant because it was all inconsequential chit-chat, Dickie screwed up his face in disgust and said that he wouldn't mind if he never ate goat curd again until the day he died!

No doubt by the time you get this letter you will have seen the picture of Mr G resting his hand on Edwina's shoulder. It was taken just at the end of the photo call when Dickie, Edwina and the Mahatma turned to walk back into Viceroy's House. I can just imagine the hue and cry! Scandalous! How dare 'that fakir' put his brown hand on her white shoulder! Already we have had a dose of such a reaction here in Delhi and it makes my blood boil.

A gentle breeze billowed the parachute silk and the shadow of George Abell flitted in front as he came in to bowl. But it was the tall, gaunt figure of Mohammed Ali Jinnah, leader of the Muslim League whom I imagined striding out of the light into the chilly gloom of the Viceroy's study. He wore a crisp cream Western summer suit and tie. With a curt nod to Dickie, he took his seat in a large armchair. All elbows and knees, his skin was yellow and taut across his cheekbones like parchment. Tapping his Pall Mall cigarette on top of his silver case three times, he lit up and attempted a smile. It came out as a grimace revealing a set of brown, rotting teeth. Unsettled by the vision, I shook my head to jolt myself back to the present.

The cricket had stopped and the interruption in the rhythm made me look up. The Maharaja was sauntering wide-legged out of the net, wiping his brow with his handkerchief. He handed the bat to George Abell and took the ball from him. They swapped pads and Abell discreetly prepared himself. No word passed between them. Smiling affectionately, the Maharaja beckoned to the boys who had been sitting cross-legged on the lawn. They jumped up in eager anticipation. He bowled deliberately short and George drove hard out of the nets. The Maharaja left it to the children to chase over the flower beds and into what passed as the rough. They tore back with matching grins on their faces, throwing the ball underarm to the curly moustached prince.

Turning, I was surprised to see Claude Auchinleck coming up the steps to the pool. From occasional interactions, I knew he was a private man, preferring quiet companions who did not push conversation. It suited me that way too, and the two of us got along quite well by not trespassing too much on each other. As Commander-in-Chief India he had his own large residence at Flagstaff House and was not seen much socially at Viceroy's House. The pool was not one of his usual haunts. Tall and athletic, he was wearing khaki shorts and plimsolls without socks, his shirt uncharacteristically unbuttoned all the way down. Taking one of the white towels embossed with the Viceroy's crest from the pile, he made his way towards me.

'Good evening, Pippi, anyone sitting here?' He nodded to the teak sun lounger next to me and I shook my head.

'Please.'

He had an angular face with a neat little moustache. Not once had I seen him smile. Stripping down to his bathing trunks, he folded his shirt and shorts and placed them neatly on the lounger. Then he showered, and with a great splash, dived into the pool.

'Poor Auk!' Lord Ismay had whispered confidentially to me one evening after a brandy. 'He's not been the same since the divorce. Awful thing when a wife carries on like that. With one of Claude's friends too! It was during the war in South East Asia Command. In the end Mountbatten packed the two sinners back to England where they shacked up in the Brighton Hotel, of all places. So humiliating for the Auk. He still keeps a photo of Jessie in his wallet. God knows why! A trollop like that deserves to be horsewhipped.'

I watched the Field Marshal swim the length of the pool in a stiff front crawl. He did not roll his head to breathe, but rather lifted it, jaw clenched. But I knew that today it was not the divorce that had brought him out here, but the issue of the former Indian National Army men who were still in prison for war crimes. Claude was adamant that they should not be released simply for nationalist reasons. If that happened, he argued, it would be impossible to maintain military discipline. He had gone so far as to threaten to resign over the matter. There had been a crisis meeting with Nehru, the Viceroy and Liaquat Ali Khan this very afternoon to resolve things. Looking at him swimming like an old bear, I feared it had not gone well.

Others began to arrive at the pool: Elizabeth Ward with her hair tied back in a pink scarf, the Viceroy's valet, Dangles and a couple of other ADCs. Out of respect for the Field Marshall, the young men waited for him to finish his exercise before getting in the pool. He swam a couple of slow breast-stroke lengths then hauled himself out at my end, water cascading off him in silver showers.

'Want a lemonade?' he called to me, beckoning to the khidmutgar.

'Yes, please.'

Flopping down on his back on his towel, his broad chest heaved with the effort of the swim. The khidmutgar brought two lemonades on a tray, placing them on the little table between us. After a while Claude sat up, put on his shirt, and raised his glass to me.

'Nehru's going to back me on the INA with the Legislative Assembly. Even the Muslim League came on board in the end, after a bit of bluster.'

'That's great! Cheers!'

He sipped his lemonade watching the lime-green parakeets with red beaks darting and swooping, tearing apart the blue sky.

'You know, Pippi, part of me wishes it had gone the other way today and they had let me pack my bags. The Indian army is the only good thing about this country, the only thing that unites and holds it all together. When the time comes I fear it will fall to me to take the knife and divide it. India and Pakistan—the whole thing is so fundamentally dishonourable, I want no part in it.'

The Indian spring passed in the blink of an eye. By April summer was already here and the mercury topped 100 degrees Fahrenheit. The ceiling fan in the middle of the anteroom to the Viceroy's study had been set to four. It tugged at the pieces of paper which I churned out of my typewriter daily. The top-secret documents were easiest to manage. Intended for posterity, they were typed on thick paper. But a mass of correspondence came in on thin airmail style paper. It would fly all over the place under the accelerated fan if not filed or weighted down.

Finishing the minutes of the Viceroy's last meeting, I looked up at the clock. The three-man Sikh delegation had been with the Viceroy for well over an hour. The second hand ticked. I wondered whether I might have time for a cigarette before they finished. Just as I reached for my desk drawer, the door to the Viceroy's study swung open and they filed out. The oldest man Tara Singh was followed by the younger ones, Giani Kartar Singh and Baldev Singh. Their arms were stacked high with boxes loaded with papers and files.

'Thank you very much for coming to see me. I appreciate the opportunity to hear your views in private.' Dickie shook hands with each man in turn. But there was no warmth between them. Atop their long beards and moustaches their eyes were fixed like bayonets. Hearing their voices, Lord Ismay came out of his office and offered the Sikhs more refreshments before they departed. They declined. Taking my notepad and pen, I followed the Viceroy back into the study and shut the door.

Dickie dithered uncharacteristically, shifting from one foot to the other on the rug. His usual dictation habit was to walk about the room whilst he spoke. He liked to use the opportunity to stretch his legs between meetings. But today, he sighed, and like a balloon deflating, sat down slowly in the armchair.

'God, I feel like a boiled egg!' he said, his face white with fatigue. Loosening his tie, he undid the top button of his shirt. 'I don't know how previous Viceroys worked in this study; so dark and with demons lurking in every corner.' He gestured at the heavy teak panelling which ran from floor to ceiling. 'Guaranteed to induce depression and despair.'

I had never seen Dickie like this. He was always the extrovert, leading with confidence and energy. I knew immediately that I had to get him out of this room. He had been closeted here in meetings day after day for weeks on end. I sensed from the mess that morale was also dipping among the staff; the enormity of the task facing us was just so great. If the Viceroy went down as well, all would be lost.

'How about we take a stroll down to the gardens? You can dictate to me there. It's almost five, should be bearable.' Nodding at my suggestion, he took off his jacket and tie and threw them untidily over the back of the chair.

After the gloom of the study, the garden was a shock of white, the sun draining the colour from everything. A couple of bodyguards joined us at a discreet distance. Keeping to the shade as much as possible, we strolled between the mushroom-shaped trees and the fountains down towards the rose gardens. Dickie walked slowly, tilting his left knee uncharacteristically out to the side which made him roll with a sailor's gait. A navy man, perhaps he was imagining himself back on the deck of a ship, or perhaps he was just trying to rein in his stride so he could think. For a long time he didn't say anything. We found a wooden bench in the shade overlooking the pond. It was too hot and the flowers, parched and bedraggled, were dying.

Everything was over-exposed, bleached to black and white, like an old photograph.

Dickie leaned back in the seat and stared across the pond, watching the malis with a wheelbarrow clearing a flower bed. When they saw the Viceroy, they put their hands together in namaste and bowed a little. Forcing a smile, Dickie returned their greeting in kind. Then slowly, meticulously, he rolled up the sleeves of his shirt.

'Today, PWP, in that meeting with the Sikhs, I realized for the first time that partition is inevitable, and if that is what the Indians want, then they must take responsibility for the decision themselves.'

Away from the incessantly ringing telephones and clatter and ping of typewriters, the silence of the gardens descended in a vortex around us.

'It would be economic madness,' I finally said. 'East Bengal without Calcutta, the amputation of trade routes in the north that have been established over thousands of years.'

He nodded. 'I quite agree and nothing in the world would induce me to countenance it, if it weren't for this horrendous communal violence. The security situation deteriorates daily. Poor Olaf Caroe looks like he is having a nervous breakdown up there on the North-West Frontier, and my Governors all tell me that we are no longer sitting on top a barrel of gunpowder, but a whole bloody arsenal ready to blow up at any time.'

I stared at the ground. A crowd of ants was scurrying about to the left of my feet.

'Ready, PWP? Have you got your pen?'

'On the 24th of April 1947 I received the Sikh delegation. Tara Singh et cetera, et cetera.' Dickie waved his hand off to the right knowing I would fill in the names, and my shorthand began to scrawl downwards on the pad on my knees. 'They were very well-informed, bringing with them boxes of copies of Parliamentary reports which they referred to at various points during our discussion. They object to the Cabinet Mission Plan which offered them no substantive protection. They told me they are raising a war fund of fifty lakhs and will fight to the last man in the Punjab rather than live under Muslim domination, which doesn't sound good at all.'

Pen poised, I waited for more but there was none. Stiffly, the Viceroy picked up a handful of pebbles and, one by one, threw them into the pool where they sank with a plop. I wrote, 'For inclusion in Viceroy's Personal Report, April 1947. End.' Meanwhile he sat there, casting stone after stone, watching the concentric circles spreading and colliding on the surface of the water.

'God knows, PWP, I have tried to bring all sides together. But I'm beginning to suspect that the one is as bad as the other. They're deliberately avoiding settlement in order to extract maximum concessions. Nehru must have his strong centralized state so he can implement his socialist economy, while Jinnah might be happy with a degree of federal autonomy. Throw into the mix Muslims and Hindus roasting each other alive in Bengal, and Muslims, Sikhs and Hindus slitting each other's throats in the Punjab.' Another stone, a larger one, a louder plop. He picked up a loose brick that had fallen from the edge of a flower bed and threw it right out to the far side of the pond. There it landed with a huge splash. 'And Jinnah is as cold as a fish. Try as I might I can't thaw him out.'

'The Muslims can be quite ideological,' I said. 'But the Muslim League ladies I have met with Lady Louis tell me that we cannot begin to imagine what it is like to be a Muslim in India. In Delhi they are regularly picked out for stop and search just because they are Muslims and are discriminated against in school and work.'

Dickie shrugged. 'That's as may be, but in my opinion Jinnah's a psychopath! He delights in torturing me with semantics. Just sits there smug, superior, all zipped up.' He sighed. 'Damn

Winston! He promised him something during the war, I'm sure of it, and the pathetic little man won't budge an inch from *Pakistan Zindabad.*' The way Dickie said *Long Live Pakistan* sounded like *Pakistan's in the bag* and I stifled a smile. 'Damn it, PWP, if only I had got this job eighteen months earlier I might have been able to do something about it. But I fear the die is cast.'

Leaning forward, he dusted off his hands, propped his elbows on his knees and bowed his head, watching the ants scurrying about their business in the gravel.

'Well, one good thing, at least Edwina seems happier. She's getting on rather well with Nehru, don't you think?'

I was caught off guard. Brow furrowed, he tipped his head sideways, looking at me out of the corner of his worried eye. I hesitated. What could I say? Her party girl reputation ran before her. I knew too much. My head throbbed. The scandal of Edwina's affair, apparently with the black American singer Paul Robeson in 1932. A libel case had been brought against *The People* newspaper and the establishment had shut the gossip down. It was all so hush-hush, I had only heard about it via my husband's Chambers. The newspaper's case floundered on its inability to identify Edwina's lover but Chambers' gossip had it that it wasn't Paul Robeson at all but a black cabaret singer, Leslie Hutchinson. And yet I truly believed Edwina had changed. During the war I had come to know a different woman, someone with a purpose in life.

'I shouldn't worry. They're both so busy. They can hardly get any time to themselves.' It was on the tip of my tongue. But that wouldn't have come out right so I didn't say it. All this ran through my mind in a fraction of a second but my hesitation said it all.

The day tipped into dusk, the light softening, colours re-emerging. In the distance an office chaprasi in his red turban hurried down the path. No doubt the Viceroy had been summoned back to the house.

'Well, I'll do my best to wrap it all up as quickly as I can. Get Edwina back to England. I promised her as much before we came out.' The Viceroy of India stood and turned to hide his face from me. I too rose, kicking myself. My indecision and silence had condemned them both. I should have said something to support Edwina, to put Dickie's mind at rest. Now the moment had passed. It was too late.

The convoy of cars carrying the Viceroy, Vicereine and their staff came to a stop at the outskirts of the village of Kahuta. The way ahead was impassable.

For the last few days I had been accompanying Dickie and Edwina on their tour of the North-West Frontier Province and the Punjab. We had left Peshawar by plane after breakfast, arriving in Rawalpindi late morning. No sooner had we reached Flagstaff House than an agitated Sir Evan Jenkins, Governor of the Punjab, was bundling us all back into cars. He was determined that we should see the riot areas with our own eyes. The twenty-five-mile drive from Pindi had taken a couple of hours.

Throats parched, and covered in dust we descended from the cars into the full glaze of the mid-afternoon sun. It was immediately obvious from the silence that all was not well. No children ran to greet us. There were no shyly smiling girls in bright skirts and veils, and no sunburnt young men driving rumbling bullock carts along the road. Only crows remained, circling over the smouldering ruins of what had once been the village.

Leading the way, Sir Evan offered no further explanation. We had been briefed on the journey and I realized with a start that was the same place where some of the atrocities Amrit Kaur had told me about had taken place. A typical Punjabi village of around three thousand five hundred souls, of whom two thousand were Sikh and Hindu and one thousand five hundred Muslim, we were told. A mob of Muslims had descended on the village in the middle of the night with buckets of petrol and set the Sikh and Hindu areas alight. As if in retribution the

direction of the wind had changed and the flames had spread to
the Muslim quarter. The whole village had been gutted.

In single file, we picked our way down the narrow rubble-
strewn streets. The upper storey of the houses had collapsed.
All that was left were the deserted blackened brick shells of
buildings. No one spoke but we were all thinking the same
thing. It was like the blitz at its worst. I could not believe that
this level of devastation had not been caused by aerial bombing.
We walked past the charred skeleton of a charpoy, through
what had once been someone's living space. At the back of
the house was a great tree. People had tied strings around it,
ring upon ring. I didn't know why—perhaps as tokens of love
that would one day be reclaimed? A woman's pink dupatta was
caught between two stones. Bending down, I lifted a brick and
freed it. The dupatta was smeared black and red with ash and
blood. Of the woman or child who might have worn it, there
was no sign.

In front of the town hall, a delegation of mostly Sikh and
a few Hindu men had gathered to meet the Viceroy. The
Muslims, they said, greatly pleased with their night's work, were
long gone with their loot. A table covered in a crisp white linen
had been placed in the shade for the Viceroy and Vicereine. Its
pretty cutwork border fluttered daintily in the breeze as Dickie
and Edwina took their seats. My ears were still popping after
the bumpy flight this morning. Everything was moving in slow
motion. Someone had managed to boil water to make tea; the
clink of glasses, hands offering and receiving, steam rising, the
soft scent of cinnamon and cloves. I wondered how it was that
a white table cloth had come to rest so pure and white amongst
such ruination.

Automatically I took out my paper and pen to keep notes.
One by one the men were making their cases, their Potohari
dialect lilting, sweet to my ears until the translation came.
'Viceroy Sahib and Vicereine Sahiba, forgive us if on this day

we cannot entertain you in our homes with food and music in
a fitting manner. Alas, you find us here abandoned, tortured
beyond endurance. Utterly bereft, all we can do is weep and beg
for your help.' And on it went. It was all an organized campaign
by the mujahidin to throw them off their land and out of their
homes. The same story, over and over. Women raped, daughters
abducted and forced into marriage, families tied together and
thrown into the flames. And what of compensation for their
losses, they asked, and what was the government going to do
about their cattle, their crops which remained unharvested,
their chickens and their shops? I wrote the words in English, in
shorthand, the brutal horror of what had happened diluted into
a record of squiggles on the page. At last a turbaned man in a
black waistcoat with a notebook bulging out of his top pocket
stepped up. My heart sank. His petition was written out on five
sheets of paper. He began so gently that the Viceroy had to lean
forward on his elbows to hear, but it was not long before the
man reached a theatrical crescendo.

'Three thousand one hundred and ninety nine forced
conversions. Allahu Akbar the Muslims say, but I say, God is
truth!

'Bole So Nihal!' he roared the Sikh cry, pointing his finger
at the sky.

'Sat Sri Akal!' came the guttural roar from his supporters.
'Sat Sri Akal!'

Encouraged, the man's oratory descended into a rant
against the Governor accusing him of siding with the Muslims
and their policy of Pakistan. But Sir Evan, who spoke good
Punjabi had turned purple with rage and the meeting ended in
pushing, shoving and near fisticuffs. Abruptly Dickie rose, face
fixed, expressionless, shoulders back and down and marched
out of the village. In the last moment one of the ADCs snatched
up the white tablecloth. It hung limp in his arms like a flag of
surrender.

There was a good gramophone collection at Government House in Lahore: all of Beethoven's symphonies, Chopin, Rachmaninov's piano concertos, Glenn Miller and a large box of popular songs. We had had yet another gruelling day on tour. I had covered miles with the Vicereine, both by jeep and on foot, visiting refugee camps. My feet ached and my heart was heavy with the wailing and crying of the women refugees. Leaving Edwina with the dinner guests, I had escaped to the library to type up the report, letters and urgent requests for medical supplies and aid that had resulted from the Vicereine's visits. Flipping through the gramophone records, I settled on the Mozart Piano Concerto number 21 in C. Slipping it out of its cover, I placed it on the turntable and stood back, waiting for the needle to reach the first thin black groove. In the darkness the orchestra commanded attention which I would not give. Then the first tickling touch of the piano keys came like a kiss, a lover laying on his hands.

Switching on the desk light under its green shade, I sat down in front of the typewriter and pulled out my notebooks. I had gone through three in the last five days. The pages were grubby with dust and heat, but there was a neat ruled line at the end of each hospital or camp visit. Wearily I began to transcribe my shorthand scribble to the blank page in the typewriter.

Wednesday, 30th April.
Wah: Left Flagstaff House, Rawalpindi, at 6.30 a.m. with H.E.
Drove 25 miles to the Wah Refugee Camp, arriving 7.30 a.m.

*8,700 refugees, mostly Sikhs with some Hindus from the riot-torn areas
of Campbellpore and Bundi. Sardar Ram Singh in charge. He had previously
run a borstal-type establishment. Camp is civil administered with army
cooperation. The latter has furnished equipment and supplies and provides a
military guard for protection.*

Here my notes broke down and my own memories took
over. Half-naked women in rags with babies at their breasts
dragging toddlers through the dust. Wailing, they threw
themselves at my feet. Some of the children's eyes had been
lined with kohl to ward off the evil eye. Their faces were now
streaked with black rivulets of dried-up tears, yet they made no
sound. I was overwhelmed. I didn't know what to do. Then I
saw Edwina ahead of me, crouching down in the dust, holding a
weeping woman in her arms. Stowing my notebook, I followed
suit, forcing the stiff-kneed ADC at my side to do the same.
Arms like sticks, long bony hands reaching up, cheap bangles
clattered as the women talked. They mistook me for the
Vicereine too. It did not matter that I was not. I was a white
woman in uniform—my St John's Ambulance fatigues, my suit
of armour. They placed their trust and hope in me.

'Please Vicereine Sahiba, there is no milk for the children
and no vegetables. Dal is running out. Please Vicereine Sahiba,
we are poor people. What have we done to deserve this? The
Government wants us to go home, but we don't want to go
home. We're too frightened. Take us away from this place,
Vicereine Sahiba. Please!' On and on it went. A toothless old
woman, eyes glazed white with cataracts, pushed a piece of blue
paper into my hand. On it was a name: Seema. It turned out
Seema was her granddaughter. She had been kidnapped by
the Muslim raiders. Wiping her tears, the old woman cupped
my fingers around the thin paper and pulled at my jacket,
begging me to find her princess, her precious one, at the end
covering her face with her dupatta. I didn't know what else to

do except take out my notebook and turn a fresh page. With the help of the ADC I transposed the name from the paper. Then came the rush: dozens more women with names of lost loved ones. So many that I was in danger of being knocked over in the crush. Sardar Singh and the ADC had to call for order, pushing the women back even as I was promising them that all the names would be taken and a proper missing persons list would be made. I meant it, but my words sounded cheap in translation. In truth, I wanted to scoop all of them, the women and children, into my arms and take them with me, away from that terrible place.

In the camp hospital there had been no control over visitors, and measles had spread everywhere, even to the maternity ward. Children with runny noses and swollen eyes, their scrawny bodies covered in spots, lay beside their mothers who were too weak or ill to shoo away the plague of flies. Now I was making notes in my head. All wards filled with dust. No sheets for the beds. Lack of clean water. Shortage of dressings.

Sardar Singh led me out of the hospital building. Outside in the shade, lines of men sat, listless, bitter, a slow cauldron bubbling with thoughts of revenge. We went into the central administration building, down a corridor and towards the open door of a small room. The heat was stifling. Behind a makeshift curtain, sitting upright on a low bed with her back against the grubby whitewashed wall, was the Vicereine. She was talking to a boy of about eight who sat beside her; a most beautiful child with a finely sculpted, intelligent face. He was long-limbed, made for running and jumping and climbing trees. He looked so fit and strong that it took me a second or two to notice what was wrong.

'They cut off his hands.' Sardar Singh said simply. 'Both sides are doing it to the children. God have mercy on their souls.'

I looked again at the stumps where the boy's hands would have been, neatly wrapped in the best white bandages

the hospital had to offer. I could not hear what Edwina was
saying to the child. Her words were being translated by a young
welfare worker who looked no more than twelve or thirteen
years old herself. The boy nodded. Leaning down to the little
wooden table, Edwina picked up a glass and held it to his lips
so he could drink. It was then that I realized the full horror of
his situation. He could not feed himself, clean himself or earn
a living. He was still alive but already dead. My mind stalled
and I groaned, sick to the pit of my stomach. Hearing me at the
door, the boy looked up with big brown adult eyes. He had seen
more than many of us here could ever comprehend and yet,
with a tiny smile, he seemed to be reassuring me: Don't worry,
all will be well.

At that point Edwina waved the back of her hand towards
us, and Sardar Singh and I retreated to the corridor.

'He doesn't speak any more, the boy. Hasn't said a word
since he arrived.'

I too was mute.

'Lady Wallace, I was wondering if you could get us some
artificial limbs?' I knew Sardar Singh was talking to me but I
heard him as if via a bad telephone line.

'Yes.' My voice was not my own. Mechanically, I pulled out
my notebook and pen from my top pocket, the same one where
I had put Jawahar's rose.

'Mohammed Hussein,' he said.

I hesitated in surprise.

'Yes,' he whispered. 'The child is a Muslim. His family
abandoned him. He was brought here, bleeding to death, by a
kind Hindu family. It shames us all.'

With my pencil that had been reduced to a stub, I scribbled
on the page, *New Hands. Mohammed Hussein. Care of Sardar Ram Singh.*
I had drawn an arrow and written: *Willingdon Hospital? Red Cross?*

With effort I hauled my attention back to the library in
Government House and the typewriter, hitting the keys with a

vengeance. I typed faster and faster, recording the Vicereine's visits to makeshift refugee camps in churches, gurdwaras and Hindu temples.

In all of them conditions seemed ideal for the outbreak of an epidemic. Overcrowding; lack of water, largely due to supplies having been cut during riots, improving but still inadequate; poor sanitary arrangements for the numbers; shortage of fresh clothing.

Harder and harder I hit the keys until my fingers hurt, on and on until I realized that the record had finished and the music had stopped. The needle hushed around and around nearing the final groove. I slumped forward, my head in my hands. After a few minutes I switched off the desk light, rose and went to flip the record over to the slow movement. At the drinks cabinet I poured a small brandy, leaving a few rupees in the mess box. Standing there in the semi-darkness, I let the gently pulsing sound rush over me, waiting for the piano entry to arrive like gentle rays of sunshine through the clouds.

Just then the door clicked open and Edwina slipped in, sitting down in a big leather armchair beside me. Sighing, she closed her eyes, drinking in the music, letting it wring the agony and exhaustion from her body.

'Escaped at last!' she said at length. 'The rest of them have turned in. But I can't sleep.'

'I know,' I replied. 'Want a drink?'

Getting up, she poured herself a soda, taking her pillbox from her pocket at the same time.

'It's like the war all over again. The two of us up late, in our khakis.'

Neither of us had bothered to change for dinner. We were still in our St John's Ambulance uniforms, covered in sweat and grime. Even Edwina's bright red lipstick had worn off by now. Soon we would be going through lists of who needed to be contacted and what needed to be done. It was an old routine.

'It's worse than the war,' I said. 'Neighbours, communities tearing themselves apart in the name of religion. Tying families together and throwing petrol over them. And the children? How can people cut the hands off a child?'

She nodded and said nothing until the music ended.

'Politics,' she spat out the word, wiping her mouth with the back of her hand. 'Men play with power like boys with toy soldiers. Grand strategies and designs, but always, always, always, it is the old, the sick, the women and children who pay the price.' She jutted a finger towards my report which overflowed out of the top of the typewriter. 'How are you getting on? Plasma needed at the Lady Reading Hospital and a new Dunlopillo mattress in the Lady Aitchison, and make sure your record in no uncertain terms my disgust at the state of the Civil Hospital in Dera Ismael Khan. I'll most certainly be speaking to Lady Caroe about that when we return to Delhi. She visited the hospital a while back. They asked for help in January, yet she has done nothing about it.'

Now it was my turn to nod. 'And we must start a central register for missing persons. The mental distress suffered by people not knowing what has happened to their loved ones is not to be underestimated.'

The telephone rang, making us both jump. Edwina's face lit up, but it was I who was nearer to the phone.

'Hello. Pippi Wallace speaking.' My new name was now firmly established in administrative quarters.

'Ah! Pippi. Good evening. Jawahar here. I was wondering if I could speak to Edwina. Don't wake her if she's gone to bed. It's just I have been waiting all day.'

'She's right here beside me—'

Edwina had already grabbed the receiver.

'Jawahar?' She swallowed the *r* on the end of his name putting the emphasis on the *h* not the *w* so it came out Jawaha. 'Yes, yes, I'm fine. It's such an unbearably sad tour. Tomorrow we head to the camp at Multan. These poor people! You really must come and see for yourself.'

Taking my drink I walked out on to the veranda. I could just hear the whispered murmur of her voice, light and fast. I sat down in a wicker chair. The wild dogs on the lawn stalked black and grey in the moonlight shadows. In a distant street there was a flash of orange followed by the loud boom of an exploding bomb.

*I*t was five-thirty in the morning and still dark. We were driving south out of New Delhi. I was sitting in the back seat of the yellow convertible, my eyes clinging to the narrow beams of headlights as if were they lifelines. There was no moon. Every now and again shadows appeared like ghosts out the darkness; Two young men and a boy, wandering cows, and a farmer driving his bullock cart to market, his dhoti and teeth briefly luminescent in the headlights. Why on earth had I agreed to this foolhardy outing?

On my return from the North-West Frontier and the Punjab, I had made some telephone calls on the subject of prosthetic hands. One of the people I had rung up was Dr Rathore at Willingdon Hospital.

'Both hands?' he had asked calmly, professionally.

'Yes. I'm afraid so. Clean cut at the wrist.'

'It makes it very difficult.' He sighed. 'In India we say that the hands are the wings of the heart. Such a beautiful and complex tool, with all the muscles, bones, arcs and planes of movement. Very difficult to replicate. The best I have ever seen is a kind of hook and I am afraid we don't have any such expertise here.' He paused to think. 'But I do know some people who might be able to help. My friend Sunny Singh is a successful businessman. We met in London years ago. His wife, Cherie, is America. Both of them are very involved in philanthropic work in India and in the US. If it is state-of-the-art prosthetic hands you are after for the boy, they are the people to speak to. As luck would have it, they have invited me to a riding party at their summer retreat, The Haven, near Mehrauli, this Sunday. I don't usually go . . . getting rather old and boring, I suppose. Why don't you tag along and I'll introduce you?'

I had stalled. The trip to the refugee camps still fresh in my mind, I wasn't really in the mood for a country house party, and with so much work to do, I wasn't sure if I could get away.

'If I might be so bold,' Dr Rathore had asserted, 'all work and no play leads to low efficiency and poor decision-making.'

'Well, it would be very nice to meet your wife.' Damn! I wished I could put those words back in my mouth the instant I said them, but they had already tumbled out like jolly fairground marbles down a chute. I had been thinking of Tania and her beautiful mother at Jawahar's house.

A pause. I heard him breathing at the end of the line.

'My wife died some years ago, when my son and daughter were just nine and eleven years old. She had a brain tumour,' he said simply.

'Oh! I'm so sorry. Please forgive me.'

Silence.

'It was a long time ago and she had suffered greatly. In the end I suppose it was a relief.'

I waited for the inevitable return question from him. But it did not come.

More silence and then he said quietly, 'Do please say you'll come, Lady Wallace. I haven't shown my face at The Haven for a while, and Cherie is not pleased. I promise that you'll enjoy the horses and the ride. The whole area is actually an archaeological paradise. To tell the truth, you would be doing me a favour.' And so I had agreed.

Black was retreating into shades of grey as we pulled into the drive of a grand white country house. We were greeted by a shrieking dawn chorus from the peacocks.

In the half-light at the top of the steps a buxom American lady in her mid- to late fifties waited by the door in snug-fitting jodhpurs and a crisp white blouse.

'Welcome! Welcome to The Haven. Howdy stranger? Sunny has been asking for you. It really isn't kind to abandon us for so long.' She reached up to give Dr Rathore a hug, offering him her cheek, French-style.

'Ah! And this must be the lovely Lady Wallace. We're all just so pleased you could come!' She held out her hand and, clasping mine in an iron grip, shook it vigorously. 'Hari has told me so much about you. You've been up to the North West with the Vicereine. We saw the pictures in the newspaper. Terrible, most terrible. I'm Cherie.' Her voice went up at the end of every sentence, making it seem a question. There must have been at least half a dozen *es* at the end of her name! Yet with her energy and informality, already she had won me over.

'Please leave your bags with the house boys. We've allocated you all rooms. You can rest after our ride, wash and change before lunch. That's when the rest of the guests arrive, the lazy ones who don't ride!'

She winked and, throwing out her arms, ushered us into the dining room. There we were introduced to two other guests, still sleepy-eyed from having risen early. They were Tim Latham, a doctor from the Canadian High Commission, and his wife, Susan. Both were tall, thin and very fair.

'Breakfast before the ride.' Cherie chivvied us over to the sideboard where several dishes of food were laid out. 'Best to start as early as we can, while it's still cool.'

Bewitched, I stared at the moist, glistening chunks of an unknown fruit, a seducing sunset orange in a silver bowl.

'Papaya,' Cherie said. 'My brother-in-law sent a box from Bombay last week. Help yourself!'

In the yard Dr Rathore embraced a small man with grey hair. Like the rest of us, he was neatly dressed in riding attire.

'My husband, Sunny,' Cherie said. 'Hari and Sunny are like brothers. Between ourselves, I think Hari is Sunny's one real friend. They don't talk business when they are together. It's such a relief for Sunny. In his line of work it's often difficult to know whom to trust.'

Sunny checked the girth of my horse himself as our party mounted up. A lithe man of about sixty, with a bouncing walk, bushy moustache and a cheeky grin, he was the antithesis of the portly looking industrialist I had imagined him to be.

'Tomahawk's a gentleman, a very steady pony. My son used to ride him for polo. Now he's getting a bit old so we keep him for Cherie.'

'I used to jump ditches and fences in my younger days,' I replied. 'I might manage to cling on!'

He smiled. The routines of getting mounted up were second nature to me. When Sunny helped me adjust my stirrups, he reminded me of my father and I felt myself starting to relax. Dr Rathore was right. I had needed to get away from the back-biting and tension at Viceroy's House, if even for only for few hours.

'This horse won't try any funny business, unlike my beautiful Indian Marwaris.' Standing back, Sunny watched me settle into the saddle. 'They're very loyal. If I put you on one of them, they'd throw you off in no time!'

A thin syce in a frayed brown shirt led a grey of about sixteen hands into the yard.

'This is Abella. My pride and joy!' The syce gave Sunny a quick leg up and he vaulted into the saddle with the energy of a twenty-year-old. 'You ignorant English call these fine royal war horses "native donkeys" on account of their curly ears!' He chuckled, tweaking the end of his moustache inwards in imitation of the animal's distinct ears. 'But that's all fine and dandy with me. If others are not interested in this magical Indian breed, and are happy to let it decline to the point of extinction, it creates a stud opportunity for me. One day there will be value in this bloodline. You heard it from me first!' He squeezed Abella with his legs. The horses were keen, and our party of seven was off at a gentle canter into the dusty pink dawn.

The tracks between the trees were sandy and just wide enough for a jeep or two horses. At first Dr Rathore kept protectively to my side. He was a different man in the saddle. The stiffness and weight gone from his joints, his movements were soft and fluid. Already he had melded with the horse while I was still adjusting to the rhythm of mine. We did not talk. There was still a hint of moisture in the air, the musty scent of night lying low near the ground. It was not autumn, but the sun-desiccated leaves had begun falling, and high in the half-naked trees the birds heralded our arrival. Rounding a corner at the canter, we startled a peacock. To escape us it took a reluctant lumbering run into a clumsy attempt at flight.

I thought at first that the bushes were burning. Not believing my eyes, I looked again and again through the trees. Everywhere there were ruins, burnished red, copper and gold by the retreating dawn.

'The Madhi Masjid,' Sunny called from the front. He wheeled Abella to the left, up a narrow track. Before us was a tumbledown fortress and a gate; with a clatter of hooves, we were in the courtyard of a deserted mosque.

'This whole area dates from the eleventh century onwards and was the centre of the Delhi Sultanate.' Tim was whispering reverently to me, ignoring the chattering hordes of monkeys running about at the top of the arches of the prayer hall.

'Muslim Turkic invaders came from Afghanistan and the North West and built over the earlier Rajput territories. Later, you will see the Qutb Minar. It is a victory tower commissioned by the slave general Qutbuddin Aibak.'

We kept our horses at a walk, as new treasures emerged one by one out of the shadows: the tomb of the court poet Jameli decorated with red and blue tiles in Islamic style; the squat square tomb of Balban, Qutbuddin's successor, abandoned to foliage amidst dilapidated walls.

'Look!' Susan pointed. 'Qutb Minar!'

A giant red sandstone tower rose from the tops of the trees.

We dismounted in the courtyard of the Qutb Minar complex. Our horses snorted and stretched their necks as we led them into the courtyard of the Might of Islam Mosque. Untying my scarf, I stared up at the ornate carvings: bells, flowers, garlands and Arabic script from the Koran. The carving here was squarer, more primitive perhaps than the Islamic art I was more familiar with.

'You can see this was the work of Hindu stonemasons.' Susan explained. She and her husband were clearly fascinated by the history of the area.

'And this! Kama Sutra carvings.' Unabashed, she pointed to a stone frieze of naked men and women.

'All sixty-four positions!' Sunny tweaked his moustache and grinned. 'The invaders built their mosques on top of Hindu and Jain temples. When your British archaeologists came along and pulled off the plaster, hey presto! Look what they found!'

'That's India for you.' Tim wiped his glasses with his handkerchief. 'Layer built upon layer. See this!'

I shaded my eyes and stared up at a great iron pillar in the middle of the courtyard.

'It would have stood in front of a temple to Vishnu. Dates from the fourth century AD. Yet it has not rusted. You have to imagine it with a statue of Garuda on the top, a humanoid bird that is the mount of Vishnu,' he clarified for my benefit.

'Do you want to go up?' Sunny asked, looking at the Minar. 'There are three hundred and seventy-five steps. You'll be exhausted, but the views are spectacular.'

'I'll take you, if you want to go,' Dr Rathore offered, unhooking his canteen from his saddle.

'We'll see you over at Metcalfe's for coffee then!' Sunny tossed another full canteen towards me. 'Leave the horses with Sunil.' He pointed to the groom who had accompanied us. 'He'll wait for you here. I guarantee you won't want to walk anywhere afterwards!'

In the end it was just the two of us who ventured into the cool, dark tower. It took a while for our eyes to adjust as we began the climb, round and round the spiral staircase. I went first, my boots scuffing on the uneven stones, my heart pounding, breath coming shorter, harder. We stopped once, and then again, leaning, panting against the wall, sipping from our canteens.

'You all right?' Dr Rathore puffed.

I nodded and smiled, legs trembling. 'Yes, just not as young as I once was.'

'Nonsense. You're a spring chicken! I'm nearly sixty!'

Round and round again, stumbling, reaching, our hands clinging to the grooves in the walls until we reached a small balcony about halfway up. From there we could see the rest of our party dismounting in front of a white ruin with an Islamic dome.

'What's Metcalfe's?' I wheezed, trying and failing to imagine a café amidst all the ruins.

'It was a tomb. That one over there. Sir Thomas Metcalfe, the British Resident at the court of the last Mughal Emperor, Bahadur Shah, converted it into his Dilkhusha. It's an Urdu word meaning "heart's delight"; it was his summer retreat. They say he built the house here so he could keep an eye on the old Emperor . . .' He shrugged. 'And soon Sunny will be reclining on a blanket in the shade of the dome in what used to be Metcalfe's sitting room. They'll all be sipping coffee brought over in flasks from The Haven, while we toil up here!'

I laughed.

'And what happened to the last Mughal Emperor?'

'He was exiled to Burma by the British because of his involvement in the 1857 uprising. He died there. Actually, he was quite a poet; wrote in Urdu.'

'It's such a contradiction, the British Raj. At home we are a liberal democracy and yet we have ruled the way we have in India. I'm sorry.'

Dr Rathore shrugged and clicked a half smile from the corner of his mouth.

'We're all full of contradictions; India too. I'm a prime example: an Indian nationalist who is very fond of England.' For the first time that day he looked directly at me, picking kindly through my wrinkles and lines with his thoughts. 'As a young man, I had very happy times in England. People were kind and generous. The England I remember is a gentle one: punting on the Cam, warm beer, soft river breezes, long summer days where the night never came, walking alone in the rain, the scent of the honeysuckle.' He looked away from me. 'What is done is done. No point in fretting over it. Soon enough we'll be the masters in our own house. Then our problems will really begin.'

We set off again, stopping more frequently to catch our breath. Higher and higher we climbed.

'Nearly there!' Dr Rathore pointed to the pillar of sunlight falling from above. 'A few more steps.' Turning, he offered me his hand, gripping my forearm when I responded. 'Careful. It's exceedingly tight up top.' He steadied me, guiding me to a narrow block. There we sat, just the two of us, perched like huge flightless birds.

Swallowed by the silence between the sky and the earth, we drank from our canteens. As the water levels fell we tipped our heads further back, catching the drops with our eager tongues.

'All those kings, generals and poets who believed they were the greatest, what are they now? Nothing but curiosities for tourists who have never even heard of their names!' Dr Rathore threw open his fist as if scattering grains on the ruins far below.

My eyes roamed over the great plain laid out before us. Hazy in the distance were the dome of Viceroy's House, the tomb of the Mughal Emperor Humayun and the minarets of the Jami Mosque. Behind them all was the Yamuna river like a silver snake. In the foreground the water tanks and ponds of Mehrauli glistened like lost pearls dropped among the ruins.

'It's beautiful,' I said.

He lowered his canteen, looking at me out of the corner of his eye.

'Jawahar told me,' he said, 'what happened to your family.' He made no further attempt at condolence or sympathy, offering instead the comfort of a quiet presence at my side.

'I always wanted to bring my wife up here. But she would never come,' he said after a while, staring straight ahead at the clouds. There were only a few in the vastness of blue. 'I blame myself for it. For years I put it all down to neurosis and paranoia. By the time I realized something was really wrong it was too late.'

I knew better than to offer platitudes in response and said nothing, waiting for him to go on.

'I was born in Rajputana. My family had land and estates. But I was never interested in the country life. I found it stifling; I was a great disappointment to my father in that sense. In the end a compromise was reached. I went off to Cambridge to study medicine and my elder brother got most of the land. In lieu, I was given a tranche of the inheritance, but an arranged marriage was part of the deal. We married after I had finished medical school in London. I was twenty-six. She was seventeen, a very beautiful girl from a noble family. She was so tiny and delicate, with long black hair down to her waist.' He stopped. 'I don't know why I am telling you this.'

'It's all right,' I said. 'Go on if you want to.'

'Well, it was a disaster from the start. We didn't have much in common. She'd never even been out of her home town, and I had grown up surrounded by men and boys; at boarding school, at university, on the estate. Never really knew how to relate to a woman. For me it was always science and sport. For her it was religious superstition. I used to read the medical and scientific journals, eager for the latest advances in science that would improve people's lives. She would tie chillies and lemons over the front door to stop evil spirits from coming in, and insist that we couldn't eat eggs because it was Tuesday, or that we needed to fast for this and that, and that she couldn't go out because the almanac said it wasn't auspicious. Pfff!' He slapped his thighs with exasperation, paused and then asked me point blank. 'Was your marriage happy, Lady Wallace?'

'Pippi. Please call me Pippi.'

'And you must call me Hari.'

'Yes, it was, although Charles was much older than me. After the children came along I resented having to give up so much of my own ambitions. There was always an undercurrent of tension between us because of that. I suppose the marriage worked because I played second fiddle to him. But he was a good man, and a kind man. He worked hard and adored the boys. I loved him.' I looked him directly in the face, noticing the grey in his bushy black eyebrows and the faint shadow of a stubble that suggested he had not shaved that morning. This made him look older than he really was as well as a little disreputable.

Taking a swig from his canteen, he continued his story, confiding no longer in me, I thought, but in the vastness of sky and plain.

'Over the years my wife became more and more eccentric and reclusive. She was always complaining of headaches. I escaped into work or sport rather than go home. If I wasn't at the hospital, I was playing polo, out riding or playing golf. In the end she just woke up one morning and couldn't move her legs. That's when we discovered she had a brain tumour. I was frantic. In retrospect I should have spotted it. All the signs were there. I got all the best experts and all the latest medical advice from London and New York. We tried various things . . .' His voice broke and he swallowed hard.

'Lady Wallace, Pippi, we call ourselves doctors of medicine, but in truth our knowledge is so limited. We are little more than Stone Age men with flint axes.'

We watched the kites soaring on the thermals, dropping occasionally in a deadly dive.

'And then one day my wife put her hand on mine. "Enough jaan," she said. "My time has come." And it had. She died a few days later.'

The heat was rising quickly now and voices echoed from far below. Cherie and Susan were standing in front of Metcalfe's place, waving and calling to us.

'Coo-eee, coo-eee, hell-ooh, hell-ooh!'

A few more minutes and it would be time to go.

'Anyway, if you can bear to hear the end of the story? I suppose my biggest regret is that I didn't spend more time with my son or daughter. My son has gone to America. We quarrelled, he and I. It was one morning over breakfast and I have not seen him since. "India is a basket case," he said. "We're deluding ourselves if we think we will ever make anything of this country after the British go. And I for one, am bloody well not going to hang around to find out."' Hari shrugged. 'I sent him to school in England, and that's what I got for my money!' He laughed; a long, rolling chuckle that made his shoulders shake. But the skin around his jaws was suddenly sallow and drooping. 'So that's that. All about me.'

'And your daughter?'

'She's married, with two children, and lives in Lahore. It was a love match, actually. I didn't object. How could I when my own marriage had been such a prison?' He paused, looking out across the great dusty plain towards the west, as if he really could see the mountains. 'Star-crossed lovers are always jumping off the top of the minar, you know!'

'Really?'

'Yes. In India there's always an obstacle to a match; wrong caste, wrong religion, skin too dark, crooked teeth! At least my daughter seems happy.'

'And do you see her?'

'A couple of times a year. I visit her, and sometimes she comes to Delhi. Both of us do our best, but it is never easy between us. I think she blames me for her mother.' Taking a little wallet from his shirt pocket, he pulled out a photograph. A tall, slim, fine-featured young woman in front of flower beds was bending, smiling towards the camera. She hugged to her two small boys, in shorts and crisp white shirts, who squinted petulantly against the sun.

'You must be worried about her in Lahore,' I said. 'The security situation is . . .' I was thinking of the houses that had been burnt down in Amritsar and the rubble from rioting piled up at the sides of the streets that I had seen in the Punjab with Edwina, of the strain in Sir Evan Jenkins's face. But I checked myself, conscious of my access to privileged information, and of the rumour and counter rumour swirling round the hotels, bars and tea rooms in Delhi.

He looked down. His left eyelid drooped more than his right, giving an impression of something that might be semi-blindness, perhaps sleep. Sighing, he shrugged again and rolled his shoulders in the way I was learning was characteristic of him.

'It'll settle down once the British have left. At the moment, it's just all the uncertainty. Pakistan's a red herring,' he said. 'Just a negotiating tactic by Jinnah to get maximum concessions from us Hindus. I don't believe he really wants it and I know Jawahar doesn't either. He believes, as do I, that the new India must have a democratic and secular foundation. Although there are others within the Congress who would have India as a Hindu nation. Such a ridiculous mediaeval notion!'

He made to drink but found his canteen was empty. I handed him mine and he took a sip, the top rattling against the can. A little water sloshed out, wetting his lips and chin. Without looking at me, he handed the canteen back and I sipped too, the water lukewarm in my mouth. We sat in silence, letting the sun burn our faces.

ack in my room at The Haven I took a shower. The water was cold, freezing cold. It made me gasp. But I welcomed it, rolling my head this way and that under the jet, letting it soak into my hair and stream over my face. Quickly, I soaped myself. My forearms, neck, upper chest and lower arms had tanned under the Indian sun. The rest of me was as lily-white as the day I left England. I turned up the shower, sharp needles of cold taking my breath away.

Teeth chattering, covered in gooseflesh, I hurried out and wrapped myself in a towel. When my body was dry, I towelled my hair dry and put on a clean pair of camiknickers and a camisole. It was then that tiredness overtook me. Turning off the ceiling fan, I lay leaden on the bed. The room Cherie had given me was a large one at the rear of the house. A low murmur of men's voices filtered up from the swimming pool in the garden. It was punctuated by the occasional half-hearted splash or shout. My eyes were heavy. The cheery blue-and-white block-print curtains undulated softly, allowing streams of hot air into the room which climbed, first caressed, then entwined my legs and arms. I still felt the canter motion of the horse within me, rocking gently like a boat on a sea. Stretching and sighing, my mind was a kaleidoscope of turquoise, emerald and blue retreating into blackness.

Knocking hard at the door, it was Susan who woke me.

'Lady Wallace? Are you ready? It's time for lunch.'

In the large dining room a buffet lunch had been laid out, a relaxed affair with people changing places between courses. There were a number of familiar faces amongst the guests including His Excellency Mr Lo and his wife. I was, however, taken aback to see the beautiful Indian lady from Jawahar's whom I had mistaken for Hari's wife.

Aware of my search for prosthetic hands, Cherie put me next to the American Ambassador. A good conversation ensued about prosthetic hands and the possibilities for procurement thereof.

'Quite a few of our servicemen have lost one hand in battle.' The Ambassador rubbed his chin. 'The tragic thing is, there were a lot of cases in the last weeks of the war, even after the Japanese surrendered. The Japs had a nasty habit of leaving booby traps, new cameras and the like and when our guys went to pick them up . . . Boom!' He twisted his champagne glass towards the ceiling.

After dessert the guests began to circulate again. The men pushed back their chairs, and lit their cigars and cigarettes. The women followed Cherie into the parlour for tea, coffee and sweets.

I found myself sitting on a sofa next to the beautiful lady. Taking the initiative, I put my hands together in the Indian-style of greeting.

'Namaste! We've not met. I'm Pippi Wallace.'

'Goldie,' she announced without volunteering a surname. She didn't smile or return my greeting, but I blundered on.

'I think I met your charming daughter at Panditji's. She told me she wants to be a nurse.'

Goldie looked down her nose at me and sniffed.

'Did she? Well, I'll thank you not to interfere in matters that don't concern you, Lady Wallace.' She sneered my name in a manner that said, and yes I know all about you too. 'My daughter is certainly not going to be a nurse.'

'Well, perhaps she might try to become a doctor then. Women should not set their sights too low.'

At this Goldie put down her teacup and stood up. I followed suit. Her beautiful brown eyes sparked with hatred. I thought she might even jump at me and scratch my eyes out with her long, red-painted nails.

'I was only trying to encourage and offer support. Medicine and public service are very noble occupations for young women. God knows, India is crying out for qualified nurses.'

'Lady Wallace, people like you and the Vicereine come over here, knowing nothing about India, and yet think it's your place to tell our girls what they should and should not do. The sooner you meddling busybodies pack your bags and leave, the better.'

'I assure you Mrs . . . Goldie . . . that is exactly what we are trying to do. The Viceroy and Vicereine, and many well-meaning people from all sides are working very hard to bring about a prompt, equitable and peaceful transfer of power. And now, if you will excuse me.' I turned abruptly and left the room.

In the hall I was surprised to find that I was shaking. I had been relaxed and Goldie had caught me unarmed and unprepared. Susan had followed me out. Taking me by the arm, she steered us to a side veranda where she offered me a cigarette. I declined.

'Don't you listen to that woman! She's just jealous.'

'Jealous? Of what?'

'Jealous of you and Hari, of course. She had just arrived when we were returning from our ride. She saw the two of you together.'

'I've never heard anything so ridiculous, and the two of us are most definitely not together. She could have ridden out with us as well. The more the merrier, it seems to me with Cherie and Sunny.'

'I know that. But they don't like it, you know, the Indian women, when we socialize on equal terms with their men. We Canadians do our best to integrate, but at mixed social events it's always the same: bitching and back-stabbing. Really, sometimes women can be quite evil.' Susan inhaled deeply on her cigarette. 'And despite your tan, you're fair-skinned, and have lovely green eyes—very attractive to Indian men, which no doubt adds insult to Goldie's injury.'

I stared at the shimmering haze of heat which hung over the garden. Once again I excused myself. I simply didn't have the time or energy for catty adolescent politics.

Down at the stables, everything appeared white in the glare of heat. Even the flies were still. I looked for the syce and found him asleep on a charpoy in the shade. He was snoring gently, mouth open, stained red with betel nut. Tiptoeing past, I located Tomahawk's stall. He had his head in the hay. I unbolted the half door and went in.

'Hello, boy. How are you doing?'

Turning, he came to nuzzle me, his nose soft and wet under my hand. I stroked his withers, murmuring sweet nothings, like a mother to her child. Flattering myself that he recognized me, I rested my cheek against his neck.

Just then Tomahawk pricked up his ears; someone was coming. I raised my head and began to make up excuses and apologies.

'Great minds!'

Squinting against the sun I saw Hari standing at the stable door. Everything about him was square, the line of his hair across his forehead, his wide shoulders which cut out rectangles and triangles of light.

'Thought I might find you here. Cherie dispatched me to get you.'

'There is something timeless about horses and stables.' I was awkward, like a child, expecting to be told off for my presumption in wandering about the estate. But he just smiled and watched me with the horse. I wanted to protest, to blurt out: 'I can't, Hari. I'm an empty shell, living on because I do, not because I want to. Leave it that way. For pity's sake, don't give me something to love, something to care about.' But I said nothing and Tomahawk swished his tail. Still Hari watched, rubbing his chin. I waited, but it did not come, the explanation of his relationship with the beautiful woman.

'The stables were always my refuge too when I was a boy. One time, I found a pigeon with a broken leg. I set it in a wooden splint and hid it in the stables where I fed it and nursed it. When my father found out he wrung the bird's neck and then beat me.'

'Oh no! Why would he do that?' I patted Tomahawk one last time.

The words were coming thick and slow between us, the spaces between them muffled with heat.

'To beat the compassion out of me. "The world is a cut-throat place and only the strongest survive. Compassion is for saints and women, not for boys who want to be men," or so my father said.'

Hari stood aside so I could get by. When I was through, he closed the lower half of the door and slipped the bolt home. Metal on metal, it sounded high and clear, a single crystal ping like the bell in a church that turns water into wine.

'Don't take it all on board, Pippi. You'll drive yourself mad if you do. I learnt that a long time ago when my first patient died on me.' He stroked the side of my arm gently, from my shoulder to my wrist. 'We all do what we can in our own ways. But India is vast, the scale of poverty and ignorance so great. You can't drain an ocean with a sieve. None of us can.'

Viceregal Lodge
Simla
Saturday, 10th May 1947

Dear Margaret,

At last we have a plan for the transfer of power. By the time you get this letter, it will all be old news. I can tell you that, generally speaking, the Provinces shall have the right to determine their own future; they will not be forced into the Indian Union. But won't bore you with more. It will all be public soon enough. Lord Ismay has already left for London with the plan for consultations. Today a big announcement is planned about a meeting on 17th May between the Viceroy and all the Indian leaders. At this His Ex will present His Majesty's government's formal plan for the transfer of power. It has been devilish hard work to get to this stage, and on doctor's orders the Viceroy has adjourned up to Simla for rest and relaxation. Most of the staff has come with him. We are all quite worn out, especially Edwina who suffers constant headaches and neuralgias.

From my eyrie of a room at the top of Viceregal Lodge, I looked up from the letter I was writing to Margaret in London and stared across the blanket of mist and rain that shrouded the Himalayas. The peaks of the mountains were only visible occasionally, appearing and disappearing as the weather shifted like a rocky reef under a dangerous sea. I had been here a week. Much of my most pressing work was done and I didn't like being idle. In the silence of the mist-cloaked mountains my head choked with memories which jostled and pressed against the inside of my skull. It was not Alan's little children who were running about on the lawns of the Viceregal Lodge, but the ghosts of my own.

Shaking my head, I looked at the clock. There were only a few minutes left before I was due to go out. I still had a sheet and a half of blank paper left to fill. Wearily, I picked up my pen and started writing again.

Simla, as I am sure you know, is the summer capital of the British Raj. High in the Himalayas, it offers respite from the crippling summer heat of the plains. Between ourselves, the Viceregal Lodge is quite hideous. With wall-to-ceiling teak panelling, it's very oppressive. I can't help feeling that Count Dracula might appear at any moment! Various guests have been invited during our sojourn, including the Chinese Ambassador and Nehru. The latter arrived in a foul mood. He tells me he was very reluctant to come. He despises Simla because it symbolizes the worst of British rule. Gandhi calls it 'government from the 500th floor,' and Nehru very much agrees with this sentiment. He especially dislikes being pulled in a rickshaw by barefooted coolies, although travelling by car here isn't to be recommended either. When we arrived, I had the embarrassing privilege of being driven through the Mall, which is the name given to the main street in Simla. The town is all mock Tudor and faux home counties, rather like an unconvincing Hollywood film set, and is built along the razor's edge of the mountain. If motor traffic were not restricted in the centre, the jams and chaos would be unimaginable. So only the Viceroy's, Governors' and Commander-in-Chief's cars are permitted to be driven through the Mall. The rest of the road is given over to pedestrians and rickshaws. The cars are forced to move at a snail's pace and everyone peers in as if one were a monkey in a zoo. It is most disconcerting. Given the architecture and weather, it would be all too easy to cocoon oneself and imagine one is not actually in India. That, I suppose, is the point of the whole place. But then one isn't back in England either. It is a nowhere land and, in truth, I feel quite lost.

Again, I looked at the clock: nearly three. Time to go. Pinning my hat on my head, I put another letter in a brown envelope into my bag. Then I took another bag full of magazines from my English dressmaker in Delhi, Mrs Pritchard. I was going to visit Mrs Jane Ovington, and deliver the letter given to me in The Savoy by Sir William Staffs in London all those months ago. The hall clock chimed a ponderous hour as I descended the great teak staircase, but no one else was about. The Viceroy and Vicereine had left earlier in the day with Jawahar, the Chinese Ambassador and a small party for tea and a walk at The Retreat at Mashobra.

When my driver dropped me at the edge of town, it was beginning to drizzle. From there I hailed a rickshaw to Jane Ovington's house, Avalon. Conscious that I was not the daintiest of women, I hired two men to pull, paying almost double the price for the ride. Nevertheless, I felt awkward in my seat as the two men set themselves into the T-bar tow, and braced themselves to take the weight. One was tall in a turban, the other short and bare-headed. They soon set up a steady pace, the soles of their sandals slapping rhythmically on the wet ground, raising little silver spurts of water. Chests forward, breathing hard, their bony shoulders protruded backward at an unnatural angle. The wind was getting up and we were heading into the rain so my face was wet. Such a strange sensation after the heat and dust of the plains. Suddenly I found myself choking on the scent of cedar and pine. It was as if I was suffocating. I couldn't breathe. Desperately, I tried to suppress the rising sense of grief and blackness. Why had it come back to me now?

'Not far now, Memsahib.' The younger rickshaw puller turned and attempted his most charming, slightly threatening, brown-toothed grin. 'Baksheesh. Memsahib not forgetting? This hard job.' I could see the heaving outline of his ribs through his thin cotton shirt as he spoke.

'Good,' I said in Hindustani, wanting the ride to be over.

'Not forgetting?' his eyes narrowed.

I smiled my Edwina smile. 'Memsahib not forgetting.'

Satisfied, he turned eyes front and I watched the bobbing back of his head, sleeked crow-black by the rain.

After a while we came to a fork in the road. A neat white sign pointed in one direction only: Tibet. I had the strange urge to follow it and never come back, but the boys wheeled the rickshaw and took the other road.

Avalon stood at the end of a narrow dirt path at the edge of a ridge where I said goodbye to the rickshaw pullers and gave them the baksheesh they wanted. The little white gate clicked in the same way as the old farm gates of my childhood. I passed under the arch of wisteria, where drops fell from the purple petals into my hair. The modest-sized house was perched at the top of a long lawn fringed with flower borders and trees. Its mock Tudor timbers were painted seaside blue in contrast to the white façade. The lawn was so steep that one got the impression the house might, at any moment, roll down it and bounce into the cloud-covered valley below. A crow cawed, a dog barked. Wiping my face with my handkerchief, I took a deep breath, pulled my shoulders back and walked up the garden path. Why was I so afraid? The fact was work was the lesser stress because people did not ask me about myself. Tea and chatter, on the other hand presented a terrifying ordeal. I only undertook this visit out of duty, because I had promised a sad, somewhat pathetic old man.

A small woman of about seventy-five with short dark hair streaked with grey waved from the veranda. Then she was hobbling down the steps to greet me. There was something wrong with her right hip, so that her body was twisted. Every step she took involved throwing her whole body forward from her shoulders in order to roll the right leg impaired by the hip. A smiling-faced cocker spaniel ran ahead. Grateful for the calming distraction, I bent down for a moment and offered it my hand to lick. He barked a little in welcome, jumping politely at my side. Then I stood up and quickened my pace. The lady, however, was determined. She had covered a lot of ground despite her infirmity, so that we met just about two-thirds of the way up the path.

'Lady Wallace! So lovely to see you! I'm Jane Ovington. Such a shame about the weather! I was hoping we might have tea outside.' She pointed to a patch of lawn under a great cedar tree. 'The views are spectacular. Never mind. Perhaps it will clear up.'

'Perhaps.'

The drawing room was bursting at the seams. There were heavy armchairs with lace antimacassars, hosts of family photographs in carefully polished silver frames on the mantelpiece, on top of the piano, the sideboard, the window sill, and knick-knacks and ornaments of every description. I turned from the carved wooden statue of Ganesh with his elephant head to the pair of black-and-white porcelain dogs perched on top of the piano. They were exactly the same as the ones my grandparents had had in their house in Cardiff.

'Do sit down. Poor you! Are you really soaked? Would you like a towel?' Mrs Ovington fussed about.

'No, thank you. I'm fine. Actually, it's quite refreshing after Delhi—all this mist and rain.' I lied to convince myself.

'Tea? Assam or Darjeeling?'

'That would be lovely. As you prefer. I really don't mind.'

Deciding on the easiest task first, I took out the wodge of half a dozen or so dress catalogues and magazines from my bag.

'A present from Mrs Pritchard at Pritchard's Couture in Delhi. I mentioned to her that I was coming up to Simla and she said you were one of her best customers.'

Mrs Ovington's small round face lit up, her brown eyes twinkling. As she reached out to take the magazines from me I saw that her fingers were badly deformed with arthritis.

'Ah, Mrs Peppermint! Quite a character!' she exclaimed. I laughed at the clever nickname, for Mrs Pritchard had a penchant for sucking peppermint sweets and punctuating her conversation with a series of tut-tuts and swallowing actions. I suspect that the habit had developed in order to keep in a set of poorly fitting false teeth.

'Indeed,' I replied, thinking of the quirky lady who, despite being in her sixties, loved to dress in the brightest of colours— oranges, yellows and purples topped off with crimson lipstick. Her looks were always carefully put together but the effect was as if someone had gaudily arranged daffodils, marigolds and roses all together in the same pot.

'Isn't she wonderful? Quite a savvy businesswoman and certainly the best seamstress I have ever met.' Mrs Ovington went on. 'She has such a flair for spotting the latest styles and adapting them to suit our lives here in India and she's a positive wizard when it comes to sourcing fabric and material. I simply wouldn't go anywhere else. I've been using her for years.' At that Mrs Ovington rang the hand bell. A house boy, who could have been any age between eighteen and thirty, brought a tray of tea, sandwiches, tiny biscuits and scones.

Mrs Ovington began to pour, her fingers like claws around the handle of the Wedgewood teapot.

'Sir William Staffs sent this,' I said, laying the letter on top of the magazines. Her hand shook a little as she gave me a cup, saucer and a napkin. Then rocking back and forth in her chair to gain momentum, she pushed herself up with her fists on the arms of her chair and limped over to the sideboard. There she picked up a photo.

'Dear old William.' She smiled softly, looking kindly at him. 'Here he is in the Punjab when he first started in the Service.'

Handing me the photograph, she sat down to open the letter. A tall, slim, handsome young man with curly black hair was standing with his bearer who was holding his horse. For the first time I saw something beyond the bumbling Sir William Staffs, the fat old man who was anyone's company for a meal and a good bottle of wine. Here was an energetic, intelligent young man from Winchester and Balliol who had given his life to the Indian Civil Service. Suntanned, fit and strong, he must have spent lonely years in the saddle, riding from village to village, town to town across the endless, flat wastes of tibbas and cactus, drawing maps, planning irrigation, solving disputes, administering the great province that is the Punjab.

By now the sun had come out and streamed through the windows, illuminating Mrs Ovington's face as she read the letter. Gone were the lines and wrinkles and for an instant she had a young face free of strain. I watched her gnarled and twisted fingers opening the small packet that had been included with the letter. She took out a ring, and held it up, briefly playing the light with its three diamonds

'We were childhood sweethearts, you know: William and I.' She removed her reading glasses. 'He proposed to me with this ring, here in Simla many years ago.' She sighed. 'I said no. I am not exactly sure why. My parents weren't keen and I was just eighteen; I suppose I was swayed by them. Anyway, I married Arthur. He was a lawyer and became a high court judge on the Bengal Circuit. It wasn't that bad. We retired up here but I have been a widow these past ten years.' Folding the letter, she put it in her pocket. Then painfully massaging the crooked little finger on her right hand, she struggled to put the ring on to it.

'Shall we take a walk in the garden? Looks like the rain has stopped.'

Hearing the trigger word 'walk', the little dog barked and jumped up, skitter scattering, tail wagging, to the door.

On the way out my eye was drawn to a photograph of a younger Mrs Ovington accompanied by a girl. They were both mounted on horses and I wondered if that was how she had hurt her hip. Perhaps she had had a fall.

'That's my daughter, Lucy,' Mrs Ovington said. 'All grown up now. Married and lives in Singapore. Had an awful time in a Jap camp during the war, but thankfully they all survived. Actually, they're emigrating to Australia next month.'

She pointed to another frame draped with black. 'And that's my son Freddie. He served with the Chindits in Burma.' She didn't say more and I didn't ask. I didn't need to.

Together we strolled into the garden. It was now a blaze of colour under the sun with yellow roses and banks of red, pink and orange rhododendrons. Picking up a mangy ball, Mrs Ovington threw it for the dog. We made our way down the garden to where it appeared to fall off the edge of the mountain. It took a while not just because of Mrs Ovington's joints and the dog's game, but because every few yards she stopped to dead head a rose, a geranium or pull up a weed. At last we reached a little wooden bench under the trees. By then Mrs Ovington could no longer disguise her pain. Her face taut, she groaned and accepted my arm to help her sit. The clouds were scudding, revealing one mountain after another, deep vistas of green, offering teasing glimpses of far-off villages, tiny people toiling in the fields and, in the distance, great peaks glistening with snow.

'It's beautiful,' I said, thinking that the Greek Gods sitting on top of Mount Olympus must have had views like these.

'That's why I love Simla—for the scenery, constantly changing, never still. I regret I never learnt to paint.' We sat in for a while.

'What will you do,' I asked, 'after independence?'

'Do?' she shaded her eyes, and looked up at me, brows furrowed, suddenly perplexed.

'I mean, where will you go?'

'Why, stay here of course. It has never occurred to me to live anywhere else. India is my home.'

He was drowning. His young face, distending white, contorting gunmetal blue, was trapped behind the window of the torpedoed destroyer.

'Mummy, Mummy!' But there was no sound.

'I'm coming.' I was swimming, pulling down hard, my arms wrenching almost out of their sockets, reaching, reaching, reaching. I could see his hand flat against the glass, the tips of his fingers, but the water of the mid-Atlantic was cold and black as death.

'Mummy!' Another young voice, a boy's, that of my other son, was calling from the end of the garden. He had fallen off the swing and cut his knee. Smoke burnt my eyes, my throat. There was a roar of airplane engines, and I sank down through darkness to the ocean bed. I was screaming, over and over, gasping for breath, cradling the horned head of a dead cow in my arms. It was desiccated white, reduced to bone yet still it bled. I thrust my right hand into the bleeding entrails of its neck. Where was it? I couldn't find it. My hand groped about in the warm, sucking mess, deeper, right up to my elbow, trying to find the artery to stem the bleeding.

'Where are you? Hurry up!' But it was too late.

I was shouting and it woke me up. It was an old dream that I had not had since I came to India, except now the ending was new. I sat upright in bed in my eyrie, covered in sweat, shivering with cold. Only when I was sure of myself did I get up. Putting on my shoes and cardigan, I wrapped myself in the woollen paisley stole I had bought in the bazaar, and tiptoed downstairs.

I didn't see him at first, sitting in the corner of the library in a big armchair, the Chinese Ambassador. The collar of his long black Chinese gown was unbuttoned, hanging to the right, revealing his vest. He raised his eyes briefly from his book as I passed. He was the only one to see me slip out of the French windows into the night. The air was cool and damp. Taking deep breaths, I walked quickly across the terrace and down to the lawns. The slim crescent moon hung half in and half out of the clouds, offering just a little light. There were no stars and the cedars sighed gently as I passed. I chose the path through the forest which led down to the edge of The Ridge. There I stood in the silence, watching the sifting shapes of darkness, wisps of mist bisecting the mountains into triangles. After I while I turned and made my way back, guided by the lights from the Lodge. They shone like beacons through the trees. An owl hooted. A bat, feather-light, brushed my face.

Suddenly there was loud bang as of a heavy wooden door being slammed. A man was coming at a half run down the terrace stairs and across the lawn. He was wearing white, but the middle part of him, the heart, in a black waistcoat was lost to the night. He seemed to know exactly where I was, making straight for me. Pulling my stole tighter over my nightdress, I looked for an alternative route back to the Lodge. But unless I was prepared to scale a ten-foot-high wall up on to the terrace, there was no other way. The man was nearly upon me but still I could not see his face. Suddenly he stopped, picked up a garden chair from a collection that had been left out on the lawn, raised it as high as he could, and hurled it against the trunk of a large tree. An arm broke off it. Picking it up, he swung it wildly, roaring with rage, beating it again and again against a tree. I stepped backwards trying to hide myself, retreating in the forest, but he had seen me out of the corner of his eye.

'Who's there?' He panted, lowering the stick.

'Panditji, it's me, Pippi Wallace.'

Jawahar's eyes bulged out of his sockets. His teeth were locked and bared. White with fury, I hardly recognized him.

Having no choice, I stepped out of the shadows. He too must have gone to bed and got up again, for he was wearing Indian-style lace pyjamas, his waistcoat thrown on, unbuttoned over the top.

'It's all over!' Viciously he flung the broken chair arm into the rough grass. It crash landed raising a few squawking birds.

'God, I hate this place. Simla.' He spat and wiped his mouth with the back of his hand. 'Be so good, Lady Wallace, as to give the Viceroy and Vicereine my best wishes. I'm leaving for Delhi. I'll not stay a moment longer.'

He turned sharply on his heels but stopped to look at his hand. Blood was dripping from his palm. He must have cut himself on the shattered wood.

'Slow down!' I said, blocking his way, reaching out but not quite touching his sleeve. 'It's one o'clock in the morning. You can't drive back to Delhi now and there'll be no trains. It can't be that bad.' I added lamely and without conviction. At the same time I had a sickening vision of the hundreds of death-defying hairpin bends on the road between Simla and Kalka.

Squinting at his wound, he pulled out a splinter, swearing softly in Hindi.

'What's happened?' I tried a different approach, warily keeping my distance.

'The Viceroy has shown me the plan for the transfer of power and I'm having none of it. That's what. A plebiscite on independence in Bengal and the provinces with the option to opt out of the union. It's a disaster. It's the Balkanization of India, that's what! I'm sorry, Lady Wallace, if I startled you. God damn it, I never should have come; tea and happy families, walking in the orchards at Mashobra! Do make sure you give my apologies in the morning to Edwina. Tell her I'll write from Delhi. She'll understand.'

'No, she won't understand and she'll never forgive you.'
Now I had his attention. Emboldened I grabbed him by
the sleeve and pulled him on to the footpath out of sight
of the Lodge. 'Think about it! Lord Ismay has already gone
to London with the plan. If you storm out now, Dickie will
have no choice. He'll have to resign. All the good work, the
rapprochement of the last months will be lost. You'll be back
to square one. Heaven knows who London will send out in
Dickie's place.'

He was quiet now. Nodding, thinking, calming. Together
we started to walk away from the Lodge and along the path to
The Ridge. When we reached a small clearing he stopped to
light a cigarette, offering me one. For the sake of friendship I
accepted, and like naughty schoolchildren we hid in the bushes,
sitting on the trunk of a fallen tree.

'When I was in the Punjab with the Vicereine I met a little
boy. He is seven years old. His name is Mohammed Hussein.
Both his hands were cut off in the communal fighting.' I was
watching Jawahar's face and he was watching mine, listening
intently. 'Dickie likes you, respects you. I know he does. The
two of you have got to make it work or there will be hundreds
and thousands more little Mohammed Husseins all over India.'

'Dickie is a good man and I like him too. At least he's a
human being, far better than the stuffed shirts we had as
Viceroys before. I could never get a word out of Lord Wavell.'

We watched the smoke from our cigarettes, rising, circling,
and dissipating into the damp night air.

'It's all over for us, you know.' I hesitated. The breeze
whispered in the tree tops. A small animal scuffled behind us in
the bush. 'We may have won the war, but we are bankrupt and
broken. If you could see London, all bombed out, whole streets,
buildings, people, their lives, just gone . . .'

'I can imagine. My daughter was there during some of the
blitz. She still has her tin hat.' He ventured a wry smile.

'Jawahar, can't you see? We're hanging on by our fingernails here in India. The British Empire? It's a façade, an illusion, a great parade held together by a few bits of ribbon and bunting, that's all.' I gestured vaguely towards the Viceregal Lodge as a symbol of British authority. 'If you can't reach agreement soon, it seems to me there is a real possibility of a complete collapse of central authority. I say this in confidence, of course. But I'm very much afraid that if the Congress and the Muslim League haggle too long, there may well be no power left to transfer at all. If we get to that point, you will have Balkanization by default.' I took a deep breath. 'You know as well as I do, it's now or never.' There it was. I had said too much, crossed the line, and he knew it.

'Thank you, Pippi. I am grateful for your frankness.' A dog howled from a nearby mountain. Jawahar dropped his cigarette on the ground, stubbing it with his sandal until no embers were left to glow. And then he sat, hands on his knees, staring at his naked toes.

'Pippi, it has been over thirty years since I first met Bapu. I was impressed and perplexed by him at the same time. And now I am a tired man. As long as I can sensibly remember, I have been fighting for independence. I have cremated my wife, lost nine years and a good chunk of my youth and vigour in British jails. I'm not getting any younger.'

'I know,' I said softly. 'It's been a long war for us too. We're all tired, so very tired. Jawahar, I am begging you, stay until the morning. Talk to Edwina. Give compromise a chance.'

We were interrupted by shouts from the house, the flash of torches coming on the terrace.

'They're coming for me,' he sighed wistfully. 'Krishna Menon is a holy terror! You go first, Lady Wallace. Protect your reputation!' We looked at each other, middle-aged, and sad, shivering in our nightclothes and laughed.

The next day dawned bright and crystal clear. For the first the time since our arrival in Simla the Himalayas were laid out in all their glory under a cloudless sky.

I was late for breakfast and the dining room was almost empty save for the Chinese Ambassador. He was sitting, contemplating his teacup in front of a portrait of the former Viceroy, Lord Curzon, in full viceregal attire: brocade, breeches, medals and floor-length cape. Already, the khidmutgar had begun to clear up. The tea he brought was strong and black, from the bottom of the urn.

'Good morning, Your Excellency. May I join you?'

'Of course, Lady Wallace.'

'Have you seen Panditji this morning?' I sipped my tea and buttered my toast.

'He was here earlier. Between ourselves, the Honourable Panditji looked as if he had spent a night boxing with the devil. Big bags under his eyes and a bandage around his hand.' The Ambassador raised a quizzical eyebrow above his heavy, round spectacles. 'Look! There he is now with the Vicereine.'

Through the long windows we saw him coming out of the house with Edwina. She was wearing a red and white flowery dress, the colours bright under the sun. Everything moved slowly in the silence, and the Ambassador and I could pick out every tiny movement, every gesture in detail. Jawahar, head bowed, hands uncharacteristically clasped behind his back; Edwina with the ball of white fluff that was Mizzen in her arms. Cautiously, three or four feet apart, they were strolling on to the lawns. She bent to put Mizzen down. Her brow furrowed, head to one side, she was looking up at him, listening, nodding.

They faced each other, their profiles towards us spectators. Her mouth was moving quickly, her hands imploring, pleading. He shrugged and they turned their backs, walking away from us. She must have given him a ball for he bowled it over arm for the dog who barked and scampered after it.

'Now that's what I call diplomacy!' The Chinese Ambassador nodded with approval. With his tiny eyes and heavy, rimmed spectacles, he was far from being a handsome man, but his voice was always measured and kind. 'Lady Mountbatten is like a beautiful pearl. Rare indeed to find such a treasure high in the mountains, so far from the sea.'

We watched as Jawahar took Edwina's arm in his and they followed the dog over the crest of the hill.

Later, when I was back in the office in Viceregal Lodge, Alan rang up.

'Pippi, what on earth is going on down there?' His voice was breathless on the line from the Viceregal Retreat at Mashobra. 'His Ex just rang. Told me that the meeting of the 17th of May with the India leaders is off. I've just announced it with a great huzzah, and now he wants to go back on it. I can't do that. All hell will break loose!'

'Panic stations all round.' I lowered my voice. 'Late last night His Ex showed Panditji a copy of the draft plan, and the balloon went up. Jawahar is having none of it.'

'Bugger!' Alan blew air down the line and I imagined him pushing his hair back from his forehead in confusion. 'What am I supposed to say? There will be all sorts of questions both in Delhi and London.'

'Can you concoct something about parliamentary time? The Whitsun recess or someone having a bad bout of Delhi belly, typhus, 'flu?' My voice trailed off with the increasing implausibility of my train of thought.

'I don't know. Bloody hell! I am coming to Simla straight
away. See you later!' One of his children was calling to him in
the background, 'Daddy, Daddy! Come and play!' Then the
click of the receiver and the buzz of the line.

'Who was that you were whispering with?' Edwina came
into the office.

'Alan. He's coming down from Mashobra.'

She pursed her lips, fixing me with her eyes which glinted
dangerously. 'Letty, why didn't you wake me last night?'

There was no point denying it—Jawahar and I in the
garden in our nightclothes, innocent as it was.

'I didn't want to disturb you. I knew you had an awful
headache and had gone to bed.'

She huffed crossly and straightened her head scarf which
she was wearing in a jaunty bandeau style to keep her hair back.

'Well, it's all sorted now. No harm done, I suppose.
Jawahar's staying on a few more hours to knock things together.
Thank God!' She parked herself on the corner of my desk and
began to swing her left foot. It beat a soft two-four time against
the wood as she talked.

'I think I've persuaded Jawahar to accept Dominion status.
It would help Dickie no end if he can be seen to keep India in
the Commonwealth. Damn close-run thing though. My oh-so-
brilliant husband was nearly hoisted with his own petard.' She
giggled. 'Jawahar is suspicious of Dominion status, of course.
Thinks it doesn't amount to complete independence.' One-
two, one-two, foot thump.

'It's a legal fudge, I suppose,' I replied cautiously. 'Strictly
speaking, India isn't a colony, it's just a vehicle. Krishna Menon
has been quite keen on the idea for a while, to speed up the
transfer of power.' I held out a cigarette as a peace offering. She
declined so I put the packet back in the drawer.

'That's as may be, but Dominion status is a complete
volte-face for Jawahar. He'll have to sell it to the Congress

and that will mean . . .' She hesitated a moment, eyes hooded, thinking. 'He's in there right now with Krishna and VP.' She meant V.P. Menon, the Reforms Commissioner to the Viceroy. 'Actually he specifically asked for you.' She stared past me, out of the window, pretending not to care. After a while she continued.

'Jawahar wants you to help VP with the new draft plan. Says he's damned if he'll trust anything that comes out of London. So it will have to be done over here. You, apparently, he does trust. Well done, my dear! One might be forgiven for thinking you are not on my staff at all these days. People seem to think they can poach you for every little job whenever they feel like it.'

Getting up, she smoothed down the red flowers on her skirt, looking at me with eyes like those of an eagle about to swoop on its prey.

'You look nice today, Letty. Is that dress new?'

'Not really. I had it made in London before we came out. Things don't stand up to the heat very well out here, do they?' She ignored my renewed attempt at reconciliation.

'Well, don't go behind my back again. Next time Jawahar needs me, you bloody well make sure you come and find me.' There, she had said her piece. She stalked out of the office haughtily, banging the door on the way out.

Sighing, I pushed back my chair and lit that cigarette. Clearly we had fallen out. Why did Edwina have to compete? It had always been like this. She could not help herself. She simply had to be the queen bee. She competed not just with others but with herself—over work, over clothes, over men, over access to power and influence. And woe betide the woman who was more beautiful, more elegant or better dressed than she was, or who just happened to stumble across her path by accident.

*I*t looked like a bomb had exploded in the middle of the room where V.P. Menon was working. Debris was scattered outwards from the centre of the conference table in the upstairs office of Viceroy's Lodge: briefing documents, minutes of meetings, tea cups and breakfast plates caked with egg, butter and jam, whisky glasses, an empty decanter, overflowing ashtrays, and more papers scattered on the floor. The room smelt of male bodies, rotten eggs and, somewhat bizarrely, of oranges. I resisted the temptation to open the windows and tidy up the cups and plates. As a woman, I was aware that there was no surer way of undermining one's status at the beginning of a meeting than to lift the teapot or pass the biscuits.

He was hammering on the typewriter and did not immediately look up. We knew each other in passing although we had never been introduced. V.P. Menon was always there but never there. He operated in the corners, in the shadows, one moment with Jawahar, the next with the Viceroy, then hanging on the shoulder of Sardar Patel. Earnest and quiet, eyes magnified by his large, round spectacles, he was the most senior of all Indian civil servants. Born the son of a schoolteacher in Kerala, he had laboured variously as a railway stoker and coal miner before joining the Service and working his way to the top.

Thumping the carriage return, he pushed back his chair and looked up. His collar was undone without a tie. The shadow of stubble was dark on his face and there were pendulous bags under his eyes.

'You've just missed Panditji.' He made a begrudging motion with his hand to indicate someone going down to the station in Simla. 'Krishna Menon's taken him to the train.'

'Her Excellency sent me. She said you could do with a hand?'

He removed his glasses, breathed on them and then wiped them with the corner of his shirt.

'Here you go.' He threw a document—its pages held together in the top left corner by a green treasury tag—over the table towards me. 'It's the plan for the transfer of power; the old one that is, that Lord Ismay took to London.'

On the front page someone had written a large NO in red letters and underscored it three times to the point of nearly scratching through the paper. I turned the page. Again, paragraphs had been struck through in red ink. The annotator had been particularly vehement when it came to the section on the plebiscite for independence in Bengal. In the margin there was a sea of angry red ink in a tiny hand I recognized as Jawahar's.

'Second Round Table Conference? Cabinet Mission Plan 1946? Simla Plan 1945? Take your pick!' V.P. threw three more briefs in my direction. 'Years of painstaking negotiation down the drain. You might as well put them in the rubbish bin. We're back to square one. I'm just drafting the new heads of terms now.' He unwound the piece of paper from the top of his typewriter, this time handing it, rather than throwing it at me.

He had set out eight bullet points on the page, not all of them filled in.

Early Dominion status as an interim arrangement based upon the Government of India Act 1935 with one or two modifications, and envisaging one or two sovereign states. If one only, power should be transferred to the existing central government. I read on. The sixth head asserted that the Governor General should be common to both states.

'I haven't got to the divisions of the army and the boundary yet.' He lit a cigarette and offered me one by cocking the pack in my direction. I shook my head. My mind whirred to translate the words to reality.

'So partition it is? All provinces must join either India or Pakistan?'

He nodded.

'No opt outs of the Union? Even for Bengal?'

'Nope. It's Pakistan or India. Provinces must vote, Princes must choose.'

'And one Governor General for both states. Who?'

'Probably the Viceroy, at least in the interim.'

I puffed out a large breath of air which rather unexpectedly made VP laugh. So that is what Edwina had been holding back just now. Dominion status by definition required a Governor General. If it was to be Dickie, this meant longer in India for her and, possibly, me.

Lighting his cigarette, VP roared like a grumpy lion for the khidmutgars to come and clear up the debris of the night's negotiations.

Standing at the window while the men worked, he offered me his hand.

'Sorry I was so curt, Lady Wallace. Temper's a bit frayed. I was up most of the night with Krishna and Panditji who was ranting and raving like a madman. In truth, a fresh pair of eyes would be most welcome. Wood for the trees and all that.'

I smiled, a big sparkly Edwina special, one even she would have been proud of.

'And we'll need to get our skates on. The new date for the transfer of power is the 15th of August.'

'The 15th of August?' My first thought was that this was later than originally planned, but VP read my mind.

'The 15th of August 1947, *not* 15th of August 1948.'

My jaw dropped.

'Who told you that?

'The Viceroy. This morning.'

'But that's just over three months away. We'll never . . . .'

'On 20th February 1947, H.M.G. announced their intention
of transferring power in British India to Indian hands by
June 1948. H.M.G. had hoped it would be possible for
the major parties to cooperate on the basis of the Cabinet
Mission Plan of 16th May 1946, and evolve for India a
constitution acceptable to all concerned. This hope has not
in the event been fulfilled; nor have the political parties in
India been able to reach agreement on any alternative plan
of their own . . . It has always been the desire of H.M.G
that power should be transferred in accordance with the
wishes of the Indian people themselves. This task would
have been greatly facilitated if there had been agreement
among the Indian political parties. In the absence of such
an agreement, the task of devising a method by which the
wishes of the Indian people can be ascertained has devolved
on H.M.G. After full consultation and in agreement with
political leaders in India, H.M.G. has decided to adopt for
this purpose the plan set out below.'

I was in full flow, knocking together a preamble to the new
draft announcement when there was a quiet knock at the door.
Alan popped his head in. His normally immaculately slicked
back hair was dishevelled, and he was mildly breathless from
running up the stairs.

'Found you at last! All alone?'

'Yup. VP's gone for a wash and shave. Krishna has been for
a confab then disappeared again.'

It was getting on for dusk when Alan and I decided to take a
stroll down the lawn. We were greeted by a glorious chorus of
birds revelling in the last moments of the day.

'Did you sort the communiqué?' I asked.

'Just been up to see His Ex. He's holding up pretty well
under the circumstances. Says it's a damn good thing he went

against the advice of his staff and ran the plan past Nehru.'
He shrugged. 'Anyway, we drafted the new press release; went
with the excuse of the parliamentary recess in London in the
end. I would have favoured a drafting technicality. But I don't
suppose it matters. We've told the truth but it's not exactly the
whole truth, and no one in Delhi is likely to believe that London
was the source of the postponement of the 17th May meeting.
It will just feed the distrust and undermine the goodwill we
have been seeking to build these past months. By the way, have
you heard?'

'What?' I said.

'The 15th of August for the transfer of power.'

'Yes. Her Ex was all buttoned up about it, but VP told me.
But why on earth the 15th of August?'

'Victory in Japan Day, the 15th of August. His Ex says it's
as good a day as any other.'

'But it's too soon,' I protested. 'It's utter madness. From a
legal point of view, we'll barely get the legislation through the
House in time. And that's not to consider the practicalities
implied by partition. No one seems to be giving them any
consideration at all: drawing up boundaries, dividing the
army and the civil service between the new states and so on.'
I was thinking of VP's heads of terms and in particular the
blank bullet points number seven and number eight. 'And this
agreement refers just to British India. It says nothing about the
Princely States, all five hundred and sixty-two of them. They
are quite entitled to become independent when we leave under
current treaties. We've no solution for them yet. What on earth
possessed the Viceroy! I don't understand?' But suddenly I did.

'Kahuta.' Alan read my mind. 'I think His Ex made up his
mind there and then in that godforsaken village, when he was
eyeball to eyeball with those Sikh farmers. He probably thinks
the sooner the better. All this uncertainty is not good for
people. We've both seen the refugees. They can't go forward

and they can't go back until there is a resolution. The 15th of August steals the initiative. At least it will have the merit of concentrating minds. You know as well as I do that if we wait for Jinnah and Nehru to agree, we'll be here until Doomsday.'

I nodded, remembering the burnt-down houses in Kahuta, the silence, and Dickie's face—expressionless, not even grim. How brusquely he had pushed back his chair to end the meeting and marched off towards the car, head down, hands clasped behind his back. Yes. I was sure of it. He had made the decision then.

'Party first. Shooting afterwards. It's not a great policy,' I grumbled through gritted teeth.

Alan met my gaze with a buttoned-up establishment look which carried the full force of school, college, Parliament and Crown. It might have variously be interpreted as, You're just a woman, what do you know, or Shut up, toughen up and don't let the side down.

'Where there's a will there's a way and it's what the Indians want: Independence. Gandhi would have us out tomorrow. What was it he said? Something about India needing to go through the flames?'

'Bloody hell, Alan!' He jerked back in surprise. I never swore. 'I'm up there now helping VP cobble it together from the debris of the Cabinet Mission plan, and Krishna and Jawahar's notes scribbled on the back of the old plan and scraps of paper. If the Indian assemblies vote for partition, we'll be setting up two completely new states in barely three months; India in a Nissan hut and Pakistan in a tent.'

PART II

Saints, Sinners, Lovers, Traitors
June 1947 to 15th August 1947

*T*oday I went with Edwina to tea with Gandhi at his cottage near the Banghi sweepers' colony. Why is it that we expect so much of the famous and the great? We anticipate that with all their ideas and achievements they must be physically bigger than ourselves and are disappointed when they are not. This was particularly the case with Gandhi. Sitting cross-legged on the floor opposite him in the small white-washed room that he used both as an office and a bedroom, I was close enough to reach out and touch him. I got the impression of shrunkenness and emaciation, a husk of a man living in the body of a child. Banghi Colony lay on the edge of the barren, dusty wasteland that encircled Delhi. It was home to the untouchable castes that Gandhi had renamed Harijans or Children of God. These people were truly outcasts living in the greatest poverty. Yet Gandhi, like Jesus, had chosen to live amongst them. At least that was what I had been told. Sure enough the Harijans lived out there, on the edge of the wilderness like animals. We passed them in the car—naked children, women dressed in rags with filthy babies on their hips standing beside huts so low they could not have stood up inside. Wide-eyed, unblinking like fish, they stared at and through us at the same time, as if we were there and not there, apparitions from another world. But Gandhi, I discovered on our arrival, was not exactly living among the Harijans. Rather, he had built his ashram on some clear ground not far from their slums. While not luxurious, the ashram consisted of rows of neat little white huts with khus cloth for windows and doors. Small barefoot boys with goat-skin bags were going around spraying water on to the cloth screens to keep the rooms cool. Telephone lines had been set up as well.

'We moved the people out last year so Bapu could come and live amongst them,' the diminutive Miss Maniben Patel explained proudly to Her Excellency as she led us to Gandhi's cottage.

'And where did they go?' Her Excellency beamed her smile.

'It is good for them. This way Bapu can educate them in our way of living.' Like all his ashramites she was dressed in homespun cotton. The keys to her own father's household that she kept on a string at her waist clinked at every step, reminding me not of a nun but of a leper.

It was dark in Gandhi's hut. He did not look up from his spinning wheel until he had rewound the thread he was pulling. Edwina hesitated, then, with impeccable judgement and timing, tapped him on the arm and told him not to get up. He gave her an impish smile, joined his hands briefly in namaste, waggled his head and put his finger over his lips.

'It is Bapu's day of silence. You can talk to him but he will not answer,' Maniben whispered, slipping back her sari pallu to reveal thinning black hair, already mostly white. She was about the same age as Edwina and me, but years of jail and hard ashram living together with the want of a good hairdresser and a bit of lipstick and powder made her look like an old woman. Except when she smiled. Then her whole face lit up and she became truly young and beautiful.

Bapu's eyes fell on me, or rather were raised up to me, for I towered above him to the point I was afraid I might bump my head on the ceiling.

'This is Lady Wallace, Assistant to the Vicereine, Bapu.' He bowed his head and returned my namaste. In that second I knew that he knew, that he sensed, that he saw. That's when I realized where the calm came from; that intangible sense of

faith in something greater that I had glimpsed in both Amrit
Kaur and Jawahar. They got it from Gandhi.

Two briefcase charkha spinning wheels were brought
out in their boxes, and a cotton-spinning lesson began. We
had removed our shoes and were sitting on the floor. There
was nothing in the room apart from Gandhi's bedding roll,
a small low writing desk and fly papers hanging at strategic
spots on the walls. It was a strange sight: Gandhi and Edwina.
He, bare-chested in his dhoti, propped up against a large
white bolster, next to her, the daisies on her carefully ironed
skirt spilling out on to the beaten earth floor. He taught by
example, showing us how to oil the spindles on which the
two wooden wheels—one bigger, one smaller—which drove
the contraption, sat. Next he put the drive string around the
wheels and fastened them to the clip which held the bobbin.
Maniben explained that these simple portable spinning wheels
had been invented by Gandhi himself. They were designed to
be cheap and productive.

'By spinning we will attain Swaraj, self-rule. Bapu teaches
that khadi and spinning are the beginnings of economic
freedom, democracy and equality for all in the country. The
true swadeshi mentality means a determination to find all
the necessities of life in India itself, through the labour and
intellect of all Indians. It teaches self-reliance and is the non-
violent way.'

I took a wodge of cotton and, copying Gandhi, attached it
to the short thread from the bobbin. He was sitting to Edwina's
left, so that he could guide her as she spun; left hand on hers as
she drew the thread, right hand on hers as she turned the wheel,
softly, gently, silently, slowly.

'Pinch, pull, quarter turn, pinch, pull, quarter turn.'
Maniben spoke for her guru. 'This is the way for the beginning.
When you get more experience you can pull and turn at the
same time.' Slowly I too began to draw the cotton but it broke.

'Keep the angle at about forty-five degrees as you pull.' The flies buzzed. The heat pressed in, but I was finding my rhythm. 'Pinch, draw, quarter turn. Rewind the cotton on to the bobbin.'

Gandhi chuckled a toothless smile, his eyes twinkling through the lenses of his little round spectacles.

'Ah, see, now you have a slub.' Maniben's commentary continued at a whisper. 'That's too much twist. Pinch, and pull. There, can you see? It's gone.'

Pull, quarter turn, pull, quarter turn. Rewind. Edwina and I were doing better, our arms arcing faster in a silent dance. Our teachers returned to their own spinning, keeping half an eye on us as if we were children. In the distance a dog barked, a child cried and raindrops fell on the cloth windows. The little boys with goatskin bags tiptoed on their rounds. Fresh tea was brought but we did not drink. I forgot the heat, the smell and even the flies. Pinch, pull, quarter turn, pinch, pull, quarter turn, rewind. Our arms flew outwards, making shadows like wings on the walls, filling the room with doves. All of a sudden my mind flooded white: Maniben's sari, yards of cotton thread, spinning endlessly the light filtering through the window above Gandhi's head, the rough plastered walls seemed to fall outwards. And as I drew on the thread, pulling out the slubs of cotton, the great knot coiled like a serpent inside me, gave way. It untangled, dissolved, just disappeared, and far away in an English summer garden a glistening pearl of water dropped from the tip of a leaf, falling, falling into a pond, and all was still.

My eyes filled with tears and I could not see. Hands reached out to me. People whispered around me, but I could not hear. Gently, Maniben took the thread from me and rewound it. My spinning must have stalled in mid-air. And then, simply, without comment or fuss, Bapu pressed a cup of tea into my hand.

They came at last, all the young women dressed in white. With expressionless faces, they called Bapu to afternoon prayer.

It was time for the Vicereine to leave. She could not be seen at one of his public meetings lest it be thought to favour the Congress over the Muslim League.

'But Letty, darling, there's no reason for you to come away with me. Why don't you go too? You can tell me about it later.' Edwina patted me on the arm, kissed me on the cheek, and retreated in a blur of yellow daisies.

I was slipping and sliding along the back seat of the gleaming milk-white Packard that belonged to the Indian industrialist Seth Birla. I was sitting between Gandhi and his young doctor, Sushila Nayyar, and was afraid I might crush them. We drove to Birla House on Albuquerque Road. Gandhi's Delhi prayer meetings were held at Seth Birla's home. A palatial place, it had a beautifully manicured garden with ornamental flower beds and a gurgling fairy-tale brook. I remembered little of the journey except the drip, drip, drip of water from the wet towel Gandhi wore like a turban whenever he went outside in the heat. Drip, drip, drip, drip on to my dress, staining purple the red leather seat. As we were getting out of the car, Gandhiji rested his hand gently on my shoulder. For a moment I thought I would not be able to bear the weight. Then we stepped out into the glare of sunlight and I knew I had changed.

*H*ari was late for our morning ride. I couldn't wait to see him. I wanted to tell him about my time with Gandhi yesterday. And how last night, for the first time in years, I had been able to pray.

The horses flicked their tails against the flies. At my side the young groom Ravi sniffed and wiped his nose on the back of his hand. We were waiting under the shade of the trees on the edge of The Ridge. Ravi's mare was young and difficult to ride. For the moment, the lowly groom was the only one she would accept on her back. And at least now she was willing to take a saddle which was progress from last week. Hari had said that Ravi was quite the best horseman amongst us and if it were not for his smallpox-scarred face he might have gone on to better things.

Yesterday the temperature had shot to one hundred and thirteen degrees. Today it was not quite 6.30 a.m. and already there was a light heat haze over the scrub. Water, which I knew was not there, shimmered along the line of trees that fluttered like a paisley border on a piece of cloth, but there was no breeze. Everything felt different after yesterday. My horse, Juno, sniffed the air. I looked again at my watch. Hari was five minutes late. My heart sank. Perhaps he was not coming?

Then, all of a sudden, there he was, cantering on Nagella, raising a cloud of dust from the direction of the polo club.

'So sorry to be late.' He was wearing a brown cotton flat cap and was covered in sweat which he wiped from his furrowed brow with his cravat. He had not shaved, and looked tired and tense. 'Gang of Sikhs took knives and cricket bats to a bunch of Muslim boys late last night. Blood all over the shop. Goddamn battlefield.'

He wheeled Nagella around to shake my hand.

'You should have rung me or sent a message. I wouldn't have minded . . .'

'I wanted to see you. It cheers me up.' He looked straight at me, holding my gaze so that I could not look away. Fear gripped me. He was looking for answers I could not give. Quickly, I shortened my reins and squeezed Juno on.

Hari was quiet. I did not press him to speak, knowing that, in addition to last night's emergency surgery, he was also worried about his daughter and grandchildren in Lahore. His son-in-law and his father were reluctant to leave their family businesses in the Punjab despite the rioting. Despite Hari's pleading they simply refused to send the women and the children to Delhi for safety. We urged the horses into a lazy canter; it was too hot to push them.

I began to talk about Gandhi and my visit. I wanted to put it all into words, to explain, to describe how Bapu had given me something—or had he taken something away from me?— and to tell him that last night I had been able to say the Lord's prayer for the first time in years. But I was struggling, my words crude and clumsy. I was so full of myself that I didn't notice Hari's face until it was too late.

'Stop! I will hear no more about that man.' Black eyebrows scrunched over his eyes and hands fisted around the reins, he glared at me. Feeling the tension, the confused horses tried for a trot. Pulling back, Hari attempted to soften his tone but spoke through gritted teeth.

'I am pleased that you have had your darshan with the great man. But honestly, that man! Without him we would not have had religion in politics. If we follow him, India will go back to the dark ages. Would you have us all impotent, sitting at home spinning and trying to cure cancer with mud packs and prayer?

'God forbid that science, medicine and machinery should raise the standard of living of the masses too high because it might lead to sin and indulgence. That man glorifies poverty and I have no time for it.'

I took a deep breath.

'We all have our shortcomings and Gandhi is no exception. But yesterday, truly, I witnessed a man of faith. There is something of the prophet in him. It is as if a light radiates from him, as if he has access to a beautiful inner resource.' Again I was frustrated with the limitations of my words which fell short of what I wanted to say. 'He has a vision of goodness and truth, a world without violence, a world where young men will not be packed into cloth planes and the bellies of iron ships and tanks to slaughter other mothers' precious sons.' My voice trailed off with my own emotions and at the sight of the veins pulsing in Hari's neck.

'Poppycock! I would have expected better of you, Pippi, a grown woman. But if you will become his acolyte and let him make you his slave then there is nothing I can do about it.' He swapped his whip from his left to his right hand; the side nearer to me.

'Look at me, Pippi!' And I did, glowering anger right back into his furious face which was black as thunder. 'I don't parade about in homespun and a silly topi, but do I love India any less? Yes, I was born a Hindu but I don't believe in religion and I eat meat. But let me tell you, I am still as much an Indian, a man of faith, a man of service as the next man. Last night . . . last night . . . I was up to my armpits in blood, trying to patch up the guts of a fourteen-year-old Muslim child. For what? For the love of India!'

This time he took his whip to his horse and galloped away, leaving me choking in the dust.

Dear Margaret,

My God it's hot here. So hot you can't imagine. Hot to the point of suffocation. Can't think, can't move and there will be no escape until the monsoons come. It's a sort of insanity, a fever, against which we all fight our own personal battles. We seek out shade which does not exist, close the shutters and put the fans on full speed. Still we sweat from dawn to dusk, and at night we wait for sleep which does not come. And when we cannot sleep we brood, we gossip and conspire. We work late, we have parties and we drink. We might be living on potatoes, cabbage water and spam here in Viceroy's House, but at least the whisky and soda are holding out! The young ADCs are the best at it, of course. Every night there is a gathering somewhere—records, dancing and a few pretty girls. You can't blame them. If it were not for the small friendships one makes along the way, the jokes, little kindnesses and gestures of hospitality, one would go completely mad.

I stopped. I hadn't seen or heard from Hari since our disagreement over Gandhi. He had not rung or sent a message. Neither had I. Both of us, I reasoned, were preoccupied with jobs, duties, with greater things. I started writing again.

On the positive side, at last we have an agreement. Hurrah! The formal announcement of the agreement for the transfer of power was made on 3rd June. Speeches on All India Radio made by Nehru and Jinnah did ease communal tensions a little, but things are still very tense. Nehru and Sardar Patel, the two big Congressmen in the Interim Government, accept partition on the basis that by conceding Pakistan to Jinnah they will hear no more of him. As Nehru privately confided to Edwina the other day, 'By cutting off the head, we will get rid of the headache.'

The Punjab Legislative Assembly has now formally opted for partition. Bengal voted the same way three days ago. The Muslim Prime Minister of Bengal, Mr Suhrawardy, and the British Governor of Bengal did try to achieve an autonomous and united province outside the Indian Union. Alas, this goal died in the face of opposition from both the major parties. The wheel does indeed turn full circle. Earlier generations of Indians bitterly opposed Lord Curzon's partition of Bengal and now, forty years later, they support the same policy. It is all very tragic. I can tell you that it has quite broken my heart to see the voting clauses I drafted with V.P. Menon becoming a reality. The greater tragedy I feel, however, would have been to impose a solution on the Muslim minority.

So, my dear Margaret, despite the best efforts of the Viceroy, partition it is to be. The gloves have come off all around us. There is no longer any pretence of loyalties to hold anything together. The other day Gandhi called Nehru 'Our King', suggesting that he ought to be criticized for making mistakes—by which he means partition. The old soul, Maniben Patel tells me, is quite broken-hearted.

And all the while the security situation deteriorates. We are under twenty-four-hour armed guard and hunkering down for a siege. As I write, the tents of thousands of Muslims are laid out around the gardens. The Viceroy and Vicereine have taken them on to the estate for protection. If you could see the people's faces—they are utterly bereft and at dusk move about like ghosts. Many of them are families of employees here who have been forced out of their homes in Delhi by mobs. Already some of them have started leaving for Pakistan.

'You wanted Pakistan. So you should jolly well pack up and go there,' seems to be the attitude of Hindus in Delhi. Even Sardar Patel has said that Muslims cannot be trusted.

It is, however, the Sikh community in the Punjab that has been sold short by the agreement. One cannot help feeling they have

been sacrificed on the twin altars of Muslim ambition and Hindu
opportunism. They number some six million and are no more than
twenty per cent of the population of the Punjab. Nevertheless, they
have succeeded in achieving influence out of proportion to their
numbers and did hold an effective balance of power within the United
Punjab. Partition means the division of their lands and territories.
Boundaries will have to be drawn in the Punjab (and in Bengal too).
I am afraid no amount of juggling the line will prevent the bisection of
their communities. Understandably, the Sikhs are reacting accordingly
and evolving more primitive remedies to protect their land and assets.
Unrest grows by the hour and power is passing to some of the wilder men
such as Tara Singh and some officers of the Indian National Army.
The outlook is grim. But bizarrely, with all this fratricidal unrest, the
British are more popular than we ever have been. Perhaps because we
are the only ones left who can keep the peace, and we are going!

You asked me in your last letter how things were between the
Vicereine and me.

Here again I hesitated. I couldn't say that she was a fickle
employer, unpredictable and moody and quite a tartar when
crossed. She could be sweetness and light one minute, and
bite off all our heads the next. I couldn't say that her marriage
seemed to be close to collapse and that despite the scandal
and political risk, she still dined with Jawahar at York Road
whenever she could. Nor could I say that she and Dickie rowed
night after night and that the rest of us did our best not to get
caught in the crossfire.

Well, you know Edwina, I wrote enigmatically. She is a
workaholic and never gives up, particularly when it comes to refugees.
She and I worked very late last night trying to track down some Sikh
women. They had been abducted by Muslims in the Punjab. She kept
on at me for days to chase it up, which I did even when I thought it
was pointless. But blow me down, in the end three girls were found and

returned to their families! She is a complete slave driver and, I don't mind telling you, some of the younger ADCs do their best not to be drafted on to her staff! But most of all, she is terribly brave, not in the least concerned for her own safety. The other day we were set to dine at the Imperial Hotel. We walked into the aftermath of an assassination attempt on Jinnah by a bunch of Khaksars. A Muslim extremist group, they demand an undivided Pakistan from Karachi to Calcutta. To them Jinnah is as much a betrayer of Muslim interests as Gandhi is to the right-wing Hindu extremists. It seems they sneaked in through the garden at the side, rushing through the tea lounge and into the lobby, brandishing belchas or sharpened spades. Then they attempted to make it up the stairs to the ballroom where a meeting of the All India Muslim League Council was in full swing. Thankfully, they did not succeed, but it took the police and tear gas to bring the incident to a close. When we arrived for dinner later that evening the whole scene was one of utter destruction: broken furniture, walls riddled with bullet holes and blackened by smoke. It could always be Edwina, of course. Any moment, she could be the one with the bullet in her head, but she arms herself with lipstick and a smile.

On a lighter note, to make you and Victor laugh, the recalcitrant Princes were the source of much amusement the other day. Apart from Kashmir and Hyderabad whose situation is particularly complex, the Viceroy has been most effective in persuading a good many of the Indian Princes to accede to either India or Pakistan. He has relied on a strategy of tactical self-interest combined with holding himself out as a role model of Prince-turned-sailor-turned-diplomat. If that fails, he smiles, pushes back the curl on his forehead and makes a gesture to indicate the chopping off of his head. He then reminds whichever Prince happens to be in his line of fire, most gently, of the fate of Czar Nicholas II, his wife and children.

The gradual removal of the Princes has indeed been a quiet and miraculous revolution. And in this the Viceroy has been aided and abetted by V.P. Menon and Sardar Patel. Imagine the Viceroy in full naval rig-out, sailing into battle alongside Sardar Patel who looks like a

Roman emperor in a toga! Alas, I fear none of them will get any credit for it, least of all the most able VP. After independence the poor chap is likely to be abandoned to the jackals.

It was most comic when the Viceroy hosted a small luncheon party for the Princes. Some of them are still resisting accession to either India or Pakistan. We aides were lined up for a charm offensive. We make virtual 'Aye' and 'Nay' lobbies for the Princes on their attitude to accession. I waylaid the splendidly attired Maharaja of Bikaner with a good cognac, as was my brief. Joining in the charade, he half-blustered, half-teased about Charles I and the Divine Right of Kings. Then he confided that deep down he had little faith in the survival of the new Dominion of India.

'Ten years tops,' he announced loudly to the assembled company. At this point he and the Maharaja of Patiala took me, one by each arm, and roaring with laughter, frog-marched me through the gauntlet of the 'Nay' lobby!

Well, my dear, I fear I have written far too much. I really must dash. Off to see my dressmaker, Mrs Pritchard, in town. The dresses I had made in London are fast disintegrating in the heat. I do so wish you could come along! I am simply terrible with fashion, fabric and style.

Much love to all.

Write soon with your news.

As ever, your loving sister-in-law,

Letty

'Ah, Letty! Where are you off too? Going into town?' It was impossible to deny. Edwina had caught me in the act of applying my lipstick in the powder room after I had dropped Margaret's letter in the mailbox by the ADC's mess. I was wearing my hat and carrying my briefcase—Charles's old one that served as my usual handbag in India, except on formal occasions. Quickly, she closed the door to the corridor. Then she looked around to make sure we were alone. Suddenly, we were schoolgirls again hiding from the school bully, Maggie Reynolds, with her wild red hair and lacrosse stick, all those years ago. Except now we were surrounded by the luxurious paraphernalia of Viceroy's House: neatly folded hand towels embossed with the viceregal crest, soaps sealed in cream paper announcing *Viceroy's House, New Delhi* in case we forgot where we were, and a couple of purple and gold vials of Yardley perfume standing to attention on a silver tray. The Vicereine of India plonked her handbag down by the sink, snapped it open and extracted her lipstick. I put mine away. Pursing her lips and blinking myopically at herself, Edwina drew on the soft red and smeared it with her finger to tidy the edges.

Out of the corner of her eye she critically appraised my reflection in the dressing table mirror. She seemed a little surprised, as if she had not seen me for a while, and I too inspected at myself afresh. Was this what Hari saw when he looked at me? A tall, striking woman with large twinkling green eyes, her black hair cropped into a little bob which curled and waved beguilingly around emerging streaks of grey. The bodice of her dress fit snugly over full round breasts and the sun-tanned skin on her forearms had a subtle sheen.

'I say, Letty, would you be a dear and drop these off on your way? It's just we've both been so awfully busy. We barely get a moment these days . . . and the way things are, I don't like to risk them with a chaprasi.' She was pleading as she pulled two letters out of her bag and proffered them to me. I hesitated: I didn't need to take them to know what they were.

Cherie had telephoned me the other day from the Haven to tell me that the prosthetic hands had arrived from the USA. 'And something else,' she had whispered on the line. 'Tongues are wagging all over Delhi. Everyone, just about everyone is talking! I thought you ought to know.' I said nothing at my end but she didn't take the cue and blabbed on. 'And she's not the only one, you know. The other week we had the American photojournalist Margaret Bourke-White over. She's the kind of woman whose reputation precedes her, if you know what I mean. Well, she was all doe-eyed as she spoke about darling Jawahar. She boasted that she was probably the only white woman to have slept between Nehru and Gandhi, on a sleeper to Simla, or so she said. I don't believe a bit of it, of course.'

I stared now at the evidence: two letters, addressed to *The Rt. Hon. Pandit Nehru, 17 York Road* in the Vicereine's scrawling hand.

'Don't look at me like that,' Edwina snapped.

'Like what?'

'Like that!'

I breathed in deeply. 'Dickie doesn't like it. It makes him unhappy.'

'Him! Unhappy! You have no idea. What about my happiness?' She was trembling, her voice rising to an uncontrolled screech before it gave out. Hands shaking, she dropped her lipstick into her open bag but she did not put the letters in.

'Letty,' she cooed, grabbing her left hand with her right to marshal herself before she smiled softly and changed tack. 'You had a happy marriage. You've no idea . . . I'm *dying* with Dickie. Day after day, year after year. It's suffocation by pomposity. God knows, I've tried. I'm here in India, aren't I?' Her steely blue gaze was a barb from which I could not escape. 'Sometimes in the evenings, at Broadlands, I liked to sit and watch the sun set over the park. I would put the gramophone on, Beethoven, Rachmaninov, Chopin. When the last light had gone I would just sit and enjoy the shadows and the quiet. But Dickie would always come crashing in and slap on the light.

'"For heaven's sake, what are you doing sitting in the dark?" That's the trouble, the heart of it. Dickie cannot and will never understand that I am not just sitting in the dark. Jawahar, on the other hand, he knows that I am sitting in the light.' She shrugged 'And guess what His Excellency the Viceroy of India is doing right now? I've just come from his study. Go on! Guess!'

I shook my head. 'I've no idea.'

'Well, he's drafting designs for new flags for the Governor General and working out orders of precedence for the Independence Day ceremonies!' She put her hands around her throat and started to choke herself, digging in her nails, gripping herself tighter and tighter until she turned red and then purple. Her eyes began to bulge out of their sockets. And when she could take no more, she started to tear at her thin brown arms with her nails, hugging herself yet abusing herself at the same time

'For God's sake, Edwina, stop it.' I snatched her hands away. Her neck was red and her arms covered in angry weals and scratches.

'I tell you, at the moment Jawahar is the only thing keeping me sane. Don't deny me that.' She was almost hysterical but the admission had the effect of calming her. Turning back to the mirror, she snapped open her gold compact and began to powder over the marks she had made on her neck and arms. After a while she said, 'Letty, do you wonder how we are ever going to go back to our old lives after India? I can't imagine how I did it all before—those interminable house parties, shoots, dinners, luncheons. Whitehall, Balmoral, the same old, narrow-minded, self-interested, self-righteous crowd, parroting the same old things.' She did a little jig like a drunken Scottish marionette. 'Tell me? How am I going to shoehorn myself back into that? Descendre pour la saison à Saint Tropez.' She pouted and shrugged in the way of une grande dame française. Then she made her fingers dance as if down a hill, such that I had to laugh. 'It's all so pointless. Futile.'

Delicately, she picked up a vial of perfume, removed the top and dabbed the scent on her wrists, rubbing them together to warm and spread the fragrance. Watching her, I wondered, not for the first time, what on earth I would do after India. Perhaps a job in Hong Kong . . .

The Vicereine of India put the final dabs of powder on her nose, sighed and rolled her shoulders.

I stared at the letters, neat, white, innocent and lying benignly next to the Yardley perfumes. *The Rt. Hon. Pandit Nehru, 17 York Road.* They were dynamite.

'All right, I'll take them.'

'Oh Letty, you are a darling!'

'But please don't ask me again. It puts me in a most awkward position.'

'Don't worry, I won't.' Her eyes narrowed and she tightened her jaw. She shoved the letters into my hand, and I left quickly, taking care not to slam the door on the way out.

There were hands on my body, feeling, undoing the top buttons of my dress and loosening my belt. Someone's hot breath was on my face, and there was a smell of peppermint. I seemed to hear a babble of voices. A sharp beam of jagged light cut at my eyes. There was the wail of sirens, then silence and darkness again. A light, just one, at the far end of a telescope, getting bigger. A huge daffodil swelling yellow, and in the middle, a rouged, powdered, crimson-lipsticked face.

'Lady Wallace! Thank God. It's Eira Pritchard.' Swallow, tut, tut. My head was pounding and I was falling, grabbing and trying to save myself. Another face, an Indian one, puffy, pushed up close. A wave of eau de cologne. Nausea.

'Gently now! She's coming round.' More swallowing and tutting from Mrs Pritchard.

I opened my eyes in shadow. A big policeman in khaki with his lathi stowed, was bending over and helping me to sit up.

'Where am I?'

'Lady Wallace, you're outside my shop, Pritchard's Couture.' Tut tut, swallowing quicker now in agitation. 'You just picked up your dress.'

My new dress? The one with the tiny grey pinstripe and the sleeves shaped like bluebells I had ordered for Independence Day?

They had eased me up now, suspended between the shoulders of an Indian man with dyed orange hair and the policeman. They helped me back into the shop and lowered me into the faux Louis XVI chair. Had it been raining? My hair felt wet but when I put my hand up to the back of my head, it came away sticky with blood.

'Went at you something terrible they did, Lady Wallace, as soon as you came out of the shop. This gentleman came to help you, but it was too late. Heaven preserve us!' Mrs Pritchard put both hands to her cheeks.

'Call an ambulance!' ordered the man with orange hair.

'No ambulance,' I said. 'Ring them at Viceroy's House.' The effort of speaking was too much, and Mrs Pritchard was not nimble enough in her orange suede shoes. I vomited first into the skirt of her dress and then into her wastepaper basket.

'Khaksars. Those sly-eyed sons of whores. They can't fool me. Khaki breeches, two of them, bearded.' The man with orange hair dictated loudly to an earnest young police sergeant who smelled of stale cooking and sweat. He had just arrived and had his notebook and pencil at the ready.

Slowly I began to remember: the shop door closing, the tinkle of the bell, the men coming fast out of the sun. At first I had thought they were just being rude, bumping into me, so I'd shouted at them to be careful. Then one of them had grabbed my briefcase. I'd held on and pushed away the smaller man. Still the larger man held on to my briefcase. Shouts in Urdu, him punching me in the stomach, both of them running away, pulling me with them. Still holding on, tripping falling, banging my head against the stone pillar of the colonnade on the way down.

'My briefcase! Has anyone seen my briefcase?'

They shook their heads.

'Ah! The briefcase. Motive, petty theft.' The young sergeant's eyes lit up with triumph at the success of his English.

'Yes,' I said with a sinking feeling at the loss of the letters. I had intended to drop in at York Road after I had picked up my dress and been to the bank. 'Petty theft.'

Edwina was dressed for dinner in a long pink-and-white flowery evening gown. A necklace of tiny diamonds adorned her slender, sun-tanned neck. I winced as she sat behind me on the edge of my bed at Viceroy's House and cleaned the cut on the back of my head. Out in the gardens the peacocks shrieked. Their call, sometimes irritating, sometimes reassuring, hacked razor-sharp at my skull.

'You're in shock, Letty. It'll pass.' She gave the bloody swab to Zamurad Khan. 'Jawahar is sending Dr Rathore over. He'll be here soon.'

My heart sank.

'You rang Panditji? He knows?'

'Actually, he rang me. News spreads like wildfire in New Delhi.'

'I'm sorry.' I said. Neither of us needed to spell out the potential political implications of any leak of personal letters between the Vicereine and Mr Nehru.

'Don't be. Mrs Pritchard said you fought back. Letty, you shouldn't have. You should just have let the letters go'. She shrugged and took out a hairpin from her head, then unwound and rewound a curl and placed it back behind her ear.

'I really love him, you know. He's my best friend in all the world.'

She meant Jawahar. I nodded painfully, the blood rushing to my ears as I acknowledged her quiet confession.

'But what if Jinnah and the Muslim League get their hands on the letters? At the very least it will put an end to Lord Louis being joint Governor General of India and Pakistan.'

'I shouldn't worry about that. I was just saying the other day that Jinnah won't settle for anything less than the Triple Crown. I guarantee he'll make himself Prime Minister and Governor General of Pakistan and be Head of the Muslim League, all at the same time'.

'Rather unconstitutional,' I quipped. 'And he calls himself a lawyer!'

'Oh, I don't think he cares about that.' She laughed with that little tinkling sound and I was shocked at how sanguine she appeared about the whole affair. 'Anyway, not to worry, Letty dear. Just get better. You look awfully pale.' She washed her hands in the little bowl that Zamurad Khan had brought for her. There was blood in the water, my blood. Edwina stood up and looked at her watch. It was almost dinner time and she had a reception to host for members of the diplomatic corps. 'The letters will be returned soon enough. Of that, I have no doubt. Jinnah might be a lawyer and a megalomaniac, but he is a gentleman.'

The sun was setting over the Mughal Gardens, bringing with it the smell of the refugee's cooking fires on the estate. Through the window I watched the smoke curl upwards, each trail a private prayer. There was a soft knock at the door and Hari came in.

'Good evening, Lady Wallace. How are you?' He addressed me professionally, formally. But his top button was undone, his tie loose, his suit creased, and his brow was wrinkled with worry and with work. His movements were slow and heavy. Everything about him was grey with fatigue.

'Dr Rathore, I'm so sorry they dragged you out here. Really, I'm fine.'

'That's for me to decide.' Lips zipped, face impassive, he removed his jacket and plonked his big black bag on the floor next to the bed. With a wave of his hand, he dismissed Zamurad Khan who was shifting anxiously from one foot to the other.

'When the Bharat Bhushan issues a summons, one has to jump to it.' Dr Rathore raised half an eyebrow in an attempt to ease the tension of the unresolved argument between us. I returned half a laugh which promptly gave way to a stifled groan of pain.

He took my pulse while noting the seconds on his wristwatch and I felt the beat of him too, busy with the stresses of the day and the drive over, slowing. Slower, slower, steadying now. One, two, three—I counted the rotations of the ceiling fan. One, two, three. In the gardens, people were moving about in the relative cool of the evening and I could hear the gruff voices of men and, in the distance, the shouts of children trying to play.

Stiffly, I bent my head so that Dr Rathore could examine the wound on the back. He was gentle as he removed the hairpins from where Edwina had pinned them. I could feel the tips of his fingers, warm and soft, pressing, testing the plates around my skull.

'That's quite a whack. You'll have a headache for quite some time, but nothing's been broken. Look at my finger. Any flashing lights, blurred or double vision?'

'A little, when I was first coming round, but not now. I vomited though.'

'That's not uncommon with a blow to the head. How long were you out?'

'I don't know. Not long, I think.'

He took out his torch and, lifting my eyelid, looked into the back of my right eye. His breath snuffled close to my ear. I stared up at the ceiling, looking past the sweaty gleaming corner of his forehead and the tuft of grey hair. At the point where the paint in the corner of the ceiling was peeling like curls, a tiny striped lizard was loitering.

'Look up. To the left. To the right. Look down.' He smelled strangely comforting, of disinfectant, of cigarettes and the accumulated grime at the end of a day. Lifting my left eyelid, he twisted his head and the torch, and I felt his hot cheek close to mine. His stomach rumbled, but neither of us commented even though we had both heard it.

'The good news is that your retinas are all as they should be.' He straightened up and stretched his back a little. The blood pressure cuff came next and both of us watched the mercury rise as he pumped it up then fall.

'Well, Lady Wallace, you have had a shock. There is mild concussion and a God Almighty bruise on the back of your head. I ought to have you in hospital overnight for observation. But given the general state of play, I can't really recommend it.' He sucked between his teeth, observing me and thinking how best to proceed. 'Ideally, I need someone to keep you awake for a few more hours, and then to wake you up in the middle of the night to make sure you're all right. You could come home with me, but I'm afraid we wouldn't be able to make you very comfortable there either. I've taken in some Muslim patients from a hospital for safety. What with all their relatives, we've got a full house: bedding rolls everywhere, in the halls and landings as well as tents in the garden. Tania, Goldie's daughter, comes to help when she can. Talented girl, she'll make an excellent doctor one day . . .' Then his voice trailed off. Unwittingly he had trespassed into the personal zone.

'Does her mother know?' I was treading carefully, fearful of landmines.

He shook his head and fastened the lid of the box containing the blood pressure gauge.

'Is there anyone reliable here, who could wake you in the night?'

'My bearer,' I said, 'Zamurad Khan.'

He frowned.

'Can you trust him?'

'I'm already trusting him with my life. A school friend of his was murdered by a Sikh mob in Old Delhi a few weeks ago.

Ever since then Zamurad Khan has been sleeping outside my bedroom door. For my protection, he said. I have tried to send him away, back to his family on the estate, but he won't go'.

"'The Viceroy and the Vicereine are very kind in letting refugees into estate, but all sorts of badmash are also coming in," the old chap was most insistent. "If some thuggi climbed in through the window, then he would have to deal with Zamurad Khan and the sword of Shah Jahan!'"

'The sword of Shah Jahan?' Again, Dr Rathore raised his eyebrow.

'Indeed, forged in the furnaces of Damascus. Apparently it's a family heirloom and he sleeps with it under his pillow!' Now it was my turn to raise my eyebrow as best as I could.

As if on cue, Zamurad Khan came into the room, carrying the dinner tray. He placed it on the coffee table in the lounge area of my room. Hot rice, fresh chapattis and dal. Again, I groaned, this time with weakness and the sudden realization of hunger.

'Memsahib, eating a little bit, please, Her Excellency saying.'

'Yes, Zamurad Khan.' I gave him a feeble mock salute and he returned an anxious half-smile. 'Hari,' I said, turning to Dr Rathore, you must stay and eat too. I know you're hungry. Don't deny it.'

He didn't. Wearily, he removed his tie. Without thinking about it and most naturally, we settled ourselves on opposite sides of the coffee table in the light of the lamp. I was in a chair and Hari chose to sit cross-legged on the floor. From my vantage point I noticed that his hair was thinning. Yet he looked like a schoolboy at the end of the day: tired and grubby, and suddenly too big for his clothes with his shirt hanging out of the back of his trousers. For an instant I saw in the face of the man the shadow of the little boy his mother would have known. Zamurad Khan returned with some pillows to prop me up, extra portions of food, water bowls and towels so we could both wash our hands. Then he went to the mess to sign out a whisky and soda for Hari on my tab.

I let Hari serve, break the chapattis, and spoon the dal.

'Best not to eat too much.'

'I know.'

For a long while, neither of us spoke. The ceiling fan whirring hypnotically above us provided an accompaniment to the silence. It pulled at the corners of the napkins on each rotation, teasing us with the promise of wind. We ate but it was obvious that Hari was exhausted. Head down, he concentrated on the business of filling himself so that he could carry on and fight another day in the ward and in the operating theatre. After the first few cautious mouthfuls, I sensed my energy was returning and that the colour was beginning to flow back into my cheeks.

At length, he said, 'Jawahar and I were young together. God knows he likes a pretty face as much as the next man, but what on earth are he and the Vicereine playing at?'

For a moment I wondered if he had somehow got to know about the missing letters.

'I got the whole story out of Jawahar. He had to tell me . . . Why else would you have been a target? Bloody hell, Pippi, if those thugs had had knives or guns, you could have been killed. People in their position can't carry on like this. It's gross selfishness. The future of India, millions of people—far too much is at stake.'

'It is precisely because they are people in their position that they carry on like they do.' I was surprised to hear myself sounding so bitter. I realized at the same time that although I had apologized to Edwina for the loss of her letters, she had not expressed remorse to me for asking me to run the errand. Despite what she'd claimed, she could just as easily have sent a chaprasi with the letters or not sent them at all.

Hari nodded and offered me a piece of chapatti. My head hurt as I shook it to decline. He chuckled grimly.

We sat back. When all the food had gone, there was nothing
to distract us except the ceiling fan. Hari sipped his whisky and
I, my tea, both of us wary and keeping our eyes down.

'It's going to be carnage, after independence. We have not
seen the worst of it yet.' This time he gulped his whisky. 'I had
to do an amputation today.' There was a long pause. 'Pippi, I
wasn't trained as a battlefield surgeon, but I'm learning fast.
Tim Latham, whom you met at Sunny's, was with the Third
Canadian Division that landed on Juno Beach on D-Day. I was
so glad to have him by my side. He is used to operating on an
industrial scale and showed me a range of new techniques.'

'Have you heard from your daughter in Lahore?'

'Yes. They still refuse to come to Delhi. Her husband's
family are typical business people! Busy securing their assets:
land and factories and so on. So stubborn. It will all calm down
once the boundary is drawn.'

'There is no guarantee Lahore will go to India,' I said. 'It
could go to Pakistan.'

He swirled the whisky in his glass as if trying to read the
future and promptly changed the subject.

'I've missed our morning rides,' he said with a forced
brightness. 'Although I certainly don't want you riding again
until I'm sure you're well. You need to take it easy for a while'.

'I've missed them too.'

'I owe you an explanation about the Mahatma.' He was
looking at me directly now, his brown eyes soft and gentle,
promising reconciliation.

'No, Hari, you owe me nothing of the kind. We British in
India, we have lived here as if we were blind. There is so much
about your beautiful and ancient land that we have failed to see
or to understand'.

The moths were gathering under the cream lampshade,
the shadows of their wings magnified to the size of bats. Hari
looked exhausted and I wanted to reach out and hold him in

my arms. But he recrossed his legs in the other direction and began to speak.

'It was late January 1944. I had gone down to Poona to the Aga Khan's palace. Mr Gandhi was in prison there with his wife, the poetess Sarojini Naidu and the famous Mirabehn. Do you know her? She is the daughter of the English admiral who became a follower of Gandhi.'

'Her Excellency gets on very well with Sarojini Naidu, but Madeleine Slade, that is, Mirabehn, has declined all invitations. They say she lives as a recluse, running a farm in the foothills of the Himalayas.'

'Well, Ba's, that is Mrs Gandhi's, health was failing. Jawahar, who was in prison elsewhere, had got permission from the authorities for me to attend her. He wanted me to get some antibiotics for her. I'd slogged my guts out to get hold of them, pulling just about every string I could find. Sunny and Cherie again! In the end, the Americans turned up trumps, God bless them! Well, I arrived in the early morning, passing through the barbed wire gates just as the mist was lifting. The palace was like something out of a fairy tale, its pretty turrets all cream and white. I thought that if this were a prison, then I too might welcome at least a short stay! The gardens were immaculate, full of flowers. There was even a badminton net stretched temptingly across the lawn. But as I got closer, no one came out to greet me. The young sepoy at my side was one of two supervised by the jemadar who guarded the prisoners.

'"This place, Doctor Sahib, it's cursed. One day, the Mahatma's secretary, he just dropped dead," he whispered lest he tempted the evil spirits. Then he took me to the mound of mud and stone which marked the cremation site of the secretary, Mahadev Desai. The flat top had been marked with the Hindu sign for Om and underneath it there was a Christian cross and, in the four corners, the star and crescent of Islam.

'After that we went round to the back veranda. They were there, like two old crones: Mirabehn milking the goats and Sarojini Naidu in a tatty pink silk dressing gown, her hair loose over her shoulders. She was stirring a pot on a little charcoal stove. Seeing them like this, I couldn't believe that they were distinguished ladies of good breeding and birth. But I knew at once from their pallor that both of them had or had had malaria.

'Jawahar and the rest of them always used to joke that it was better to keep one or two of us medics healthy and on the outside to treat them when they got sick!

'The two women stared at me in disbelief and asked me what I was doing there and whether I had come to save them. Mirabehn looked puzzled and shaded her eyes against the sun.

'I told them that Jawahar had sent me to see Ba.

'There was a rush of pink to their cheeks, as is always the way with the hope of people who have been incarcerated for a long time.

'I said that I had some brought antibiotics in case they were needed.

'Oh! Pippi! You should have seen their faces. "Antibiotics!" They put their hands up and recoiled in horror as if I were the devil incarnate.

'"That's no good," Mirabehn had said, "Bapu will never allow it."

'"Let's ask him, shall we?"'

'After a long wait, the Mahatma finally agreed to let me see Ba.

'"Well, if Jawahar has sent you, then I suppose you must."

'Then leaning on his stick, he turned his back on me and sauntered off into the garden.

'I went with Mirabehn into Ba's room off the veranda. Flowers had been laid out in rangoli patterns on a small table by the bed. Mirabehn said she arranged them every day in different rooms in the house to keep up her spirits. She thought that Ba's depression was the worst of it, compounding her very real physical ailments. She said that on occasion Ba could be distracted by playing carrom or be tempted into trying to hit a shuttlecock over the net to Bapu. The hilarity that inevitably followed apparently gave her some hope and strength to carry on.

'Oh, Pippi! It was such a shock to see the wife of the Mahatma like that: as tiny as an eight-year-old girl huddled in the bed. She had the saddest eyes of anyone I had ever seen, as hard and impenetrable as millstones.'

He sipped a little more of his whisky and watched the moths that had now become trapped under the lampshade. When he was ready he continued.

'I had treated Ba once before and she had always been suspicious of me, preferring Ayurvedic medicine. Nevertheless, she allowed me to examine her. She had had a weak chest since she was a child. The condition certainly had not been helped by years of hard living in ashrams and prisons. The diagnosis was not easy. I suspected that she had had a minor heart attack, but she definitely had pneumonia. It was that that was in danger of killing her. I recommended an injection of antibiotics. It would buy her time and I planned to request an immediate early release on medical grounds. I would remove her to somewhere healthier where with good nutrition, we could nurse her back to health.

'"The war is nearly over," I said as I took her tiny hand in mine. "India will soon be free. Don't you want to live to see that glorious day?"

'We argued and cajoled at length as with a child. Mirabehn even told Ba that in Vedic times doctors used to give injections with cow horns. She went as far as to admit that she herself had had quinine injections for malaria. This was much against her convictions about non-violence of course, but it had brought her fever down. Eventually, Ba agreed to having the injections provided her husband gave permission.'

Hari sighed and rubbed his neck and shoulders. Night had clamped down around us like a cage in Viceroy's House. In the gardens, someone was playing a flute. The notes seemed to stick on the warm air, elongating the lament.

He finished his whisky with one last slug and stared up at the lizard still loitering in the corner. It stared back with unblinking eyes.

All the time Hari had been talking he'd been staring into his whisky glass, but now he looked directly at me.

'Pippi, I understand that your audience with the Mahatma gave you some sort of peace. I am glad for it.' He smiled softly, rocking the empty glass in his hand. 'And history and the world will judge him to be a great man. Of that I have no doubt, and indeed he is. He gave us Swaraj, and united and galvanized a weak and passive people into action and resistance. But that man they call the Mahatma, he believes that injections are violent and against the law of Satyagraha. What kind of truth is that?' His eyes burned with fury, once again demanding an answer of me which I could not give.

'It is ignorance, pure and simple. He had it within his power to use the latest advances in modern medicine to perhaps save his wife, to give her at least a chance to recover. But he refused to do so.'

To my astonishment, Edwina was right in her predictions: her letters to Jawahar were returned. I found them early one morning in my pigeon hole, in a brown envelope zealously sealed with brown tape. Mr Jinnah had duly appointed himself Governor General of the new Dominion of Pakistan. The consequence was that a very reluctant Dickie was left to take up the post of Governor General of India following the transfer of power. Some of the less important and high-profile members of staff, including me, would have to stay on into 1948 as part of the Governor General's team. We would remain in Viceroy's House until the summer of 1948. After independence, Viceroy's House would be renamed Government House.

In the days and weeks following the assault, the other staff initially treated me with kid gloves. Always territorial about their responsibilities and resenting my intrusion with regard to their mistress, Edwina's two female secretaries were particularly solicitous about my welfare. This was despite the rush towards the transfer of power and the absurd level of work in all departments.

'Take it easy. Best not to overdo it. Knock off a bit early, why don't you?'

The reality was that more and more relief work began to come my way. As Amrit Kaur put it gently at one meeting: 'Because it's seen to be women's work and none of the men want to touch it with a barge pole.'

The situation had become increasingly desperate. Thousands of refugees poured daily into Delhi from the Punjab and many more were stuck in camps in the Province. Despite my best efforts, I found it an impossible task. Everything was made worse by the lack of cooperation between the various agencies and the general hogging of resources in the run-up to the transfer of power. I spent hours on the telephone, begging, sweet-talking, blackmailing, bullying anyone who the Vicereine, Amrit Kaur and I thought might be able to help. We needed blankets, clothes, food, tents, vaccines, powdered milk and medicines. People were dying for lack of them. I couldn't give a tinker's cuss whether something 'belonged' to India or Pakistan: the supplies needed to be released before it was too late.

'Damn it! We'll have to do something about this.' Edwina thumped down her teacup at our regular morning staff meeting in the shade by the swimming pool. I had been telling her of my latest frustration in trying to get the army to hand over medical supplies. She took off her spectacles, squinted, cleaned them on the hem of her dress and put them back on again.

'What we need is a united agency for refugees. That way, we can fund it from the top-down and make sure the money reaches various societies and organizations. Then they can deliver help promptly where it is needed.'

It was a simple administrative structure, of course, to coordinate and streamline. But in the chaos and haste to help, none of us had seen it. And yet I couldn't see where, so late in the day, the money could come from.

'After independence,' she announced, 'I'll speak to Jawahar and get him to sort something out.'

I looked at her in the early morning light, unmade up, craggy, old, and thought that there had always been more to Edwina than met the eye.

You'll never guess who turned up the other day! I found him washed up by the ADCs' mess. The house boys had taken his luggage and he was quite abandoned with no one to greet him. Funny though, coming

*straight from London, it was he who seemed the foreigner, as white
and pasty as English autumn mist. He hasn't changed a bit. His glasses
opaque and slightly grimy, he was standing there, slowly turning his
bowler hat round and round in his hands, as if waiting for a bus! I know
you always said he was a man of the 'highest calibre' and 'supremely
efficient'. But for some reason he has always reminded me of a badger.*

I did not write 'Dearest darling' in my diary any more. It was not
a conscious omission. It had just happened. The pain of loss
was there, of course, and always would be. But now it was a
dull ache rather than an all-pervasive twisted agony, a torture
from which there was no escape. India had created a distance
between us, and if Charles had not gone, he had begun to fade.
I still saw him striding jauntily down Argyll Street, resembling
a walking deck chair in his striped MCC blazer. At the corner,
he still turned, tipped his hat to me, waved and smiled.

And yet when writing about Cyril Radcliffe it was to Charles
that I addressed myself. Cyril had been a contemporary of mine
at Oxford and a former pupil of my husband's at his Chambers.
A brilliant young man, he had always been marked out for great
things. A career at the Bar, a fellow of All Souls, he had also
served as Director General of the Ministry of Information
during the war.

The day I came across him in Viceroy's House he had
blinked in surprise as if he were not quite used to the startling
Indian light. He greeted me in Welsh for, like my father, he
hailed from North Wales. It had been a joke between us since
our student days.

'Helo Letty! Sut wyt ti?'

'Da iawn, diolch.'

He grabbed my hand and kissed me formally, once on
each cheek.

I had not seen him since Charles's funeral. There was an
awkward moment when I thought he might say something,

perhaps offer me his condolences. But we were so far away from it all now that the moment passed.

'SA to Her Ex,' I teased him with a line of jargon. 'Special Assistant to the Vicereine. She and I were at school together you know,' I tagged on by way of clarification.

His mouth opened and closed and I saw him as a goldfish out of water, but one that sweating profusely into his collar and armpits. His suit was quite unsuitable for the Indian heat.

'What on earth are you doing here?'

He flashed a very faint and quick smile, a rare thing for this man who had always been so earnest.

'For my sins, I have been appointed to chair the Boundary Commission for the Punjab and Bengal. But what a pleasant surprise to find you here, Letty! Antonia will be delighted to have your company. She's shipping out any day now.' He was talking about his wife.

'Antonia is coming out? Surely there won't be time?' My mind was doing the calculations. It was already the 8th of July and Independence Day had been set for the 15th of August.

'What do you mean?' His eyes narrowed and he gave the bowler hat on his head a quarter turn.

'There are less than six weeks to the transfer of power and the boundary must be drawn before then. If Antonia is coming by boat, she will barely get here before having to turn back home.'

'Six weeks? I was under the impression I had six months, at least, to do the job.'

I hesitated, lowered my voice, and guided him out into the gardens where we had less chance of being overheard. 'Perhaps I'm wrong, but my understanding is that the Boundary Award is to be announced before the 15th. Have you seen the Viceroy yet?'

He blinked, pulled at his sweat-drenched collar, and gave his bowler another quarter turn. The colour drained from his face.

Zamurad Khan told me that it was the hottest summer in seventy years and worried that the monsoon would be late. To focus minds on the countdown to the transfer of power the Viceroy had had a set of calendars printed and distributed to all the offices in Viceroy's House. The days announced themselves in bold: 1st August, fourteen days to the transfer of power; 3rd August, twelve days to the transfer of power. As each white-hot day melted into the next, furiously, hopelessly, we tore off the stupid sheets. Muriel Sparks made hers into neat little Japanese-style boxes in which she kept her treasury tags. Alan, Dangles and even Lord Ismay made paper airplanes which they hurled about the place in an effort to lighten the atmosphere. I screwed mine up into tight little balls and tried to pop holes-in-one in the wastepaper basket on the far side of the office.

I didn't see much of Hari any more. The heat and my concussion had put paid to our morning rides, along with the fact that I had been his patient, however briefly. I had recovered well and he had called twice to check on my progress, but this had put a professional barrier between us. We spoke occasionally on the telephone, usually about relief work. Both of us were tired, preoccupied, struggling against the tide of futility, the unsaid always masked behind the formal requests and polite turns of phrase. We were like codebreakers, each searching for a nugget of something in the subtlety of tone or expression of the other, all the while knowing that on all fronts we were fighting battles we were only going to lose.

In the weeks of July and early August I ended up keeping Cyril company when we were both off-duty. Usually we walked on The Ridge in the relative cool of the evening. We were like two orphans making the best of one another; there was a quiet trust between us in the way of people who had been young together and were now getting old.

I wrote again to Charles.

You will understand that the judicial nature of the Boundary Commission necessarily imposes a requirement of social isolation on Cyril. If he goes out to dinner he is besieged by people lobbying for the Sikh, Muslim or Hindu case. You will remember him as a dry character. He has but one joke and tells it at least once or twice a week. You've probably heard it before: the story of how he and his tutorial partner at Oxford invented a Greek historian called Aristomenes of Tauromenium. They used to spout him as an authority to a particularly doddery tutor. The old chap would nod and say, 'Ah, I had forgotten that.' I too pretend to forget that Cyril told me the same joke just a few days ago and laugh in the hope that it will cheer him up.

The poor man really is caught between a rock and hard place. I have watched his illusions gradually fall away. He is meticulous in everything he does and a credit to your training and to your Chambers. Rising above the fray in true judicial fashion, he has carefully defined the terms of reference for the Commission. He even took me along as a witness to meetings he had first with Nehru and then with Jinnah. Before he began his work he asked both men point-blank whether there actually needed to be a physical border between India and Pakistan. The expectation is that the new Dominions will live in peace in the way of the U.S.A. and Canada. Both men were taken aback by the question, insisting that a formal border must be drawn.

In addition to Cyril as Chairman, there are four nominees on the Commission: two from the Muslim League and two from the Congress. All of them toe their party's line which means that Cyril is effectively making the decisions alone.

You know Cyril, stoical to the end. In truth, I think that deep down he is one of the unhappiest men I have ever met. There is never any hint of joy or merriment. Perhaps happiness does not matter to him. What is important is courage under fire, not letting other men down, and doing the best job one can despite impossible odds. It is the quiet courage of your generation, which you will recognize as born of the Great War.

Occasionally, however, on our walks he does let things slip. One of the Muslim nominees said that it was not that he did not want to be more accommodating. It was just that he could not be so for fear of his life. Furthermore, Cyril tells me that the maps are inadequate. Surveys were stopped during the war, so the Commission works off documents that are too large in scale and well out of date. The census figures too, which are all important for deciding the religious make-up of each district, are unreliable. Needless to say, there is a good deal of gerrymandering going on as each community seeks to maximize its territorial claim.

Sometimes we meet for dinner in Cyril's bungalow. There are others there too, his Secretary, Chris Beaumont and a young Indian ADC. We all have Oxford in common so we talk about that, punting on the Cherwell, mutual friends and so on. Thus neutered the conversation goes round and round from one College to another, from one Oxford pub to the next in a ridiculous long-distance pub crawl. Imagine the men arguing about which one has the best bitter! Cyril, it turns out, is an Eagle and Child man!

I looked up at Dickie's calendar which announced: *9th August, five days to the Transfer of Power.* Below, in the Mughal Gardens, the fountains tinkled and the colours thickened towards dusk. I ripped off another page, another day from the year. Viciously I tore it and tore it again into strips, strips and yet more strips. When I finished, I gathered up the scattered mess and scrunched it into ball. Standing up, I hurled it towards the basket. I missed.

'Bugger,' I swore quietly. There had been a lot more swearing in Viceroy's House over recent months and it had become infectious. Not even I had proved immune. But I was unsure why I felt so angry. To calm myself I wrote again in the vain hope that words might put things right.

Delhi is alive with rumours and counter-rumours about just where the boundary will fall. The Hindus have convinced themselves that Lahore will be given to India and the Muslims are sure it will go to Pakistan. Meanwhile the fate of millions hangs in the balance and the pressure has begun to show on Cyril who is too tired to walk far of late. The Commission is due to report any day and the whole process has taken on a pseudo-scientific air. Each side is convinced there is an answer which can be correctly determined and that the Chairman will declare in its favour. It is all baloney, smoke and mirrors, of course! From what I have gleaned of the workings of Cyril's mind over the last weeks, the overriding factor has been a fair division of the so called 'contiguous majority areas'. Tell me, why must men create a euphemism to hide the truth, to make themselves sound grand and important? Here it means division on religious lines. This imperative is balanced with a need to preserve the infrastructure—both economic and physical, including canals and dams—as best he can. In truth, there is no magic formula. There are no right answers. Whatever Cyril comes up with, however diligently and judicially he works, communities will lose out. A scapegoat will be required and he will be damned.

yril worked and lived in a neat white bungalow on the estate. The long green blinds outside the windows were at half-mast. The left one was slightly lower than the right, so that from the outside the building appeared to be crouching like a lazy animal taking a prolonged siesta into the late afternoon. I had cycled down from the main house for my usual pre-dinner stroll with Cyril. Temperatures had begun to dip a fraction and normally the estate came to life at this time; chaprasis running messages, the changing of the guard, smoke from the kitchens, the malis turning on the hose pipes. But today it was as if a great veil had fallen from on high, muffling everything, leaving me with the impression I was a bit player in a silent film.

Chris Beaumont was standing on the veranda of Cyril's bungalow in front of the door, blocking it. Arms folded firmly across his chest, he shook his head as I approached: he was very obviously cross. He was in conversation with V.P. Menon who was dressed for squash and had his racquet tucked under his arm. There was much shaking of heads and shrugging of shoulders by both of them. VP took a step towards the threshold but Chris stood his ground. VP hesitated and at the last second offered Chris his hand. The offer was accepted and VP turned curtly on his heels and left.

He and I crossed each other on the garden path—me pushing my bicycle, and VP with his chin in his chest—and mumbled greetings.

'Lady Wallace.'

'Mr Menon.'

'If anyone asks, you didn't see me. I wasn't here.' There was the crunch, crunch of his footsteps on the sandy path, the swish of a swinging racquet, and then he was gone.

Chris let me in and bolted the door. It took a few seconds for my eyes to adjust to the gloom inside the hall.

'What was that all about?'

'Nothing much. Just VP pushing his luck. Nehru had sent him over but he's no fool; knew damn well he couldn't speak to Sir Cyril. Apparently, Bikaner has got his knickers in a twist about Ferozepur.'

I knew that the Maharaja of Bikaner was very agitated over how the boundary might affect the rivers and canals in his state. But I giggled at the thought of him all knotted up in a pair of oversized pink laced bloomers. Chris sneezed and wiped his streaming nose with his handkerchief. He had a cold and was clearly too far gone with fatigue brought on by weeks of stress to laugh at his own joke.

I changed tack.

'Where is he then?' Most days Cyril waited for me with his study door open and when he saw me locked up and came out. The need for secrecy during the preparation of the Boundary Award meant that I was never invited into the room but I knew that maps, papers and reports were stacked up in great piles inside like mini skyscrapers in a child's model city.

'He's out back. I'll just get him. Why don't you wait in the study?'

Today, the room was tidy. All the papers and general debris of his work had vanished, rendering it as pristine as a hotel room ready for the next guest. Cyril's trunk was sitting in the corner. Embossed with his initials CJR, it was old and battered enough to date from his school days. On top of it was what I knew to be a red, green and purple Persian carpet, neatly folded into a square, wrapped in brown paper and tied with string.

The Chairman of the Boundary Commission came huffing
and puffing into the room, wiping the sweat from his brow
with a handkerchief. His face was so blackened by soot that he
looked like an engine stoker.

'Sorry, Letty, I was just burning the last of my papers. Best
to do it myself, under the circumstances, don't you think?'

He offered me a lemonade from a tray on the table, drained
one himself, poured another, drained that, sighed and wiped
his mouth with the back of his hand.

'All done?' I asked.

'Done and dusted.' He picked up a neatly bound report
from the centre of his desk, considered it briefly in his hand
and passed it to me.

'Here it is! I've had to give Lahore to Pakistan, of course.
India keeps Calcutta. It's not fair if she gets them both.'

The glass shook in my hand. In my attempt to control it
and juggle the report I spilled some lemonade on the carpet.
I was finding it difficult to breathe and locked my knees to
counteract the wave of panic that was manifesting itself as
weakness in my legs.

'Of course.' I tried to sound cool and disinterested. But my
mind had run to Hari and the photograph of his daughter with
the two curly-haired little grandsons that he kept in his wallet,
next to his heart.

'That's good. So the Award will be released before the
15th of August then?'

'One would have thought so. Evan Jenkins is crying out
for it up in the Punjab so he can deploy forces in anticipation
of trouble. The war of succession, he calls it, and Campbell-
Johnson is backing him. But His Excellency wants to sit on
the damn thing until after the formal transfer of power, or so
I heard.' He tapped the side of his nose and lowered his voice.
'Between you and me and these four walls, you understand . . .'
He dusted the remaining soot from his hands. 'But that's not

my problem. I'm all set with Aladdin's Original Flying Carpet.
Shame I can't fly out on that!' We looked at the brown paper
parcel containing the neatly folded Persian carpet. I had helped
him choose it in old Delhi, and I chuckled at the memory of the
shopkeeper's sales pitch.

'Alan bought one from the same shop, different colours
and design to yours and his was also Aladdin's original.'

I managed to keep the little joke going to calm my nerves
and to give myself time to think.

'Well, I intend to station myself at Palam and wait for
the earliest flight out of this Godforsaken country. I'll go via
Timbuktu if I have to.'

'You don't want to stay until the 15th to see the festivities?' I
handed the report back to him. To my astonishment, he threw
it casually on to his shiny mahogany desk where it slid to the
end and nearly fell off.

'No, thank you very much, Letty. God knows I've done
my best, but when this thing comes out, there will be eighty
million people with a grudge against me. I don't want them to
find me.'

At dinner, I could not concentrate. Plates clattered, faces
contorted into a blur and the half-followed conversations
might as well have been in Arabic or Russian for all the sense
they made to me. The Boundary Award was top secret. What
could, or should, I do? If I warned Hari about it so that he
could help his family, I would not only be betraying my country
but my friend Cyril too. What was Hari to me anyway that I
should even contemplate such a risk? Perhaps Hari's daughter
had already come to Delhi, although I thought that unlikely.
Last week he had told me on the telephone that her father-in-
law had nailed a sign to the gate of their compound in Lahore:
Hindu, Muslim, Sikh, Christian, Parsee, we are all brothers
here. Despite the escalating violence, the old chap had decided
to batten down the hatches and ride it all out.

When I picked up the telephone in the lobby next to
the mess after dinner, I realized I was shaking. I had judged
that that would be the best place to talk. It was film night at
Viceroy's House and everyone was gathering to get a drink
before it started. Anything I said would be lost in the general
post-dinner hubbub.

'Delhi 617.' My throat was dry and the operator asked me
to repeat the number. As I waited, each whirr and click on the
line hit me like a sledgehammer.

The servant answered the phone and I heard the thump,
thump, thump of his limp as he went down the hall to find his
master.

'Good evening, Pippi. How are you?' Hari's voice was
clipped, irritated.

'Fine. Fine. Sorry to call so late. I need to see you.' I cupped
the receiver in my hand and turned to see if anyone was
watching. 'Can you come over now? Back gate as usual. I can't
talk on the phone.'

'Can't it wait until tomorrow? I've just come home.'

'No, it can't. I'll see you in half an hour.' I pressed down
on the cradle and cut him off. The line, dead, buzzed in my ear.

If the afternoon had been quiet, the night most certainly
was not: a baby was crying, a dog was barking and a lone peacock,
who for some reason had not yet roosted, was shrieking bitterly
over and over again. My bike rattled. The chain needed oiling
and it clanked on every third rotation. I thought it odd that I
had not noticed it earlier in the day. The lights on the main
roads of the estate were surprisingly bright and I knew what
was out there. Hundreds or thousands of pairs of eyes would
see me on my way from the house to the back gate at this hour:
estate staff, men of the bodyguard, refugees, some in tents and
others sleeping along the verandas of the bungalows and in the
archways and corridors. I had passed Claude Auchinleck in
the corridor on my way out and Dangles was with an officer's

daughter in the corner of the mess. He had winked at me and given me his beautiful young man's grin as I passed.

My heart was beating wildly in my chest and I felt sick. My mind seethed with visions: the ravens on the green at the Tower of London; St Paul's Cathedral in flames; mediaeval paintings of hell, showing devils and witches, naked men contorted on the rack; a figure in a shiny black plague mask descending through the clouds to peck out my eyes. It was not too late to turn around and go back to watch the film. I could have a brandy and banter with the rest of them. I could tell Hari that there had been 'a misunderstanding on high, crossed wires: 'Terribly sorry, do let me buy you a drink instead.'

In defiance of regulations, the sentry was sitting on his stool by the barrier at the back gate, smoking. Rotate, clank, rotate, clank. I got off my bike and he stood up at my approach, hastily stubbing out his cigarette with his foot and coughing as if that would clear the air of all traces of smoke.

'Dr Rathore is coming.' I was breathless with fear. 'My bearer is unwell.' I swallowed hard on the lie. The Naik came out of the guardhouse where a chess game was underway. I could see that many pieces were left and that the black bishop and knight were positioned for checkmate. He knew both Hari and me from our morning rides and merely nodded at my explanation, clicking his fingers and lazily stretching his hands above his head. Just then Hari's convertible purred up to the gate and stopped. The hood was closed but its brash yellow colour had been transformed into an eerie purple by the light from the roof of the guardhouse. The sentry lifted the barrier and looked casually inside the car. Recognizing Hari, he waved him through. Abandoning my bike against the wall next to a broken wooden table and empty gas canister, I went round to the passenger side and climbed in. The windows were open but the full heat of the day had built up inside. It was stifling.

'Pippi, what on earth . . .?' Hari was tight-lipped, his fists clenched round the steering wheel.

'Drive! Slowly, up to the dispensary!' I fixed my eyes on the road. 'If anyone asks, Zamurad Khan is unwell and you've come to see him.' It was an unlikely excuse. He knew it and squinted suspiciously at me out of the corner of his eye, switching down a gear.

'My God! You're trembling . . . What's the matter?'

On our left, just past the stables, a group of Muslim men in white skull caps were sitting cross-legged in front of a tent. Smoking and playing chess, their eyes lifted and glinted as we passed.

'Pull up here.' I hadn't wanted to tell Hari while he'd been driving. He parked in the shadow of the dispensary. We got out and the doors clicked shut far too loudly. Instinctively, we made for the front door and the safety of the veranda but a rope had been tied across the top banisters. Following it with our eyes we saw that it had been fastened to the top of a cooking pot which was deliberately precariously balanced to fall and make a warning noise. On the veranda behind the rope two Muslim women in burkas were asleep with their children. They had put the babies and a thumb-sucking toddler between them and two older children clung to their backs like little monkeys. Dried leaves crackled under our feet as we tiptoed away. A child stirred in its sleep, flicking a hand as if swatting a fly. We sneaked between the oil tank and the side of the dispensary. But the passage stank of urine so we moved on to take shelter under the trees in the shadows at the back of the building.

'Lahore,' I whispered. 'It's going to Pakistan.'

'It can't be.'

'It is. I've had it from the horse's mouth. Don't ask me how I know. If there's a leak and they trace it back to me . . .'

I could see only the whites of his eyes, flickering in the night, and his teeth bared in a grimace, like a wolf.

'Are you sure?'

I tried to say yes, but the effort of the betrayal had taken all my strength. I just nodded. It was done.

Hari exhaled very slowly, then reached out and pulled me to him. Simultaneously ashamed and relieved, I rested my head on his chest. I desperately wanted to cry but no tears came.

'What are you going to do?' My voice was weak and croaky.

'Fly up first thing. Bring my daughter and the children back with me. By force if I have to. I'll take a man with me. Fortunately, I have money and connections—that helps.' I raised my head, searching for expression amongst the craggy black and grey mountains and ravines of his face.

'Go, go and bring them back safely! God be with you.' I started to pull away thinking he would want to get back to the car. But Hari gripped my upper arms tightly, pushed the hair back from my forehead and kissed me on the mouth. Shocked by the ferocity of our coming together, we pulled back, but could no longer help ourselves. In our fear and loneliness, we held on, digging deeper, clinging on. We stood, rocking back and forth gently, the rhythm soothing, comforting, as if we were tired children on a garden swing.

$\mathcal{S}$o, this was it: Freedom! Formality, restraint, order, precedence, planning were now subsumed by great oceans of exuberance and joy. I peeked out from a window in the Council House. It was as if all the people in the world, all the souls that there had ever been and ever would be had come out to celebrate India's Independence Day. I had come down earlier by a back way from Government House. The crowds then had not been too bad. But now people were converging from every side, pushing and shoving in an effort to come inside to witness the historic speeches. The circular Council House was besieged. Mountbatten, in the new role of Governor General, and his wife were due to arrive any moment but, as things stood, there was no way they would be able to enter. On Jawahar's orders, policemen had attempted to open the great door but with a mighty roar the crowds tried to rush in and the men were forced to put their shoulders to the door and heave it closed again. Jawahar went out via a side door with Sardar Patel and other members of his Cabinet to try to ease the situation. Another roar, another barrage of people. Everyone wanted their piece of history, to touch Nehru or Patel, to shake their hands. For a moment, both men were lost, drowned in the crowd. I was afraid a riot would break out. The policemen were hitting out with curses, grins and lathis. Miraculously, sufficient order was eventually restored for Dickie and Edwina to be able to get inside.

The speeches began. Sitting a long way from the dais, I heard them in fragments, like a disrupted radio broadcast with the static coming from the buzzing of the fans and the noise of the crowd. Dr Prasad read out a series of congratulatory messages from all over the world but forgot the message from President Truman. It was left to the American Ambassador to cough and splutter loudly in order to rectify the situation. When Dickie got up to speak there was the usual prelude of flashing photographers' bulbs. He conveyed the message from the King and paid tribute to the leadership of Patel and Nehru. But it was his solicitude for the Mahatma that drew the loudest cheers and it was sometime before he could continue. He finished with a promise to leave by April 1948 and stated that no pressure whatsoever would be brought on India to stay in the Commonwealth: that would be entirely India's own decision. Then it was back to Prasad who gave a lengthy address, speaking first in Hindi and then in English. His speech was mostly inaudible in either language, but at the end a few sentences emerged loudly and clearly:

Let us gratefully acknowledge, whilst our achievement is in no small measure due to our own sufferings and sacrifices, it is also the result of world forces and events, and last though not least it is the consummation and fulfilment of the historic traditions and ideals of the British race. The period of domination of Britain over India ends today, and our relationship with Britain is henceforward going to rest on a basis of equality, of mutual goodwill and mutual profit.

And thus the day went on with a crazy momentum of its own. Alan, ever with an eye for public relations, had scheduled the Mountbattens to meet five thousand school children gathered at the Roshanara Gardens so that they could give out sweets. The atmosphere there was akin to that of a gigantic afternoon fête. There was singing, dancing, a red-and-gold merry-go-round and a whole host of stalls and sideshows, including a near naked fakir. As we passed, the man appeared to gleefully bite off the head of a snake. The children had all turned out in their best clothes. The girls, with bright ribbons in their pigtails and plaits, were unfazed by the heat. They giggled and cheered in the hope that Edwina might come over and talk to them. When she did, they offered her little posies of flowers, brown paper bags of nuts, fruit, and pencil drawings. I followed in her wake. She piled the flowers and sweets into my arms until I was weighed down like a donkey and had to start handing the gifts out again.

Then it was back to Government House in the late afternoon for a quick tidy before I needed to be on parade again. This time it was at Princes Park for the flag raising. I was in the ladies' party with Fay Campbell-Johnson and Ronnie Brockman's wife, Marjorie. We were greeted by smiling young air force officers proudly heading their various white-taped lanes. I heaved a sigh of relief when they gave us tickets for our designated seats in the stands. But as soon as we entered the arena and headed for what were supposed to be the reserved areas, the illusion of order collapsed into unfettered confusion. In the stands there were easily four or five people on every chair, perched on the arms, on the backs, upon each other—men, women and children of every age and caste. We were swallowed up by the happiest of human hubbubs, all fixed on one prize. Their aim was to get to the tiny island on which stood the flagpole. Desperately, I held on to Fay's arm and we pushed forward together.

'The BBC van,' she shouted as she tried to hold on to Marjorie. But she was spun away from us by the momentum of the crowd and disappeared into the maelstrom.

'Make way for the Memsahibs,' someone shouted and for a few yards our passage was a little easier. But some fool was trying to ride a bike and the back wheel came between Fay and me. In the end, she too was torn away.

Everyone was smiling and laughing, including me. I was being pushed and shoved, battered and bruised, but I didn't mind a bit!

'Jai Hind, Jai Panditji,' people shouted. Nehru had hauled himself up on to the central platform only to launch himself off again. There was another roar as they held him up. He walked on one shoulder to another, took the topi off one man and banged it down on the head of another. For once, my height was an advantage and I could see that he was moving to try and rescue Pamela Mountbatten. She, like me, had got caught in the swirling crowd. At that moment, I was trapped by an ebbing current. It dragged me around and away from both the flagpole and the BBC van where I saw that Marjorie and Fay had both managed to find refuge. The crowd roared again and rotated on its axis like a giant wheel. I glimpsed the ADCs in white, followed by the fluttering lance pennants of the Governor General's bodyguard, then the carriage with Edwina and Dickie and more bodyguards and horses.

Taking a leaf out of Jawahar's book I removed my high-heeled shoes and started to walk over and through people. At first, I clambered over knees and then over shoulders as people lifted me up.

Hari saw me first and he waved and shouted from his horse. But I didn't recognize him.

'Pipeee! Pippeee!'

At the back of the cavalry was a group of men dressed for polo. They were wearing brightly coloured turbans wrapped dramatically in assorted styles. Two of them were waving at me now, beckoning to me, urging me over. The crowd saw them and shouted encouragement to me.

'Make way for the Memsahib!'

I recognized the horses first and then the men: Hari and Sunny. They were heading the group of riders from the Polo Club.

'Jai Hind, Mountbatten ki jai, Pandit Mountbatten!' The crowd was jumping, waving and chanting itself into a frenzy.

'Come on!' Hari reached out while Sunny bellowed affectionate abuse at the crowd in Hindi, eliciting more laughter.

'Jai Hind!'

Hari had me by the hand.

'The stirrup, put your foot in the stirrup!' He had taken his foot out to free it for me. Someone shoved me unceremoniously on my behind and pushed me up into the front of the saddle. I landed half on and half off Hari's lap, my skirt hoisted high above my knees. No one minded, no one cared, and everyone cheered.

'Jai Hind, Memsahib ki jai!'

'Jai Hind,' I shouted.

'England ki jai!' they roared back.

The light was fading and soft rain began to fall. It felt like a benediction after the searing heat of the day and we lifted our faces in thanks. From my vantage point I watched Jawahar trying to reason with the crowd. He was valiantly trying to clear a way for the Mountbattens to go from the landau to the dais for the flag raising. When words failed, he kicked out, threw a few punches and banged yet more topis on heads for good measure. But it was all to no avail, so in the end he gave up and climbed into the landau to join them. The order was given and the Indian flag was raised, saffron, white and green. Dickie stood to give the salute from the back of the carriage, and just at that moment, as if by magic, a rainbow appeared in the sky.

Up in the saddle, Hari and I readjusted our positions as best we could. He retained the stirrups and the reins. There were about a dozen or so men in the troop. Young men and veterans from the Polo Club, they had informally augmented the ranks of the Governor General's bodyguard. As the procession moved off, we kept tight ranks so as not to be broken up by the crowd. Unable to get back to his car, Jawahar was sitting cross-legged on the hood of the Mountbattens' carriage. The people in the crowd nearest to the horses tried to push back and keep their distance, but with thousands behind them eager to press forward, they were in danger of falling beneath the carriage wheels or the horses' hooves. Next to me a young woman in a purple sari with a baby was pushed up against a horse. Her smiles and laughter turned to screams of terror. She tried to save herself but she couldn't because she had no free hands. Hari's horse started to spook and it took all his skill to keep the animal steady. At the last moment, the woman, who must have been no older than sixteen, shoved the baby into my arms. I watched helplessly as she disappeared into the crowd. I held the child, a grubby little boy with kohl around his eyes, but I worried that I would never see the mother again.

'Catch her! That woman! For God's sake, don't let her go.' Sunny had turned around in his saddle and was madly gesticulating to the younger men behind. One of them managed to haul the woman up on to his horse. She sat there like a fragile rag doll in his arms, half hiding her face with the pallu of her sari and waving shyly to me.

By the time we'd returned the baby to his mother and brought the horses back to the Club, where it had been insisted that we dine, it was late. Before dropping me off at Government House, Hari took me to his home. He wanted me to meet his daughter and grandsons whom he had managed to evacuate by air from Lahore five days ago. As we drove along, he told me that after his arrival in Lahore, Sapna's husband and father-in-law had hastily negotiated a house swap with a Muslim business associate in Delhi. Three days ago he and his daughter had been to inspect the property and the deal, such as it was, had been finalized. The Muslim family had already left for Pakistan and he was paying for a guard for the house in the interim. His daughter's husband and father-in-law were still holed up at Lahore airport but they had secured flights that were due to leave the next day.

The heavy iron gates to Hari's house were closed. Hari honked the horn three times and we waited. A few minutes later the left-hand gate swung open a foot or so and an elderly Sikh man peered out cautiously. Hari waved a hand and both gates were opened. As we drove in I saw half a dozen or so men of different ages in pyjamas. They were armed with an assortment of cricket bats and hockey sticks. The nails they had hammered into them glinted in the car headlights like Christmas tinsel.

As far as I could make out, Hari's house was very similar in style to Jawahar's bungalow except that there were tents all over the garden.

'It comes to something when Muslim patients are not safe in our hospitals, when thugs and hoodlums choose to prey on the sick and injured. I've taken in those whom I can. I've some patients downstairs, and upstairs there are new Hindu refugees from my son-in-law's family in the Punjab. It's not ideal, but so far, here at least, the peace has held.' He placed a hand on the small of my back. A tall young woman with a shawl over her pyjamas came out on to the portico and stood there with her arms folded. Her long hair was twisted into a plait which tumbled to the front over her left shoulder. I recognized her from the photograph. Hari snatched his hand away from my back but it was too late. She had seen, seen whatever it was that was between us, even if we ourselves didn't know what it might be. She gave a tiny gasp, her eyes widened and she looked first at her father and then at me.

'Sapna, this is Lady Wallace. I was telling you about her.' Hari sniffed in embarrassment. Awkwardly, I joined my hands and greeted her with a namaste.

Sapna hesitated, then shyly offered me her hand which I shook.

The house smelled of cinnamon, cumin, milk and sugar. Someone had been making cakes, but the party, if there had been one, was over. There were bodies everywhere: in the hallway and in the sitting room which had been laid out with camp beds and charpoys in the manner of a hospital ward. Every available space was occupied with someone sleeping, a cloth bag, a small suitcase, a cardboard box—people's lives packed up in a hurry. For the second time that day, I removed my shoes and we tiptoed through the hall to the back of the house. The Sikh servant, Sandeep, came with us. His limp made its irregular thump on the boards which disturbed such sleepy silence as there was. An old man coughed and opened his eyes; even in the gloom I could see they were misty with cataracts. He had wrapped himself in a flowery red blanket and his bare feet, sticking out of the bottom, resembled those of a large crow. A set of false teeth grinned fiercely in a metal cup by his head. Hari touched him on the shoulder as if he were on a ward round.

'Got back to sleep, Chacha. All is well.'

We sat on rattan chairs in the garden, looking up at the stars. After the cheering and shouting of the day our ears were ringing with the silence. Sandeep brought tea and little sweets with pistachio nuts which I nibbled at politely but for which I had no appetite. Just over two years ago I was sitting in my garden in Argyll Road on a night not too different from this one. It was Victory in Europe Day and the streets of London were overflowing with people rejoicing. But with two sons dead and an ailing husband, I had not felt able to celebrate. Now, as I sipped my tea in India, I had a vision of countless displaced people all over the Punjab and Bengal: of families separated; children, mothers, fathers, brothers, sisters, missing or dead; people sleeping on strangers' floors, in refugee camps or under the stars. They had lost everything in the haste to transfer power. Until tomorrow, when Radcliffe's Award would be announced, none of them would have any idea of where the boundary between India and Pakistan might lie or what their future might hold.

Hari snipped the end of a cigar and lit it. Tipping his head back, he inhaled deeply and puffed the smoke slowly into the night. Someone in the neighbourhood set off some fireworks.

Little fountains of silver, purple, orange and green banged and
fizzed into the night.

'Papa, I thought you said you'd stop smoking when India
was free.'

Sapna, bless her, tried to lighten our mood.

Hari chuckled.

'Yes, Daughter, but not tonight. Tomorrow, darling,
tomorrow, I will stop.'

Sapna took me upstairs to see the children. Curly-haired, as
I guessed their grandfather had once been, they were sleeping
together in a double bed. The elder one was lying with limbs
akimbo. The younger one was making little suckling noises
with his mouth and clinging on to a ragged blue elephant
that was worn out with love. They had kicked off the sheet.
I couldn't help myself—I reached out and stroked their feet.
Then, together with Sapna, I replaced the sheet. Two women,
mothers, we stood at the head of the bed, listening to the
children breathing.

'My father said you also had two boys ...' She stopped not
needing to say more.

'Yes.' I replied. 'But they are with me no more.' My eye
fell on the rocking chair at the head of the bed and on a pair of
knitting needles that had been stuck into a ball of red wool and
left on the seat. I imagined Sapna had been sitting here earlier
that night, waiting for her father.

'You've been knitting?'

She picked up the needles and wool from the chair and
handed the work to me. Half of the back of a child's jumper
had already been knitted.

'Something from nothing,' I whispered, fingering her neat
stitches.

She nodded. 'Delhi winters are cold. I found this old wool
of my mother's when I got here. It's calming. It keeps my mind
off ...' A tear rolled down her cheek to her chin and dropped to

the floor where it darkened the rug. More tears followed. She tried to choke them back and I took her in my arms.

After a while, she said, 'Don't tell Papa I was crying. He says it's bad for the boys.'

'Don't worry. I won't say a thing.' I wished that I too could cry, but I was arid inside. My tears had dried up a long time ago.

Back in the garden Hari was restless.

'Let's go over and see the Bharat Bhushan. He must be back by now.

'Maybe,' I hedged. 'There was a big reception at Viceroy's ... I mean Government House this evening. I was supposed to be there.'

'Instead you spent it with me and my family?'

'Yes. I suppose I did. It just happened.'

He put his arm around my shoulders and led me to the back of the garden. We went through a little archway where he switched on a light in the wall.

'My swimming pool. My little indulgence in life. Can't live without it you know! Usually I keep it full all year round, but with all the strangers in the house I thought it better to drain it. On top of everything else, I don't want a drowning.'

A heavy green tarpaulin had been drawn over the pool and carefully tied and weighed down with bricks. Hari sighed. 'Everyone in Delhi thinks I'm barking mad. I even swim in the winter. Filthy British habit I acquired as a medical student in London. Then, I used to go swimming in the Serpentine! But now it just serves to remind an old man that he's still alive.' He gave me an affectionate squeeze and tried to pull me closer but he knew I was tense.

'What is it?'

'Hari, I need to ask you something.'

'Fire away.'

'Goldie. What is there between you? She and I had a run-in that day at Sunny Singh's. I need to know.'

'Ah! That.' He exhaled some stale tobacco breath. 'It's complicated. She's divorced . . . Well, not really. Separated, I suppose, divorced that is, in a peculiar Indian way. It was a scandal for a while. But I always thought that if the two of them had managed to work out a modus vivendi whereby they didn't end up murdering each other, and could pretend to be a happily married couple when occasion demanded, jolly good for them. Her husband lives in Bombay with his mistress, while she lives her own life very comfortably here in Delhi. Despite the gossip, or perhaps because of it, Goldie's parties are quite the place to be seen. After my wife died, Goldie was kind to me, took me under her wing if you like. I suppose I was flattered. My wife had been so pious and here was a famous beauty—what did she see in this duffer of an old medic? One thing led to another, but I soon came to see that she wasn't for me. Charming, stunningly beautiful, but she was only interested in shopping and being seen in all the right places with all the right people.' He sat down heavily on a deck chair and I perched on the foot of a sun lounger next to him.

'Once, we went for tea at a friend's house. Goldie brought her own blend and proceeded to lecture our host's wife on how to make tea: the correct temperature for the water and the exact height for pouring and so on. And Goldie would only drink her own special tea. Utterly ridiculous, of course. A woman like her has never made a cup of tea in her life! That was the last straw for me and we had a huge row. But she wouldn't let go; every day there was a barrage of letters and telephone calls, even suicide threats.'

'And now?' I was not ready to let him off the hook just yet.

'It's over, Pippi, I promise. I'm only sorry you got caught up in the aftermath. She's found someone else to worship her. Someone much richer and more successful than I am, who is happy to take her to New York and Paris. But she's cross with me for encouraging and supporting her daughter in her medical ambitions. Well-born Hindu girls are meant only for marriage. They're not supposed to soil their hands with work.'

He stood up and unnecessarily smoothed down his jodhpurs.

'As I said to you at Qutb Minar, I am not very good with women. Perhaps I am better alone.'

He took my hand and waited for me to withdraw it but I didn't. He led me through a hole in the wall at the back of the pool area which was connected to a narrow passage between several gardens. The trees were blocking the light from the stars. I couldn't see to put one foot in front of the other, but he knew where we were going and I followed him.

After a minute or so we emerged into the back of 17, York Road. Light streamed out of the windows on to the lawn. We heard Jawahar first, shouting in Hindi, and then saw him in his study. He was holding the telephone and gesticulating wildly for the benefit of an audience on the other end of the line. Through the open French windows, he caught sight of us holding hands and beckoned us in. Face tense with worry and anger, he delivered one last tirade and slammed down the receiver.

'Lahore,' he whispered, holding out his arms to embrace first me and then Hari. 'Lahore is burning. Our freedom will mean nothing if this is to be the price.'

PART III

Exodus
21st September 1947 to end November 1947

$\mathcal{E}$dwina, Jawahar and I were squeezed into the cockpit of the Governor General's Dakota, squinting as it flew towards the sun. Far below, churning up clouds of dust and snaking all the way to the horizon were lines of refugees. Our inspection party to assess the refugee situation in the Punjab was made up of staff from the Governor General's office as well as from the office of the new Indian Prime Minister.

Jawahar had his arm around Edwina's shoulders. He was gripping the top of her arm so tightly that his knuckles were white. He had hardly let go of her all day and had clung to her hand. We had all seen. It was as if she propped him up, and without her he could not go on.

'Shall I take her down, sir?' The pilot addressed the Prime Minister. But Jawahar had no voice. He merely nodded and folded his chin to his chest to disguise his anguish.

The pitch of the engine changed as we descended, the dial counting down to 200 feet. There were two columns of refugees passing each other on either side of the road. One was made up of Muslims walking out of India and into Pakistan. In the other, Sikhs and Hindus were coming out of the East Punjab and making for Delhi. Staring down at the endless lines of people, my first ridiculous impression was of rush hour in Oxford Street. But instead of cars and buses there were lumbering bullock carts, herds of cattle and hundreds and thousands of trudging nameless people who were not going home. As we flew overhead, they craned their necks and looked up at our plane, shading their eyes against the sun. I wondered if they still had faith. Part of me hoped that they did not. For if they were looking to us—the gods, the new ones and the old ones, peering down from above—for salvation, they would be disappointed. It was only too evident that the scale of the communal violence and migration was beyond our powers to control.

As the sun began to set, we flew over Balloki Head, the actual border. The bottleneck of refugees floods resembled a white river over the plain. A small shanty town had sprung up. The refugees were jostling and pushing to get over the bridge which had not been built in contemplation of such an exodus. Men on horses were riding up and down the densely packed lines. Cattle had been abandoned because they couldn't be herded across the bridge. It was difficult to make out much amid the chaos, but as the pilot banked the plane and turned it towards the coming night, I saw an old purdah carriage. It had bright red and orange curtains and was lying on its side. Next to it a young child sat alone, apparently abandoned by the side of the road.

Back in the cabin of the Dakota, most of the rest of the party were asleep. Amrit Kaur, now the Health Minister in Jawahar's Cabinet, sat behind me, next to Lord Ismay. They were snoring in soft unison. Edwina too was exhausted, her head slumped on Jawahar's shoulder. It seemed that only Jawahar and I were still awake.

He was calm now, impassive, his eyelids hooded, flickering slightly as he read *The Little Clay Cart*. I recalled him at the largest of the camps we had visited on this trip. It was just over the border in the West Punjab, full of Hindus and Sikhs who had been driven out of their homes in Pakistan. They were waiting for onward transport to Delhi. Gone were the joyous, cheering crowds of the 15th of August. A large group, made up mainly of men, had greeted Jawaharlal Nehru, the Jewel of the Nation, in stony silence. Quiet at first, the crowd had quickly become restless and started to seethe as he moved among them. Anger and hatred quickly bubbled to the surface in hisses, boos and bitter murmuring.

Then someone shouted, 'Nehru Murdabad!' and another threw the first stone.

Jawahar turned white, a flurry of emotions on his face, realization followed by shock, fury and terror. There were no bodyguards so we were on our own. Grabbing Edwina by the hand, he snatched a stick from a young man in the crowd and weighed it visibly in his right hand.

'Oh my god! They are going to stone him to death,' Amrit Kaur shouted, seizing my arm. We were standing just behind Jawahar and Edwina. Another stone, and another; the little ones fell like hail.

'Keep smiling,' I hissed to her, urging, 'do as Edwina does.'

And that's what we did, gritting our teeth into smiles, acting as if nothing was amiss. Edwina offered a hand or a namaste to people in the crowd. She continued having a little word here, another one there, and cocked her head charmingly from one side to the other, all the while dragging Nehru and his stick along with her. In that way she led him, and us, to the safety of the camp commandant's hut. She had saved the day.

As I sat in the gloom of the aircraft cabin, a wave of anger built inside me. It came to me as white, boiling dust, tight in my chest, and rose rising higher and higher until I felt sure I would choke on it. As my eyeballs pulsed with fury, I stared at my hands balled into fists. They rested on my notebook in which I had written strings of useless shorthand notes, the usual ones: names and more names, of loved ones lost, of supplies required, blankets, clothes, tents, lentils and fresh vegetables for the children, powdered milk, saline, cholera vaccines, standpipes, water tanks.

In my mind everything was dust. There was no escaping it: in the camps, on the roads, in the tents, in our office and even in Government House. It was as if a great veil had come down to obscure our vision. It was here now, in the cabin, circulating like autumn mist in the dim light. It was thick in my hair and grey over my shoes and socks. It was inlaid in the seams of my St John's Ambulance uniform, and encrusted my papers, maps and notebooks. I had taken out my comb to brush my hair, then dusted off my skirt, but it had all been to no avail. Dust. It drained the colour from my memory.

In the camps, seas of white tents stretched as far as the eye could see. The canvas flaps were strangely still, for there was no breeze, and the false clouds that promised rain rose high in the sky as the soldiers dug pits and emptied sacks of lime over a pile of corpses. All of it was playing in black and white like a newsreel. Rationally, I knew there was colour in insanity, hatred, suffering, war and disease. But it was as if my mind had chosen to dilute the memory and, to protect itself, bleached itself clean.

I balled my fists tighter in an effort to contain my rage, my nails pressing into my flesh. My anger was beyond words. I knew that I would never be able to even begin to express it in my notebooks or diaries. Everything flashed in my mind like a series of camera snapshots. In the camps, thousands of brown eyes, emptied by despair, looking at me. Gandhi spinning, the sunlight falling from the window to frame a halo around him. Jinnah with Miss Jinnah who had worn diaphanous purple in the Rose Garden at Viceroy's House. Dickie inspecting the troops in naval whites, his medals glinting in the sun. Jawahar, the rose in his buttonhole, sitting doe-eyed at Edwina's feet.

Words jumbled with emotions in my mind. They led to the sinking sense of utter futility that I knew only too well, and of which I was so afraid. I forced myself to get up and go to the back of the cabin.

As I approached Jawahar he lifted his eyes from his book. Setting it down, he tenderly supported Edwina's head, laid it back against her own seat and covered her with her fox fur. He found me in the tiny makeshift galley where I was attempting to calm myself by pouring tea. I had the thermos flask in my hand and he picked up another cup for himself and held it out to me. My hand trembled with emotion as the liquid glugged temptingly out of the glistening silver innards of the flask. It steamed softly in the cold air.

'Any sugar?' he mouthed against the grinding roar of the engines. Sugar was not his preference or mine. Yet I found some and dropped two spoonfuls into his cup. Leaning back on the bulkhead, he absently clinked the spoon. In the dim cabin light I was shocked to see how haggard Jawahar had become. In the few weeks since Independence, the handsome, youthful Jawahar, always so popular with the ladies, had aged twenty years. His cheeks were hollow, eyes dark and sunken, his hair had greyed and he was balding on top. Exhausted, spent, used up, he had become a man who had witnessed the destruction of his life's work. I picked up my own cup and added sugar too. Leaning against the cold, vibrating bulkhead next to him, I stirred my tea, imagining the thousands and thousands of tiny grains dissolving into nothing. Far below us was yet another column of refugees. This time it was marked out by pillars of fire rising from cooking fires into the night.

$\mathcal{L}$ightning tore the sky, which, although it was still day, was as black as night. Thunder boomed and the rain poured down, the drops so large that they bounced like coins. And the whole torrent overflowed in waterfalls from the gutters of Government House in Delhi. At last the temperature dipped and the humidity rose. But this year no one had celebrated the arrival of the monsoon.

Dear Margaret, I wrote, then put down my pen. I stared up at a patch of damp in the corner of the room, already black with mould from previous rains. What would I tell her? That the new India was in desperate straits and that the battle for Delhi was on? That half a million refugees were converging on the capital with nowhere to be housed and nothing to eat? At least fifty thousand Muslims had fled their homes in the city, fearing for their lives, and were holed up for safety in the old mediaeval fort of Purana Qila. Perhaps I could tell her that there had been a complete collapse of law and order in Delhi and in the Punjab. That on our daily hospital inspections Edwina and I had had to dodge snipers' bullets and pick up dead bodies from the streets and take them to the mortuary. Or that trains carrying refugees from both sides had been ambushed, and their human cargoes—men, women and children—had been massacred like cattle by gangs in a frenzy of inter-communal madness. To make matters worse, the normally strong Delhi Garrison had been so depleted, having mostly been deployed to contain riots in the Gurgaon area, that the city had been left virtually unprotected, and the Governor General had had to put his own bodyguard at the disposal of the Garrison Commander. And finally, perhaps I ought to mention that the two new Dominions were on the verge of going to war over the state of Junagadh? With a majority Hindu population and completely surrounded by other states that had acceded to India, the Muslim Dewan there had decided to throw in his lot with Jinnah and Pakistan.

I sighed and shook my head in an attempt to clear it. The sound like buzzing bees in my ears, the smell of lavender, and bittersweet bile, tasting of summer, of raspberries, iron, rust and blood, rose in my mouth. I wrote none of it. All I knew was that I did my best, from hour to hour, from day to day. Each vaccine provided, each blanket dispatched, each little life saved represented a small victory in a war against I knew not what. Against insanity, against the demons within myself? Perhaps both.

And yet they claimed it was not a civil war, even though it felt like one. I couldn't tell Margaret that Prime Minister Nehru and Deputy Prime Minister Patel had invited Dickie as the Governor General to chair an Emergency Committee to deal with the crisis and that he had agreed, provided that the fact was not made public. The committee, made up of Nehru, Patel and key members of the Cabinet, had been meeting on every second day. The Indian men grim-faced, at the end of their tethers; Dickie, calm and in control, for it was no longer really his fight. Nor could I tell her that Dickie had reinstated his old wartime South East Asian Command procedures; daily briefings and a command and control map room to plot the flow of refugees and identify trouble spots. It would be equally impossible to tell her that there was real fear that in the chaos Delhi would be lost. I knew that less than a month after Independence the new government could be forced to evacuate the capital and that if Delhi fell, India would be finished.

Eventually I picked up my pen and wrote slowly, without interest or passion.

The situation here is pretty grim, as you have no doubt read in the papers. But we are holding up well. The general consensus amongst outgoing and new governments alike is that we all have to do our bit to uphold authority wherever and whenever we can. Edwina really is a trouper and an inspiration to us all. A new United Council for Relief and Welfare has been set up which she chairs. It brings together fifteen organizations to pool their efforts and really is a tribute to her initiative and drive. She never takes no for an answer. Only yesterday she stood up for her case, insisting to Nehru that the provision of milk powder for infants should be a Government responsibility and not dumped on her Council and charities. Needless to say the poor fellow, startled by her affectionate onslaught, had to back down!

Again, I paused. I was tired, my words limp and lame. Margaret would have to remain ignorant of the fact that the two lakhs of funding for the Council had come from Sardar Patel's budget and had been facilitated by Edwina's friendship with Jawahar. I scratched my head.

Despite it all there are bright spots in the darkness. I cling to the hope that cool heads and common sense will prevail. We are getting a lot of help in relief work from so many unexpected quarters: the Chinese, the Canadians, the wider diplomatic and the religious communities. Even my dressmaker has pitched in. She has turned out to be a quite a Mrs Fix-It, sourcing all sorts of supplies from heaven knows where! And in our trials it should not be forgotten that Bengal, which has been a hotbed of riot and inter-communal butchery, is relatively quiet. This is thanks to Mr Gandhi and the former Prime Minister of Bengal Mr Suhrawardy. One a Hindu, the other a Muslim—together they have worked nothing short of a miracle in Calcutta to keep the peace.

The telephone on my desk rang. One, two, three, four, then I picked it up.

'Good afternoon, Lady Wallace,' tut tut, swallow. 'It's Eira, tut, Prichard.' I reached for the accounts ledger for the United Council for Refugees and Welfare; a neat black book embossed the crest of the Imperial Bank of India with its two lions.

We sped quickly through the platitudes. For my part I informed Mrs Pritchard that Lady Mountbatten was visiting camps in the Punjab with Amrit Kaur.

A series of awkward tut tut, swallows followed, more than the usual and almost to the point where I thought I could actually smell peppermint coming down the line.

'Do you want the good news or the bad news first?' asked Mrs Pritchard.

'Good news,' I said without hesitation.

'The blankets and shoes for the refugees have arrived from Bombay. We have them in the warehouse in Delhi and can deliver them tomorrow.'

'That's great. Lady Mountbatten will be pleased. I will arrange final payment straight away.' I looked down at the ledger entries.

Bombay Milliner's Company: Blankets, Rs 529.

Bata Shoe Company: 10,000 canvas shoes, Rs 5,000.

Tut tut, swallow. Tut tut, swallow.

'And the bad news?'

There was a long pause.

'I've had it out of Simla. There's terrible, it is. Filthy Sikhs on motorbikes tearing down The Mall, firing at anyone and anything. I didn't want to tell you, see, tut, until I had confirmed it. But some customers of mine were evacuated to Delhi and I had it from them and it's in the paper too, it is.'

'What is?'

Tut tut, swallow. 'Mrs Ovington. Poor dear. She's shot herself.' Tut tut, swallow. 'There's terrible.' A sniff, and I realized that Mrs Pritchard was crying. 'Her bearer said she took her pre-dinner gin gimlet down to the end of the garden to watch the sunset as usual. When he heard the shot he went running, but it was too late.' Tut tut, swallow, sobs. 'It was with her husband's revolver, they say. They were making repatriation arrangements, you see, for Simla residents to go . . . home . . .'

I heard but I didn't hear. The bees were buzzing once more on the lavender. Her words had landed in my mind with a dull thud, as if they were insulated behind thick board.

'Yes. I see. I'm so sorry.' I asked about the funeral.

'They had it in Simla last week. Not much time. They were all evacuating, and there it is, so it is.' Tut tut, swallow.

I put down the receiver. Lighting a cigarette, I thought about Mrs Ovington, her dog, the peace of the mountains and her gnarled and twisted fingers hooked painfully round the handle of her bone china teacup. And in the background, my own voice echoed around the rocky outcrops of my grief, 'Where will I go? What will I do?'

*M*ajor General Pete Rees, head of the Governor General's military emergency staff, was not afraid of getting his hands dirty. He had the bonnet of the car up and was checking the oil with the Gurkha rifleman. Now he was fiddling with the string on the plaques bearing the Governor General's Crown which were tied on to the front and back bumpers of the old Buick 8. It was a rental car out of the pool.

'How's that?'

'Left hand down a bit . . . there.'

He fastened the string, straightened and patted the couple of strands of hair that remained on his pate. In that moment I saw it, a flash of it, exhaustion and disillusionment. We were all feeling it, but he had hidden it better than most.

'That's better. Can't have you going about the place with wonky crowns!'

I smiled, but pulled nervously at the tops of my white gloves and smoothed down the skirt of my St John's ambulance khakis. I had made an effort for this afternoon, curling my hair under my cap and applying lipstick. Zamurad Khan had had my uniform cleaned, pressed and re-pressed. All this I had learnt from Edwina, and I didn't want to let her down.

'Lady Wallace, you don't have to do this.' Pete's eyes were kind, his voice soft with a subtle hint of Welsh about it. It reminded me with a pang of my father.

'I know, but the refugee situation in Purana Qila is dire. Lady Mountbatten was most keen that I should go in her place as soon as possible.'

His eyes narrowed and he peered down the bridge of his hawk-like nose.

'That's as may be, but you need to be aware that Purana Qila has become a fortified Muslim ghetto. It is not just women and children who have taken refuge in the fort. There are armed men too. The place is bristling with weapons. The other day, Patel was all for sending in a battalion to clear out the armed Muslims. God knows who put that idea into his head. It's a sure way to provoke a massacre.'

'I'll be fine,' I insisted. 'I am on a humanitarian mission representing Lady Mountbatten and the United Council for Relief and Welfare. I am going in at the request of the Purana Qila Medical Committee.'

Pete Rees sighed and adjusted his belt.

'Well, I don't like it. You're not going to Purana Qila alone. I'm sending Captain Fraser of the 6th Gurkhas with you. He's one of the best. He'll look after you. I've also got two armoured personnel carriers in the vicinity, just in case.'

Sitting in the back of the Buick 8 with the taciturn Captain Fraser, my confidence ebbed. Only three days ago a delegation from the Delhi City Health Department had had to abort a visit to the Muslim refugee camp at the last minute for fear of their lives. Such was the suspicion and distrust between Muslims and Hindus that it was seriously hampering relief efforts. Why had I agreed to this? For the refugees? Or had it been for Edwina? Or perhaps for Hari? Or had it really been for myself?

Yesterday morning Hari had rung me on behalf of a former Muslim colleague of his, Dr Tariq Ali, who had volunteered to go to Pakistan and had found himself holed up in the Purana Qila camp. The Indian government had temporarily stopped refugee trains from Delhi to Pakistan because of the massacres en route. As a result, more and more people had come to the camp with nobody knowing how long they would be there. They really were on their own, Doctor Ali had told Hari, with no meaningful help forthcoming from either government. And any Hindus or Sikhs who came near the camp, even well-meaning ones, were likely to have their throats cut. In light of the deteriorating nature of the Purana Qila situation, Dr Ali had wondered whether Lady Mountbatten might visit as a neutral party to help organize aid. Since Edwina was in the Punjab, it was agreed that I would go in her place rather than wait for her return.

Approaching the fort, we passed a little lake which acted as a semi-moat. I stared up at the massive ramparts, and realized that the elevated site covered quite some acres and was more like a small walled city. The car turned up the hill towards the main gate with its bastions of red sandstone topped by ornamental canopied turrets. Parts of the ancient stonework had tumbled down, and grass and trees now grew in the gaps. The mid-afternoon heat and monsoon humidity blurred everything around us. The red of the sandstone was washed out in yellow and blue; Turner would have painted it just like that if he had ever come to India, I thought.

Captain Fraser craned his neck to look out of the car window and frowned. He was a man in his early thirties, yet experience and a lifetime in India showed in every sinew of his body. You could see it in the way he held his head, just a little too upright, in his loose marching walk and in the small click he made out of the corner of his mouth at the end of a sentence. He had been formal and minimally polite to me in the way of a professional. I knew that he would do his duty to the last in spite of his evident disgust with the whole situation, specifically his mission to nanny me. If I had asked him, he would no doubt have blamed the Viceroy for his haste in winding up two-hundred-plus years of British Raj in barely three months.

Frowning, he said something in Gurkhali to the havildar who was sitting in the front seat next to the rifleman driver. The havildar responded by pointing out several strategic points on the ramparts.

'Snipers and machine gun posts.' Captain Fraser translated for my benefit but I was hardly reassured.

The driver honked the horn. Our way up to the gate of the fort had been blocked by streams of refugees with their baggage, tongas, bullock carts, and lines of jeeps picking people up, dropping people off, delivering supplies. There were even a couple of camels. The monsoon rains had reduced the unmade road to mud. Wheels were spinning, tempers flaring, camels grunting, and it was obvious that there was no way through. My heart sank as I suggested we get out and walk. There was no sign of Hari's friend, the Chairman of the Purana Qila Medical Committee, who was supposed to have met us.

Slipping and sliding in the mud, skirting puddles and stray dogs, Captain Fraser and I picked our way nervously uphill.

'Lady Wallace! Lady Wallace!' At first there was just a hand waving beyond the white awnings of the jeeps, dancing like a fairground puppet above people's heads. It descended at a pace from the gate towards us, until at last it emerged from the chaos, bringing with it a portly man. He was running helter-skelter towards us with galoshes and black pin-striped trousers rolled up to his knees. Watching him half-jumping, half-skipping the puddles, I feared he would not be able to stop and would slip and slide all the way to the bottom of the hill.

'Tariq Ali.' He held out his hand which I grabbed as he wobbled on the edge of a large puddle like an egg. 'I am so pleased to see you! Dr Rathore promised me, he promised me you would come. Thank you! Thank you so much!'

My heart sank with the weight of his expectations.

I told him that Lady Mountbatten was very sorry that she couldn't come herself and that she had asked me to give him her best wishes. I added that we would do what we could to help.

Pausing to catch his breath, he pulled out a crumpled handkerchief from his pocket and used it to wipe the sweat from his face. A man of about sixty, with plump round cheeks and a bald head, he had somehow managed to retain the innocent look of a boy. Amazingly, he was clean-shaven despite the circumstances.

'The rest of the Committee is waiting inside. I do apologize. They won't come out. They're afraid. But if you ask me, the worst of it is within ourselves.'

As we passed under the great red sandstone arch into the fort, the stench of human excrement took our breath away. But we did not get far. We were stopped by a group of half a dozen or so bearded men brandishing an assortment of rifles and revolvers. A hostile crowd quickly gathered around us and an exchange followed that I did not understand. Dr Ali remained calm and soft-spoken in response to their barrage of questions. I made no attempt to intervene for in relief work the best results were always achieved by rising above politics. But it soon became apparent that Dr Ali was losing his case and that we would be turned away. Suddenly, a torrent of Urdu came from Captain Fraser at my side. Taken aback, the simultaneously amused and bemused young men relaxed their grip on their rifles, and their angry faces seemed to soften a little under their beards. They argued a little more for the sake of it, but, miraculously, then chose to let us through.

'Well done! How did you manage that?' I whispered to Captain Fraser.

He shrugged and waggled his head with a modest smile. 'Didn't think I was from Dundee, did you? My family are the Frasers of Quetta. Urdu, Pushtu and whatnot. I generally get by.'

Dr Ali led us up a narrow winding staircase in the eastern bastion. We emerged into what might have been a room in the guardhouse once. There was only one slit window and a paraffin lamp had been placed in the centre of a table, its light

augmented by a few candles. Smoking while they lounged
on a crazy assortment of deck and shooting chairs were the
members of the Purana Qila Medical Committee. Swatting the
flies away from my face, I sat down at the head of the rickety
wooden table. Their faces pressed in and they looked at me with
suspicion. I couldn't blame them. Who was I after all—a white
woman who represented the wife of the Governor General of a
departing colonial power? There were nine of them and I knew
that they were desperate.

Barely a week or two ago they had been successful professional
gentlemen comfortable with their families in middle-class lives.
Now they were refugees, grubby and unshaven, their shirts
unwashed, unironed. They had no idea where their next meal
would come from, if at all, and had been reduced to begging,
living with disease, fear and violence.

    Dr Ali called the meeting to order. There was no point
in beating about the bush. They had no medical supplies to
speak of. The hygiene situation was critical and without swift
intervention there would be a cholera epidemic and thousands
of deaths. I asked if they were registering the refugees. He
said that they were doing their best, but that they needed a
loudspeaker with which to attempt to impose order. They had
asked both governments for one but neither side had responded.
There was a sigh of relief when I told them that the United
Council for Relief and Welfare would supply a loudspeaker as
well as two thousand cholera vaccines plus syringes and needles.
We would deliver on the morrow, with more as needed. Sitting
at my side in the role of ADC, Captain Fraser made a list in
his notebook. This had the effect of triggering the doctor's full
shopping list. They spoke quietly, efficiently, each word heavier,
more hopeless than the last: sulphaguanidine, sulphonamides,
carminative mixture, saline, Dettol, bandages, cotton wool,

aspirin, Lysol, boric acid, Atebrin, gauze, field dressings, silver nitrate, carbolic acid, mepacrine, Argyrol.

'Paraffin oil, feeding cups, milk powder and perhaps a generator, if I can get my hands on one?' I suggested from experience and they nodded.

'And Christian and Anglo-Indian midwives, doctors and nurses.' Dr Ali was sweating with tension and exhaustion. He said, 'We cannot send our women out to hospital and we only have one female Muslim nurse for the whole camp.'

A man pushed back his chair with a dramatic scrape and stood up. He was tall, bespectacled and younger than the rest.

'It's a disgrace, cancelling the trains and leaving us here to die slowly and painfully of hunger and disease,' he shouted. 'What the hell are the governments of India and Pakistan playing at?'

I took a deep breath and told them that while I could not presume to speak for either government, I could assure him that there were good men on both sides. I added that, like all of us around the table, everyone was doing their best and that, like us, they were at the end of their strength.

I got up and said that I thought it would be best if I saw the situation with my own eyes.

We didn't go back to ground level. Instead, Dr Ali led us up to the ramparts. The acrid stench of stale excrement rose on the moist afternoon heat as if from a giant dung heap. I had to bite down to control the reflex to vomit and I told myself to keep breathing, just keep breathing. Forcing my mind to be rational, I tried to assess the scale of the human catastrophe that was playing out below. Purana Qila was rectangular, probably just short of a mile long and half a mile wide. It was surrounded by walls fifteen to twenty feet high. There were only two permanent structures inside the walls, a small hexagonal building and a mosque. The monsoon rains had flooded large portions of the enclosure and reduced the area available for use.

From above it looked like a crude map of a strange world with people marooned on an assortment of continents and islands. In some places the population was so dense that there was no room for anyone to sit down. Men, women and children were forced to stand like gannets crowded together on rocks. Tents of all sizes and descriptions had been erected on drier ground and all around the ramparts. Those who had managed to get a more elevated spot were the most fortunate. From the tents and across the walls hung a limp assortment of clothes and blankets drenched by yesterday's rain.

Mentally, I assessed the area and tried to make a head count. Captain Fraser did the same and briefly we compared notes: Thirty, forty, fifty, sixty thousand? More? Helpless, we stood in silence, watching the swallows as they darted and fluttered along the tops of the walls. An entire makeshift city was laid out in front of us. Yet the myriad people made barely a sound; only the occasional bark of a dog or the wail of a child managed to pierce the thick blanket of fetid air.

Climbing down to ground level, we came across a group of men urinating against the wall. We turned away quickly. Continuing our progress, we balanced on duckboards and squelched over the pieces of newspaper that formed makeshift, largely useless, pontoons over the puddles and mini lakes.

'Watch out!' shouted Dr Ali suddenly as he grabbed my hand and pulled me away from the large human turds that were floating and slowly dissolving in the muddy water.

'We've dug two sets of latrines, but the trouble is that there are no sweepers and they're overflowing. The women, in particular, won't use them.'

'No sweepers?' I queried?

'Yes, Lady Wallace. They were too frightened to come.'

It took me a few seconds to realize what he was getting at. In India, the night soil was usually collected by untouchables, the lowest Hindu caste.

A thread snagged inside me. It frayed and jerked with exhaustion and frustration. Then Hari's warning voice came to me: You can't drain an ocean with a sieve. But I couldn't help myself and I turned on Dr Ali.

'Why don't you clear the worst of it yourselves?' I stared at the shit at my feet, and at the groups of morose men who were standing idly by.

'But we are Muslims, we . . .' He blinked quickly with fatigue and distress.

I shrugged.

'For heaven's sake! Who is going to clear your night soil when you get to Pakistan?'

I knew that I was being rude. Dr Ali had every right to be cross, but he merely shook his head as if I had raised a valid point.

'I don't know. I've never thought of that before.'

'I'm sorry,' I said and told him that I would see about arranging for a contingent of sweepers, perhaps under a Gurkha guard. I looked at Captain Fraser. He had attempted to lock down his face to show no emotion but a muscle in his right cheek was twitching.

He nodded. 'That might be a way forward.'

The women's tent was dark, the heat overpowering, the air rancid. They had opened the flap just far enough to let in sufficient light to function. At first I just saw the whites of their eyes flickering in the darkness. About twenty women sat on the tarpaulin surrounded by small children. They reached up, pulled at my skirt, patted my knees, clasped my hands and would not let go. I hunkered down to talk to them. The pretty young Muslim nurse who was acting as my translator shot me a look of distaste because it obliged her to do the same.

'It's the children. It's the children. They're getting hungry, getting sick.' The women's voices were high-pitched with a metallic timbre. It was a refrain I had heard thousands of times, both in India and in London. And although these were brown faces, thinner, more gaunt and suffering a harsher poverty than their English counterparts, they were not so very different from those white faces in the East End, women who had been bombed out of their houses during the blitz. And then it dawned on me that although Purana Qila was full of children, I had not seen even one at play.

'Vicereine Sahiba, the water is dirty and we have to use it to cook. Just last night a baby died.'

One by one they pushed the children forward, as if I, a white woman in uniform, could offer a miracle cure. Younis, aged two, listless and dehydrated, was running a temperature. Noor, whose hair had been uncombed for days and was falling out of her plaits, had lost one of her green ribbons. She had diarrhoea. As we examined her, her bottom lip quivered and she wept soundlessly, as if she had learnt to stifle her pain. Her mother was too exhausted to offer comfort, and the child was left to rock herself back and forth, back and forth. For the first time during all my relief work both in England and India, I wished that I had not come. In their confusion and despair these simple women had appealed to me as 'Vicereine Sahiba', as if I were an angel descended from heaven. But what good was there in offering hope where there was none to be had?

Allahu Akbar. Allahu Akbar. God is Great. God is Great. From the mosque came the call to the afternoon prayer. But the women merely lowered their voices a little and carried on imploring me, grasping my hands and tapping my knees with their bony hands.

I shivered and frayed a little more inside.

'Please, Vicereine Sahiba, my daughter gave birth yesterday, but we have no clothes for the child.'

'Please, Vicereine Sahiba, my mother is a diabetic. We have no medicine left . . .'

'Please, Vicereine Sahiba, my husband went out and never came back . . .'

When I asked them about the latrines they wailed and shook their heads.

'How can we go? All sorts of peeping Toms. Best to do it in a bucket in the tent and tip it out later. And we cannot wash. We have only one set of clothes, so when we menstruate, we soil ourselves and are ashamed.'

It was a relief to get out of the tent and into the open air, but my head was ringing with the women's pleas. The young nurse, however, appeared unmoved by what was going on around her. She was shaking her head in evident disgust.

'Lady Wallace, you are not believing everything those women say. They're poor and uneducated. They know quite well you are coming, so have dressed themselves in rags, wanting you to take pity.'

I looked at her with utter incredulity. Just then I heard singing and a man's voice in a plaintive chant that was floating out of the misery and abject squalor. Swiftly, I dismissed the young woman by thanking her, and left her to find the men.

Dr Ali and Captain Fraser were standing and smoking with the same group of armed men who had stopped us at the gate. Except that now the ruffians had their rifles slung on their backs. Captain Fraser was over six feet tall and with his shock of blond hair, he ought to have stuck out like a sore thumb. But I could see instantly from the movement of his mouth and the loose, lazy way he was holding himself that he was not speaking in English. Somehow, despite his genetics, he had blended in to almost become one of the gang.

Catching sight of me, Captain Fraser put his cap back on and dropped what little was left of his cigarette, stubbing it out with his foot.

'All sorted, Lady Wallace. They will accept a Gurkha escort for the sweepers.' The men smiled and nodded. Thanks to Captain Fraser of Quetta, for a few moments at least, the soldiers were real people again, happy-go-lucky lads who ought to have been learning a trade, not fighting civil wars.

Again I heard it, over and over, the wailing lament that seeped through the heat and the stench.

'Music?' I cocked my head to one side and wondered if I were going mad.

Dr Ali giggled at my apparent confusion. 'Yes. It's the Sufi musicians. They're starting a qawwali at the mosque, making solace for our souls. Come!' He threw out his arms to the side in the manner of a generous host who was inviting me to supper at his house after all was over and everything forgiven.

The red sandstone mosque had five arches, the middle one decorated with white marble inlays which winked in the late afternoon sun. A group of ten musicians was sitting on a tatty carpet just outside the mosque, in front of the middle arch. The singers were accompanied by an accordion and two men playing percussion—one the flat-topped tabla, the other the double-ended dholak.

Was the music a prayer, a seduction or an enchantment? I didn't know, but it beguiled me, it beckoned, it called in a way that left me no choice. Quietly, men were gathering from all over the fort. They found dry patches on which to sit or, where it was too wet, squatted on their heels or sat on old newspapers, buckets, cooking pots, bits of corrugated iron, boxes.

'Usually qawwali doesn't begin until much later in the evening,' Dr Ali explained. 'But here we have extenuating circumstances. This group goes from one Sufi shrine to the next, singing our devotional songs. Unfortunately, they have got stuck on this side of the border with us.'

The lead singer, an old man, was wearing a black turban and was bedecked with a crazy selection of semi-precious stones: red jasper, amethyst, malachite, topaz. The larger pieces, he wore in a long necklace. The smaller ones were set in silver chains which formed a glove-like bracelet that fell over his right hand. To my mind he didn't look like a singer at all but more like a pirate, perhaps a gypsy. And yet his singing cast a spell on the gathering. As his eyes rolled back into his head, leaving only the whites, he set out the tune. This was picked up and repeated by his chorus of younger men and boys who clapped on the off-beat and drove the music on.

Allahu, Allahu. God is He, God is He.

Without waiting for the end of the song, Dr Ali had removed his galoshes and was padding barefoot across the carpet to give money to the musicians. Quietly we took our places on a white sheet that had been laid out under the middle arch of the mosque. I felt awkward at first since I was the only woman there, but no one bothered to give me any attention. A white woman in uniform was hardly a lady and often an exception in India. But when I looked up I saw hundreds of veiled heads peeping down from the gallery above. I was not alone after all. A small boy offered tea in murky chipped glasses. Captain Fraser gave him a few annas and took three cups. He drank readily and without fear of disease but I chose to leave my glass untouched. For my benefit, Dr Ali translated an Arabic inscription on the wall of the mosque.

As long as there are people on earth, may this building be frequented and people be happy and cheerful in it.

Suddenly the song died. There was no winding up, no final drum roll, no grand finale. It just stopped, leaving the silence begging for more.

Then another song began, the lead musician's husky gravel-like voice raking against the sky, beseeching, begging, imploring. My arms and legs were getting heavy now. I could not resist. There was so much I didn't understand, but did I need to? It had been over a year since I had walked out of church in Oxford before the end of the Credo. Yet, already, this gypsy, this pirate, this saint, he had me in his thrall.

The chorus picked up the words, chanting them over and over.

The wedding night is here at last.
I stay up all night with my Beloved

Dye me, Master
Dye me, the same colour as You.
Dye me Master
Dye me, the same colour as You.

This time, Captain Fraser translated, his eyes half-closed. It was an extraordinary sight. Although he still wore his soldier's uniform and had the face of a white man with blond hair, all that was English in him had gone, obliterated by this *something*, that, having been called, now descended, quietly, invisibly all around.

Oh! cloud of mercy
I pray for your generosity.
Please, patter a few raindrops on my head.

The sky had turned apricot, burning to red with the setting sun. More men had come, and women too, shy with their scarves over their faces, dragging children and supporting the sick and the lame: thousands and thousands, their faces wet with tears.

The singer's voice cracked as he set out the pattern of a new song.

Kill me if you must, then watch me die.

People groaned and began to sway, their faces contorted as if they might pass out with grief, but the singer held them, suspending them with his notes, wringing them, torturing them, then at last gently nursing them back into themselves.

Kill me if you must, then watch me die.

Was I the only one left untouched? God knows I wanted to, but still I could not cry.

The journey had come to its end, and the train had been shunted into a siding at Delhi Main. The dusty pea-green engine was resting its exhausted nose against the buffers. The smell of smoke and steam hung in the hot night air. A floodlight had been set up on a gantry and, like a fallen moon, it illuminated the scene in a beam of ghostly white light. All was still. There were no passengers. There was no hustle and bustle, no chatter of monkeys or tweeting of birds on the roof. There were no huddles of people sleeping wherever they could lay their heads. The platform had been cleared, leaving only Gurkha sentries stationed every ten yards or so along its length. The silence swallowed and stifled everything.

Jawahar emerged out of the darkness with his entourage, looking flustered. I imagined that he too must have been called away from dinner, just like Edwina and I had been. Edwina went over to greet him. Heads bowed, they whispered to one another reverently, like mourners gathered in a church for a funeral. The Gurkha officer in charge raised his hand and pointed into the blackness down the tracks. A motley gang of Indian workmen dressed in loincloths was shuffling slowly towards us. Their heads bound with turbans, they seemed to be porters, or sweepers, perhaps. They knew what they had been called out to do and had covered their mouths and noses with cloths. They were the vanguard. Lumbering slowly, bringing up the rear, were three empty army trucks. My heart sank. Time was running out.

I was carrying my first aid bag with its tatty red cross. No one stopped me as I jumped down from the platform, crossed the tracks and climbed up into the rear carriage. Dimly, I heard the havildar shout, but it was too late.

It was as if I had run into a brick wall. All I could do was scream, except that no sound came. For a moment, I was a child standing in the meadow behind my father's house. It was full of purple and pink poppies, their heads dancing in the soft summer breeze. I was looking back at the house on the crest of the hill, trying to get there. But the poppies had suddenly become vicious, binding my legs, and with my hands over my ears, I let out a silent scream.

Bodies upon bodies were piled up. Pinned by the mass of corpses, a man was hanging as if crucified on the window bars. Fixed in the moment of death, his left knee was raised, still climbing, still running. Below him, there was a pile of women with their children heaped up behind them like dominoes: dead, their mouths open, perfect rows of milk teeth glistened icicle white in the eerie light.

The carriage door clanged behind me and the havildar came in. He was an older man, his chinstrap tight over his chin. We stood knee-deep in dead bodies, holding each other's gaze as if there were some lifeline between us. We were witnessing something so terrible that each of us needed the other to affirm that what we were looking at was real. To my left lay a little girl, peppered with shrapnel; an old man with his innards hacked out, tumbling like chains over the face of someone else, dry now, and infested with flies. I tried to work out what might have happened, how it might have played out. The victims had all been Sikh and Hindu refugees on their way from the Punjab. The train had been attacked and strafed with bullets. Then the murderers must have climbed aboard to the finish the job by hand.

I hefted my medical bag. Looking down at my pretty white dress with tiny pink roses, realized that I was still dressed for dinner. I was not in my uniform. I was unarmed.

No words passed between us, the Gurkha havildar and me, as we picked our way through the carriage. My legs were leaden, hard to lift and move forward, as if I were wading upstream against a raging torrent. The bodies too were heavy, dead already for a day at least, pale green and blue in the half-light. At times, it took both of us to shift them and clear a way. We had no voices. My tongue was stuck to the roof of my mouth. But somehow we managed to murmur, to call softly, to invent a strange language in this no-man's land somewhere between insanity and grief in which to talk to the dead. Checking, turning, feeling, touching as many as we could; our progress was slow, through the flies, the heat, the gloom, the stench. And every one of them, every man, woman and child was stiff and as cold as stone. The rear door of the carriage clanged again. Two young riflemen peeked in, their mouths covered with khaki neckerchiefs. Under their wide hats they looked like Asian cowboys. But the havildar, old enough to be their father, gently raised his hand to spare them and warned them away.

My head was now full of noise, hissing, scratchy static, punctuated by screeches and whistles, a wireless untuned. I knew that I would never write any of this, not in my diary, not in my letters, not in my reports. Yet I also knew that every detail of every contorted, tortured face would remain in my mind and could never be forgotten.

Together we waded through and climbed up the flow of death. The path taken by the murderers gradually became clear. They had got in at the rear of the train and worked their way towards the engine. The biggest piles of bodies were therefore at the front of the carriages from where the poor souls had tried to escape. The rear door to the next carriage was hanging open and we stepped across the junction plate. A wild dog had his nose in the naked torn breasts of a woman. The havildar hit him across the side of the head with the butt of his rifle and beat him again and again. The dog moaned pitifully. Panting, the havildar grabbed him by the scruff of the neck, and drawing his kukri, quickly, professionally, slit the animal's throat. Wide-eyed, the dog first growled, then rasped and choked as blood spurted in fountains from the severed arteries in his neck.

Huge black crows had also invaded the carriage. Along with the dog and flies, they had pecked and sucked on open wounds, eyes, mouths, innards. Gorged, fat, sated, our arrival had done nothing to deflect them from their feast. Banging, clattering, we drove them away as we went along. Cawing, the winged monsters fluttered up, out of the open carriage door. Suddenly a body tumbled from a bench. A hand reached out and grabbed my skirt. It belonged to a boy of about sixteen or seventeen who was lying in the shadows beneath a seat.

'Maa, Maa,' he croaked, his brown eyes bloodshot, but blinking.

'He's alive.' I had found some words and forced them into a voice. 'There's one here. Alive!'

'Hush, it's all right, I'm here. I'm here,' I said, as I bent over the body. He was thin, wiry, a farm boy most likely. His face was cut, battered and bruised, as if he had put up a fight. He was covered in blood, but in the half-light I couldn't see where it had come from.

'Don't just stand there! Get a stretcher.' My voice cracked as I attempted to shout at the dithering havildar. He took a torch from his belt and flashed it at the boy's head. I gasped at the sight of the wound. The back of his skull had been hacked away—neatly, as chance would have it—perhaps with an axe or sickle, almost as if it had been surgically trepanned. His gently pulsing brain was infested with flies.

The young riflemen with their neckerchiefs over their mouths lifted the stretcher gently down from the train and up on to the platform. The boy was groaning with pain and would not let go of my hand. His own hand was thin but still warm, rough and calloused with work, the nails black, encrusted with dirt. Around us the night had closed in and the station was as still and quiet as a cathedral. At the back of the last carriage, the coolies had started unloading the dead. They were throwing them like sacks of potatoes on to the trucks where they landed with dull thumps.

'Maa, Maa,' the boy repeated, and other words I did not need to know to understand. But when the havildar put a water bottle to the boy's mouth, blood gurgled over his stubble. Everything was disjointed, out of time, out of place, nothing connected, each minuscule movement highlighted at half-speed, each word standing alone in my mind. Edwina was patting my arm. Beside her stood Jawahar who was weeping. Resting his hand on the boy's shoulder, he bent down to talk to him. Recognizing the Prime Minister, the boy attempted to rise, still clinging to my hand. They backed up the ambulance and lifted the stretcher carried by four Gurkhas, although the boy was nothing but skin and bone. Hundreds of people, I realized, must have crammed into that train, a thousand perhaps, yet only one had survived.

'I'll go with him to the hospital,' I said.

'Take him to the Willingdon,' Edwina ordered. 'It's the best, and if you have any trouble, tell them I said so.'

Jawahar nodded and ventured a slight smile. 'Thank you, Pippi. The boy's name is Vijay. It means victory.'

In the ambulance, my hands shook but I managed to get a drip up. All the while I murmured wordless words, made what I thought were soothing noises and hummed quietly as I stroked Vijay's forehead. I noticed that he had a birthmark the shape of a heart on his right forearm.

'Maa, Maa.' There was fear now in his voice. Wracked with pain, he somehow summoned the strength to cling more tightly to my hand.

'It's all right, I'm here. This time Mamma is here.' I told him. I looked for morphine to ease his pain but I had long since given away the last of my supplies.

Then I started to sing quietly: 'Bugeilio'r Gwenith Gwyn',
the Welsh love song my father had always used to comfort me
as a child. I had sung to my own boys whenever they had been
sick or afraid.

> *A young and foolish lad am I*
> *I live life as fancy*
> *shepherding the white wheat*
> *whilst another does the reaping.*
> *Why will you not follow me?*
> *Some day or another?*
> *For in my eyes, my dearest maid,*
> *you are fairer, fairer daily.*

I sang it very softly in Welsh and the boy calmed and tried to
smile, so I carried on. But the ambulance swayed as it took a
sharp corner and lurched over the potholes in the road. I was
thrown away from the stretcher and the boy's hand was jerked
away from mine.

'Bloody hell!' I banged on the partition and shouted at the
driver in my best Hindustani. 'Be careful, won't you!'

When I looked back, Vijay's eyes had closed.

> *As long as seas are made of brine*
> *and as long as my hair keeps growing,*
> *and as long as a heart beats in my breast,*
> *to you I will be faithful.*

Tim Latham was on duty at the Willingdon when they carried
Vijay in. He greeted me with the news that Nehru himself
had called ahead so that we would be expected. Stethoscope
round his neck, spectacles balanced on the end of his nose,
he was impassive. He examined the boy meticulously, feeling
his neck and his wrist in search for a pulse. He gently opened

the boy's shuttered eyes and flashed them with his little torch. The Canadian said nothing; he had no need to. I stood there with Vijay's bony farmer's hand limp in my own.

'No! No! No!' Someone was shouting all of a sudden, screaming, and I realized with a shock that it was me. I pulled at Tim's white coat and pummelled his arm. 'Try again. You must be mistaken. He's alive, alive.'

They fetched Hari. The bulk and height of him were exaggerated by his white coat as he strode forward, frowning from under the arch at the bottom of the corridor. Seeing me, he did a double take as if he couldn't believe his eyes. He took careful note of the gaping hole in the dead boy's head, then gently uncoupled our hands.

'Come Pippi. Come with me.' Putting his arm around my shoulders, he led me away. I had neither the will nor the desire to resist.

He took me into a small dark office with blinds at the window, dismissed the orderly and locked the door. I started to shiver, to shake, and my teeth began to chatter.

'No, no, no!' I balled my fists in fury and turned them on myself, beating my chest, the side of my head, boxing my ears, tearing my hair. Hari seized my wrists. He was strong, but deliberately he only partially restrained me.

'Hit me, Pippi! Go on, hit me!'

And I did, again and again in my rage, my fists battering his broad chest.

'Go on! Is that all? Give me more!' He parried a few blows, let a couple fall, then wrestled me to a stop and held me tightly to his chest. There I buried my head. The dam had broken. They came now, in gulping, choking waves—unstoppable tears. A stream, a river, an ocean of grief poured down my cheeks, washing blood down my neck and chest into the top of my dress.

'I couldn't save them. My boys . . . my beautiful boys. They died alone, in fear, in pain.'

'Hush, jaan, hush. Please don't torture yourself.'

'Sometimes, at night they call to me from the flames or from the bottom of the sea. "Mummy, Mummy." And every time I try. Oh God, I try with all my might! But every time I fail. I can never get to them.' Blood rushed to my head and the strength went from my legs. Hari caught me and cradled me gently to the floor. 'My boys, my beautiful boys,' was all I could say.

He stroked my hair, kissed my forehead and rocked me.

'Hush, jaan, hush. You were there for him tonight, in the end, for that boy and he knew it.'

'Yes,' I whispered. 'But it was not enough.'

It was hot but I was cold even though I had been wrapped in a blanket. Hari made me sit in his office chair. I was mute, utterly drained to the point where I feared that this time there might be no return and insanity would finally have its victory. Everything that had been going on around me had happened not to me but to a stranger who had taken up residence inside my body. Hari unlocked the door and called for the orderlies who brought bowls of water and tea.

He handed me a cup.

'Drink.'

Fighting nausea and the desire to wretch and vomit, I took a tentative sip, welcoming the warmth as it seeped into my veins.

'Now let's get you cleaned up.'

The water was warm, and the towel soft. It smelled of soap flakes, of safety and somehow of a family and a home. I lifted my face to Hari who gently wiped round my eyes, my forehead and chin.

'There, that's better . . . Now your hands?' I held them out and was shocked to see them stained blackberry red and purple, my wristwatch caked in dried blood. Removing it, he put it in his pocket and wiped the tide mark away from my wrist. I washed my hands in the bowl. Then he knelt at my feet. I wanted to kiss the small bald patch hidden on the top of his head as he struggled to undo the buckles of my sandals. They were the high-heeled white ones I had bought from Mrs Pritchard. I liked to wear them in the evenings and they been whitened just the day before. I reached down to help Hari, and rested my hand on his cheek which was gleaming, polished with sweat. Without looking up, he put his hand on top of mine and held it there for a while to comfort himself. Then we turned our attention to my sandals which he was dangling by the ankle strap. They were red, soggy, still squelchy with blood, beyond repair. Bewildered, I stared down at the feet and legs that were attached to me. The havildar and I must have waded through a river of blood.

*T*he tall, green-eyed white woman was wearing cheap Indian canvas shoes. Her fashionable summer dress was covered in blood and she was standing under the chandelier in the lobby of the Imperial Hotel. I stared at her in the mirror. Her shoes were frayed and an odd unmatched pair. I realized with a shock that the woman was me.

If the staff in their crisp white livery with shiny gold buttons raised their eyebrows a little, they did not make a fuss. Hari had got it all in hand—booking two rooms for the night, ordering beer and food. It had been a relief to let him take charge, for a while at least. He was leaning on the counter in the hotel, finger in one ear, talking discreetly into the receiver. He had already rung Government House and his home. Now he was speaking to Jawahar who was having supper with Edwina at York Road.

A peal of laughter propelled a woman into the lobby. She had dared to wear slacks in the evening and a bright silk scarf cleverly tied in a revealing halter-neck style as the top. But strangest of all was her hair. She was not old, probably younger than I was, yet her hair was completely white, so white that it hinted at pale blue.

'Oh! My Gawd! What's happened to you?' She made a beeline for me. There were about half a dozen mildly sozzled white men with her. They followed in her wake. I recognized many of them, for they were the foreign correspondents of Western news agencies. From there it was not difficult to deduce that the woman was the American photo-journalist Margaret Bourke-White. She was famous, at least as far as Cherie was concerned, for her sleeping arrangements on the way to Simla.

Hari was quick off the mark and tempted the woman from her path with key words. 'Delhi Main, train full of dead bodies. No survivors.' The journalists took the bait and scattered to fetch notebooks and cameras like a pack of bloodhounds that had scented a trail. At the last second, Margaret Bourke-White turned and said, 'I'll send a dress up for you, honey. We're more or less the same size.' She flashed a wide all-American grin at me.

Hari and I found a quiet corner at the back of the hotel overlooking the pool. Hands folded in my lap, I sat in a rattan chair. Water tinkled clear and pure under an illuminated fountain and fireflies flitted around the ornamental hedges which were garlanded with fairy lights. Looking up, looking down, I was not sure which was which, for the stars had fallen into the indigo water of the pool.

The house boys brought us some food—a vegetarian Indian platter—and Hari let them serve.

'When was the last time you ate?' he asked.

'Around noon. What time is it now?'

He looked at his watch. 'After ten.'

I stared out across the pool and watched the wild dogs prowling in the shadows at the bottom of the garden. I sipped my beer, waiting for it to soothe and calm.

'Eat!' Hari urged. I did my best but choked a little on the mushrooms which felt like rubber in my mouth.

'That's good.' He smiled. 'You're looking better already.'

'You look exhausted,' I said in reply. His skin was sallow almost jaundiced, his brow permanently furrowed.

He wiped up the last pieces of potato with his chapatti.

'Why did you do it? Go into that carriage . . .' His voice trailed off at the sight of my face.

'I had to,' I said. 'Already the men were coming to clear the bodies. They don't always look.' But he didn't understand what I was trying to say so I tried again. 'One night during the worst of the blitz I went to a street of houses that had taken a direct hit from a German bomb. Gas mains had been broken and the fire raged all through the night. Emergency services had had to work well into the next day to put it out. They had given up looking for survivors. But there was one ARP warden, an old Cockney, who wouldn't stop.

'"I've got a feeling about this one," he said to me. "I know it in my bones." To tell the truth I was dead on my feet. We'd been up all night, but I stayed with him into the following afternoon picking through the rubble. And he was proved right. In the last house, away from the heat, we found two children: a toddler and a baby. Their mother had taken them into the kitchen at bedtime, put them under the special metal table that served as an air-raid shelter, and told them not to come out. A street blasted to smithereens and under it all, these children were still alive.'

Someone had put on the gramophone on in the bar. The sound of the piano accompanying the song drifted out into the garden.

> *I can't begin to tell you how much you mean to me*
> *My world would end if ever we were through.*

Bing Crosby's voice was soothing, mellow, as familiar as that of an old friend. The snare drum tapped. Again, I found myself crying.

> *How happy I would be*
> *If I could speak my mind like others do.*

I wiped my tears with the back of my hand.

'Come on,' Hari said, his voice very deep and soft. 'Time to sleep.'

In the hotel bedroom it was as if snow had fallen and silenced the world. All was muffled, still, miraculously at peace.

We were awkward in the quiet, marooned by uncertainty and exhaustion between the settee and the coffee table.

'It's a lovely room,' I whispered, looking at the watercolours of Indian landscapes on the walls and the cream bedspread that had been folded back for the night, revealing pristine white sheets. I told him that I thought it was quite like Viceroy's House in a way and blathered on.

'The Imperial was designed by D.J. Blomfield, an associate of Edwin Lutyens. Art deco style.'

Hari sat down on the settee and then promptly stood up again. I turned to draw the curtains which had been left open despite the fact that the bed had been turned down.

'Thank you for bringing me here,' I told him.

'You just need a bit of a break, time to recover. Edwina will understand.'

I was far from sure that she would, for she never stopped even during the worst of times. But I said nothing, and stared out of the window. The horizon was red with flames. Instinctively, I braced myself for the sound of air raid sirens, anti-aircraft fire and exploding bombs. But there was nothing. This was a war of stealth fought between communities in narrow alleys and over rooftops.

'Oh God, when will it end?'

Sighing, Hari came up behind me and rested his hand on my shoulder.

'I didn't think I would ever say this, but the Mahatma is the only one who can stop it now. They say he is planning to fast unto death.'

'But he is so old and frail, he will surely die.'

'Maybe that is what it will take: the ultimate sacrifice.'

We stood together in silence, watching the skyline.

'Must be time to turn in,' Hari said. 'My room is just down the corridor.'

'Please don't go. I don't want to be alone.' I startled myself with my frankness.

'Darling, you are terribly upset. You're in no fit state to make that kind of decision. I don't want to take advantage.' He was right of course, but his friendship and kindness towards me only served to prompt more tears.

Taking off his tie, he ran me a bath and knelt by the tub, stirring the water with a long back brush.

'When my children were small I used to love bath time. My daughter had this little wooden duck. It was such fun! I used to get completely soaked with all the splashing and my wife and the maid would get cross and chuck me out.'

'Well, I'm chucking you out now!' It was a weak joke and he smiled. Before I could stop him, he had picked up a bottle of bath salts and tipped a little into the running water. My chest tightened with panic at the thought that it might be lavender.

'Sandalwood,' he said, almost as if he had read my mind, and closed the bathroom door. 'Throw out your dress when you are done, and I'll give it to the dhobi.'

I wallowed in the warm water but my head was full of memories: face after face, severed limbs, dogs mauling naked bodies, pubic hair. The images stuck in my mind like Goya's lithographs of war. I took a deep breath. The sandalwood smelled sweet and woody, of vanilla and prayer but for some strange reason it made me think of orange groves. I focused on the thought of the shiny fruits ripening in the sunshine, the breeze in the trees and, in the distance, the soft shushing of a warm sea. I was walking down a hill into the blue when exhaustion suddenly hit me, heavy, like a shutter coming down. It was time to collapse into sleep and I thanked God for it.

In the bedroom, Hari had fallen asleep on the bed, fully clothed. Mouth open, he was snoring gently, puffing a little at the end of each exhalation. He did not stir when I pulled up the sheet.

We found each other in the darkness in the early hours of the morning, the tips of our fingers roving gently to trace the contours of each other's faces, eyes, noses and softly begging mouths. Hari had not washed and he was all beer, sweat and masculinity, his stubble rough on my cheek, on my breast, the inside of my thigh.

'Are you sure?'

His voice was distant and sounded gruff. I nodded. He could not see but he knew my answer. It had been months in the making and yet it happened quickly now. We did not grab, did not push or force, but let the magical moment of surrender lead us and build its own strength. Afterwards, I lay with my head on his chest and listened to the beat of his heart.

'I never thought . . .' he eventually said, 'I thought I was too old. I never thought I could be so blessed.'

'No,' I said. 'I am the one who has been blessed, blessed by you.' Tears rolled down my cheeks and he savoured them with the tip of his tongue. I faltered then. 'Is it right? How could we make love at such a time?'

'Yes, jaan, it is right.' His words vibrated deep and long in his chest. 'Nothing is more right. It's a promise, a gift, a reason to go on.'

Part IV

The Balance of Madness
Christmas 1947 to 21st June 1948

I had not felt like this since I'd been the back legs of the donkey in the school nativity play. It was a strange, uneasy sensation, something to do with being present but unseen, a symptom of the utter incredulity at playing a ridiculous role in a great charade. I was hidden with the women behind a purdah screen in the City Palace at Jaipur. Below me, the Maharaja of Jaipur was sitting on his golden throne beneath a solid gold sun in his Durbar Hall. Either his diamond encrusted turban had slipped or the polo-playing soldier–Prince had set it at a deliberately rakish angle. A handsome man in his mid-thirties, he appeared bored as ranks of noblemen dressed in gold and scarlet filed past, dropping gold and silver coins into a red velvet blanket at his feet. This was the 'nazar' or symbolic tribute. The Maharaja's full title was Lieutenant General His Highness Sarmad-i-Rajahai Hindustan Raj Rajendra Shri Maharaja Dhiraja Sir Sawai Man Singh Sahib Bahadur of Jaipur, but Dickie and Edwina just called him Jai, another name that meant victory.

Behind the purdah screen, the Indian noble ladies were dressed in their finest silk saris bedecked with diamonds, emeralds and rubies. I felt quite old and plain in my velvet evening dress and single string of pearls. Never mind the Independence of India, the Silver Jubilee celebration of the Maharaja of Jaipur was, without a doubt, the social occasion of the year for these ladies. It might have been 1947 and India a constitutional democracy, a new Dominion within the Commonwealth, but there in the City Palace I felt as if I were an extra on a film set for Arabian Nights. To my left, at

one end of the balcony, sat the Maharaja's older first wife. She
was dressed in a red sari covered in glinting silver pennies and
wore a veil. To my right, at the other end of the balcony, was
Ayesha, the Maharaja's second wife. She was the younger sister
of the Maharaja of Cooch Behar. Ayesha's and Jai's had been a
love match. They had chased each other from London to Paris,
from ski resort to yacht and finally, despite much opposition,
got married. Wearing a peach-coloured sari, her long hair loose
over her shoulders, she looked like a schoolgirl and was most
elegant and beautiful.

'We have prayed for this for twenty-five years,' the state
singer repeated over and over in Indian classical contralto.
'Everyone is intoxicated in happiness of the jubilee.' The
dancers swayed, hesitated and swayed again, and on it went, on
and on. People started to twitch, and I began to suspect that
something had gone wrong. At last the great doors at the end of
the hall were opened and in stepped Dickie and Edwina. They
were the ultimate professional royals and this was a repeat
performance: Dickie in full naval whites, medals lined up all
the way across his chest, and Edwina in the gold shift dress she
had worn for the Governor General's swearing-in ceremony on
Independence Day.

'I don't care if they do notice,' she had said to me over
breakfast. 'I'm jolly well going to get the wear out of it.' She stood
now by the dais, her thin arms thrust down by her side to control
her nerves, her jaw locked, chin stuck forward at an unflattering
angle. The trumpets blared a fanfare. The Governor General
hung the sunburst Star of India around the Maharaja's neck and
then patted him affectionately on the shoulder.

Later in the day I ran into young Mr Singh. As ADC to the
Silver Jubilee guests he was responsible for the sporting
entertainment. I had met him at a duck shoot the previous day.

The shoot had been held on the lake by the Summer Palace and the beaters in motor boats had chased hundreds of poor birds into the guns.

'It's a disaster,' he wailed, 'I have failed to equalize the balance of madness.' He pushed his shiny black hair, which he wore slicked back like the Maharaja, off his forehead.

'What disaster?'

'The elephants. One of them has gone mad, but the other has not.'

I shook my head with incomprehension.

'The elephant fight, it will have to be cancelled.'

After the duck shoot, I couldn't say that I was disappointed at his news. But young Mr Singh was so utterly crestfallen that I agreed to go with him to inspect the elephants.

On the way to the pens he explained his dilemma.

'Several months ago, we selected two of the biggest males in the state of Jaipur and put them into solitary confinement in preparation for the Jubilee fight. Bulls, you know, are liking mischief-making in the river with the ladies.' Young Mr Singh shook his head and winked at me. 'So when we keep them alone, starve them if you like, they go a little crazy.'

I heard the mad elephant trumpeting, moaning, long before I saw him. As we rounded a corner, there he was, standing in his pen. His four great feet were tethered to concrete blocks. Frenzied, he was straining at his great clanking chains. At the far end of the block of pens was the other elephant, head down, stubbornly calm in the face of months of torture. This one too was lashed to four large concrete blocks, but he was rocking gently in his chains. His head had drooped as if in defeat and tears seemed to be falling from the corners of his sad, sad eyes.

'I really have done my best to bring the elephants to madness on schedule,' young Mr Singh lamented. 'We have given this one steroid injections and used whips but all to no avail. Such a shame, it would have been fun for the guests.'

As far as I was concerned, the visit to the elephants could not have ended too soon. Afterwards I went to look for Edwina and found her lying on her bed, holding an ice-pack to her head. Her large suite in the royal palace overlooked a courtyard on one side and had a balcony with a jathi screen on the other, the city side. Her gold dress was crumpled over the back of a chair and she was wearing safari trousers and a shirt.

When I came in, she opened half an eye.

'The elephant fight is off. One has gone mad as required but the other has not,' I whispered. 'Just thought you might want to know.'

'Thank God for that!' Gingerly, she sat up. Her brow was furrowed, her pupils contracted in pain. She was all skin and bone. Not for the first time I wondered how and why she kept on going. What was it that drove her, enabled her to always get out there and smile? She would never say no to people in need. On top of that she maintained a punishing social schedule, hosting dinners and receptions, travelling all over the country, setting foundation stones for colleges and hospitals, visiting slums and making speeches. The Governor General and his wife were scheduled to leave India in the summer and Edwina's diary was full to bursting up until the last moment. I took a deep breath before I spoke again.

'Edwina, I'm worried about you. Shall I speak to Muriel about the diary? See if we could cut you some slack for a couple of weeks?'

Her gold charm bracelet jangled as she waved an arm dismissively in the air.

'Don't worry about that. These damn royal occasions and house parties are such a farce. I always feel so false.' She stood up and drank a glass of water. 'You know why they had to keep on and on singing and dancing this morning at the ceremony?'

I shook my head.

'Dickie's valet had packed the wrong set of medals! Typical Dickie! He refused to go on parade without them, so we had to send the plane back to Delhi to fetch them.' She blew out a long breath of air and massaged her temples. 'Jawahar would have a fit if he came up here and saw them all carrying on as if nothing had changed.'

'What about the Star of India?' I ventured. 'Aren't we too carrying on as if nothing has changed?'

'Oh! That bit of tin and white paint!' She shook her head and it made here wince with pain. 'By the way, Letty, have you seen this? God, I'm so angry it makes my blood boil.' She picked up a neatly typed letter from the desk and shoved it towards me.

'Yes, it came up in the mail bag from Delhi yesterday. I deliberately put it on top of your pile.' I took the letter. It concerned Lady Mountbatten's nomination of Amrit Kaur for Chief Commissioner of the St John's Ambulance Brigade in India.

'I just want to let you know quietly before anyone else does,' Hon. Mrs Copland-Griffiths from the St John's Ambulance headquarters in London had written. I saw that Edwina had marked the offending paragraph in the margin with three long red dashes. 'There is likely to be stiff opposition to your proposal. It is generally felt that since we are a Christian organization, people don't want non-Christians involved in running it.'

'But Amrit is a Christian,' I protested, 'just an Indian one.'

'You know as well as I do it's not about Christian or non-Christian. It's because she's Indian and they don't like the colour of her skin! What on earth do those people think has been going on out here? Don't they realize the world has changed?' She snatched the letter back from me and placed it for future reference under a paperweight on the desk.

'But what can we do about it?' I asked. The St John's Ambulance Brigade was an organization we both cared deeply about. 'If we can't find someone of calibre and influence to take over, St John's will be finished in India after we leave.'

'There's nothing for it, I am going to ask Dickie to roll out his cannons. I'll get him to write them a stinking letter, that's what. Not sure what good it will do though. In the end the Brigade will end up merging with the Red Cross in India, such a shame.'

We walked on to the balcony and listened to the birds, the distant tinkle of bicycle bells, and admired the pretty pink city of Jaipur, bathed in the gentle winter sunlight.

'We go between so many different worlds in India, see so many extremes,' I said. 'Sometimes I am not sure what is real and what is not.' I put my finger in the carved curl of the ornate lathi screen that separated us from the outside world.

Her nails painted red, Edwina likewise put a finger in one of the holes in the carvings. She was taking deep breaths as if she were a prisoner craving air and freedom. 'I think the answer is that it is all real and unreal at the same time: war, death, suffering, joy, love, happiness. We cannot have one without the other.' She paused, rubbed her side, then took some more deep breaths.

'Fancy a bit of Christmas shopping in the bazaar? If I don't get out of this cardboard palace, I'll soon be as mad as that poor elephant.'

We escaped by the side stable gate, giggling like schoolgirls because we had got away without a security escort. I could sense that the cool, fresh air would do Edwina good. Putting on her little round sunglasses, she swung her arms and set off at a cracking pace.

Then suddenly, 'So, how's it going with Hari? she asked. 'Tell all!'

I hesitated. I wished I could see her eyes.

'Fine. He's a kind man, a good friend.' The warm winter sun was forgiving on my face and I cautiously ventured more. 'And I care about him.' But no sooner had my words left my mouth than I regretted sharing such a confidence with Edwina.

'It'll never work, you know. Jawahar is convinced that he and I must function in our own orbits or we'll make each other very unhappy.'

Why did she have to knife me? My heart twisted and knotted in my chest. Did my happiness have to come at the expense of her own? It was, of course, impossible for the former British Vicereine to stay on in independent India; if her friendship with Jawahar became public knowledge it would fatally undermine her husband's position of impartiality and the whole basis of the transfer of power. It was equally ridiculous for the first Prime Minister of India to think for even a moment about residing anywhere other than India. But Hari and I were nobodies. Why could we not be together if that is what we both really wanted? After all, the world was changing, wasn't it?

'Have you discussed it?' She pressed her advantage. 'What about the job at Hong Kong University that I wrote you a reference for?'

'They've offered me the post.'

'Well, there you are then . . .' We strode on a few more paces. 'Everyone is leaving, you know. No one, just no one, is staying. The Indians don't want us here any more. Quite the best thing, Letty. I wouldn't want my old friend making a fool of herself.'

At that point our conversation was interrupted by shouts from both front and rear. The local children were racing, helter-skelter up from the bazaar to greet us, and young Mr Singh, followed by Dickie's Special Branch detective, was running down from the palace.

'Lady Mountbatten, Lady Wallace, I really must protest . . .' Young Mr Singh was red-faced and out of breath.

'I'm so sorry,' Edwina laughed. 'Have we really been very naughty?'

'Yes, yes, very, very naughty indeed. His Highness will have my guts for garters if he finds out that I have let you go gallivanting about, unescorted!'

We proceeded with our escorts and the giggling, jumping, skipping children down to the bazaar. On the corner of the square, Edwina stopped at a sweet shop. Despite the protests of young Mr Singh, she bought a large selection of delicacies for everyone.

'Don't fight now, share!' Headache forgotten, she was happy and relaxed amongst the children, breaking the cakes into portions and delivering them into their grubby outstretched hands.

'Special ghewar!' The shopkeeper smiled, displaying a perfect line of gleaming white teeth. 'Normally we make them in January for the harvest festival but this time we made them early to celebrate the Jubilee and Christmas.'

'Happy Christmas!' the children chanted, licking the pistachio nuts off the tops of their sticky cakes. 'Everyone is intoxicated with happiness at the Silver Jubilee!'

After the war years in London, the bazaar was entrancingly illicit. The stalls and shops sold fruit and nuts, brightly coloured block-print cottons, carpets and blue pottery. In a sari shop we sat cross-legged on the floor while the proprietor laid out rolls and rolls of silks and cottons: reds, golds, greens, purples, oranges, all the colours of the rainbow and many in between. I bought a length of pale blue silk embroidered with silver for Margaret in London. Edwina chose a selection that could easily be made into Western dresses for her daughters. As we were paying, we were interrupted by a distinctive but familiar voice.

'Well, hello there! Dr Livingstone, I presume!' Margaret Bourke-White let loose her huge American grin. Edwina instantly switched on her own charming light-bulb smile. Platitudes ensued.

'I just loved your gold frock this morning. I was wondering where I might get something similar.'

'The fabric was a gift. These things are one-offs, you know.'
And so it went on, the two women sparring, duelling with
inflections, nuances and smiles.

'Jawahar was just telling me all about you the other
night,' drawled Ms Bourke-White. 'Such a charming man.
We had dinner together—macaroni cheese, a most sweet
and informal affair.'

I wondered how mature women who ought to know better
could sink to such a level and squabble over a man, even if the
one in question was the Prime Minister of India.

'Trollop!' Edwina hissed when at last we got away. She
made her right hand into a claw. 'I can just feel her getting her
pincers in to me for a story. Whatever she writes about me, I
guarantee it won't be nice.'

As afternoon tipped into evening, the temperature dropped,
so I bought a cheap paisley shawl and wrapped myself in it.
Edwina had gone back to the City Palace with our purchases,
the Special Branch detective and young Mr Singh. I wandered
around the shops and alleys, stopping only to buy a packet
of pistachio nuts which I munched on my progress. With an
overwhelming majority Hindu population, this area of India
had been left largely untouched by Partition. Girls in bright
red saris gossiped and dawdled their way home with little milk
pails. Young men loitered, leaning on their bicycles, and old
men smoked in the corners of their shops and played cards. As
the simple age-old rhythms of daily life played out around me,
I puzzled over the future.

Hari and I had avoided discussing it. Probably, I reasoned,
because when we were together we were just happy to escape
with the horses to The Ridge, eat a simple meal and lie in each
other's arms. We were both busy with work and he had been
preoccupied with resettling his daughter and the other refugees

he had taken into his home. Unbidden, the thought occurred to me that perhaps he saw no future for us at all. He was enjoying my company while I was here, but would not mind too much when I left. Suddenly I realized that I had become lost in a narrow alley lined with shops and that the light was fading fast. I knew that Edwina had been right when she said everyone was leaving, and that the Indians didn't want us here any more. Yet the prospect of returning alone to England, to old age and a mire of grief, filled me with dread. I turned left and right and left again and found myself on the threshold of a Hindu temple. Light from candles was streaming out into the dusk. A toothless old man wrapped in a shawl against the coming night beckoned me in. I removed my shoes. The stones of the temple floor were worn black with the passage of bare feet. The courtyard was small, filthy, crowded and filled with glittering glaring eyes, incense and smoke. I thought that Roman temples must have been something like this. To the left, stood a huge gold statue of the Nandi bull, garlanded in fresh flowers. Reaching up, the old man pulled a string to ring a bell.

'I am telling God that Memsahib is here. If you whisper in his ear, he will listen.'

*I*t was after 6 p.m. and I was about to shut Edwina's office in Government House for the day when the telephone rang. I hesitated. Perhaps it could wait until the morning, but I thought probably not. Either it was Edwina or Muriel who was accompanying her on her current tour of Madras. I ignored it for the usual three rings, but that proved to be too long. It set off a chain reaction all the way down the corridor, one phone tripping the other, going off like a series of landmines.

The moment I answered, even before he spoke, I knew it was Hari.

'Jaan, it's me. Gandhi's been shot. At a prayer meeting.' He was out of breath. 'Jawahar just rang. I'm going over now, to Birla House, following the ambulance.'

'Is he alive?'

'I don't know.' The line buzzed dead in my ear and I could smell lavender.

Doors were banging, voices shouting, men were running, the ADCs in their leather shoes, the chaprasis in their soft sandals, except that this time no one was running to catch the mail bag for London. I too ran down to the Governor General's office where everyone was in the anteroom: Alan, Ronnie Brockman, the whole of Dickie's staff.

'He's dead. I've just heard it on the radio.' Pearce, Dickie's driver, was red-faced.

'Who did it?' Again, I sought an answer. He shook his head.

'God help us if it is a Muslim.' Alan was so agitated he was jiggling about like a small boy needing the bathroom. 'It'll be all out civil war and there'll be nothing anyone can do to stop it.'

Dickie came striding out of the door of his office. He was still in his riding clothes and was chewing on his lower lip. Tense, he spoke in short staccato sentences.

'He's dead. No confirmation yet as to the identity of the assassin. Rumour is it's a Hindu.'

His eye fell on me.

'Have you spoken to Edwina?'

'Not yet.'

'Ring her! Get her back here ASAP. Fly her through the night if necessary.'

He took a deep breath and tried to arrange his hair which was sweaty and dishevelled after his late-afternoon ride.

'Just been on the phone to Rajagopalachari in Calcutta. He was most insistent. Could be a conspiracy. Must take utmost precautions with Nehru's security. We're done for if we lose him too. He'll have to address the nation. Not much time to think about it. Everything depends on what he says. The next few hours will be make or break'.

It was decided that we would go over to Birla House to pay our respects. Fifteen minutes later when we went out to the cars a crowd of staff had gathered at the bottom of the steps to glean news. Chaprasis, khidmutgars, cooks, the men who arranged the flowers, the malis, the little boys from the tennis courts—their faces pinched, they were all twitching and restless with fear. Zamurad Khan was among them. Dickie circulated, patting shoulders and shaking hands. I went over to the old bearer who was trembling with terror. We fixed each other with our eyes.

'Make sure your family is on the estate tonight. The guard has been doubled and there are Bren guns on the main gates.'

'Yes, yes. All here.'

I touched him lightly on the arm and he looked hard at me.

'Take care, Lady Wallace.'

News travelled by word of mouth at lightning speed in India. By the time we reached Albuquerque Road crowds of young men had already gathered. Such was the crush around the gates of Birla House that the cars had to honk their horns repeatedly to get through. Miraculously, in the darkness the guards recognized the Governor General's Crowns and let us in.

'It was a Muslim who did it,' someone shouted from the crowd.

'Don't be a fool!' Dickie roared. 'Don't you know it was a Hindu?'

But we didn't know, and I was terrified.

In the confusion, no one came out to greet us. The front door of Seth Birla's expansive white mansion had been left open, so in we went.

Following the sounds of chanting and wailing, and the scent of incense, we found the place. Sandals were lying abandoned in an untidy pile and bending down, we too removed our shoes. Inside the small side room which had been the Mahatma's bedroom, there were about forty people, including Jawahar and Sardar Patel. They were weeping. In the far corner lay the frail body of Gandhi. Covered in a blanket, his head was being cradled by one of his female followers. The women were all wrapped in shawls against the cold and they chanted prayers and *Ram, Ram* in a forlorn rhythm. The mourners shuffled up to make space for us, and together, British and Indian, we stood in silent homage. How strange he looked, this little man, without his steel rimmed glasses that had become so much a part of him. And yet his face, though pale under the bright lights, was at peace, almost as if he were sleeping during a fast and would soon wake with his impish smile to chide us all again. My legs shook with fear for the future. I was utterly bewildered by what had happened. But in that moment there was also a sense of something else—victory, perhaps, rather than defeat. That the strength of this eccentric little man's ideas and ideals, from the very force of the devotion he commanded even here and now, might, just might, prove too strong for the assassin's bullets and the ideas they represented.

Outside, however, a storm was brewing and the room was in the eye of it. The crowd continued to press in, hundreds of faces peering through the French windows, banging and shouting. I feared that the wooden doors would not be able to hold much longer. Jawahar wiped his eyes and came over to embrace Dickie. We followed them, the Governor General and the Prime Minister, out into the main hall and left the women to weep and pray. The members of the Cabinet began to adjourn to another room and Dickie went with them. Jawahar also followed, but stopped en route upon seeing me. If, once upon a time, all those months ago at breakfast in York Road, there had been something young and bashful, something of a boy about him, it had all gone now. The responsibility for the future of India rested solely on his shoulders. Without the Mahatma, Jawahar was alone, old, inexpressibly sad and careworn. Suddenly there was a loud crash and then another one. The crowd was breaking down the windows.

I saw the question flickering in Jawahar's eyes and hurried to answer it.

'Edwina's coming. I've spoken to her. She said, "Don't fight with Patel."'

He snorted a little and touched me briefly me on the shoulder.

'If I might be so bold Prime Minister,' Alan interjected at my side. 'We are rather in danger of being overrun.'

'It's all under control.' Jawahar rubbed his chin with his hand. He spoke quietly, slowly, with immense effort and self-control, for he had loved Gandhi. 'The body will be laid out on a table in the garden tonight for the darshan. The funeral will be in the morning.' With that he turned and left to join his Cabinet. It was then that I saw Hari. He was standing with another man in the corner of the hall, both of them dishevelled, blood on their shirts.

'Who did it?' Alan asked Hari.

'A Hindu, a member of the Hindu Mahasabha,' the other man said.

Absurdly, I sighed with relief for the Mahasabha was a right-wing Hindu organization. So, it hadn't been a Muslim after all.

'I did my best,' the other man said, ringing his hands. 'But there were no medical supplies in the house, nothing at all.'

'It would have made no difference. There is nothing you could have done.' Hari tried to offer some comfort. 'The Mahatma was shot three times in the chest at point-blank range,' he added for our benefit.

'But what monster could have done such a thing? Still I don't understand.' The other man, also a doctor I realized, began to cry, wiping his tears with the back of his hand.

Once more we were interrupted, this time by the screaming and shouting of the women in the room where Gandhi was lying. Several of them were dragging a big woman out of the room, battering her with their fists. The unmistakable white mane of Margaret Bourke-White was gleaming in the midst of the mêlée. They were fighting over something, trying to grab it and Margaret was hitting out valiantly, trying to keep hold of whatever it was the women wanted from her.

'Get out! How dare you! Have you no shame!' The women shouted in English and Hindi. At last they overwhelmed her. Tearing the camera from her hands, they triumphantly ripped out the film and let it uncoil to expose it to the light.

'Jesus H Christ! What kind of chicken shit is this?' Margaret bellowed. And the women, aided now by the guards, wrestled her, kicking and swearing, out of the front door.

'Come on!' Hari profited from the distraction to grab my hand and lead me away into the shadows of the corridor. Together we found a door into the garden where we weaved our way through the crowds. Towards the back of the garden there was a tiny chink of light, wavering and golden in the black Indian night. It was drawing the crowd towards it and we found ourselves carried along. Someone had set a candle on the spot where Gandhi had died. The small patch of dust had been marked off with a humble line of short sticks laid in the shape of a triangle as if by a child for a game. A large empty tin can, such as might have contained tinned peaches or condensed milk for a mess, had been kept on the precise spot where the Mahatma's head had fallen. Kneeling around it were men and women of all faiths and social classes. Sikhs with turbans, Muslim men in white skull caps, rich and poor, united in sorrow, they reverently scooped up small handfuls of bloodstained earth into their handkerchiefs to carry away and preserve.

I crossed myself and prayed almost silently, 'Agnus Dei qui tollis peccata mundi, dona nobis pacem.' I did not know what else to do.

The crowd began to murmur, whisper, shift, then retreat. A new current carried us towards the front of the house where Jawahar had perched himself precariously on the top of the wall by the front gate. My heart jumped into my mouth. Gaunt, ashen, perfectly illuminated by a street light, he was another easy target for any assassin's bullet.

'Oh God!' Involuntarily, I put my hand over my mouth. Hari placed his arm around my shoulders and held me tightly.

A hush fell upon the crowd as Jawahar began to speak. 'Mahatmaji is gone. The great light is extinguished. Darkness of sorrow and distress surrounds us all. I have no doubt he will continue to guide us from the borders of the Great Beyond. But we shall never again find that solace which we did by running up to him for advice at every difficulty.' At this point his voice broke. He tried to carry on but had to give way to tears. Only with a supreme effort did he manage to utter his closing words.

'We can best serve the spirit of Bapu by dedicating ourselves to the ideal for which he lived and the cause for which he died.'

This time it was I who did the driving. Taking the wheel of Hari's yellow convertible, I patiently cajoled our way through the endless stream of mourners coming to Birla House. Hari was slumped in the front passenger seat, hands neatly folded in his lap, staring straight ahead. I did not want to use the horn and it took us a long time just to go a few hundred yards. Then Hari began to weep. Tears poured down his face, and dripped unchecked off the end of his nose.

'Perhaps,' I ventured, 'now the killing will stop.'

He nodded, his brow furrowed with pain, but said nothing.

At the gate to his house, I did not need to honk the horn. Sandeep had been looking out for Hari and opened the gate. The tents had all gone: the refugees had all been relocated over the last few months. The grounds of Hari's house seemed a vast expanse in the headlights. Under the portico, the Sikh servant embraced his Hindu master and the Englishwoman. We went together into the empty house.

'I need to wash,' Hari said, his words distant, mechanical. He didn't go upstairs to the bathroom, but out to the garden instead. I followed. Despite the fact that it was winter, the swimming pool had been filled. All was calm, still, black as the night. We were alone with the water under the silent stars. The click and clank of the pool lights being switched on was brutal, almost disrespectful. Hari started to undress, stripping off his bloodstained shirt and trousers until he stood in his underpants. It was January and I was shivering with cold, but he did not seem to feel it. He stepped under the shower, raised his head, and let the water caress his brow. It flowed in a silver sheen to coat his body, droplets glistening like tiny diamonds in the black hairs on his chest. He began to rub himself, to clean himself, vigorously washing his hands and forearms as if he was scrubbing up for an operation. At length, he turned and looked at me. Stepping out from the shower, he held out his hands like a child for me to inspect.

'I can't get rid of the blood,' he said. 'I know there is none there, but I still can't get rid of it.' I turned his palms over in mine and stroked them. They were brown on the back and pink on the underside. I lifted them to kiss.

But Hari pulled away and switched off the shower. Then he dived quickly into the pool and shot from one end to the other like a shimmering fish. The bulk of him was lost in the water and just as on horseback, he was loose, light and elegant. He swam a couple of lengths to get warm, water dripping from his arms in trails of silver pearls. Panting, he came to rest at the top of the pool in front of me. There he cupped the water over his head, again and again, and washed himself in a ritual way and prayed.

Looking up, he raised his arms to beckon me in. I unbuttoned my jacket and dress, stripped down to my camisole and camiknickers and slipped into the water with him. The cold was biting and I cried out but he was there to catch me. He was warm and he held me, washing me, cupping water over my head.

Asato Ma Sad Gamaya
Tamaso Ma Jyotir Gamaya
Mrityor Ma Amritam Gamaya

I raised my head to the stars. We were weightless, floating, and he lifted me. There was no effort and no more pain.

There were very few British staff left now in India and I was one of the last. Our last weeks at Government House had flown by at a whirlwind pace. There had been visits to Srinagar, Baroda, Panipat, the Refugees Handicraft Shop in Connaught Place, meetings of the United Council for Refugees, meetings on the placement of returned women, lunches, receptions, farewells and more farewells. It had been a gruelling fourteen months and now it was nearly over. We were all utterly exhausted. Even the stalwart Ronnie Brockman had been off sick. Yet, somehow, Edwina still managed to paint on the lipstick, and carry on smiling and shaking hands. And so did I. At her request, I managed to squeeze a free day and night into her schedule. Jawahar arrived to fly her up to Naini Tal to visit Sarojini Naidu who was now the Governor of the United Provinces. The two women had worked closely together and become good friends. It was precious time with Jawahar and Edwina returned exhausted and emotionally drained. We didn't speak much. Whenever we did, she would pull at the St Christopher medallion around her neck and tug needlessly at her wedding ring. We talked in lists, clipped and efficient, avoiding personal issues, and dealt with diaries, logistics, guests and planning. I dared not push her for I knew that she was distraught at the thought of leaving India and Jawahar. She knew she had no choice. For her there was no way out.

Restless and unable to sleep, I sat for the last time at my desk by the window in my bedroom in Government House. Tomorrow it would all be over. Dickie would relinquish his post. Mr Rajagopalachari would be sworn in as the new

Governor General, and the Earl and Countess Mountbatten would leave India and, with them, me and their few remaining British staff.

I sighed and took out some writing paper. Unlike Edwina, I was a nobody. No one would mention me in history books, no one would remember me, miss me or even notice me. But now, suddenly, at the eleventh hour, I had been given a choice

Through the open window the night was retreating by degrees, lifting veils of grey from the great imperial mirage, shadows beyond shadows, lawns, fountains, trees, flowers. In the distance a raucous peacock heralded the dawn. A breeze suddenly came from nowhere and rippled the reflection of the moon on the silver surface of the ornamental pond. Then, equally suddenly, all was still. In that moment of pure silence, in that second, I knew. The decision I had been agonizing over in private these last days had been made. Tomorrow I would start the next chapter of my life although I still did not know whether Hari would be a part of it.

Slowly, I filled my fountain pen, waiting for it to draw up the black ink from the bottle. As the first orange of dawn seeped up from the bottom of the Mughal Gardens, I began to write.

The first two letters were easy: one to Amrit Kaur, accepting her job offer to work with refugees and the St John's Ambulance and Red Cross here in India; the other to Dickie. I kept the latter letter simple and formal. I told him what an honour it had been to serve with him and Edwina during their time in India and thanked them for their support in my darkest hour and for all the many kindnesses they had shown to me. It was the third letter, to Edwina, that presented a challenge. What would be the best way to tell her my decision? I knew her so well. Whatever I said, however I told her, in her current state of mind, she would not take it well. She would certainly be cross that I hadn't gone to her to discuss the job offer when Amrit had first raised it with me three days ago. But how could I have done that? I had not even made up my own mind then and perhaps I had been afraid that Edwina might lean on Amrit and persuade her to withdraw the offer. Once I had formally accepted the job and Edwina had left India, it would be too late for her to interfere. Edwina would also have been angry if I had gone to tell her that I had decided to turn down the job in Hong Kong that she had kindly written the reference for. I knew that I was letting her down on that. But most of all, it was likely that she would be jealous, even incandescent with fury, because I was being given an opportunity to stay on, perhaps with Hari, when she herself would have to leave India and Jawahar. It was this last potential reaction that most perturbed me. Edwina was still a woman with real influence. Deep down, I was afraid that she might find a way to mess things up for me out of spite, to deny me this chance. I scratched my head and watched the malis turning the fountains on early for the Mountbattens' last day. In sequence the water spouted, spluttered then shot high into the orange sky where the moon was still hanging as if it too didn't want to miss the final curtain.

'Dear Lady Louis,' I wrote, calmly, formally. I thought it might be easier if I kept some sense of distance. When I was finished I licked my finger to moisten and secure the seal on the envelope and placed the letter on top of the other two.

I was surprised to be interrupted by Zamurad Khan bringing my breakfast on a tray. Normally I ate in the mess, but there were so few of us left now.

'What's all this?' I asked as I put the letters into my briefcase.

'Today is the last day old Zamurad is serving Memsahib. Special treatment!' He tried to smile but his face was long and grey. 'And I have brought you farewell gift.' With a magician's flourish, he placed a small cardboard box about an inch square on the tray front of me.

'Open it!'

'Zamurad Khan, there is no need a present,' I protested, but I did as he commanded, holding the box in the palm of my hand and removing the top. A ruby and two pearls had been carefully nestled in a square of green silk.

'Ruby and pearl from the hilt of the sword of Shah Jahan.' He smiled proudly. In the early sunlight, the ruby glistened pomegranate red.

I was horrified.

'Zamurad Khan, it is far, far too much. I cannot accept this.'

He frowned. 'My wife, she asks me, what is Lady Wallace going to do in England all alone with no husband and sons to protect her? *Inna Lillahi wa inna ilayhi raji'un.* So, this morning she took kitchen knife and removed these from the sword for your dowry.'

Registering my shock, he sought to reassure me. 'Not to worry. Taken from back of sword only.'

'Dowry! Zamurad Khan? I am too old for that!'

'My wife, you know, sometimes she surprises me. Last night she becomes revolutionary! She has seen pictures of Memsahib with Lady Mountbatten and bigwig Congress ladies. She says that Lady Wallace is very beautiful, like a goddess.' He raised his left eyebrow, feigning surprise that his wife should even have thought such things. 'And, so she says, Lady Wallace is not to grow into lonely old widow. Lady Wallace is still young and must find good man and marry again. Such things are possible in England and there is no shame. And that is what she says.'

'And what do you think, Zamurad Khan?' I said.

'I think it is very bad mischief of Lady Mountbatten, Rajkumari Amrit Kaur and such other English-educated riff-raff ladies, making my wife and daughters-in-law think about leaving purdah for the sake of our new India, and doing such other things to make my life complicated in my old age!' He was shaking his head and his index finger by way of admonition which I wasn't convinced was entirely pretence. All the while I was trying to push the cardboard box with the ruby and pearls back into his hand, but he would have none of it.

'So, Wallace Memsahib is not arguing and is accepting this gift. Not from my family but from Great Emperor Shah Jahan.'

Facing defeat, I played my final hand.

'But I won't be going back to England so I don't need a gift.' I shook my head and finger back at him. 'I'm going to stay in India, at least for a while. I've got a new job!'

'Mashallah, Lady Wallace! Mashallah!

*I*t was still early morning when I made my way down to Dickie's study. The Governor General's last day in India was packed with engagements: a drive through Old Delhi with his wife and daughter in an open-top car, a farewell lunch for personal staff, a civil farewell, a farewell dinner by the Prime Minister and Cabinet, and a final farewell reception in the Mughal Gardens, to which seven thousand people had been invited. If I were to have any chance of a quiet word with either Dickie or Edwina, I needed to get in before the crush.

Passing through the corridor and into the anteroom to his office was like walking into a peculiar jumble sale. All the portraits of former Viceroys and Vicereines and the assorted pictures of landscapes that were not hung had been stacked against the walls. In the midst of the stacks were two large gilt chairs with faded green upholstery. Brown labels had been carefully tied around the elegantly scrolled arms.

Thrones x 2, 1911 Durbar, someone had printed in a neat, decisive hand.

The door to the study had been left ajar and Dickie was relaxing in khakis at his desk. Ridiculously, he reminded me of a giant pixie camouflaged against the light green walls of his study. I tapped lightly on the door. Seeing me, he turned on the charm switch to somewhere between public and private, which was the setting reserved in varying degrees for friends and staff.

'Pippi-ee WP! Good morning! Bright and early as ever! Come in!'

I pushed at the partially open heavy teak door. A small mountain of cardboard boxes behind it kept it from opening fully.

'Good morning, Lord Louis!'

'Bit of a tip, I'm afraid.'

'What's happening to the paintings?' I gestured in the direction of the anteroom.

'They'll stay. They belong to India. It's up to the Indians to decide what to do with them. The boxes are going home with me though.'

He used his chin to indicate the boxes behind the door. He had labelled each of them himself in red ink.

South East Asian Command/Navy utmost IMPORTANCE,
Bikaner, Hyderabad, Kashmir/Princes Assorted
INDIA misc FOR MYSELF

'I am, however, leaving the new GG the air conditioner, a prerequisite for good administration in India. I wrote a memo myself on the subject and gave a copy to Nehru! All government offices must have air conditioners which promote regular office hours and clarity of mind.' He laughed at himself. I smiled politely and looked at the floor, awkward now that it had come to the point.

'But what is it, Pippi?' His eye fell on the letter in my hand. I gave it to him. 'And somewhere I have got one for you,' he said. Going back to his desk, he picked up a letter from the top of the tray. 'Well, spit it out!'

'I want to thank you, Lord Louis, for doing me the honour of allowing me to serve with you and Lady Louis.'

'Quite frankly, I don't know what we would have done without you, Pippi. You have been the best Special Assistant without Portfolio I have ever worked with, stepping into all the breaches like you did and keeping Edwina afloat.'

I hurried to bite the bullet.

'Lord Louis, I'm not going to come home with you tomorrow. The thing is, Amrit has offered me a job to continue refugee and welfare work here in India. And I've accepted.'

He was taken aback, and rubbed the back of his neck before quickly recovering his composure.

'I can't go back to England. I just can't . . .'

'My God, of course you can't Pippi! I understand, and Amrit is a sharp one for asking you to stay.' There was such softness in his eyes that I wondered briefly why it was that Edwina, his own wife, seemed unable to find just a little something in him to love.

'Have you told her yet?' He meant Edwina.

'No. I wanted to tell you first.'

He nodded and then said, hesitatingly, 'Break it to her gently, Pippi, and wear your tin hat. There'll be fireworks.'

'I will.'

'Ayoooh! Neola!' A streak of silver lightning and a chaprasi charged into the room, followed by one of the little ball boys from the tennis courts. They were chasing the mongoose which had been adopted by the Mountbattens' daughter. The cheeky animal made three circuits of the room tailed by the chaprasi and the boy. At last it jumped on to the Governor General's desk where it stood on its hind legs, as if to address the nation. But the first and last British Governor General of India was too quick even for a mongoose. He grabbed it by the scruff of the neck and promptly stuffed it into an empty cardboard box, before quickly battening down the lid. I felt relieved, for this spoilt mongoose had a propensity to bite anyone who was not its mistress or her bearer. Order was once more restored. The servants retreated, taking with them some of the boxes on Dickie's orders.

'Here! Keep the devil in there!' Dickie got me to hold down the top of the box with the mongoose scrabbling about inside. 'I've got just the job for him.'

He opened the top drawer of the desk and pulled out a brown file labelled *Operation Madhouse, Top Secret.*

'Let him out!'

Cautiously, I opened one flap of the box and Neola, which is Hindustani for mongoose, popped up like a cheeky jack-in-the-box.

'Here you go! Be a good chap and shred this for me!' Dickie pulled the first of two sheets out of the slim file, tore it vertically down the middle and put one half into the mongoose's paws.

The two of us stood over the box and watched the excited Neola gnaw the correspondence: *in view of Mr Churchill's position . . .* The typescript parted, separated by a bite from *meeting Mr Jinnah.* The signature of the previous Viceroy, Lord Wavell, was scissored into big black free-standing letters which floated to the bottom of the box.

'I just want Edwina to be happy. I always have,' Dickie Mountbatten said to no one in particular. Perhaps he was addressing me, the mongoose or himself. 'I am stubborn and selfish, more interested in my gadgets and genealogy than romance, but she is all I ever wanted. We fell in love here in India when I was ADC to the Prince of Wales. Actually, it was the Prince that lent us the key to his bungalow!' Dickie gave the second strip of the document to Neola and looked around the room as if he were seeking to rewind time.

'I know. I was there on your wedding day.'

Perhaps I sounded wistful but Dickie gave a little puff as if to say that it all had been a long time ago and in a very different life, as indeed it had.

'Edwina is such a conundrum. She didn't want to come to India. We had to drag her out kicking and screaming.' Neola took the second sheet from Mountbatten's big hands and set his teeth to work on it. *Attlee . . . Labour party . . . in the event of . . . imperative . . . timescale . . . The British Government cannot commit forces beyond...* I was glad I couldn't read the full document. Now, no one else would be able to either.

Dickie hadn't finished.

'When I decided to bring forward the timetable for the transfer of power, it was of course because of the rapidly deteriorating security situation and the influence of Ismay, Auchinleck, Abell and the Governors' Conference. But perhaps in some way I had also had Edwina's unhappiness in the back of my mind. Before we came out I had promised her that I would wrap everything up quickly.'

'Oh!' I was shocked by his confession and even more that he had trusted me with it. I recognized at once that it was potential dynamite. What if it ever got out that the last Viceroy of India had advanced the date for the transfer of power from June 1948 to August 1947, with all the implications for the bloodbath that ensued, partly because of a promise to his wife to wrap things up quickly? It was on the tip of my tongue to say that he must never tell anyone, that he must not even think of it. But already his jaw had clenched as if he had mentally retracted the statement. I knew that he had realized that he had revealed too much and I said nothing.

'Sometimes I really don't understand her at all.' He looked me squarely in the eye for a long time like a small boy who had repeatedly done all the sums right only to have them spitefully marked wrong. And yet we both knew why Edwina didn't want to go back to England now.

'I like him, you know. He's the best of the bunch. We couldn't have pulled it off without him. I count him as a friend.' There was no need to ask who he was talking about.

The last sheet had gone from Lord Wavell's file and Neola was finishing off the cardboard title page *Operation Madhouse Top Secret His Ex Eyes Only* with methodical razor bites. When it had finished, the last British Governor General of India pushed the animal's head down and shut the lid of the box. He blinked quickly, decisively, and I saw that his eyes had become calculating, steely cold.

'Well, I suppose it's time to say goodbye.' I offered him my hand. He took it and leant forward to kiss me formally, once on each cheek. For a moment, I thought that this German Prince was going to click his heels.

'You are coming to the dinner tonight?'

'Yes,' I said, 'I have been invited. And to Palam in the morning to wave you off. Can't miss that!'

He smoothed the difficult curl that always fell forward back to his head.

'Good luck, Pippi! We shall expect to see you at Broadlands, and when you come, make sure you bring Hari with you!'

I must have looked surprised for I did not think he had known about our friendship. He grinned at me and almost winked.

'Don't worry! Won't tell a soul. And it is good to know the two of you will be here to support Nehru.'

Now I was blushing, a full red, neck to ears, a young woman's blush. I picked up his letter and awkwardly took my leave.

The teak door swung slowly on its hinges as I closed it behind me. Through the diminishing crack, I saw Louis Mountbatten sit down heavily at his desk. He took out the paper knife to open my letter, and lowered his head to read. I knew that he would never be able to escape India, not for the rest of his life, not even after his death. There would always be recriminations over the question of responsibility for the decision to divide India into the two new nations of India and Pakistan and the communal carnage that ensued. Disaster, catastrophe, civil war, hell on earth: what were the words that might allow me to talk about the things I had seen? There was simply no way to describe what had happened when a line had been drawn on a map, to divide and uproot communities that had been living in one place for generations. Young, old, sick, insane had all found themselves in refugee camps in a country a thousand miles away from all they had known.

Everything had become so utterly senseless; a raging, flaming, rolling cycle of madness that had seemed to spawn out of the dust and the air, feeding upon itself, gorging on greed, revenge, fear, poverty, religion and power. In the end, none of us had been able to stop it, except perhaps one eccentric frail old man with little round spectacles, a pocket watch, a spinning wheel and a loincloth—the Mahatma, the Great Soul, Gandhi.

I was a coward and I was ashamed of it. I went first to the office before I could muster enough courage to go and seek out Edwina. The place was deserted, silent, still: no ringing of telephones, no gruff men's voices, no laughter or pinging and clickety-clack of typewriters. I thought of all the different jobs I had done over the past year, the tedious routine, the fill-ins, the chores, the panics and the crises. In the end, I was back in the office where I had first started out as Special Assistant to the Vicereine. The door still squeaked slightly on its hinges and the heat made me gasp. Dickie had always had the air conditioner humming along quietly in the background in his study. I hurried to open the windows and turn on the ceiling fan. As always, it was temperamental and it took two short sharp tugs on the cord to coax it into action.

Muriel had already packed up her desk. Even the boxes that been here yesterday were gone. Slowly, I eased back the heavy office chair, sat at the desk, and telephoned the home of Amrit Kaur. I knew the number by heart and I listened to the deep cat-like purr as the dial of the telephone slowly returned to zero. Each time asking me if I was sure, if I was sure. I cradled the receiver to my head, expecting to wait, but the phone rang barely once before it was picked up.

'Hello. It's Pippi Wallace from the office of Lady Mountbatten. May I speak to Rajkumari Amrit Kaur please?'

'I'm sorry, Lady Wallace. She's in a meeting.'

'Will you tell her that I would be delighted to accept her offer and that I'm putting a letter in the post today?' There was a pause, a kerfuffle. I heard Amrit's sweet voice with her precise

Oxford English far away in the room across the hall that I knew was her study.

'Tell Lady Wallace, I am delighted and I shall see her tonight.' I imagined Amrit's infectious giggle and big half-surprised smile which always reminded me of Gandhi. The thought of him brought a wave of weakness, a wobble in my legs and I steeled myself, like we all had had to do, and carried on.

'One moment please.' There was a scuffling of slippers on a wooden floor and more voices. A door banged and the secretary was back on the line. 'The Minister for Health said that you will be welcome to move in here for a while if you have not made alternative living arrangements.'

'That is very kind. Please tell her I have a place.' I was lying. 'Goodbye.' I kept the receiver at my ear and pressed down the bar to end the call. Then I dialled the Imperial Hotel to reserve a room.

And so it was done. My future, in the short-term at least, was settled. There remained only Hari and Edwina to tell.

I rang Hari next. The shadows of the night had long gone but daylight had brought with it renewed doubts. Hari and I had always avoided the subject of the future. Perhaps it was because the burdens of my grief and our previous marriages still weighed too heavily upon us, perhaps because we were just too old, and old people didn't fall in love and live happily ever after. And perhaps Hari's family would not welcome me, a white woman, a Britisher.

I breathed deeply and, for the last time in Government House, picked up the receiver and rang Hari's bungalow. Again, I had no need to look up the number. But this time no one answered. The phone rang and rang. I knew where the phone was. It always stood on the table in the hall between the drawing and dining rooms. Patients, colleagues and friends, they had always been able to call Hari Rathore at all hours of the day and night, asking for help and advice. I had never known a call to go unanswered. Another five rings. Perhaps Sandeep was in the garden? The polio-induced paralysis in the servant's leg slowed him down, especially on the steps. At length, reluctantly and yet relieved, I placed the receiver back in its cradle, comforting myself with the thought that I would meet Hari at the farewell reception that evening.

To distract myself from my doubts and a sense of rising uncertainty, I turned my attention to clearing my desk. The task didn't take me long: my fountain pen, a pot of ink, an airmail writing pad with one remaining leaf, a stack of personal letters from Philip and Margaret fastened with red ribbon, and my leather diaries with the last entry made just yesterday. Unhooking the elastic binding, I flicked through the letters I had once written to my husband, Charles. Left to the mercy of Indian heat and humidity the pages of the book had already buckled and yellowed. They crackled like some ancient document. Wiping the sweat from my brow, I wondered what I ought to do with my personal papers. Should I burn them, or send them to my solicitor in London for safe-keeping? Eventually I put what I wanted in my briefcase. Before I finally buckled the strap, I took out the letter I had written to Edwina in the middle of the night. Placing it on the desk, I smoothed it with the flat of my hand.

So, this was what the collapse of an empire looked like—an empty office with a lone widow and a letter. Now that it had come to it, the whole thing was bizarre, like the last day of the summer term at school, or coming down from Oxford. Almost everyone had already gone, the place was virtually deserted. Promoted immediately after Independence, the Indian ADCs had left to take up new commands in the new Indian forces. Pete Rees, and Field Marshall Auchinleck had departed last year. The Field Marshall had been so sickened by Partition that he had turned down the offer of a knighthood. Alan, Fay and the children had left just a few weeks ago, terribly disappointed at having to miss the final show. I imagined Pete digging his garden in Monmouthshire, and Alan knocking on doors in Whitehall, looking for a job or prospecting for a Parliamentary seat. How small and insignificant England must seem to them after India.

Stretching my arms, I leant back in my chair. For better or worse, it really was over, and I was left with a strange sense of anti-climax, fear and anticipation. There was nothing now to do but watch the ceiling fan: whir, whir, whir, click. It still wobbled slightly on its axis and made its arthritic sound on every fourth rotation.

The drawers of the metal filing cabinets in the corner of the room stood open as if they had been tipped out and emptied in haste. I went over to inspect them, pulling them out and feeling in the gaps at the back and underneath in case anything important had been overlooked. A family of spiders had already moved in and constructed three small webs in the bottom drawers. Respectfully, I closed the drawers and left them undisturbed.

Who, I wondered, would come after us? They were all probably waiting in the Secretariat just down the road, young, moustached, keen Indian officials leaning on mountains of boxes, having a gossip and a smoke. Tomorrow, after the Rajaji had been sworn in as Governor General, they would move in. Telephones would ring and typewriters would clatter and ping once more. Old problems, new problems—everything would change, but perhaps not much.

And what would happen to Viceroy's House, its vast estate with its thousands of staff? They said that Jawahar's government was likely to move the capital south again, that New Delhi was too far north. I imagined Government House, the symbol of the British Raj, abandoned to rack and ruin, the great dome fallen in, creepers climbing through the windows, flowers and trees growing out of the walls, and monkeys holding court in the Durbar Hall.

Then I thought of that day, riding at Mehrauli, the mosques, temples and palaces crumbling into dust and Shelley's poem we had recited as children in school.

My name is Ozymandias, king of kings:
Look on my works, ye Mighty, and despair!'
Nothing beside remains. Around the decay
Of that colossal wreck, boundless and bare
The lone and level sands stretch far away.

So many memories, too many ghosts. Slowly, I took the last sheet from the airmail pad and picked up my pen for the final time.

Welcome!
    A few bits of housekeeping.
    1. *The fan is rather temperamental. The cord needs two short*
       sharp tugs.
    2. *Keys for filing cabinets in top right-hand drawer.*
    3. *We had a nest of cobras in the washroom at the bottom of the*
       corridor last rains. The snake man cleared them out. Watch
       out for that!
    Good luck!
    Jai Hind!

Swallowing hard, I hesitated at the door to Edwina's apartment. Our relationship in India, that of employer and employee, had been tricky even though we had known one another ever since we were friends together at school. Such friendship could not be easily written off. Two rolls of carpets were leaning against either side of the door like silent sentries. Edwina had ordered them to be removed nearly six months ago when her beloved and elderly dog, Mizzen, had become incontinent. The staff must have brought them back, ready to roll them out in the room for Rajaji, the incoming Governor General. It was stifling in the corridor even though the Mountbattens' summer apartments were on the north side of the house. I struggled to think clearly. How on earth was I going to break it to Edwina, tell her that I had decided to stay on? I still hoped for some words of encouragement from her, that she might be happy for me. But I feared she would see my decision to stay as a personal betrayal.

I knocked gently, three times.

'Come in!' Her voice was light, her tone sharp.

Edwina, Countess Mountbatten of Burma and wife of the last British Governor General of India, was without make-up, her brown hair still in rollers from the night. Hunched over her dressing table, she was writing frantically while the fan above her head turned languidly, in defiance of her haste. She was grasping the pen with a childish fist and making notes along the margins of what I suspected was the guest list for the evening's farewell reception. She scrawled another hasty note before squinting at me through her thick spectacles.

'Ah, good morning, Letty!' Her jaw was set tight, her face blotchy and shiny with sweat. She was now the only person in India who still called me by that name. It felt as if it had belonged to someone else in a past life. 'Where is everyone? Have you seen Muriel?'

'I passed her in the corridor. She's on her way up.' I sniffed the air which, strangely, smelled of mango.

With a tut of disapproval, which I took as applying to all her remaining staff for slacking, she turned away from the dresser to face the room and held out the paper she had been working on. Taking it from her, I saw that by using arrows up and down the list, she had taken the liberty of amending the seating plan for the Cabinet dinner tonight.

'Dickie between Amrit and Indira, then Rajaji, and make sure they put me next to Jawahar. The rest, you can do what you like with. I really don't care.' Her voice trailed off and she turned to face her mirror, mechanically pulling out the clips from the front of her hair where they had been placed the night before to train it back in curls from her forehead. As ever, her nails were a beautifully manicured red, but I saw that her hand was shaking as she dropped the clips one by one into a little carved wooden box sitting amid a crowd of pill boxes.

A door slammed at the end of the corridor, disturbing Mizzen. He got up unsteadily from his basket at the end of her bed and, dragging his hind legs, crawled over to Edwina and lay down beside her.

'Dickie and I are going to serve the hors' d'oeuvres ourselves to guests tonight. People will appreciate it, don't you think?'

I nodded and wondered what the great and good in London would make of it: the white serving the brown. I was certain she would not escape the salvoes on her return. Taking off her glasses, she gestured to a box of mangoes on the floor next to the dressing table that I had not noticed before.

'Jawahar sent them as a farewell gift. They're from Lucknow. And this.'

I saw that she was holding a copy of his autobiography in her lap. Jawahar was looking contemplative on the cover, wearing his trademark white Gandhi cap and black sherwani jacket. His hands were curled softly on the arms of the chair in which he was posed. Eyes dipped a little, he gazed sage-like into the distance.

I thought she meant that he had given her a copy of the book. But she opened the palm of her hand and showed me a tiny gold coin. As I leant forward to take a closer look, she snatched it away, as if I had been about to steal it from her.

'It's to go on my charm bracelet.'

Rather viciously, she started pulling the rollers from her hair, quickly unravelling it into set-piece curls at the side of her face and the nape of her neck.

All the talk of Jawahar had not made my task any easier. I needed to get on with it and say what I had come to say.

'I'm going to give Jawahar these as my farewell gift.' She took out an enamel and gold box from her drawer and an emerald ring. 'Eighteenth century, French, from Versailles.'

Her voice had risen in pitch as she spoke, as if she had been asking for my approval. But I hesitated to give it.

'Perhaps it's a little too much? He might be embarrassed.'

She blinked in surprise.

'Yes. You're right. I shall tell him that he must sell them if he ever needs money.'

The idea that the Prime Minister of India might need to sell belongings to get money seemed ridiculous to me, but keen to raise my own matter I offered no further counsel.

'Jawahar says I should put Mizzen down.' She nodded her head towards the dog. 'Put him out of his misery.' Her face contorted and a deep furrow formed between her eyes.

'I think Panditji was suggesting that it might be kind.'

Edwina put a new hairpin in the front of her coiffure and began to dab on face cream, energetically smoothing it into her skin. While she was waiting for it to soak in, she attended to her eyes, adding a touch of blue and grey eyeshadow on her lids and flicking mascara on to her lashes. A cloud of powder flew up into the air as she picked up her puff and liberally applied the powder to her forehead, cheeks, nose and chin. She looked so white that she reminded me of a portrait of Queen Elizabeth the First I had seen in a gallery in London before the war. The final touch came with the brush from the rouge pot, expertly applied to her cheeks. I opened my mouth to speak but she got in before me.

'Oh God, Letty, I feel like I am being torn in two! We have vowed to each other that duty must come before desire.' She took a pile of letters from a drawer in her dressing table and proffered them sneakily, almost like a bribe that if I took, might make everything right.

'I know,' I said briskly. I wanted to put my arms around her and tell her that I understood, but the wheel had come full circle and it was now my turn to be cruel to be kind.

'Edwina, I'm really sorry to do this now.' I pulled my letter from my briefcase. 'I want to thank you for everything and for bringing me to India on your staff. It has been a great honour to work with you. After my boys and everything . . . Well . . . You gave me a chance to break free of my grief, to move on. I will always be grateful to you and Dickie for that.'

'What's all this about?' She took the letter from me but made no attempt to open it.

'I'm not flying back with you tomorrow.'

She stared at me blankly as if she hadn't heard me, then shook her head in disbelief.

'Of course you are. Don't be silly! If this is a joke, I'm not in the mood.'

'No, really, it's true. I've been offered a little post here in India and I've decided to accept it.'

'Well, that's ill-advised and you jolly well know it. Anyway, you've got a job lined up in Hong Kong. I pushed the boats out to get you that one, even though I really need you back in England with me, doing relief work.'

'I know you did and I am grateful. It's all been terribly last-minute. I was only approached a few days ago and decided to accept the job just last night. It really is quite the best thing for me.'

Her eyes narrowed and became cold and calculating, the way they had when Dickie's French mistress Yola Letellier had visited last winter and had wrapped herself languidly and elegantly in a fur coat. And now that she was so emotional about Jawahar, I realized that she was jealous again. I feared our friendship would be lost forever.

'Well, good for you!' She looked me up and down like a school headmistress inspecting me for mucky shoes, while she pondered my fate.

'It's that man, isn't it? Jawahar's friend . . . What's his name, Doctor Whatsit?' Of course she remembered Hari's name. She had a knack for remembering names and had met him and joked with him on many occasions. 'No good will come of it. You won't be received anywhere in London if you take up with him. Heaven knows what his family or your friends will say!'

She bit her lip, knowing that she had struck below the belt and that she was being contradictory and hypocritical, condemning my relationship with Hari in terms that she would not apply to her own with Jawahar. Yet she was furious, so much that for a second or two I thought she was going to jump out of her chair and slap me. I was annoyed by her pettiness even though I knew that it was born of physical exhaustion and her feelings towards Jawahar.

'Actually, I am not staying on for Hari.' I had wanted to spare her the details for a little longer, but I decided to give it to her straight, even though I knew it would hurt. 'Amrit has offered me a job working for her at the St John's Ambulance and Red Cross, continuing your good work, in fact.' With the last, I had offered her a sweetener but it didn't sound as conciliatory as I had intended.

Edwina had been so preoccupied with work, Jawahar and herself that she had not anticipated any of this. I watched in horror as her face collapsed in upon itself. She had to swallow hard several times before she could speak.

'Well, well, aren't you the dark horse!' Unscrewing her Elizabeth Arden lipstick, she applied big red dots to her lips, spreading them with her finger. 'At the very least you might have had the courtesy to tell me and seek my opinion on the matter. I expected better of you, Letticia.' She didn't call me Letty, and hissed as she saw my reflection in the mirror.

'Edwina, don't be like that! I did not solicit this job.'

'Not solicit, not solicit?' Her voice trembled with uncontrolled rage. 'You've been plotting behind my back, plotting all this time to betray me.' She took a few moments to calm herself. 'I needed you in London for a few months before you left for Hong Kong. I'd been counting on you to sort out all my India papers. After all I have done for you, you treat me like this!'

I was aghast. I had known that Edwina would be upset, jealous even, but now I realized the true extent of the anger and distress I had caused. I remembered our first afternoon in India when I had found her locked in the bathroom, eating chicken, and I had vowed to do my best to support her in her difficult, seemingly impossible, role as Vicereine. Was this how it was going to end between us?

'Edwina, I have not betrayed you. I never would! Amrit came to me just a few days ago. She floated the idea informally at first, and I told her that I needed to think about it. Can't you be just a little bit happy for me? It is a tribute to you that she has asked me to stay on.'

She got up slowly, stiffly, smoothed her skirt and adjusted her necklace, deliberately taking her time so I would stew. Pursing her lips, she went over to her bureau by the window and picked up some papers in a large brown file.

'Here you go! I was going to give this lot to Amrit myself this evening, but you can run one last errand for me.' She almost threw the file at me. Flicking it open, I found that it contained hundreds of notes in Edwina's handwriting on committee meetings, memos, lists and reports, the Red Cross, St John's Ambulance and the United Council for Refugees and Welfare.

'That should keep you busy. And don't you ever, ever . . .' Underneath all the powder, her face was turning crimson. Hand at her throat, she tugged at her St Christopher and gasped for breath, 'Don't you ever ask anything of me again!'

She drew her shoulders back and straightened to her full height. I saw that she was struggling to stay rational. Part of her had heard what I said and knew it to be true, the other part wanted to tear me to pieces and feed me to the dogs. With distain, she offered me her hand, as if I were simply one more person in a long reception line. For the last time, I dipped into a curtsey and accepted her hand.

I turned to take my leave, knowing that I had burnt my boats, but felt that I should give her some advice and reassurance.

'Edwina you must get a good rest when you reach home. You've worked so hard and the people of India, Jawahar, especially Jawahar, they know it. Truly, you are loved; you have nothing to prove to anyone.' I wanted to say more, but it was all far too complicated and I had run out of words.

Mizzen, a dog of duty, got up and struggled to escort me to the door. I bent down to stroke his head, briefly holding my hand over it like a priest giving a blessing. The dog looked

up at me with sad brown eyes as if he had understood what
had happened.

As I closed the door, I saw that Edwina was wincing with
pain and had put her hand on her left hip. Taking a towel, she
was like an old woman as she wiped up the drops of the dying
dog's blood-flecked urine from the marble floor.

$\mathcal{L}$ight was spilling in delicate fountains from the crystal chandeliers in the state dining room. It scattered tiny rainbows on the faces, medals and ermine of the few former Viceroys whose portraits had been left on the walls for one last night. Tomorrow, I had little doubt, these remaining gentlemen would be removed, mothballed and relegated to a dingy back room somewhere on the estate.

They were a select band, the guests at this final farewell dinner: Dickie and Edwina, Rajaji, the Prime Minister and his Cabinet, some members of their families and a few remaining British. I was honoured to have been invited. I had been placed at the far end of the table next to Baldev Singh, the new Defence Minister, who was brooding morosely under his tight turban. Worries about war in Kashmir with Pakistan and the state of Hyderabad which had still not acceded to the Indian union were etched on his brow. We chatted about his family, his wife and boys. When he asked me about my plans I explained quietly that I would be staying on.

'Good,' he said, his expression lost in the forest of his beard, his face reflected back at him from a silver tureen. 'We need all the help we can get.' He sighed. 'We have fought long and hard for it, and tomorrow we will truly be masters in our own house. But I fear we have been in opposition too long. Now we will have to take responsibility for our own mistakes. We are not used to that.'

The conversation in the room was strangely subdued, interrupted only occasionally by isolated tinkles of laughter. All eyes were on Edwina and Jawahar who were sitting side by side in the middle of the table.

Tonight, her last night, Edwina looked stunningly beautiful. Her skin, lightly tanned by the Indian sun, was glistening against the white silk of her dress. She wore a sparkling necklace of diamonds and emeralds. And yet she and Jawahar both looked utterly forlorn. Eyes downcast, they picked at the food on their plates, Edwina with her left hand, Jawahar with his right. Were they perhaps holding hands? What a consummate actress she was! However dark, grey and grim she felt inside, she still managed to paint on the glamour and exude the charm. But this evening, despite her best efforts, the façade had cracked and all of us could see it.

The khidmutgars cleared the plates after the main course and I realized with a pang that tonight was my last night too, my last one in Government House. Tomorrow, I would sleep in the Imperial Hotel, alone with the consequences of my decision. Wistfully, I stared up at the huge Indian tricolour which was hanging from the ceiling. Saffron, green and white; the spinning wheel that used to stand at the centre of the flag of the Indian National Congress had been replaced by a twenty-four-spoked Ashoka chakra. The spinning wheel, it was believed, would be too feminine a symbol for a nation. It was in this room that Hari and I had first met. I imagined him now, striding out of the flag, coming towards me, smiling, or was he frowning? I couldn't tell. Such a gentle man, such a strong man, a big man, and I softened at the thought of him.

'You're not eating, Lady Wallace?' Baldev Singh waved his spoon in the direction of the milk pudding. It was topped with ground pistachio nuts and small pieces of mango which fanned out like the sun's rays. The truth was that I felt sick to the pit of my stomach. What would Hari say when I told him that I would be staying on? Slowly, I picked up my spoon and made an effort to eat. Baldev talked about growing up in the Punjab and the family's horses. I reciprocated with tales of my own childhood holidays in Pembrokeshire with my grandparents. After what seemed an age, it was time for the speeches. Napkins fluttered, chairs were pushed back and the incoming Governor General, Rajaji, stood up. He spoke softly, kindly, quite informally, like a grandfather at a family gathering, and thanked Dickie and Edwina for their dedication and service to India. It struck me that people on the outside of events and those in the future would never be able to understand what the people in this room represented. The eclectic group gathered for the occasion was made up of natural enemies who, not long ago, had been consumed by mutual hatred. Yet, somehow, through terrible trial and adversity, and most of all a shared belief in greater ideals, they had become friends.

Next it was Dickie's turn and he responded in kind, paying tribute once more to the Mahatma and Nehru. By the time Jawahar rose, stiff and shy, everyone was very emotional. At first, he addressed his remarks to Dickie, for Jawahar was one of the few men who had truly grasped the complexity and gravity of the situation that had faced the new Viceroy in the spring of 1947. He went on to thank various people individually, even me, before abandoning his notes and looking down at Edwina with love in his eyes.

'The gods or some good fairy gave you beauty and high intelligence, and grace and charm and vitality—great gifts—and she who possesses them is a great lady wherever she goes. But unto those who have, even more shall be given; and they gave you something that was even rarer than those gifts—the human touch, the love of humanity, the urge to serve those who suffer and who are in distress. And this amazing mixture of qualities results in a radiant personality and in the healer's touch.'

He hesitated and rubbed his chin with his hand, looking first at her and then down at his feet.

'Wherever you have gone you have brought solace, and you have brought hope and encouragement. Is it surprising, then, that the people of India should love you and look up to you as one of themselves and should grieve that you are going? Hundreds of thousands have seen you personally in various camps and other places and in hospitals, and hundreds of thousands will be sorrowful at the news that you have gone.'

No one could move. Out on the patio the band was tuning up, discordant trills, scales, a trumpet testing a few bars of 'Auld Lang Syne'. Jawahar, finally unable to control his emotions, turned on his heels and left the room. Edwina burst into tears.

As soon as I could I escaped to the terrace. Drying my eyes, I took deep breaths of the night air, but it was much too hot to help clear my head. In desperation, I lifted my eyes to the stars, as if they might offer me a sign, but of what I was not sure. Conjurers juggled fire and the band played a familiar Indian folk song whose name I thought I might yet learn. The glittering people circulated like miniature galaxies and constellations, revolving around each other and around the khidmutgars with their trays of drinks and nibbles. The bearers looked smart with their spare hands neatly tucked against the backs of their striped cummerbunds.

It was never difficult to find Hari in a crowd. He stood head and shoulders above the average man and was waiting for me exactly where he had promised to be: by the seat to the left of the first fountain. I hesitated. He was dressed not in his usual Western suit but a crisp white Indian kurta-pyjama topped with a purple silk waistcoat which shimmered under the lights like the back of a mandarin duck. He was deep in conversation with a group of men. From the movement of his lips and waggle of his head, I knew that he was speaking Hindustani. Although I had managed to find time for some lessons and my knowledge of the language had increased in leaps and bounds, I still could not hold more than a basic administrative or social conversation. The truth was that I was afraid. My head was spinning, with wine, with nerves. Seeing me, Hari nodded discreetly in acknowledgement and disengaged himself from the conversation. There were just a

couple of steps between us. His black bushy eyebrows made
him look tense and fierce. I stopped, but at the last moment he
smiled and I gained the courage to go to his side. People were
looking at us. Friends, acquaintances, many I had worked with
in various capacities, all were heading towards us to chat, no
doubt to bid me farewell.

'I need to talk to you,' Hari whispered, firmly grasping my
elbow and steering me away from the crowds.

In silence, we headed down to the long rose garden far
from the lights. It was quiet, the music and chatter muffled by
the red sandstone walls. Without touching, we sat side by side
under a pergola hanging with grapes and jasmine. In the stillness
the tension between us was almost unbearable. We both had
something to say but I asked myself if what either of us wanted
to say was what the other wished to hear. I knew I was in love
with Hari. I was beguiled and terrified by the feeling which, at
the same time, offered comfort and security. Confused, I still
said nothing and wondered how the silence could be broken
and the tension eased. To my relief, it was Hari who did so,
clearing his throat and shuffling his words as he spoke.

'I know it's impossible, out of order, perhaps . . . India is
a difficult place and it's never going to be plain sailing. And of
course, there will be those who will turn up their noses and say
that we ought not . . .' He twisted his hands, looked at me, and
then looked away. He took my hand then released it.

In the half light, in the shadows I tried to see his face, but
why did I need to? I had traced it a hundred times in the darkness
with my fingers: the lower lip that was so much thicker than the
upper one and protruded, almost petulantly, when he was cross or
worried . . . and the tiny dimple in his chin which caved in when
he laughed.

In that moment I realized that he had been plagued by
the same doubts as I had been. 'I've got something to tell you,'
I finally said.

'Oh! Damn it! Pippi, will you marry me?'

I couldn't breathe, I couldn't speak, but when my questing hands found his face, words exploded out of my mouth.

'Yes, yes, Hari, oh yes!'

'Oh God, really?'

'Yes.'

He drew me to him and buried his face in my hair, relishing the smell of me as he breathed me in again and again.

'I have been so afraid, so afraid that you would say no, that I would be alone again. All these years, long, long years.... And then you just turn up, one fine morning, in Viceroy's House looking for a Maharaja!'

I laughed.

'I've waited a lifetime to find you. I couldn't bear to lose you now.' He kissed the top my head and then placed more kisses on my eyes, nose, cheeks, mouth.

'I've been such an ass, dithering all these months. In the end, it was Sapna. "For heaven's sake, Papa," she said to me, "stop mooning about the place like a lovesick elephant. Just go and ask her". We could live in London as well if you want, part of the time, perhaps. With airplanes, these days, it's much quicker. Whatever you want.'

Words came readily now, thick and fast, almost too fast as Hari tried to pour out his desires and plans for our future together.

'Oh Hari, the thing is, I'm staying on in Delhi anyway. Amrit has offered me a job. I'm not naïve enough to think the role will last forever, but it's a start at least.'

He pulled me closer again, squeezing me tightly. 'Now I will never let you go.'

'If I am to live in India, you will have to teach me the names of the flowers and the trees.'

'Done,' he said, laughing again.

'It feels so easy,' I whispered.

'It is, jaan, it is.'

Arm in arm, we walked back towards the house, the music, the lights, and upwards to the stairs. The band was playing Glen Miller's *In the Mood* and Hari puffed out his chest.

'And now I am going to tell everyone. I want to show you off.' My thoughts turned to Edwina and Jawahar and their unhappiness. But I could not stop Hari even for a few more hours. With a wide grin and twinkling eyes, his hand danced from the small of my back up to my shoulder and back again. He had become irrepressible, ebullient, full of energy and youth. I realized with a shock that it was I who had done this to him and that he had given it back to me. It was a strange, overwhelming, flooding feeling that had been long forgotten and which I had been frightened and reluctant to indulge: joy. He told Sunny Singh and Cherie first. Cherie did a little jig and I stepped into a whirlwind of handshakes, hugs, kisses, backslapping, jokes, surprised congratulations and merriment.

At midnight, the band played *Abide with Me* and silence fell as everyone remembered Gandhi, whose favourite hymn it had been.

It was after three when we went to my room to pick up the bags which I had prepared to take to the Imperial Hotel with me. But Hari was having none of it and insisted that I go home with him.

'Is that all?' he said, looking at my suitcase, briefcase and soft holdall bag.

I nodded. 'Not much to show for a year in India, is it?'

'Well, you do have me. That's a bonus, I suppose!'

For the last time, I closed the door to my room. The alcove where Zamurad Khan had insisted on sleeping during the worst of the troubles was now dusty and bare.

'I might have to do something for my bearer and his family,' I said. 'They'll be laying off staff at Government House. He's a Muslim, vulnerable and old.'

Hari touched me lightly on my arm.

'Of course. Don't worry about that now.'

As we left Government House, I glanced up at Edwina's apartments. The lights were still burning. Was Jawahar with her I wondered? My heart ached for them, imprisoned by duty, by fate.

Back at York Road we collapsed, exhausted, on to the big double bed, sleeping like logs for a few hours. Shortly before dawn we washed and dressed, enjoyed a quick breakfast and then drove out to Palam. The landscape around the airport was barren, unforgiving, almost desert-like. Already the sun was burning hot and a light breeze had whipped up some dust. The parades, inspections, twenty-one-gun salutes, speeches, parties and fly pasts were no more. Only the key players in the tragedy were left, standing like chess pieces waiting for the final moves to be played. Hari and I joined the line. I bid farewell to Muriel Sparks, Edwina's long-suffering secretary. We had never really warmed to one another but had managed to get on. We kissed each other on the cheeks now and she invited me to tea next time I was in London. Dickie, Edwina and Pamela were passing slowly down the line, shaking hands. Photographers lunged in for the intimate moments: Jawahar, fatherly, his arm round Pamela, was giving her a hug; Edwina was embracing Rajaji; Jawahar lifting Edwina's hand to kiss it. But even as Dickie and Edwina climbed the steps to the Dakota, the press pack were already leaving. The story was old news and they were rushing back to Delhi to secure the best spots at Rajaji's swearing-in. The plane revved its engines. As the last moment, just as they were about to remove the steps, Muriel reappeared at the airplane door. Urgently, she beckoned to me, and shouted my name. The wind swirled my skirt as I ran across the tarmac and climbed the steps. There were four steps up for me, two

steps down for her. She pushed something small and warm into
my hand.

'It's for Panditji from Lady Louis.'

Shading their eyes with their hands, everyone watched as I
returned and spoke quietly to Jawahar.

'You're not going, Pippi?'

I shook my head, wanting to spare him the full explanation
at this point.

'Edwina wanted you to have this,' I said. I imagined her
taking her seat in the Dakota, bursting into tears and removing
her precious St Christopher medallion, embossed with a picture
of the Saint carrying a child over the river.

As discreetly as I could, I dropped the little gold necklace
into his outstretched palm.

He smiled wryly. 'Oh God, I hope she doesn't expect me
to wear it.'

'I think she just wants you to have it. It belonged to her
father.'

The Dakota had slowly made it on to the runway. People
started to turn away, but Jawahar didn't move, so everyone
else had to stay. They fidgeted. He remained motionless. The
engines roared and the plane carrying the last Viceroy and
Vicereine of India lumbered into the air. Jawahar raised and
waved his hand. He was still waving as the plane circled west to
chase the dawn.

Part V

Marigolds
New Delhi
22nd February 1960

'There!' the little boy said in Hindustani, jabbing his stubby index finger into the heart of the drawing room. It was the language the other must have addressed him in when asking for me. Removing my reading glasses, I squinted against the light. They had come with the morning mist—I supposed that the one must have found the other wandering about in the back garden. They were holding hands, peeking in through the French windows like the coy New Delhi winter sun: the little boy with his toy engine and the old man, who had come out without a hat.

I had not heard them coming. But then I had heard nothing else that morning, not the glorious chorus of the birds in the trees outside the bedroom nor the throat clearing and soft off-beat thud of eighty-three-year-old Sandeep dragging his polio leg. Every morning he limped about pulling the curtains and blinds and opening the windows of the bungalow to let in the air. I had not even heard the soft crunching of the wheels of Hari's car as it had pulled out of the long drive. My students' essays were unmarked and jumbled together in a ragged pile. I had abandoned them the previous evening when the news came in. The letter of condolence I had been trying to compose since before dawn lay unfinished on my desk.

I hadn't recognized him at first. He was wearing an old cream English woollen coat over his usual attire and had a shabby tweed scarf around his neck and lower face. Shading my eyes against the sun, I looked and looked again.

'Jawahar!' Surprised and taken aback at seeing him unannounced at this early hour, I called him informally by his given name. 'What on earth?' And yet I already knew. Jumping up, I rushed across the room, arms outstretched. Stepping over the threshold, he put down a large battered green dispatch box, and bent to remove his sandals At the sight of the box my heart gave a thump and blood rushed to my head. Even after all these years, it was still a call to action.

'Panditji, please. There is no need.' I addressed him formally now, my knees cracking arthritically as I too knelt, trying to stop him from taking off his heavy black sandals. The front of the sandals was made of plaited leather and the back straps were buckled around his ankles. He was wearing thick black home-knitted socks against the winter cold. The thread around the left big toe was wearing thin and would soon need to be repaired.

'Don't,' he said softly. He leant gently on my shoulder to steady himself, reminding me of Bapu. 'Jawahar,' he said. 'Call me Jawahar! That is why I have come.'

He held out his arms and murmured as we embraced. I was taller than he was so the tip of his chin rested on my shoulder. He smelt of cigarette smoke, shaving cream and the leftover chill of the winter night. We stood silently together for a long time, my palm between his shoulder blades, his cold hand resting on the nape of my neck. The little boy, unsure if he would be allowed to stay and sensing that something was wrong, tugged at my skirt and pushed in between us. He too needed comfort although he didn't know why.

We pulled apart and I caught my breath. The handsome energetic widower, adored by the people and seemingly blessed with eternal youth, whom I had first met thirteen years ago, was now old. Thin and frail, walking with a stoop, he had gone completely bald on top and what was left of his hair around the side of his head was snow white. Today his cheeks were as grey as mud. His brown eyes had sunk back into sockets that were purple and black, as though someone had beaten them in with their fists. I had seen him like this once before. But now

I suspected it was too late. He had the look of death about him. This time there would be no saving him.

He tried to speak but no words came. This great orator, who had led a nation to independence not just with the beauty and power of his words and ideals but at great personal cost, could only open and close his mouth like a gasping fish. Looking down at the boy, he ruffled the little one's curls. Then taking a freshly pressed handkerchief out of the top pocket of his padded jacket, he carefully unfolded it and wiped the child's winter nose. That simple act appeared to give him some strength and when he looked up the words came.

'There is hardly anyone left now.' He paused and I put my hand on his arm. 'No one left now to call me by my name . . . now that she has gone.' He choked a little on the reality of the fact that Edwina Mountbatten, the last British Vicereine of India, had died the previous day. It had been a terrible shock for all of us. She had passed away suddenly in her sleep while touring with the Red Cross and St John's Ambulance in Borneo. 'Jawahar,' he repeated in a daze, as if in confusion he was trying to affirm his own continued existence. 'And Pippi, you say it just as she does; in that light, cheerful English way without the r on the end!'

And I understood why it was that he had come.

'Have you had breakfast?' I asked.

He raised an eyebrow and attempted a grin, perhaps at the memory of a long-ago morning when it had all begun.

'No,' he whispered.

'Then you must stay and have some with me.' It was the set response, defined by custom and time between us.

At this invitation, he picked up the dispatch box, and touching his elbow, I led him to the sofa in the middle of the room. Gently, I took his frayed English coat which smelled of moth balls and which was such an uncharacteristic garment for him to wear. Helping him remove the scarf from around his

neck as if he were a child, I folded it with the coat and laid them
over the back of a chair. Privacy was precious for this man and
I didn't want to rush to call the house boy. Sitting down, he
placed the box securely on his knees, his hands sitting sphinx-
like on top of it.

Risking privacy, I decided to ring for breakfast while
Jawahar watched the little boy playing at his feet. His father, our
driver, had made the boy a wooden toy train and designed the
engine like a box with a hinged lid. The child had collected an
assortment of treasures and placed them inside: sticks, pebbles,
fallen leaves and feathers. He was busying himself opening and
closing the lid with a muffled bang. Every time he took an item
out of the box, he reached up and put it into the outstretched
palm of the old man. Then he stood back, breathing hard with
both concentration and a stuffed-up nose, observing intently as
the other carefully laid out his precious objects on the lid of the
dispatch box and created patterns around the faded gilt coat of
arms of the last Viceroy of India.

'I gave them all the slip this morning with my woollen coat
disguise, the whole damn lot of them!' Jawahar was looking at
me but I knew that he only half saw. 'I walked from Teen Murti
with just one bodyguard, much to his chagrin. "The whole way,
Panditji?" the poor fellow had kept saying. "Oh dear, dear,
Captain Sir won't like it! There will be the most terrible trouble
on this account. And what if someone recognizes you?"'

I managed a smile, imagining the poor policeman shaking
his head and trailing the long boulevards of New Delhi in the
wake of the seventy-two-year-old Prime Minister with his
dispatch box 'the whole way' up York Road to our house.

'Soon they will be here, Pippi, mark my words! Come to
take this errant knave home! And then my daughter will tell
me off.' He wagged his finger and head in contrary motion.
'"For God's sake Papa, you can't go about being so selfish!
What if something happened to you? You tell me? What will

India do then?" As a matter of fact, she has always said that and I have always replied, "When I go, just stuff me into my best sherwani, stick a red rose in my buttonhole and prop me up on the front bench. No one listens to me any more and most of India will not even notice I've gone."' There was a twinkle in his eyes, and for a moment I glimpsed the witty Jawahar of old who used to leap about, the life and soul of the party. But the humour was a feint, a ruse to avoid the matter in hand and he couldn't keep it up. His eyelids drooped and he was once more the fragile, hunched old man, a husk of his former self, exhausted by the vicissitudes of politics and power, the gap between his vision of India and the harsh realities, and the sudden and unexpected death of a woman who, against all odds, had been a most dear friend. He fiddled with a pebble on top of the dispatch box and rearranged it on the Viceroy's faded gilt coronet. Then he handed it back to the little boy who had already begun facilitating the return trip for his treasures.

'I cannot believe Edwina has gone.' He choked on her name and could say no more.

'It was a terrible shock to us all. Edwina and I were friends as children.' I knew that he was aware of that and I had no idea why I had felt the need to mention my own relationship with Edwina. Perhaps it had been to fill the pain of silence, perhaps because she had been so much a part of my life too, perhaps because she had been only fifty-eight years old, the same age as me and too young to die. 'We went round to Teen Murti as soon as we heard,' I said, 'but they said that you had gone to the Toynbee Lecture.'

He nodded. 'If it had been I who had gone first, she would have carried on.'

'Yes.' I confirmed. 'Edwina always drove herself. She never knew when to stop. It was her greatest strength and her greatest weakness.'

Under Sandeep's stern supervision our young house boy brought in the breakfast tray. Sandeep's turban sat unusually low on the old Sikh's brow, pushing his forehead down into his eyes so that he bore some resemblance to a Neanderthal man. His evident disapproval of the unexpected arrival of a guest, however familiar, was exaggerated by the downward flow of his wispy white moustache and beard around his pursed lips.

'The bread is not fresh. The baker's boy is late again this morning. So unreliable. Apologies, Panditji. Madam, if I had known . . .'

'Don't worry, Sandeep! I'm sure it will all be fine.' I gave him my biggest, most charming Edwina-style smile. But in my distress I couldn't quite pull it off and the old servant just shrugged and limped out of the room.

Seeing the food, the little boy shunted his train round the coffee table to where I was kneeling and backed himself on to my knee in anticipation of a snack. I was too soft with him and I knew it. But I couldn't help myself, especially since his mother had just had another baby and had little time for him. I started to butter the toast and to draw out the marmalade. The knife scraped noisily over the crusty bread while the grandfather clock in a corner of the room chimed a quarter to eight.

'Eat!' I offered the toast to Jawahar who was still clinging to the green dispatch box like the little boy to his train. He placed the plate on top of it, but he didn't eat. Unlike other Indian leaders, Panditji had always worn his heart on his sleeve and over the years I had come to know the many moods which passed over his face. They could change with the speed and unpredictability of English weather: rain clouds forever chasing sunshine and shadows, freezing snowstorms, blazing summer heat and, sometimes, the gentle breezes that rippled and creased his forehead.

Watching him with wide eyes, the little boy, in contrast, was busy eating. He was stuffing the long soldiers I had cut for him from the toast into his mouth the marmalade and butter oozing shiny and golden orange around his lips.

'I wasn't expecting it,' Jawahar said. 'Barely two weeks ago I was holding her hand in mine. She had been at my side in New Delhi, at the Republic Day Parade, at the Mughal Garden Reception'.

In my mind's eye, I captured Edwina that night, as I knew he too was doing. She had been wearing her long pink satin gown with its impeccably cut bolero jacket. His hand was on the small of her back and she dipped her head graciously when he whispered something in her ear. With the tip of his index finger, he gently tucked an escaped grey curl behind the garland of flowers that she was wearing in her hair. He smiled contentedly like an old guru as he guided her through the crowds of mutual friends.

Politicians, generals, businessmen, civil servants, the great and the good of the Congress Party, had all gathered on the terrace at the back of Rashtrapati Bhavan, the President's House, which had once been Viceroy's House. Suddenly the photographers rushed forward because they saw Edwina shaking hands with Marshal Voroshilov, the Russian President, who was on a state visit to India. And I remembered how the British High Commissioner at my side had sucked his teeth with disapproval.

'Bloody hell, Pippi! Someone needs to get to Lady Mountbatten and tell her a few home truths. London is not going to like this one bit.'

He was right, of course. Thirteen years had passed since Indian gained independence. The last British Vicereine's visits to the country and her close friendship with Prime Minister Jawaharlal Nehru in particular probably no longer served British interests. But then Edwina had never cared too much about what people thought. She had always done her own thing.

That night was no exception. She had just carried on
smiling and laughing and mingling through the Mughal
Gardens. Her gold charm bracelet chinked in time to the lilt
of her voice as she made little circles in the air and talked
with her hands. Suddenly, she saw me waiting in line. She
stiffened almost imperceptibly, nodded, forced a smile and
then quickly looked away. The fountains sparkled and the
people chattered perhaps remembering other nights, other
parties. And for those who had eyes to see, standing in the
gaps between them and in the shadows of the trellises and
rose bushes were the lost ones, the ones who had gone to
Pakistan and never come back.

'The operator just said, "Telephone call from Broadlands,
England."' Jawahar continued and brought my mind back to the
present. 'I thought it must be her. Oh, how it always lifted my
spirits to hear her quick happy voice from far away. I thought
that perhaps she had returned early from Borneo. And then
Dickie's voice came on the line. "Look here, Jahwaralal . . ."'

This time I managed a proper laugh as Panditji gave his
impression of Dickie, struggling to pronounce his name
properly. In all the years, he had never managed it. Sometimes it
had been Jaharlal, sometimes it had even sounded like Narwal.
But as Jawahar had once said to Edwina and me, 'Don't tell
him! It will ruin the fun!'

'And then Dickie told me. "Awful news. No sense beating
about the bush. Better sit down, old friend. Better coming from
me. I don't want you to hear it from the press. Edwina is dead."'

The tears slowly built behind my eyes as Jawahar spoke and
I hurried to pour the tea. It would not have done to cry and we
didn't. It was how everyone had survived, for if we had cried we
would have never stopped. Lifting the teapot, I was reminded
that I too was no longer young. The skin on my hands was thin
like rice paper, almost translucent, and in places the blood was
damned up in tiny veins. I wanted to ask Jawahar for more

details of the circumstances of Edwina's death. It was odd that she had died so suddenly, so mysteriously. She had not always been the most stable of people. But now was not the time, so I said nothing and waited.

'Heart attack, they said. She'd been at a St John's Ambulance reception and hadn't been feeling well. Apparently, she'd had an eggnog and an early night. They found her in the morning . . . dead in bed.' He swallowed hard, and the Adam's apple in his throat bobbed up and down. He tried to say something else but couldn't. I sensed that he was holding something back.

I handed him the teacup on the saucer, swapping it for the untouched plate of toast. It rattled in his hands but I was relieved to see him take a sip.

'She fell out with me, you know—Edwina.' Today it was not just Jawahar who felt the need to confide. 'It was silly really. There was no need for it. It was a bit better in recent years when she visited India. But even so, I wish we could have sorted it out sooner . . .'

He looked at me over the top of his teacup, and recognized the shadow of his own grief in me.

'She just couldn't stand it, all of this'. He gestured with his spare hand and looked around the room. I knew that he was referring to my life here in India after Independence. 'Sometimes, despite our best intentions, we can be so small. Even I was jealous, just a little, at times.'

'Were you? Jawahar, I had no idea. I am so sorry.'

'Don't be, Pippi. Being happy is not a fault.'

He sipped his tea again and the little boy got up from my knee and returned to his engine, pushing it around the legs of a spare chair. 'Choochooo! Psssht. Tuktuk.' His little lips let loose a quiet assortment of sounds and words that sometimes were Urdu, sometimes Hindi, sometimes more Punjabi, and sometimes English, a mishmash of all the languages of our unorthodox household.

Finishing his tea, Jawahar placed the empty cup back on the coffee table and picked up the plate of toast. He was staring at me, long and hard, as he had done the first time, that morning, years ago, measuring me up, checking that I was still the person he thought I was.

'There can be no rest, Pippi. They won't ever let me stop.' The grandfather clock ticked and he nibbled on his toast, eating because he had to, without pleasure in the taste. 'As a matter of fact, Pippi, sometimes I even hanker after the solitude of a British jail. There at least there was time to read, write and think.' The grandfather clock ticked on. 'They all have a vested interest in keeping my nose to the grindstone, even my own family. They say that I am the centre of the great wheel. Without me all their carefully arranged spokes will lose their place.' He sighed and looked around the drawing room of our bungalow which was almost identical in design and aspect to his old house at 17 York Road. 'As a matter of fact, I miss it, you know—York Road. Teen Murti is far too big.' He still called it York Road, not Motilal Nehru Marg as it had been renamed after his own father post-Independence. 'Life was simpler then; the gate being left open, even at night, no guards and people just coming and going; you and Hari all shy, holding hands like young lovers, Dickie, even dear old Patel!' Saying her name was much effort for him and he distracted himself with a touch of sarcasm at the memory of his old political rival, chewed on his toast and swallowed hard as if he were eating stones.

It was in that moment I saw them, all the invisible shackles, balls, and chains that constricted and burdened this lonely, old man and locked him to his fate. Like Sisyphus, he had every day to put his shoulder to the boulder that was India. Every day he had had to heave it up and up the slope. And when it rolled back, as it was bound to do, he had no choice but to pick himself up and labour again.

There was a rusty click when he opened the dispatch box and timidly lifted the lid, as if he were somehow afraid of what he might unleash. Slowly, he turned the box around to reveal its contents, deliberately offering them to me. Quickly, I pushed the breakfast tray down to the far end of the coffee table so that he could lay the box in the space created. It was full of letters. Hundreds of them in different sizes and shapes, all neatly tied up in batches of twenty or so with lawyer's red tape. And I realized immediately what they were. He had no need to say anything. Here was his confession. That was why he had come.

'All this time? All these years, Panditji?' I said. I knew these letters were the sum of Edwina's correspondence to him. And somewhere in a box or drawer on the Mountbattens' country estate, Broadlands, in England, was the other half from him.

'Yes.' He whispered, his voice soft, almost feminine with old age. 'Two a day, at first, after she left. I would work all day and unburden myself to her at night. Then once a day and then, with the pressures of state, sometimes just one or two a week. She would tell me off for that!' He hesitated, as if having come so far, he had become unsure of how much to trust me with. 'Always in diplomatic bags, always under a double cover. We were so afraid of letters falling into the wrong hands, communists perhaps. Look!' He selected a bundle of letters and handed them to me. 'She made me number them, so that we would know if one went missing.'

I was reluctant to intrude, but he stole a march on me, deftly untying the tape and letting the letters drop into my lap. They separated with a gentle rush, like slowly melting snow from the branch of a tree, and came to rest on my knees and on the floor around me. Seizing the opportunity, the little boy abandoned his train and moved to pick them up. Meticulously, he delivered them alternately, one to me and one to Jawahar.

'Precious,' I said. Widening his eyes, the child nodded and stroked the soft watermarked paper of one letter with the tip of a finger. Taking it from him I noticed that Edwina had written *To The Prime Minister* on it in her spidery writing, while the next one had been addressed *To Himself.*

'May I smoke?' Jawahar asked. He knew very well that he could and had done so on many occasions in our house, but it was a mark of the man that still he sought permission. I assented and taking the matchbox from the drawer in the coffee table, I struck a match for him. He leant forward to cup his hands around the flame and I felt the warmth of his breath on my hands and face. Sitting back on the sofa, he drew up his legs and crossed them beneath him. Inhaling and exhaling, he watched the curls of smoke rising and dancing as if he might somehow conjure the tall svelte figure of Edwina out of the air.

'I think,' he said, his voice thin and quiet as if coming from a far off place, 'It was that she was my escape and I was hers. Writing to her, being with her—it was always dreamlike, a state most unbecoming of a Prime Minister.' He exhaled slowly. 'But in truth, Pippi, I think I am only incidentally a Prime Minister.' He was losing himself in a reverie and I realized that for him, I too was now only incidentally there.

'I would send her poems: Yeats, Swinburne, Euripides, Auden, Blake, the Song of Solomon and poor ham-fisted efforts of my own. I would lose myself in tales of myths and legends. I would write about the Buddhist caves of Ajanta and the Temple of the Sun in Orissa, where there is no sense of shame or hiding anything. Ah! Pippi, you should see the faces of the Bodhisattvas on the walls at Ajanta. They are thousands of years old yet still so real and alive, looking down at me, each one a jewel in itself. The women are painted with such beauty and such grace, they make me feel pain at the vulgarity and cheapness of the life we see.' He heaved another sigh and tapped the ash off the tip of his cigarette. The little boy had stopped playing so that he could watch and listen.

Then, unexpectedly, Jawahar started laughing, long
and loud, apparently for no reason, as if he had gone a little
insane. 'God forgive me, Pippi! I even used to look forward
to Commonwealth Conferences being in London! Do you
know why? Because I could bunk off on weekends down to
Broadlands. She would be waiting for me, skipping about on
the doorstep, giddy and excited like a schoolgirl. And me, I tell
you, I was probably much the same! And every time I would
be surprised how at home I felt there, deep in the English
countryside with the smell of freshly mown grass in my nostrils,
and no one able to reach me from the utter madhouse that is
Delhi.' He raised his palms to the ceiling and rolled his eyes in
an exaggerated gesture of despair. I was reminded of another
beleaguered old man, the penultimate Viceroy of British India,
Lord Wavell, who had also used the term madhouse for India,
many years ago. 'And so you see, Pippi, Edwina and I . . . we
would have two whole days to walk along the river, ride across
the fields, laugh and cry, hold each other, and talk and talk.
Always we talked. And the joy of it was that, for a short time at
least, we were free, we were together.'

At last great tears rolled down his cheeks and fell like
pearls on the front of his jacket. And while for him there
was no shame in this, I remained unsure. Still entrenched
in my obstinate Englishness, I didn't know what to do. My
awkwardness left the silence to itself and in the stillness I
understood, perhaps for the first time, what it was that had
bound them together. A love of the Mahatma, and India for
sure, but it had always been something more than that. He had
thrown open the shutters for her, shown her another world,
made her understand that she was worthy of love, and she in
turn had held him in her arms, stroked his head and given this
tortured man a taste of peace.

If I didn't know what to do at the sight of the great man
in tears, the little boy did. It was he who came to my rescue,

picking up his wooden train and standing in front of the old man. He put his tiny hand on Jawahar's knee, the pudgy baby dimples around his knuckles offering themselves like tiny kisses. Gently, he reached up and lifted the toy into the old man's lap.

'Is this for me?' The old man smiled through his tears and the little boy nodded.

'Don't cry,' the child said. It was the longest sentence in English I had ever heard him string together. And then the most amazing thing happened. He clambered on to the old man's lap, took the handkerchief from the pocket of the Prime Minister's jacket, and offered it back to its owner to wipe his eyes.

The grandfather clock sounded a regal eight.

'Who is this boy?' Jawahar asked.

'Zamurad Khan,' I replied. 'He's the grandson of my former bearer at Viceroy's House and named after him. Old Zamurad waited for him. He died the day after the boy came into this world.' I hastened to take from him the handkerchief, soiled now from the wet nose of the child and the tears of the man.

'Well, Zamurad Khan,' Jawahar said to the boy. 'Shall I tell you a story?'

The boy nodded, and with the practised skill of a grandfather the old man settled both boy and train into the space between his knees. Then he popped open the top of the train and peered inside, as if looking for the story, unfolding it in his mind, and taking it out.

'I am going to tell you a story, a very old story, written by a king a long time ago in the ancient language of India called Sanskrit. It is called *The Little Clay Cart*. Are you ready?'

'Once upon a time there was a man called Chārudatta who lived with his wife and little son. Now Chārudatta who lived was a good man and a kind man and he liked to help people. Before long he had given all his money away to the poor. But

it surprised and upset him that many of his old friends wanted
nothing to do with him because he was no longer rich. Ah! "He
whose sometime wealth has taken wing, finds bosom-friends
grow cold."

'One day Chārudatta's little son was particularly upset
because his father could not afford to buy him a little golden
toy cart he wanted. Instead he had to make do with a little
clay cart.

'But all was not lost for there was one friend who still
loved Chārudatta and that was the lady Vasantasenā. Ah, my
Zamurad! I tell you, she was the most beautiful, gracious and
kind lady.

'Then one night there was a great and terrible storm. The
peacocks saw it coming first, raising their heads and lifting
their fans and letting out great shrieks. Clouds, black as wet
tamala leaves, the rain coming down in sheets and my, how
the cold wind did beat.' Jawahar blew to make the sound of
the wind and little Zamurad snuggled deeper into his arms
for protection. 'And yet even this great tempest did not stop
the lady Vasantasenā from coming to Chārudatta. And in his
sadness, the sight of her and her kindness and understanding
made his heart overflow with joy.'

Little Zamurad listened as the old man continued with the
story. He told him how the courtesan's jewels placed in the
little clay cart were stolen. He told him about the evil, half-
mad courtier of the king who tried to woo Vasantasenā and
who, when he couldn't get his way, strangled her and left her
for dead. Gradually, Jawahar approached the denouement,
sanitizing and simplifying the classic story for the child.

At the happily ever after, I watched them, the old Kashmiri
Brahmin whose face had graced the front of newspapers all
round the world, cradling an unknown little Muslim boy who,
lulled by warmth and the lilt of the other's voice, had begun
to doze. And when at last the child was asleep, the old man

placed a kiss on the top of his head and then he, too, let his eyes close.

> *'Fate plays us like buckets at the well,*
> *When one is filled, and one an empty shell,*
> *Where one is rising, while another falls.'*

I managed to get up off my knees by the coffee table and drag myself to the chair next to the sofa, but I was overwhelmed by the weight of sadness. Once again, I had reached a point in my life where I felt used up, utterly spent. What was the point of going on? The end result was always the same. It was not just for Edwina that I was grieving but for the loss of our youth and ideals, for the wanton death and destruction we had been unable to stop, and for the people we had tried and failed to be.

And so we slept. I didn't know for how long. Maybe a few seconds, maybe a hundred years, an hour or a day?

It was the great noise outside that woke us. There was a roar of car engines as they came rushing up the drive. Doors were slammed, men's gruff voices shouted and boots stomped.

Through the glass door to the hall, I saw the burly figure of Panditji's head of security, his revolver out of its holster, cocked in the air.

'Where is he? Is he here? Take me to him!'

'Of course he is, and Panditji is always perfectly safe in my house.' Sandeep was not one to be deterred by his age or infirmity. Waving his stick, the old Sikh squared up to the big policeman. 'And no thanks to you lazy lackeys! Didn't your mothers teach you to knock? Where are your manners?' He pointed at the men's boots with his stick. 'God help us, if the defence of Mother India depends on the likes of you goondas!'

I raised my hand to the glass door to signal it was all right. Then I smiled a charming smile, just as Edwina might have done, to indicate to the big policeman that he should not come in. He scowled under his thick moustache and, having satisfied himself that Panditji was indeed in my drawing room, holstered his pistol.

Slowly, Jawahar raised his chin from his chest and began to move the sleeping Zamurad. Carefully, he laid him on the sofa and covered him with his old tartan scarf to keep him warm. The child was snuffling and making gentle suckling sounds through his lips. For my part, I pulled up a chair to the side of the sofa to keep him from rolling off. He had been struggling to shake of his winter cold and I knew that it would do him good to let him sleep a while

'Well, Pippi, I suppose I should give myself up and go quietly so I can stop Sandeep and Handoo coming to blows?' Jawahar attempted a half-smile, but the sagging skin around his jowls did not seem to want to respond.

'It might be wise, Panditji!'

We embraced. He was warmer, softer now, his muscles more relaxed.

'What about your scarf and handkerchief?' I asked, although I didn't need to.

He grinned just for a fraction of a second, the shadow of the cheeky grin of a boy, and then it vanished.

'I'll take the coat, but you keep the rest, Pippi,' he said. 'Then, one day, I shall have to come back to pick them up.'

I smiled. That too was an old joke, an old routine left over from the younger people we had once been, when there had been more hope in our lives.

One by one, we gathered Edwina's letters, tied them up, and put them back in the dispatch box. Picking up the box, Jawahar leant on my arm and we took a few steps towards the door. Suddenly he stopped.

'Dickie said that they were going to bury Edwina at sea. That it's what she wanted . . . But why would she want that?' He was a man of great intellect and imagination but I could see that although he professed to believe in science, not religion, he was distressed at the thought of the woman he had loved being tipped into the cold grey grave of the English Channel.

'She was always terrified of being incarcerated in the family vault at Romsey Abbey,' I said simply.

He nodded in acceptance of my explanation.

'I think,' he said, scratching his chin. 'I shall send an Indian frigate to escort the burial party, to scatter marigolds on the waves. Do you think that would be all right?' His face was so grey, it was almost as if he was drowning alongside her.

'Yes.' I patted his arm as though I were his mother and he, my son. 'It would be completely appropriate. She loved India. After all, she was the Last Vicereine.'

He nodded again as if making a mental note to himself to make that happen. Then we passed out into the hall and through the crowd of policemen bristling with humiliation.

'Panditji,' the chief said. 'I really must protest.'

'Don't start!' Jawahar growled into his chest like an old bear and, for a moment, I thought that one of the Prime Minister's infamous fists would shoot out of the cuff of his coat and break the poor policeman's jaw. In the old days the press had even had a euphemism for the younger Jawahar's tendency to lose his temper and wade into the fray: 'The dynamic character of the Prime Minister restored order.'

Finally, in the shade of the tall white pillars of the front portico, he hugged me, letting his cheeks rest against mine, first on the left then on the right, reluctant to release me. And then he turned away. Head bowed, shoulders hunched, he shuffled to the rear door of the big American car. The red-faced young officer who had accompanied him on foot that morning was holding it open for him. With every step he took, Jawaharlal Nehru, first Prime Minister of the Republic of India, died a little and something of me died with him.

ACKNOWLEDGEMENTS

*T*he Last Vicereine is a work of fiction imagined around the events that occurred during the transfer of power from the United Kingdom to India between 1947 and 1948, and some of the key historical figures involved in them.

Pippi, Hari, Zamurad Khan, Goldie, Mrs Pritchard, Tariq Ali, Jane Ovington and their families and associated minor characters are all imaginary figures. Any resemblance to any person either living or dead is purely coincidental. The well-known historical figures portrayed in this book are my artistic interpretations of the characters based on my readings of the readily available histories, biographies, autobiographies and primary historical sources of the period. I am of the opinion that a sufficient period of time has now elapsed to make it possible to tell the story of the great friendship between Jawaharlal Nehru and Edwina Mountbatten in a fictional format.

I include a general bibliography that will be of interest to readers who wish to know more about the events and individuals referred to in this book.

In writing this novel I supplemented my own research in India with contemporaneous eyewitness accounts from a variety of sources. I am particularly indebted to the accounts of Margaret Bourke-White and Alan Campbell-Johnson. I am well aware that both of them had their own perspectives.

Nevertheless, elements of their recollections have proved invaluable and have been included at various points in this book. Particular acknowledgement should be made to Alan Campbell-Johnson's account of the viceregal swearing-in ceremony, the Viceroy's visit to Kahuta, discussions at Simla in the run-up to the transfer of power, and Independence Day events in Delhi, as well as to his recollections of everyday life in Viceroy's House and assorted diplomatic, political and social encounters. Both Campbell-Johnson and Bourke-White witnessed refugee columns in the Punjab from the air and their accounts influenced my descriptions of the mass migration. Bourke-White was present in Jaipur for the Silver Jubilee Celebrations in the winter of 1947. Some of her recollections of events, in particular her description of the mad elephants and her phrase, an 'equal balance of madness', have been used in the novel. Bourke-White and Campbell-Johnson were also both witness to the events in Birla House in the immediate aftermath of Gandhi's assassination. I have used and adapted elements from both of their accounts.

The pet mongoose is mentioned by Lady Pamela Hicks in her autobiography, *Daughter of Empire: Life as a Mountbatten*.

For Jawaharlal Nehru's telling of the story of *Little Clay Cart* I relied on Arthur William Ryder's 1905 translation.

In writing this novel I spent time at the Mountbatten Archives at Southampton University, going through papers of both the Earl and Countess Mountbatten of Burma. I am grateful to Professor Ian Talbot, the librarian and staff at Southampton for their help and permission to consult the available documents. At the time of writing, the personal correspondence between Edwina Mountbatten and Jawaharlal Nehru held at these archives was still held under an embargo. For the content and general tone of their letters, I have therefore been forced to rely on the groundbreaking work of Janet Morgan in her biography *of Edwina, Mountbatten, A*

Life of Her Own. Some of the content of the correspondence was published in her book with the kind permission of Rajiv Gandhi. It should be noted that Janet Morgan's work was completed at a time when the private letters from Jawahar to Edwina were still held in the Mountbatten family archives at Broadlands and before they were placed under embargo in the archives at Southampton University. The rest of the letters are, I am told, still in the keeping of the Gandhi–Nehru family.

I could not have written this book without the support and encouragement of my family. A special thank you goes to my father, Edgar Jenkins, for his unfailing belief in my abilities, his patient copy-editing and invaluable feedback on the first draft. My husband, Steve Tsang, and my son, give me the space and time in which to write. They put up with all the usual writer's ups and downs and accompanied me to India to do research. I asked a lot of our young son during this trip. He was stoical in the face of a new and challenging environment, Indian railways and two bouts of Delhi belly. I am very proud of him. I must also thank a number of friends with whom I tested out ideas and enjoyed many conversations in the course of writing this book, or who supported the project in assorted practical ways, particularly during my research trip to India: Professor Katharine Adeney, Yeshwanti Balagopal, Prithvi Chandrasekhar, Zulfiqar Haider Khan, Clare Kittmer and Rahul Yadav. A big thank you must also go to Kate Furnivall for her rigorous feedback and most generous encouragement and support. Finally, I could never have managed to bring the book out in India for the seventieth anniversary of the independence of India and Pakistan without my wonderful editor, Tarini Uppal, and the hardworking team at Penguin Random House in Delhi. Thank you all for making a dream come true.

NOTES

On Krishna Menon, p. 13

Hall, Ian. '"Mephistopheles in a Saville Row Suit": V.K. Krishna Menon and the West'. In *Radicals and Reactionaries in Twentieth Century International Thought*, edited by Ian Hall, pp. 191–216. Palgrave Macmillan History of Intellectual Thought, 2015.

On riots in New Delhi between Sikhs and Muslims. p. 38

Von Tunzelmann, Alex. *Indian Summer: The Secret History of the End of an Empire*, pp. 166–67. Great Britain: Simon and Schuster, 2007.

On Gandhi's relationship with Manu, p. 61

Alexander, Horace. *Gandhi Through Western Eyes*, p. 210. London: Asia Publishing House, 1969.

On the opinion expressed about the situation of Muslims in India during this period, p. 91

Vicereine's report of her meeting with Fatima Jinnah, 24th April 1947. Papers of Countess Mountbatten of Burma MB1/Q38. In the archives at Southampton University, UK.

On the set up of the ashram at Banghi Sweepers' Colony, pp. 147–48.

Bourke-White, Margaret. *Half Way to Freedom, A Report on the New India in the Words and Photographs of Margaret Bourke-White*, p. 81. New York: Simon and Schuster, 1949.

On the comments about Gandhi, pp. 153–54

Bourke-White. *Half Way to Freedom*, p. 230.
Von Tunzelmann. *Indian Summer*, p. 174.
For a discussion on Gandhi bringing 'spiritual sensibilities' and religion into Indian politics, see: Von Tunzelmann. *Indian Summer*, p. 230.
On his glorification of poverty, see: Misra, R.P. Editor's forward to *Rediscovering Gandhi, Vol. III, Satyagraha Gandhi's Approach to Conflict Resolution*, edited by R.P. Misra. p. xxv. New Delhi: Concept Publishing, 2008.
On Mirabehn/Madeleine Slade's complex relationship with Gandhi, see: Grizutti Harrison, Barbara. Introduction to *The Spirit's Pilgrimage*, by Mirabehn. Arlington, Virginia: Great Ocean Publishers, 1984.

On Sardar Patel, p. 218

Campbell-Johnson, Alan. *Mission with Mountbatten*. p.190. Great Britain: Robert Hale and Co., 1951.

SELECT BIBLIOGRAPHY

Alexander, Horace. *Gandhi Through Western Eyes*. London: Asia Publishing House, 1969.

Bourke-White, Margaret. *Half Way to Freedom, A Report on the New India in the Words and Photographs of Margaret Bourke-White*. New York: Simon and Schuster, 1949.

Campbell-Johnson, Alan. *Mission with Mountbatten*. Great Britain: Robert Hale & Co., 1951.

Chester, Lucy P. *Borders and Conflict in South Asia, The Radcliffe Boundary Commission and the Partition of Punjab*. Manchester and New York: Manchester University Press, 2009.

Collins, Larry and Dominique Lapierre. *Freedom at Midnight, The Epic Drama of India's Struggle for Independence*. Great Britain: William Collins & Co. Ltd, 1975.

Evans, William. *My Mountbatten Years, In the Service of Lord Louis*. London: Headline Book Publishing PLC, 1989.

Goldberg, Vicki. *Margaret Bourke-White, A Biography*. London: Heinemann, 1987.

Hough, Richard. *Edwina, Countess Mountbatten of Burma*. London: Sphere Books Limited, 1983.

Mason, Philip. *A Shaft of Sunlight, Memories of a Varied Life*. New York: Charles Scribner's Sons, 1978.

Mason, Philip. *The Men Who Ruled India*. London: Pan Books Limited, 1987.

Moon, Penderel. *Divide and Quit, An Eyewitness Account of the Partition of India*. Oxford: Oxford University Press, 1998.

Morgan, Janet. *Edwina Mountbatten, A Life of Her Own*. London: Fontana, 1992.

Nehru, Jawaharlal. *Jawaharlal Nehru, An Autobiography.* London: Bodley Head, reprinted 1982 with forward by Mark Tully.

Nehru, Jawaharlal. *Mahatma Gandhi.* Calcutta: Signet Press, 1949.

Ryder, Arthur William (trans). *The Little Clay Cart.* Cambridge: Harvard University Press,1905.

Sahgal Nayantara. *Jawaharlal Nehru, Civilizing a Savage World.* New Delhi and London: Penguin Books, 2010.

Singh Sarila, Narendra. *The Shadow of the Great Game, The Untold Story of India's Partition.* London: Constable, 2006.

Symonds, Richard, *In the Margins of Independence, A Relief Worker in India and Pakistan,1942–1949.* Oxford: Oxford University Press, 2001.

Von Tunzelmann, Alex, *Indian Summer, The Secret History of the End of an Empire.* London: Simon and Schuster, 2007.

Ziegler, Philip, *Mountbatten.* New York: Alfred A. Knopf, 1985.